BEWARE THE DRAGON

BOOK 3

THE FALLEN KNIGHT

PETER WACHT

Beware the Dragon
By Peter Wacht

Book 3 of The Fallen Knight Series

Cover design by Ebooklaunch.com

Published in the United States by Kestrel Media Group LLC.

ISBN: 978-1-950236-62-6

eBook ISBN: 978-1-950236-63-3

Library of Congress Control Number: 2024926948

❋ Created with Vellum

ALSO BY PETER WACHT

THE FALLEN KNIGHT SERIES

The Death of the Dragon (short story)*

The Dragon Awakens

Duel With a Dragon

Beware the Dragon

The Dragon Returns

THE REALMS OF THE TALENT AND THE CURSE

LEGEND OF THE DRAGON LORD

A Painful Truth (short story)*

Stealing the Light

Sacrificing the Queen

Roar of the Broken Bear (Forthcoming 2025)

Rise of the Dragon Lord (Forthcoming 2026)

THE TALES OF CALEDONIA

(Complete 7-Book Series)

Blood on the White Sand (short story)*

The Diamond Thief (short story)*

The Protector

The Protector's Quest

The Protector's Vengeance

The Protector's Sacrifice

The Protector's Reckoning

YOUR FREE STORY IS WAITING...

This eBook is a prelude to the events in *The Fallen Knight Series* and is free to readers who receive my newsletter.

Join Peter's newsletter and get your FREE short story.
PeterWachtBooks.com

1

THE OCEAN DOESN'T FEEL RIGHT

raig frowned, eyes narrowing. He gave a short wave as he pulled back on the throttle, the cabin cruiser slowing to little more than a drift. With a deft touch he turned the wheel just a hair to starboard then cut the engine entirely, guiding rather than motoring the craft into its slip in the Kraken Cove harbor.

The Safe Haven, Hestia's inn and his first destination that morning, was perched on the cliffs above.

Walking out to the bow, he threw the line to a scowling Seamus McCracken. The salty mariner caught it with barely a glance.

While Seamus tied the line to the cleat, Draig trotted to the stern then jumped to the dock, rope in one hand. In the other he held the blackthorn shillelagh that was never far from his grasp.

Once moored, he turned. Waiting.

His friend wouldn't be there unless he had cause to be. And, with Seamus, the cause rarely was a good one. But Draig understood that they needed to dance first, Seamus preferring to tiptoe before kicking him in the gut.

With a rare smile, Seamus stood there admiring Draig's restored 1923 cruiser with its hull mahogany on oak and gleaming brass railings and cleats. It was more than sixty feet long. A fully extendable awning covered the aft deck. A real beauty.

"Still can't buy her from you?"

Draig shook his head. "Not until I'm done with her."

"When will that be?" Seamus already knew the answer.

"I don't know."

"Helpful as always."

"I do what I can," Draig replied, cracking a small smile.

"To make my life difficult," Seamus muttered. "If you're not going to give her up, when are you going to name her?"

"When she tells me her name." A mysterious glint danced in Draig's eyes.

Seamus gave his friend a questioning glance. "She's going to tell you her name?"

"She will. When she's ready."

Seamus shook his head, only slightly amused. "Barely past breakfast and you're already irritating me."

"And you're here to greet me when you shouldn't be." Draig's smile was gone. His countenance serious. Challenging. "You're supposed to be out on a job."

"I felt the need to get back to town sooner than I anticipated."

"This can't be good." Draig and Seamus walked farther down the pier, stopping in front of the *Kraken*, Seamus' deep sea fishing charter, which was just one slip over.

"You're not happy to see me?"

"Not with that expression on your face."

"My expression?" wondered Seamus.

Draig nodded. "Usually you're grumpy and dour, as if the world is about to fall on your shoulders."

Seamus wasn't offended, because Draig was correct. He lifted an eyebrow. "What do I look like now?"

"Grumpy and dour as always, but that the world already has fallen on your shoulders." Draig shrugged. "Either that or you've caught a case of the crabs."

Seamus snorted out a laugh. Unable to stop himself. "It's not the crabs. I'm careful about that."

"And for that I'm grateful." Draig studied his friend, Seamus' unease almost palpable. "So the world already has fallen on your shoulders."

Seamus nodded, not disputing the claim. "That might be a very good way to describe it."

"Describe what?"

Seamus ignored Draig's question, not yet ready to jump into the reason for his early morning visit. "Where are those mangy mutts of yours? Nasty beasts all three."

"I don't know that Butch, Cassidy, and Sundance would appreciate your description of them. You know how sensitive they can be."

"I do," Seamus admitted. "That's why I didn't say what I said where they can hear me. I'm more than familiar with their work and have no desire to be their next victim."

"They're not as bad as you think, Seamus."

"I don't know about that. As I said, I'm more than familiar with their work."

Draig smiled. This was one of Seamus' more common complaints, keeping in mind that he had many, and that he was more than willing to share all of them with Draig. Again and again and again.

Nevertheless, Draig sensed why Seamus had chosen to start with this one.

He was nervous, which was exceedingly rare for him.

Just as rare, his friend also was ... concerned.

For Draig. Even more so as to why Draig's dogs, who were overly protective and quite handy in a scrap, weren't with him.

The most obvious source of Seamus' worry would be the events of the last few days. Draig didn't believe that was the cause, however. There was more to it than just that.

Rather than going straight to the heart of the matter that Seamus wanted to raise, Draig understood that it was better to allow his friend to get to it in his own time. It would slow things down, true, but he had learned through experience that it was better not to press.

Seamus didn't like to be rushed. If he was, he became even more difficult than he usually was.

"You just need to spend some time with them, Seamus." Draig gave his friend a smile, his reddish-orange eyes sparking with amusement. "Get to know them. They like you."

"They like me?" Seamus was surprised by that comment. Usually, he and Draig's dogs kept a wary eye on one another. Trusting, but only to a point.

"They do," Draig confirmed. "Almost as much as they like their favorite chew toys."

"Funny," Seamus grumbled, shaking his head in feigned irritation while trying not to smile. "That makes sense, actually. Usually, I don't do well with your kind. That alpha response has a tendency to get in the way."

"My kind?" Draig wondered. Not concerned or offended by Seamus' comment. More that his friend was taking so long to get where he wanted to go. Clearly, something or someone had spooked Seamus. And it took a great deal to do that. "We're friends, aren't we, Seamus?"

"We are," Seamus admitted, "albeit reluctantly."

Draig chuckled at that even as his eyes narrowed. Seamus was grouchier than usual. That wasn't a good sign. This definitely wasn't the way that Draig wanted to start his morning. Adding another challenge to his already long list.

"You're not just here to start my day off on a good note." Seamus didn't miss Draig's sarcasm. "What's up?"

Seamus sighed, then kicked at an imaginary pebble on the dock. "Normally I wouldn't bother you with something like this."

"But clearly this something is bothering you. Spill it," Draig prodded.

Seamus frowned, still trying to figure out where he wanted to start. He opted for the longer way around. "I was coming down the coast from Canada early this morning."

"Another smuggling run?"

"Just business," Seamus replied, giving Draig a deceptive smile and a shrug.

Draig wasn't taken in by the poor attempt at subterfuge. With Seamus, smuggling and business were one and the same. Feeling the press of time, he tried to nudge his friend along. "You were sailing down the coast from Canada ..."

"I was," Seamus confirmed.

"Then what's the problem?" Draig didn't understand why Seamus was hesitating. Usually, he had no problem telling him what he thought. About anything. Even when Draig told him that he didn't want to hear it. "You've made that run hundreds of times."

"True, but never like this."

"Seamus, you're dancing around like a middle-school boy too frightened to ask a girl to dance." Draig's tone demanded an answer. "What's the problem?"

"I don't know if it is a problem."

"If it's not a problem, then why did you wait for me to get here this morning?"

"That's a good question," Seamus admitted.

"Seamus." Draig's tone hardened in an instant, his eyes flashing dangerously. "I didn't get a lot of sleep last night, I've got more to deal with today than I want to, and I'm beginning to lose patience."

Seamus held up his hands, seeking to stave off Draig losing his temper. Knowing what that could look like and not wanting to bear the brunt of it. "I just don't want you to think that I'm crying wolf. That's all."

His friend's comment stopped Draig from pushing harder. The Werewolves were well out of Kraken Cove when he came down from the mountain yesterday and should be gone at least for a time, but he hadn't checked on them since late last night.

Draig did so then. Reaching for the Grym, he used the Power of the Ancients to extend his senses in all directions around the seaside town. One mile, then two. Five. Ten. Twenty miles. Fifty.

Nothing.

Just as he hoped and expected. The Renegades turned tail and fled after he killed Raik. In fact, he couldn't sense a Werewolf in the state. A good result. Those Weres wouldn't be coming back anytime soon, which meant he wouldn't have to worry about the blood debt between them until the pack rebuilt its strength. And that would take some time.

"Instead of beating around the bush, Seamus, just tell me what it is that's bothering you. Then I'll judge if you're crying wolf or not."

"I just don't want you to give me that look."

"What look?"

"The one that suggests that I'm full of it."

"You are full of it, Seamus," Draig replied more sharply than he intended. "You know it just as well as I do."

Seamus stared at his friend, his eyes shifting in color. From a deep ocean blue to a dark grey. At the same time, the mariner flexed his fingers and lifted himself up onto his toes. The energy flowing within him began to seek a release. To take shape.

He prevented the shift from occurring, although his glare continued for several seconds more before Seamus took a deep breath and settled back down onto the soles of his feet. He took several more deep breaths, pushing the air out through his nose, to calm himself.

"Only you can get away with doing that to me," Seamus grumbled once he was certain that he was back in control of himself.

"I'm honored." Draig grasped Seamus' shoulder and gave him a friendly squeeze, a form of apology for almost setting off his friend. "Now what's got you all hot and bothered? Not another mermaid I hope."

Once again Draig's humor made Seamus smile. It also helped him to relax just a little bit more.

"If only," Seamus mused. "Did I tell you about the time I found that mermaid ..."

"Seamus."

The mariner nodded, realizing that he couldn't delay any longer. So he just said it. "The ocean doesn't feel right."

Draig nodded slightly as he thought about what Seamus told him. Not out of concern. Rather curiosity. Understanding just how hard this was for his friend. "The ocean doesn't feel right?"

"That's what I said," Seamus confirmed.

"What does that mean? The ocean doesn't feel right."

"I'm sorry, but that's the best that I can explain it." Seamus shrugged, hoping that the movement of his shoulders explained to Draig why he was so hesitant to mention this to him in the first place. "It's just a feeling, no more than that. I wish I could tell you more, but I can't." Just then a cold gust of wind swept off the water of Kraken Cove, sending a chill through the both of them. "The ocean doesn't feel right. That's all that I wanted to tell you."

"And that's why you were here to greet me? That's why you returned sooner than you planned?"

Seamus nodded and shrugged again, hands now in his pockets. Looking for another imaginary rock to kick into the water. "Yes."

Draig didn't say anything for a time, thinking about what Seamus had told him. Even more, examining his friend, who appeared to be more than just a little out of sorts. Seamus never would have interrupted a run up the coast unless he believed that it was absolutely necessary. Not with the profit to be made.

"When you say the ocean doesn't feel right, do you mean like a storm coming in?"

Seamus considered Draig's question, his head moving slightly up and down as he considered the possibility. "That might be the best way to put it."

"But?" Draig caught Seamus' hesitation.

"But it's not an actual storm."

"A metaphorical storm?" Draig prompted.

"What do you mean by metaphorical?"

Draig didn't bother to reply. If he tried to explain it he'd just end up down the rabbit hole.

"A premonition, perhaps?" Draig suggested, trying hard to understand when Seamus didn't seem to understand himself.

"That's an even better way to describe it." Seamus smiled, then chuckled softly, an uncommon event for him. If Draig hadn't struck gold, he had come close.

"Talking with you can be like pulling teeth," Draig grated.

"One of my better qualities," Seamus said with a wink, apparently feeling better now that he had told his friend what he wanted to.

"Have you ever had a feeling like this before?" Draig was still trying to get a better sense as to what Seamus was so worried about.

Seamus usually wasn't worried about anything. Especially

when he was out on the water. Because on the water, there was little that could challenge him.

"Only a handful of times," Seamus replied. The mariner's eyes took on a glazed cast, seemingly captured by memories that he would have preferred to keep buried.

"What happened when it did?"

"Nothing good, I promise you that."

"Can you be any more specific, Seamus?" Draig was working hard to maintain what little patience he had left. "Anything you can share could prove helpful."

"The eruption of Krakatoa comes to mind," Seamus muttered, images of that event flashing through his mind. "Death. Destruction. Devastation. Mayhem. On more than just a massive scale. A global scale. And bad news for all the Teg." Seamus shivered as he came back to himself. "Nothing good for the Teg, that's all I can tell you. I don't know why I felt it. All I can tell you is that I did."

"Not a pleasant picture you're leaving with me," Draig admitted.

"It wasn't meant to be. I'm sorry. But you asked."

"Why are you telling me this now, Seamus?"

"This feeling that I get ..." Seamus' voice trailed off, then he shook his head as if he were trying to clear it of thoughts and memories that wouldn't leave him alone. "Whenever the ocean has felt like this, whatever the cause, it's never taken long for that cause to be revealed."

Draig's frown deepened. So a potentially catastrophic event and Seamus could tell him little more than that, other than it was imminent. Wonderful. Definitely not how he wanted to start his morning. "Thank you, Seamus. I appreciate you telling me this."

"I had to, Draig. We're friends after all, albeit reluctantly as I said." Seamus grinned, though that grin quickly was replaced by his more common grimace, which was caused by what he wanted to say next. He started and stopped several times, requiring a good bit of effort to put his concerns into words. "I just wanted to warn you. This feeling ... it's coming from my world, from the ocean, but I don't know the cause. I do know – and don't ask me why because I can't tell you – that it relates to you directly."

Recognizing his friend's discomfort, rather than pressing Seamus further, Draig nodded. He doubted that Seamus would be able to offer any more detail than that.

Still, what Seamus had revealed was quite helpful. It served as additional confirmation as to what he had learned in the Circle atop the Druid's Peak and the decision that he needed to make. A decision that he didn't want to make.

"Thanks Seamus." Draig clapped him on the back. "You're a good friend."

Seamus nodded. "Don't go spreading that around. I have a reputation to maintain." He jumped over the railing and landed on the *Kraken*, feeling better once he was floating atop the water. "If you need anything, you know where not to go."

Draig smiled. Grouchy and dour. Crusty. Certainly antisocial. But still a friend. Seamus was ready to assist despite his words to the contrary.

Draig reached for the Grym again, searching once more, taking more time, focusing on Kraken Cove and the town's surrounding environs. Extending his search all the way to the Druid's Peak to the west and then past his home, Raptor Bay Lighthouse, to the east and well out into the Atlantic Ocean.

Nothing.

All seemed to be well.

There was no reason for him to be concerned.

At least none that he could identify.

Of course, that didn't mean that he shouldn't be worried.

Seamus was many things. But Peter from the fable he was not.

2

NO ROOM AT THE INN

Seamus' warning kept playing through Draig's mind as he climbed the stairs that led up the cliff from the beach to the Safe Haven.

"The ocean doesn't feel right."

Draig shook his head, unable to contain his smile that was a mix of both humor and frustration. Just as clear as always with Seamus. And just one more thing for him to worry about.

Still, despite Seamus' lack of specificity, Draig couldn't ignore the warning. Even as he turned his focus to that morning's primary task.

He had tried to get the information he wanted from Melissa yesterday evening on the way back into town after defeating Raik and sending what was left of his Werewolf pack running with their tails between their legs.

Melissa had been less than accommodating. Revealing some but not all of what she was dealing with, and by association what he was dealing with, since he had given in to his need to dig deeper into the mystery and helped the Witch.

After Seamus' warning, which he believed was connected in some way though he had no evidence to support that claim, he had to make Melissa understand that her withholding critical knowledge put them both at risk.

Draig knew that Melissa was hiding from him pieces of what she was truly about. And he knew that she knew that he knew she was hiding those pieces from him.

Yet she still refused to reveal any of it despite all the problems that she had caused for him and several of his friends.

Selfish. That was the only way to describe her actions.

He couldn't ignore that. Although it was a sign of desperation as well.

He had seen it many times before, and he could thank his father for that last. A natural result of the work that he had done for the King Teg for so long.

Draig needed to know what Melissa was hiding from him. He suspected, but with what he had in mind for dealing with what threatened him and those Teg residing in Kraken Cove, that wasn't enough. He required confirmation. Preferably before he put his plan in play.

And if he didn't get that confirmation?

The result he expected based on Melissa's remarkable obstinance. A result that he didn't want. Nevertheless, if it came to that, he would do what he needed to do, just as he had done in the past.

He didn't want to do that. He wouldn't enjoy it. But he wouldn't have a choice.

Draig stopped abruptly, halfway through Hestia's rose garden that ran along the northern side of the inn.

All the garden gnomes placed here, several dozen in fact, faced the Victorian house built on the edge of the cliff.

That was strange.

He had never seen that before.

A mistake perhaps?

He doubted it. Hestia didn't make mistakes.

Draig continued through the garden to the front of the bed

and breakfast. All of the gnomes set in the garden beds that ran all the way down the driveway to Market Street were facing toward the Safe Haven.

More than strange now. Worrying.

Draig trotted up the steps.

The front door was open.

Hestia never left the front door open.

Ever.

Grasping his shillelagh in a tighter grip, he pushed the door open with his walking stick and stepped into the foyer. The counter greeted him, half the keys to the various rooms still hanging from their hooks.

Melissa was still here. Her key wasn't on its hook.

Draig peeked into the dining room. No breakfast to be had.

That didn't surprise him. It was just after eight.

In the Safe Haven, if you weren't down for breakfast by eight, you didn't get breakfast.

Hestia never failed to leave for her morning hike right after that.

So all seemed to be as it should.

Then why did it feel otherwise?

Draig stepped around the counter and glanced through the door into the small office that butted up against the stairs.

Not a piece of paper out of place on her desk. Not a speck of dust to be seen.

Just as was always the case.

But Hestia never, ever left the front door open.

Draig reached for the Grym for a third time in just the last few minutes, extending his senses throughout the Safe Haven. He couldn't do it from outside the inn because of Hestia's many wards.

Draig's shillelagh flashed. The illusion fading and revealing his gleaming sword, he raced up the stairs two at a time.

"Perhaps you could put some clothes on. It's time to go."

Melissa jumped a few inches off the ground upon hearing the quiet, insistent, and totally unexpected voice. Walking out of the bathroom wrapped in nothing but a towel, she had been drying her hair, eyes on the carpet.

"Who in all the hells are you?"

She removed the wet towel from her head, trying to understand how someone had gotten into her attic room without her permission. Hestia had said that was impossible.

Yet Melissa could barely contain her shock at finding a woman sitting comfortably in front of the bay window, legs crossed, one arm draped over the back of the couch, as if it were Melissa who had invaded her space.

"Who I am doesn't matter. What matters is that I'm here."

The intruder pushed herself up and took a few steps toward Melissa, who naturally stepped back closer to the bathroom door. She wanted to keep some space between them. If she didn't, Melissa would have fewer options than she already had.

She didn't get very far.

Two men she hadn't noticed appeared behind her, blocking her path. She could have sworn the pair hadn't been there before. It was almost as if they materialized out of thin air.

And maybe they had.

Three more men appeared right in front of her. One by the door to her room. Two others standing in a position that ensured she was boxed in with no avenue for escape.

The men looked quite similar in appearance. Nondescript. Normal if she could use that term with Teg who appeared and disappeared in a flash. Barely noticeable because they seemed barely there.

So much so that Melissa had a hard time seeing them even when she was staring directly at them. It was easier when they moved, but negligibly so. More like a flicker of motion that the eye still wanted to ignore.

She had heard of men such as these. How could she not since she traveled on occasion along the darker lanes among the Teg? But she had never come up against them until now, and gratefully so.

Warlocks.

The small mark that resembled an evil eye and was tattooed just above their right cheekbones confirmed it.

Seers of things in the dark that any sane Teg sought to avoid. Unseen unless they chose to be seen.

Using the Twisted Grym to blend themselves into their surroundings so that they were all but invisible.

The perfect assassins, preferred on certain jobs by those of the Tylwyth Teg who could afford their outrageously priced services.

"Get dressed, please."

Melissa pulled her eyes away from the Warlocks standing to her front and shifted her focus to the woman. Taller than her by a few inches. Wearing all black. Dressed like a runner. Her black hair kept out of the way with a ponytail.

A good disguise for Kraken Cove, but Melissa could see beyond what the woman wanted her to see.

A Witch, just as she was.

Stronger than she was, Melissa feared, though there was only one way to find out.

"I wouldn't do it if I were you," the woman said, seemingly reading Melissa's mind. "It won't end well for you."

"Do what?" Melissa filled her voice with a false innocence.

The woman obviously was used to being in command, used to killing or kidnapping, so clearly this wasn't the first time she and her Warlocks had been employed on a job like this.

Melissa detected the power that radiated from her. Maybe not a Witch. The power reminded her of ...

"Get dressed. Now," the woman ordered. She smiled, though her eyes didn't. "You have two minutes. Then we leave. Clothed or in a towel. Your choice."

Melissa searched for some way to extricate herself from a situation for which she was sadly unprepared. "Just let me grab the clothes I left in the bathroom."

She made a move toward the open door, steam still wafting out from her hot shower and into the colder attic room.

The two Warlocks at her back closed ranks.

"Take what you need from your suitcase. You can get dressed right here."

"You expect me to change in front of them?" Melissa barked, hoping that the shock she infused in her voice might gain her some leeway.

It didn't.

"Take it or leave it," the woman shrugged. "I don't care if you're dressed in a towel or clothes when we leave. I only care that we leave. Time is pressing. You have two minutes as I said."

"I can't believe that you would ..."

The woman cut off Melissa's protest. "Ninety seconds."

Seething with anger because she worried about what would happen if she gave free rein to her fear, Melissa dropped the towel that she had used to dry her hair. Then she reached for the pile of clothes on top of her travel bag.

She got dressed as quickly as she could while still trying to maintain her modesty, not allowing the towel wrapped around her to fall until she had only her socks and running shoes left.

"I can't believe that you couldn't give me just a few minutes in the bathroom."

"We know who you are ... Witch," the woman said.

"Takes one to know one."

"That it does," her kidnapper replied, offering her a brief nod of respect.

"And who am I since you know me so well?" Melissa bent

down. Pulling on her socks and then her shoes, she tied the laces. All the while her thoughts focused on how to make her escape. Various ideas running through her mind. None of them all that appealing.

"You're the Witch who has caught the eye of my Dragon."

Melissa pushed herself back up, giving the woman a quizzical expression. "Your Dragon?" She didn't quite understand, until she did. "You mean Draig?"

The woman's dark eyes flashed, hints of anger in the back. Or perhaps jealousy. Melissa couldn't tell for certain, the woman closing herself off just as quickly as she revealed herself.

"My Dragon, yes."

"That's why you're here? Because of Draig?"

"Unfortunately, no," the woman replied with a smile that threatened to curl Melissa's toes. "If only I was. I have such good memories of spending time with him in this very room."

"Good memories?" Melissa wasn't quite sure what the woman was talking about, but she could guess, and she really had little desire for details. Although she did want to extend the conversation. Every second she gained might be another second that she could use.

"Very good memories indeed. And a good thing for you that I didn't find him here with you."

Melissa nodded, remembering that flash in the back of the woman's eyes. Jealousy for certain. Perhaps she could play off of that.

"Well, I'm sorry to say that you just missed him." Melissa offered the woman a sly smile and then a wink.

The woman's eyes narrowed. "Is that so?"

"It is," Melissa replied, crossing her arms in front of her chest. "He left no more than thirty minutes ago." Her smile widened. "After his shower." She tilted her head down, as if she was sharing a secret with the woman and trying to keep it from the five Warlocks pressing in close. "He was dirty. Very, very ... dirty."

Her kidnapper's jaw tightened as her eyes flashed. The woman clenched her right hand into a fist then reached for her. "You little bit ..."

Getting the reaction that she wanted, Melissa didn't hesitate. Calling on the Grym she sent a blast of energy right at the woman's feet.

Melissa turned away and closed her eyes, seeking to avoid the full effect that the blinding power would have. The woman and her Warlocks, if they survived, would be dazed and disoriented, if not unconscious, unable to stand against the force she employed.

If she had learned nothing from Draig in the last few days, it was that it was better to provoke and then attack, because it was always better to attack than defend.

She could ask questions later. Although she really didn't have any questions for this lot. She just wanted to get away from them.

And she believed that her surprise attack would give her the chance to do that.

The flare of bright energy fading, Melissa turned back around and opened her eyes.

Her jaw dropped, smile disappearing, replaced by a look of dejection.

The woman laughed at her crestfallen expression. Other than the scorched carpet where the blast struck, nothing had changed.

The Warlocks still surrounded her, and they appeared to be even less pleased than they had been before her attack. The shield of protective energy continued for several seconds more, her kidnapper wanting to show Melissa the real power that she was up against, before she released her hold on the magical construction, the energy flickering a few times before disappearing.

"That was a big mistake, Witch," the woman murmured, shaking her head in mock disappointment. "Although I can't say that I'm surprised. We were warned that you were less than trustworthy."

"Look ..." Melissa sought desperately for some other way to extricate herself from her dilemma, but nothing was coming to mind, and clearly the woman's patience, little there to begin with, had run out.

"We were told to take you, Witch. What condition you are in when we deposit you where you need to be was never discussed." The woman nodded as she studied Melissa, clearly thinking of revenge for the failed attack ... even more for her alleged indiscretion with her Dragon. "I think we'll have a little fun with you first. So you can't give us any trouble along the way."

"I was hoping that I wouldn't see you for several more decades, Callie."

Draig stood in the doorway, sword in hand.

And he was less than pleased.

In fact, he was pissed.

3

QUITE AN ENTRANCE

A charged silence descended in the attic room, all eyes going to Draig.

The Warlocks -- before still as statues, clearly not concerned about Melissa -- shifted uneasily from one foot to the other, a few flexing their fingers as if they were preparing for a fight, all of them already touching the Twisted Grym.

Uncertain.

Anxious.

They had been warned that the Dragon lived in this town. Although they were assured that they would not have to stand against him, obviously their intel was quite poor. Their source fallible.

The Warlocks standing near the door took several steps back, desiring more space, because that meant more time – a half-second at most, but against the Dragon they would take that -- to do what might be required of them. Wary of the gleaming blade. Even more so of the Dragon's fiery eyes.

"I was hoping you might make an appearance." Callie eyed Draig appraisingly, although she made no move toward him. She knew what he was like when in a mood such as this one.

Still, that didn't stop her from nodding appreciatively. "You look well. Very well."

"As do you," Draig replied, inclining his head, his eyes never leaving the Warlocks closest to him.

"That's kind of you to say, Draig." Callie's smile broadened. "Yet still my feelings are hurt. You are not happy to see me, which I can't really understand since in the past we always enjoyed ... one another's company. Considering how well we know each other, I should be offended."

"But you're not." Draig's expression didn't change. He understood that this was all part of the game that Callie liked to play. Besides, a little extra time before all hell broke loose wouldn't be a bad thing.

"I'm not, you're right," Callie purred, "because now I'm even more intrigued."

"That's what got us into trouble the first time."

"My interest in you?" Callie chuckled. "You didn't seem to mind that I was interested in you. Or for that matter how I expressed my interest. In fact, I seem to recall you enjoying my interest quite a lot."

"Not your interest in me," Draig clarified. "Rather your interest in what I could do for you."

"Now you're just picking at what we had together, Draig."

"And whether you could get me to do what you wanted."

Callie's expression shifted from one breath to the next. Her smile faded, a cunning look taking its place. She ignored Draig's accusation. "After all the things we've done together, after all the things we've done to one another," Callie giving Draig a wink that Melissa couldn't fail to see, "this is how you treat me? I am so disappointed. Even devastated."

"I'm treating you better than you deserve, Callie."

"Draig, did you want to introduce us?" Melissa sensed the tension building between the two, and it was making her exceedingly uncomfortable. She was searching for a way out of this mess, and with five Warlocks bunched around her, she was hoping that Draig could provide it.

"You've already been introduced. Callie is an old flame."

"I'm so much more than that, Draig," Callie countered. "Really. You need to give me more credit."

Draig smiled then, although there wasn't a hint of warmth to it. "You're right." Draig's eyes flashed. "Callie is an old flame who tried to kill me."

That got Melissa's attention. She took a step farther away from the woman, only succeeding in bumping into the two Warlocks at her back.

"Draig, you give me so little credit," Callie complained, although her tone suggested that she was enjoying the clash taking place between them. "Old flame? I am so much more than that. We had almost reached the point of picking out place settings."

"That never would have happened, Callie."

"Believe what you want, Draig. I had you wrapped around my finger to the point where I could get you to do almost anything I wanted," Callie bragged.

"That's what you believed, Callie."

Callie chuckled at that. "That's what I knew, Draig. I was this close." She lifted her hand, her forefinger just a hair away from her thumb. "This close to getting what we wanted."

"Getting what you wanted," Draig corrected.

"Is there a difference?" Callie mused.

"Not for you. For me, yes."

"And that's why we needed to take a break from one another."

"It was more than a break, Callie."

"You keep telling yourself whatever you need to, Draig."

"Even after all this time, you continue to delude yourself, Callie."

Her eyes sparked dangerously, though her anger faded just

as quickly as it appeared. "Now that I've found you, Draig, we can rekindle that special connection that we had."

It was Draig's turn to chuckle. "Even after you tried to kill me, you expect all to be forgiven between us? You're asking quite a lot."

"Draig, really, you're making this more difficult than it needs to be," Callie tsked. "You and I both know that if I wanted to kill you back then, I would have. There was no cause for us to part as we did. There was no cause for us to part at all."

"Leave while you can, Callie," Draig ordered, ignoring her comment. Tiring of the conversation. Certain that he had gained the extra time that he needed. "Take your Warlocks with you."

"Another of your ultimatums, Draig?" Callie shook her head in amusement. "You so did like to tell me what was going to happen, didn't you? Yet little of it ever came to pass."

"Not an ultimatum, Callie, just a promise. Leave now. I won't give you another chance."

"You think you can challenge me and five of my Warlocks?" Callie scoffed.

"There's only one way to find out."

Not bothering to wait for a reply, Draig crouched down so swiftly that he appeared to be more a blur. Slamming the hilt of his sword onto the floor, a wave of shimmering energy erupted from the blade and smothered the room.

4

CHANGING TIDE

Caught flat-footed, the wave of energy blasted the Warlocks backward. Each one skidded across the floor, not coming to a stop until they slammed into the wall or tumbled over a piece of heavy furniture.

Farthest away from Draig, Callie avoided the same fate. Turning away, her magical shield taking shape just as the edge of the wave hit, the brunt of the blast washed over her rather than hitting full force.

Although standing against the power Draig employed proved to be a challenge. The explosion of energy pushed her backward even as she kept her feet, her legs smacking into the couch in front of the bay window.

Melissa attempted to protect herself in the same way, but she wasn't as quick as her eager kidnapper. Already falling backward when she finally got her shield in place, she dropped to the floor with a heavy thump, grateful that she didn't follow the Warlocks caught in the blast.

Nevertheless, she experienced enough of the surge before she fixed her barrier in place to feel dizzy, disoriented, and slightly sick, all of her senses muddled, as the energy cascaded over her.

Despite her confusion, she reared back when a large shape appeared just above her, worried that it was one of the Warlocks. Struggling to manage the Grym when her brain was short-circuiting, she rubbed her eyes, attempting to clear her double vision.

Thankfully, it worked, the effects of the blast lessening. She grinned. Not a Warlock. Draig knelt in front of her, offering her his hand.

She didn't take it so much as he took hers, pulling her to her feet.

Draig was telling her something, though Melissa couldn't make out what it was.

While she struggled to make sense of Draig's words, her ears still ringing, her head pounding as if she had been hit with a hammer multiple times, her vision cleared except for the black spots that danced at the very edge.

She frowned at him, trying to understand.

Melissa couldn't hear what he was saying, and her foggy brain still wasn't working as she wanted it to.

She turned away from him, pressing her fingers against her temples. Rubbing. Trying to stop the pounding in her skull.

Draig was still shouting at her. She remained deaf to whatever he was explaining, however. She could only see him motioning. Toward the door maybe?

Bending over, hands on her knees, she gave in to the urge rising up within her, freeing that morning's coffee and scone from her stomach.

That helped. Now she felt a little better.

With her stomach settling, some clarity and understanding returned. The fog disappearing. The ringing fading. Her vision no longer speckled. Finally, she heard what Draig was telling her.

"We missed our chance. We'll need to fight." Then he turned away from her and called over his shoulder. "Just like in the hollow."

Melissa nodded and then immediately regretted the action, a wave of dizziness threatening to send her back to her knees. She reached out a hand, steadying herself.

She could function now, just not as well as she would have liked. Or rather she hoped that she could. Taking a few deep breaths, she straightened, the last of the cobwebs clearing, though at a painfully slow pace.

Her anger helped.

At this woman and her Warlocks.

At Draig.

He couldn't have figured out some other way to get to her other than knocking her on her ass?

Melissa didn't have a chance to make her displeasure known. Hearing the sound of steel striking steel behind her, the hair at the nape of her neck standing on edge at the use of the Grym, Draig employing blade and magic to defend them from that direction, she realized that she had no time to delay.

She had her own battle to fight.

Two Warlocks stood in front of her, each one holding a long, curved knife in one hand, spheres of energy crafted from the Twisted Grym in the other.

Not thinking, relying solely on instinct, she called on the Grym.

The buckler she used so effectively against the Berserkers appeared on her left forearm, the magical dagger she favored already in her right hand.

Melissa lifted her shield and deflected the flashing orb the Warlock on her right flung at her, the energy smashing into the ceiling and leaving a large hole in its wake.

Hestia was not going to be happy, Melissa mused. But she had no time to worry about that.

She pivoted, bringing her shield around, redirecting another sphere that smashed into the fireplace and scorched the brick.

Not wanting to remain an easy target, Melissa took two quick steps forward and closed with her pair of attackers.

She hoped that if she could get in close, she could limit their use of the Twisted Grym and force them to rely on their daggers.

That wouldn't guarantee her success, of course, particularly with how she was feeling, but it would improve her odds.

Melissa recognized immediately the additional risk associated with her strategy.

The Warlocks enjoyed a unique advantage thanks to their skill in the Twisted Grym, flashing in and out of existence whenever they liked. There, then not. Never in the same place twice.

Melissa had no clue as to where they would appear once they vanished in the blink of an eye.

Frustrated by that realization, worried, and admittedly more than just a little frightened, Melissa pivoted. The tight movement allowed one of those shrieking orbs to pass her by, the frigid cold of the magic sending a chill through her body.

She didn't stay still, however. Continuing her motion and spinning all the way around, Melissa raised her buckler just in time to catch the Warlock's dagger before it punched between her ribs.

It seemed that the Warlocks had taken their leader's words to heart. Less concerned about the condition she was in when they took her. More concerned about getting away from Draig and still meeting their charge.

That first attack done, just as quickly as her adversary was there, he was gone. Winking out. Fading into the background.

Not knowing from which direction the next attack would come, guessing and hoping that she was right, she slid a few feet to her left. Melissa assumed that the Warlock who vanished couldn't come at her from the direction she chose because his partner had just appeared in that space.

She slashed with her dagger, forcing the Warlock she could see to step back.

The ball of energy dancing atop his palm winked out, the Warlock hissing in pain. The pale-faced fellow whose features were difficult to discern uttered a sharp expletive.

Melissa struck true and cut across his other hand, her blade slicing away two of his fingers much like a warm knife through butter. His dagger dropped to the carpet.

She was about to step forward, wanting to take advantage of the brief window of opportunity she earned, steel aimed for the wounded Warlock's ribs just below his heart.

Halfway through the motion, she almost lost her footing when she tried to arrest her lunge at the very last moment. A flash of light to her right was the only warning that she received, but it proved to be enough.

Her slip became a controlled fall. Dipping her arm with the shield toward the carpet prevented her from tumbling to the ground. At the same time, she raised her dagger, catching the Warlock's weapon just in time, the steel sliding across her magical blade rather than across her hip, a shower of sparks flashing in front of her.

Melissa glanced to her other side. The wounded Warlock was none too happy, his face a mask of rage. Never expecting that taking her would prove to be so difficult ... or come with such a high cost.

Then he was gone. Disappearing in a heartbeat.

But before he did, she caught the look in his eyes. He no longer had any intention of trying to capture her. Not now. Not after what she did to him.

The Warlock had a new goal regardless of what his

employer wanted. And he was going to come for her while she was occupied with his partner.

Remembering where he had vanished, Melissa shifted her focus back to the Warlock above her.

Her eyes widened. A ball of the Twisted Grym, white mixed with black, floated above his palm.

Worse, his arm was already moving toward her.

Realizing that she had no chance of getting away, she did the only thing that she could. Rolling across the carpet, she lifted her shield.

The sphere slammed into her buckler, knocking her onto her back.

Still, she would take that result compared to what it could have been.

She was alive. That's all that mattered.

She just needed to get to her feet.

Although she realized that was going to be a challenge.

She rolled to the other side.

The wounded Warlock flashed right in front of her, just a few feet away, a sphere of tainted energy streaking down toward her. Then the Warlock was gone just as quickly as he appeared.

Melissa rolled to the other side, not having the time to raise her shield and defend herself.

She was either lucky or fast. Probably a little bit of both, she concluded.

The orb plowed into the carpet where she had been just a moment before, the Warlock's aim off because of his anger and his gruesome injury.

Growling in frustration, feeling like a target in a shooting gallery, Melissa pushed herself to her feet as quickly as she could, grateful that the two Warlocks opposing her didn't attack right at that moment when she was most vulnerable.

Aggravated by the reality of her circumstances, she had no

choice but to step back. Getting in close wasn't working. All she had succeeded in doing was to make them angry.

The Warlocks were too disciplined and too skilled. They knew what they were doing.

With her two opponents appearing and disappearing on a whim, and she having to divide her attention between them, she couldn't be as aggressive as she would have preferred. Instead, she narrowed her objective to avoiding a knife or a blast of the Twisted Grym in the back.

But she feared that she wouldn't be able to hold the pair off for much longer. She was still feeling the effects of the blast that announced Draig's arrival for the combat, and Draig wasn't in a position to help her as he fought to keep the other three Warlocks off her back.

Melissa growled in frustration again.

This was getting ridiculous. A no-win situation.

This was not how she wanted to spend her morning.

"Paint them!" Draig called over his shoulder.

He didn't bother to turn around, focused on his trio of attackers. Excalibur sang as it sliced through the air, Draig creating small shields of energy that moved with him to defend against the Warlocks' unceasing magical attacks.

Melissa nodded, cursing herself for a fool.

Of course!

A streak of bright, fluorescent yellow streamed from her palm. Moving her arm in a wide arc, she painted the space around her.

Success!

Both of the Warlocks took shape in front of her. The one who stood just to her right as well as the one who had faded into the background, invisible if not for the stroke of her brush.

Both visible. Vividly so, in fact.

Neither of them would be able to disappear on her now. Even if they employed the Twisted Grym, the wounded one doing that now, she could still see him. Or at least where he was, the streak of yellow energy not disappearing when he did.

Now she had a chance. Brief though it may be.

Understanding that eventually the two would force her back onto the defensive, she decided to make the most of however much time they would give her and jumped back into the clash with a renewed purpose.

Dagger flashing in front of her, she sought to knock the wounded Warlock out of the fight for good while keeping the other on his toes.

Angry that they had lost their most important advantage and slightly off balance as a result, the two Warlocks evaded her attack, then stepped back, ceding more space.

Melissa didn't follow them, because she sensed the mood of the combat had changed, the Warlocks attacking Draig disengaging as well.

She and Draig had earned a brief respite. Even better, Callie, who had watched the fight with a smile on her face when it first began, now was scowling.

Clearly, her Warlocks had not achieved the result that she desired.

Pity for her, Melissa snorted.

She glanced over her shoulder.

"Why did you do that?"

"Do what?"

"Hit me with the Grym like that?"

"That wasn't my intention. Nevertheless, you handled it well. Just as I knew you would."

Melissa grunted at the compliment. Then she noticed his smile. "Are you enjoying this? Getting pounded with the Twisted Grym." She wasn't quite ready to let go of her anger.

"No, not really."

"Then why are you smiling?"

"Because we're not on our own any longer."

"What do you mean ..."

Melissa never had the chance to finish asking her question.

She ducked and turned to the right at the exact moment a shard of energy streaked over her shoulder and slammed into the Warlock with the badly wounded hand, sending the man flying back through the air and crashing against the wall with a back-breaking crunch, body sliding to the floor in a pile of loose limbs.

"You rotten jackasses think you can do this in my inn!" Hestia roared, her voice reverberating off the walls of the attic suite.

The kindly old woman was gone, replaced by a spitfire whose rage knew no bounds. Hair standing on end, sparks of energy dancing between her fingers, the wrathful goddess had emerged from beneath the innkeeper's demure facade.

The Warlocks who were still standing turned as one to face this unanticipated threat.

"Leave off, old woman," Callie ordered. "Your time is past. Walk away. We'll be out of your hair when we're done."

Hestia snorted, more in contempt than disbelief. "You're no more than a child, Calypso. You always have been. So much power. So much skill. But only playing at the edges because you didn't have the courage to look at yourself. To see who you truly were. Instead, you prefer your illusions. Your schemes."

"Leave now," Callie spat through gritted teeth. "I will give you no more warnings. We are not here for you."

"No, but you are in my inn, and you have broken my rules, which are sacrosanct. Even worse, you are once again trying to work your spell over someone I care about."

"Leave now, old one. Your time is done. The Dragon can't stand against us. Neither can you."

"Sad, really. So much promise. Squandered." Hestia shook her head. "And even after all this time, you don't know the Dragon. Or me. You don't know what we are truly capable of."

"Kill her!" Callie screamed, her face a mask of rage. Not wanting to hear any more. Hestia's words striking much too close to home.

Hestia didn't give the Warlocks the chance to do as ordered, firing one shard of energy after another at the tainted wretches foolish enough to invade her home.

The Warlocks dodged as best as they could in the confining space. Diving over furniture. Scrambling and crawling unceremoniously across the floor. Not having the time to set themselves and respond effectively.

They realized immediately that the old woman who had joined the fight was stronger than they were and that trying to stand against her was a very bad idea, evidence of that conclusion the unmoving bag of bones crumpled against the base of the wall.

"Stand and fight, you cowards!"

Hestia cursed up a storm as she flung the Grym at the Warlocks, earning a few glancing blows but nothing matching the success of her first strike.

The Warlocks faded in and out of existence. Always moving. Always evading. Yet though they stayed alive, they had no avenue for escape.

Hestia was furious and with good reason. Sensing the use of so much of the Twisted Grym in the Safe Haven, she had raced back from her hike. No one not invited should have been able to enter her inn. Yet these pasty bastards had.

That could mean only one thing.

Calypso didn't have the skill or strength to do this on her own. The only conclusion that made sense was that she and her Warlocks were working with one of the Ancients. Only they had the ability and the knowledge to disable her wards.

"That's the best that you can do, you scummy fools!" Hestia grumbled.

A few of the Warlocks threw spheres of energy at her. Bright white streaked with black sizzling through the confines of the attic.

Hestia hated that tainted energy with a passion.

She didn't bother to step out of the way. The Warlocks popped in and out of existence so quickly, concentrating more on keeping themselves alive than on their attack, that their aim was poor. And when it wasn't, she was more than ready to show them the error of their ways.

There was no way that she was going to allow a single one of the pretentious dolts to leave her premises alive.

Maintaining her assault to keep the Warlocks on their toes, whenever one of the corrupted orbs actually came close to striking her, she used it as an opportunity to demonstrate that they were messing with the wrong Teg.

Reaching out, Hestia caught the tainted energy with her free hand, shielding it with the Grym, transforming it, burning away the corruption within it and leaving nothing but the pure Power of the Ancients in its place. Then, reshaping it into a spike, she threw it right back.

A process that took no more than a few seconds and only a handful of the Teg could accomplish. Also one that gave her some satisfaction.

Because she hated the fact that these useless fools had forced their way into the Safe Haven. She was angry with herself as well. There was a weakness in her security system that she would rectify when this was all over.

However, she couldn't deny the fact that she was relishing the fight. It had been too long since she had matched herself against those who sold themselves to the darker side of the Grym. Too long since she had the chance to demonstrate what she could do with the Power of the Ancients.

Even so, she had no desire to allow the clash to continue for any longer than was necessary.

Especially with the dark-haired beauty standing in the back of the room, her eyes blazing with an uncontrollable fire. She had seen that expression the last time Draig challenged Calypso.

The result had been close to catastrophic, and she had no desire for that to occur here in Kraken Cove.

"They're in the way," Hestia complained to her two guests who had just appeared at her back. "I can't deal with them as I want to so long as Melissa and Draig are in their midst."

"We'll take care of it," Tom promised.

"If you could give us a path," Harry requested.

The Three Brothers, dressed sharply in cleanly pressed grey suits, starched white shirts, and thin black ties, fedoras perched on their heads, each stood at Hestia's shoulder. Calm. Composed as always. Completely at ease with the battle of blades and magic taking place in the only room on the top floor of the Safe Haven.

"With pleasure."

Hestia grinned wickedly. She shifted the form of her attack, sending long sheets of energy flowing toward the Warlocks.

The sheets weren't designed to kill. Rather to hinder. And they did. With great effect.

Try as they might, the Warlocks couldn't escape them, the thin folios billowing and following them wherever they went in the room, whether they were visible or not, inevitably the magic wrapping itself around its victims.

The Warlocks struggled to break free, but they couldn't. Neither blade nor Twisted Grym could slice through the glimmering sheets that functioned much like a boa constrictor, slowly but surely tightening their grip.

"You incompetent saps!" Callie screamed, not quite

believing how easily Hestia had knocked her Warlocks from the fight.

She remedied that in an instant. Directing a hand toward the Warlock closest to her, she beckoned with her fingers. The blankets of energy refused to budge at first, ignoring her command, still tightening around the struggling Warlock and compressing his chest, making it harder for him to breathe.

"Damn hag," Callie muttered. Redoubling her efforts, she beckoned again.

This time the magical sheet couldn't resist her call, unwrapping itself, hanging in the air for just a moment. When Callie closed her fist, Hestia's magic vanished with a pop and a flash.

Callie did the same again. And again. Then once more. Until her four assassins were free from the grasp of Hestia's power.

It had taken her less than a minute to release her underlings, but that was all the time that the Three Brothers needed.

When the Warlocks attempted to get back into the fight and challenge the Dragon and the Witch, Tom and Harry were waiting for them.

They waded in among the Warlocks with a dexterity completely at odds with men who appeared to be little more than accountants.

As if to play into that charade, Tom and Harry each pulled from the breast pocket of their suit jackets what appeared to be pencils.

They were anything but, however.

In an instant, the pencils lengthened into two-foot-long steel spikes, a small hammer balancing the other end.

Neither Tom nor Harry hesitated. The Three Brothers made excellent use of their speed, fighting as a team to cut down the Warlocks one by one.

They started with the Warlock closest to Melissa, Tom stabbing with his spike, the man dancing back as fast as he could.

Recognizing the danger he faced, the Warlock tried to disappear, calling on the Twisted Grym.

It did him little good. The streak of yellow Melissa had applied gave him away regardless of his unique ability.

Harry took full advantage. Stabbing with his spike right where he thought the Warlock's kidney was on the left side, he felt that brief moment of resistance then heard the squeal of pain he was listening for. Smiling with a grim delight, he was certain that he hadn't missed his target by much if he missed at all.

Before Henry pulled his spike free, Tom finished the Warlock. Flipping the weapon in his hand so that the hammer was facing forward, he punched down. The sickening crunch told Tom all that he needed to know. Another Warlock removed from the fight.

The Three Brothers already were turning, picking their next target without having to say a word. It was as if they worked with a single mind. Moving with the same deadly grace. Advancing toward the Warlock on Melissa's other side while leaving the other two for Draig.

The Warlock jumped back, avoiding the spike targeting his eye. Then again the jab from the other side, the Three Brothers moving one right after the other, their stabs no more than blurs, not connecting but not having to, forcing the Warlock back against the wall.

That's where they left the Warlock. Stuck to the wall for just a few heartbeats. Spikes punched through both eyes and into his brain, the Warlock slumped when Tom and Harry pulled their weapons free at the same time.

With two quick steps they bracketed Melissa, bloody magical steel at the ready.

"What are you doing?" Melissa demanded.

A pair of Warlocks remained, although neither of them demonstrated any real interest in challenging the sharply dressed men who had killed two of their brothers in less than a minute.

"Protecting our investment," Tom replied in a casual tone.

"Besides, Draig would be very angry if we let anything happen to you," Harry added, "and we don't want Draig angry with us. It never ends well when he gets angry."

"If you would please, Melissa," Tom said, using his free hand to grasp her elbow. Gently, of course. Guiding, not forcing.

Harry did the same on the other side. "Hestia has requested a clear space, and she's another of the Teg that it's best not to anger."

Melissa grudgingly acquiesced as Tom and Harry stepped back toward the bathroom, clearing the center of the room and giving Hestia the angle that she desired.

With Draig already moving, having eyes only for Callie, Hestia didn't hesitate.

Three spears of energy shot from each palm. One right after the other.

The unlucky Warlock Hestia targeted dodged the first one. And then the second, although he couldn't avoid it entirely, the white-hot energy cutting across his hip, causing him to stumble and hiss in pain. The third did him in, finding a home in the center of his chest and striking with such power that it pinned him to the wall. The other trio of spears wasn't necessary, although all struck home and offered Hestia a quiet satisfaction despite the smell of burning flesh that permeated the room.

"You will die, old one," the last Warlock hissed, trying to project a confidence that he didn't feel. Not with all his comrades lying dead around him, except for the one slouched against the wall.

He stood on his own in the center of the attic, black flames of the Twisted Grym dancing across his palms as he tried to appear unconcerned by the ease with which Hestia had dispatched his friends. The beads of sweat dripping down his forehead and the shakiness of his hands told a different story, however.

"You dare to challenge me." Hestia's tone was frigid, insulted by the threat and far from cowed. "You should have never come here, Warlock. You will pay for your stupidity."

"I do challenge you, old one. Are you too frightened to face me?"

The Warlock stepped forward as if he was about to enter a boxing ring, assuming that his adversary would step forward as well to meet him so that they could engage in a proper duel. Hoping that his insult goaded her into action, because if she made the mistake of doing as he wanted, he felt certain that he could catch her in the trap he planned to spring.

Hestia stared at the Warlock, not quite believing what she was seeing and hearing. He thought that he was her equal? That she would deign to engage in an honorable combat with him?

It was time to dissuade the fool of that notion.

She did so with an immediate finality, sending a blazing stream of the Grym right at him.

The Warlock's eyes widened in disbelief. Caught off guard, he never expected that she would ignore his challenge and not bother to follow the niceties of a legitimate duel.

The fire surging toward him, the Warlock pulled in as much of the Twisted Grym as he could to craft a protective barrier of energy.

He breathed a sigh of relief when he completed his task just in time.

It did him little good.

Hestia was too strong in the Grym, her stream of blazing power shattering the Warlock's shield. The energy was so hot, so potent, that rather than flinging him backward, it burned through his chest and out his back, scorching the wall behind him.

The Warlock dropped his chin, staring in shock at the smoking hole in his body as his heart beat its last. Then he fell onto his back with a resounding thud.

"That was quite impressive, Hestia," Tom said.

"Indeed," Harry continued. "Truly a remarkable display."

"Thank you," Hestia replied with a slight nod. "Very kind of you to say."

She scanned the room quickly. The Warlocks were no longer a threat. The only challenge left was removing their bodies.

"Should we help Draig?" Tom asked.

Draig and Callie were engaged in a duel that more resembled a dance. Gliding more than walking, demonstrating a prowess that was both eye-catching and unnerving as their blades, Excalibur in Draig's hand, Callie gripping a long dagger in each of hers, flashed through the air, every time the gleaming steel met flashes of light sparking.

Hestia shook her head. She had never liked Calypso, recognizing her for what she was the first time she laid eyes on her. But this wasn't her fight.

"Better to let Draig deal with her. If we interfere now, we could distract him, and she's never been one not to pounce on a weakness. It's too much a part of her nature."

"I have so missed our little tussles, Draig," Callie purred. A spark of delight flashed in the back of her eyes. With the lift of an eyebrow, she lunged then stepped back swiftly. She knew as soon as she attacked that she was going to miss her mark, Draig shifting out of the way with a breathtaking speed. But that didn't bother her. "With words. Blades." She blew him a kiss. "Bedsheets."

"You have a very selective memory, Callie."

"That's the way I like it." Callie slashed, targeting his throat.

Draig barely needed to move. Turning his blade with his wrists, Excalibur met her long dagger, a bright light flashing when the magic met. He didn't bother to reply to her comment, knowing that she wasn't finished with what she wanted to say.

"You can't tell me that you didn't enjoy our time together."

"I never denied it," Draig acknowledged as he stalked around her. His flinty eyes, not a hint of amusement to be seen, never left hers.

Callie's delight was evident as she turned with him, tracking his movement. Despite the serious circumstances of her latest meeting with Draig, she was enjoying herself more than she had in years.

"Then why not give it another go?" She lunged again, blade in her right hand aimed for his left hip.

Draig ignored the stab, not feeling the need to defend himself, already having read her attack for what it was.

A feint.

Understanding in an instant that she wanted him to move toward her. Because if he did, she could stab him in his hip or his thigh with the dagger in her left hand.

Not a killing wound perhaps. Certainly a disabling one.

If he had fallen for the ruse.

He didn't.

He had battled Callie too many times. He knew her habits. Her tells. Some that even she didn't know.

So, he continued to glide around her. Slowly. Focused. Wary. Understanding what would happen if he rushed his decision making.

Interpreting her motives. Reading her intentions. Knowing that what he saw with Callie was never what he got.

"Are you seeking to replace me, Draig? Is that why you're making the mistake of getting in my way?"

"I seemed to get in your way quite a lot when we were together. Why would now be any different?"

Callie thought about that, then shrugged. She couldn't deny his claim. "True." Then she gave him a devilish smile followed by an alluring laugh. "Of course, that only made things between us more fun. More ... exciting." She bit her lip saying the last, understanding full well how her doing that used to affect him. Hoping it might help her now as well.

Callie lunged again, so fast that any other Teg wouldn't have stood a chance.

This time Draig responded, pivoting, allowing the blade in her left hand to run past his hip. In the same motion, he swung down with Excalibur and knocked away the dagger in her right hand that would have punched right into his gut if he hadn't anticipated the real attack.

"It's been way too long, Draig," Callie said, stepping back and putting some space between them. "You're the only one who ever gave me a real challenge." She continued to spin just as he did, though she in a smaller circle as he moved around her. "How have you survived without me? Life must have been quite boring for you."

Draig smiled at that. He had always enjoyed Callie's dry wit, if for no other reason than it often matched his own. "It's been a struggle. One day at a time."

"That doesn't seem to be the case," Callie responded. "You're with the Witch now? Really? Most definitely a downgrade when you could have someone like me."

"You keep telling yourself that, Callie. Whatever helps you get through the day."

Draig's words were quiet, but he infused them with a faint hint of scorn. Just enough, in fact, to draw Callie's ire, which was exactly what he wanted.

She was impetuous by nature, often giving in to her urges before thinking, and he sought to make use of that weakness now.

"Once I get rid of this new Witch of yours, she'll no longer be a temptation," Callie promised with a low growl, her expression changing. The first touches of anger coloring her cheeks. "There will just be you and me. You will have no choice. We will be together again, just as we were meant to be."

Callie attacked with a remarkable speed, so fast that her movement was difficult to discern much less defend against.

Draig was ready. Instead of staying where he was and parrying the slash aimed for his throat that would have been followed by a second aimed for his thigh, he spun away and sliced down with his blade.

Callie stumbled, having no other option except to drop the dagger in her right hand, the power of Draig's blow too much for her. If she tried to maintain her grip, then he would have forced her off balance more than he already had, and she couldn't allow that. She'd never be able to recover in time.

Desperate to keep him back, knowing that she couldn't reach down for her dropped dagger, she slashed with her other blade, the glowing steel a bright blur as she swung in a back-handed arc.

Her dagger cut through nothing but air.

Draig already had glided away from her, beginning his slow circling again, though not before kicking her dropped dagger against the far wall. And this time, he was closer to her, tightening the snare, no more than a blade's length away.

"Tempting," Draig replied, "but I can't go back to the way it was."

"I will admit you have some cause to be concerned," Callie said, sensing that the conversation between them was coming to an end. Realizing as well that just as in the past, he was proving difficult. She couldn't seem to find the edge that she needed to have any chance of getting the better of him. "As you might assume, that is not easy for me to admit, but you're right."

She gave him a warm smile as she struggled to think of some way to extricate herself from her current predicament. She had hoped to distract him, then wound him. Not kill him, of course. Not unless she had no other choice.

But he wasn't giving her the opportunity that she was seeking. Just like him, she knew from experience. Never willing to budge. Never willing to give her an inch when that was all that she required of him.

"I can change, Draig. Just as you have, or as you seem to believe you have. You know I can."

Draig heard every word Callie spoke. It was no more than background noise, as he had little reason to believe her.

With good cause, because he saw the truth in her eyes.

Draig halted his motion with a deceptive grace. He whipped Excalibur through the air, parrying the dagger aimed for his heart.

Just as quickly as Callie lunged, she glided back. She understood the danger of getting too close. She couldn't afford to get locked into a battle of strength with him.

"Everyone can change, Callie, but I don't think you want to."

Instead of being angry at his comment, she laughed softly. "You're the only one who can see through me, Draig. You're right, of course. Why would I want to change? There'd be no fun in that."

Callie followed Draig as he began to move around her again. Her eyes crinkled, just for a second, catching the very end of the larger clash when Hestia eliminated the last of her Warlocks.

Not a good result, although she couldn't say that she was

surprised. She had expected as much when Hestia forced her way into the battle.

Thanks to the innkeeper, what should have been an easy job was only getting more difficult. Perhaps even impossible.

Calypso didn't care that her henchmen had died. If they couldn't take care of themselves, then they were of no use to her.

But their failures put her in an unfavorable potentially untenable position.

Standing against Draig was bad enough. She knew what he could do that other Teg couldn't. She had seen what he could do. What he would do if he believed there was a need.

And now she needed to deal with Hestia at the same time?

The old one hated Callie with a passion. She couldn't be reasoned with. She couldn't be manipulated. None of Callie's charm or magic worked on her.

That was challenge enough. Worse, though, was another hard truth.

Callie had believed that if she could use their past history against him, she might stand a chance against Draig. Unfortunately, he was doing an excellent job of dissuading her of that perspective during their combat.

If Hestia joined the fight against her, then she had no potential advantages to employ. Callie was an excellent fighter, both with the blade and the Grym. But there would only be one outcome for her if she had to test her mettle against both the Dragon and the Sorceress.

Callie dodged to the side, no longer able to think about how to escape her conundrum. For the first time, Draig attacked, surging forward, an economical slash of his gleaming blade forcing her to retreat toward the wall.

Rather than stepping back and allowing her to recover, Draig continued to advance. Another slash. Then one more.

Efficient movements. Designed for a specific purpose.

Callie blocked each one, though she was having a difficult time defending against his sword with just a dagger. The challenge deepening the more he pressed her.

Then it hit her.

Draig wasn't trying to harm her. That much was quite obvious. No, he was simply trying to move her.

Just a heartbeat later she felt the wall against her back.

Yet Draig didn't halt his attack as she anticipated. Callie lifted her dagger quickly, catching Draig's blade before he could cut across her shoulder.

Now she was stuck. There was little else that she could do. With Draig pressing Excalibur against her steel, keeping her in place, she had to focus all of her strength on keeping his long blade from getting any closer to her.

A stalemate that could quickly slide toward a devastating loss.

For her.

Refusing to give up, Callie fell back on some of her other skills. If she couldn't beat him with the blade, perhaps she could get the better of him in another way.

"I knew you wanted me, Draig." Callie's eyes flashed, and not with a sarcastic edge this time. She opened her mouth slightly and placed the tip of her tongue on her upper lip, making sure that she caught his eyes. "That you just had to get close to me."

Draig didn't smile at her quip. He didn't say a word.

No more than a few inches separated them now, and that distance was decreasing with every passing second. Draig continued to push Callie's dagger back toward her, and what irritated her the most was that it didn't even seem like he had to put much effort into the task.

Especially when Callie pushed back with all the strength she had left, desperate to break free. Searching for just a little breathing room with which to maneuver.

It was wasted toil. She realized that immediately, but still she tried. She had many faults, more than she cared to list. Lack of determination was not one of them.

She redoubled her efforts and still enjoyed little success. It was like she was trying to move a brick wall.

"You might as well give in, Draig."

Callie grunted out the words. He was barely flexing his muscles, yet still he brought his blade closer to her, meaning that her blade was just a knuckle away from biting into her own flesh. There had to be some way to get out of this. There was always a way!

But what?

When Draig was in a mood like this, she had learned that there was little that she could do to stop him.

"Surrender, Callie." His voice was quiet. Calm. Cold.

"Why would I do that?" she asked in a chuckle that came out more like a wheeze, the strain of fighting him becoming too much for her. "I have you exactly where I want you."

"Don't make me do this, Callie. There's another way to end this."

"I knew you still cared about me," she whispered, her lips curling into a slight smile.

Trusting that Draig was speaking the truth, that he didn't want to harm her, she dropped her dagger.

Her smile broadened, pleased that she had been right. Rather than pressing his steel against her throat, he took a half step back, not wanting to hurt her.

Callie followed him, reaching out with a hand to grasp his shirt, holding him in place as she leaned up and kissed him on the lips. Hard. Biting his lower lip before letting go.

"Until next time, my sweet."

Then in a bright flash of white light, she disappeared.

5

THE KISS

"We shouldn't have left you here by yourself," Tom said. "We're sorry about that."

He and Harry sat at the dining room table, finally eating breakfast, both on their second cups of coffee, having missed their chance twice earlier that morning.

"We would have been here sooner," Harry confirmed, nodding an apology to Melissa, "but we got back late from our run and Hestia was gone. We did as she instructed. We went to Tia's Bakes to grab a bagel. We came back as quickly as we could once we realized the threat you faced."

Blaming herself for the ruckus in the attic, Hestia had broken one of her cardinal rules. She had warmed up that morning's peaches and cream French toast for the Three Brothers. A reward acknowledging the contribution they made to clearing the Safe Haven of intruders.

"Why did you even bother to join the fight? You didn't need to."

Calypso had come there for her and no one else. If Draig hadn't shown up when he did, and then Hestia and the Three

Brothers, the Sorceress would have succeeded. Melissa didn't understand the Three Brothers' motivation for putting themselves at risk.

"Several reasons," Tom admitted in between bites of cream cheese, peaches, and Challah bread that Draig had baked for Hestia the day before.

Melissa stared expectantly as her two companions continued to eat. Almost a minute passed before she realized that she needed to press a little harder.

"Are you going to share those reasons?"

Harry shrugged as he wiped his mouth with his napkin. "You already know the reasons."

Melissa leaned back in her chair. Eyes crinkling. Thinking. Worrying. "We share the same employer currently. You're here because of him."

"That in part, yes," Tom confirmed. He reached for the serving spoon and scooped another helping of the breakfast casserole onto his plate.

"There's more?"

"Of course there is," Harry replied, serving himself another helping as well when his brother was finished. "The fact that we both have contracts with the same employer is relevant yet not determining. If that was our guide, then we would have already taken you from Kraken Cove and delivered you to him."

Melissa nodded, beginning to understand. "The pact you put in place with Draig? The standard rules nonsense when you first arrived in town? About behaving yourselves?"

Tom chuckled softly, the first time either of the brothers had displayed any emotion other than their usual disconcerting seriousness.

"The standard rules don't apply to what just happened in your room. The standard rules don't apply to you. They apply only to our interactions with the Dragon."

"You helped me because of Draig?"

It was Harry's turn to chuckle softly. "In all honesty, you really didn't need our help. You were in good hands."

"You're losing me." She leaned forward then, placing her elbows on the table. Tired of dancing around the issue. "Right now, you sound just like Draig, and I can't say that's helping this conversation." Her rising exasperation was quite clear in her voice. "Is there any chance that either of you could talk plainly? It's been a bit of a morning."

Tom studied Melissa for a few heartbeats. His eyes tightened ever so slightly. Whatever good humor he had been experiencing slid away just as fast as it appeared, his expression sober once more.

"As Harry said, you were in good hands. You didn't need our assistance. At least not directly."

Melissa nodded as it became a bit clearer for her. "You were helping Draig."

"We were," he confirmed.

"Why would you do that? Is giving aid a requirement of the standard rules?"

"Far from it," Harry replied, taking the last bite of his breakfast, then gazing at what was left of the casserole. From the hint of temptation on his face, it appeared to be quite the struggle for him not to partake of a third portion.

"Then why? As I said, and as you just admitted, it wasn't really your fight."

Tom's gaze became shrewd. "You ask a lot of questions."

"Some would say asking questions is the only way to gain real knowledge."

Tom nodded, not bothering to respond to Melissa's comment or her smirk. She was quite pleased with herself. He would allow her that for now. Engaging in a philosophical dialogue with the Witch would only serve to tie him into knots.

He didn't have the desire or the energy for that. There were other matters that he and his brother needed to address.

"Have you ever pondered why we're called the Three Brothers?"

Melissa wondered first if he was simply trying to sidetrack her. His expression not changing, remaining just as unreadable as it usually was, she chose to take the bait.

"I have. Ever since I met you and Harry."

"You can ask the question," Harry prodded. His expression was the same as his brother's. Indecipherable.

"It just doesn't make sense. Why are you called the Three Brothers? Not the Two Brothers? Or the Twins?"

"Because we had another brother," Tom replied.

"He died?"

Harry nodded. He didn't say anything else.

"You're going to make me ask?" Melissa's aggravation only worsened, but she had no choice except to play along. "How did your other brother die?"

"Draig killed him," Harry replied in a serious tone, not a hint of emotion in his voice.

"Draig killed your brother?" She couldn't believe what she was hearing. How could these two be so calm about that? Among certain Teg, such as the Weres, family came before all else. Right or wrong had nothing to do with it. Vengeance was required at the loss of a family member. And she sensed that family was important to the Three Brothers. She corrected herself. To Tom and Harry. Calling them the Three Brothers seemed more than just a little incongruous. "If he killed your brother, why do you treat Draig with the respect that you do?"

"Why would we not?"

Melissa shifted her gaze to Tom. "That's not an answer. I know Draig is the Dragon, but why not go after him like so many other Teg have for what he's done. You just said he killed your brother."

"Draig did us a favor," Tom explained.

"He did you a favor?" Melissa sighed. Talking with these two was like pulling teeth. Based on that alone, she could understand why they got along with Draig despite what he had done. "What does that have to do with him killing your brother?"

"Dick deserved to die," Tom explained.

"Dick deserved to die?"

"Dick deserved to die," Harry confirmed with a nod.

She was afraid to ask the next question, but she couldn't stop herself. "Why did Dick deserve to die?"

"Dick was a dick," Harry explained. "Draig named him well."

Melissa held up her hands, trying to get a handle on a conversation that was quickly leaving the rails. "Wait a second. Draig named your brother? He named him Dick?"

"An apt choice in our opinion," Tom replied. "Archibald just never fit him."

Melissa pondered that admission. "Did Draig name you two as well?"

"He did," Harry confirmed with a nod.

"Tom, Dick, and Harry? That's what Draig named you three?"

"He did." Tom shrugged, the most expressive movement she had ever seen him make besides that smile of a few minutes past.

"And you were all right with Tom, Dick, and Harry?"

"We were. I never cared for Bartholomew. Harry never cared for Barnaby. And Archibald ... well, it doesn't matter what Dick thinks now. Dick was a dick, so definitely the right name for him."

"I'm having a hard time believing this."

"You're trying too hard to understand," Tom said. He gave her a smile, another reaction that she never expected from him.

"Questions can lead to more knowledge. You're right. But they can also lead to greater confusion."

"Fair enough," Melissa sighed, unable to argue with Tom, who appeared to be quite pleased with himself, although it was very difficult for her to tell, his smile fading just as quickly as it appeared. "You like the fact that Draig named you based on a phrase used to denote the common man? From what I saw when you fought the Warlocks, you and Harry are anything but common."

"Thank you." Harry was smiling now as well, though only for a second. No more than that. "Because of our profession, we prefer to appear common. No different than anyone else. Besides, we never understood why our mother named us as if we were lords living in 19th century England. We were born and raised in New Jersey."

Not wanting to fall any deeper down the rabbit hole Melissa tried to return to her original question that had prompted this curious and somewhat disconcerting dialogue. "Draig killed your brother because he was a dick?"

"Only in part," Tom clarified.

"You're going to have to give me more than that."

Harry nodded, acknowledging the truth of her statement. "Tom is right. Dick was a dick. We didn't like him. We never liked him even though he was our brother. But he was our brother."

"You're not telling me …"

"Patience, Melissa," Harry interrupted in a quiet voice. "I was getting to that."

"Just as Draig said."

"Just as Draig said?" Melissa asked, turning her focus to Tom. "What did Draig say about me?"

"This isn't high school. You can ask him yourself."

"Tell me." What could Draig have been telling these two about her?

"That you were always in a rush. That you needed to know everything that very instant even if it was better that you didn't know."

"That was it?" Melissa frowned. She would have a hard time disputing Draig's perspective, so she didn't bother. Although she had a very good reason for being in a rush while visiting Kraken Cove.

"That was it," Tom confirmed.

Melissa nodded to Harry, giving him permission to continue.

"Dick was a dick, but that wasn't the reason Draig killed him. Dick also made a mistake."

Tom nodded sadly. "We were on a job. The Teg who hired us didn't give us all the facts."

"We never worked for him after that," Harry cut in.

"Hard to do after we killed him," Tom clarified.

Melissa quirked an eyebrow. Was that an attempt at humor? Before she could find that out, Tom provided more clarity, such as it was.

"But that isn't relevant. What is relevant is that because our employer did not tell us all we needed to know, during the job Dick was cursed."

"Cursed?" That caught Melissa's attention. She had more experience with curses than she would have liked. She knew just how dangerous they could be.

"Cursed. And as you likely know because of your background, oftentimes there are no cures for curses. That proved to be the case for Dick."

"We did what we could for Dick," Harry said. "We really did. We didn't like him, but he was our brother. We didn't want him to experience the horrible death that awaited him."

"Draig killed him instead? Just like that?" Draig was the Dragon after all, the former assassin of Arthur Pendragon, so she couldn't say that she was surprised by his action.

"He did, but it didn't happen as you might think. He needed some convincing before he agreed. Once he did his own research and realized that nothing could be done for Dick, he agreed to fight our brother in a duel."

"Dick knew that he was going to die," Melissa murmured, the pieces coming together for her.

Tom nodded. "He did. Draig gave Dick the honorable death that he desired. Dick didn't want to die from the curse. Draig gave him a death that didn't last for days with unending pain and torment. Our brother died with a blade in his hand fighting the Dragon. He couldn't ask for more than that. Neither could we."

"Compassion from the Dragon," Melissa mused. "Who would have thought?"

"A compassion that you're benefiting from now as well," Tom pointed out. He pushed himself up from the table, his brother doing the same.

"We will adhere to the standard rules while in Kraken Cove, have no fear of that," Harry reiterated.

"But please understand that you won't be able to escape our mutual employer." Tom's eyes contained a touch of sadness. There then gone just as quickly, the façade falling back into place. "Harry and I are certain that we were not the only Teg given a contract to find you. If it's not us who takes you to him, it might be somebody worse. I would avoid that risk if I were you."

"When you're ready," Harry continued as he followed his brother out of the dining room, "give careful consideration as to whom you want to escort you. Some of the other hunters might not be as respectful or as professional as we are."

Unable to miss the warning, Melissa could only stare as the Three Brothers left. They were quite the pair. Respectful yet frightening at the same time. A rare and highly effective combination.

"You heard?"

"It's an old house," Hestia replied as she pushed open the swinging door that led to the kitchen and walked into the dining room, clearing the dishes from the table. "Voices carry."

Melissa smiled, only believing that in part. Having no doubt that in the Safe Haven Hestia listened to whatever she wanted to whenever she wanted to.

"That's why they feel like they owe a debt to Draig?"

"So smart yet so naïve," Hestia replied with a warm smile, not an ounce of insult in her tone. "Your mother kept you hidden from the Teg world for longer than she should have."

"What do you mean by that?" Melissa bristled.

"No reason to get angry, love. It's the truth, and I'm sure your mother would agree with me now."

Melissa shook her head. Primarily because she couldn't disagree with Hestia like she wanted to. Also because she had a hard time staying angry with the Sorceress. There was a natural warmth to the innkeeper that couldn't be denied. "What's your point?"

"Tom and Harry are professionals. They knew that Dick was going to die, but he was their brother. They didn't like him, but they couldn't do it themselves. Draig did it for them and in a way that addressed Tom and Harry's guilt and Dick's desire for a clean end. Of course they feel like they owe him. How could they not?"

"I understand that, but it doesn't make sense," Melissa growled. She seemed to be saying or thinking that a lot that morning.

"It makes perfect sense," Hestia replied as she picked up all the dishes and nudged the swinging door open with her shoulder. "If you haven't figured it out yet, Draig isn't as complicated as you think he is."

"Not complicated? The man is nothing but a morass of complications and contradictions."

"You're seeing what you want to see, love, not what is actually there," Hestia called as the door swung shut behind her. "Honor is one of Draig's defining characteristics. Just as it is with the Three Brothers."

Melissa didn't have time to ponder what Hestia told her, Draig appearing in the hallway just beyond the dining room.

"Do you have a minute?"

Based on the sharpness of his gaze, a touch of worry shot through her. "I guess," she admitted reluctantly.

"It's a beautiful morning. Why don't we talk in the garden."

Melissa pushed herself up from her seat. Slowly. Her trepidation solidifying within her.

Inside the inn, she was safe. Or at least as safe as she could be, Calypso proving that Hestia would need to up her game.

Outside, she would be alone with the Dragon. And though he was smiling, his eyes were not. His reddish-orange orbs burned with a scorching fire.

~

"You seemed to enjoy that kiss." Melissa tried to offer a comment that might deflect whatever was on Draig's mind, anticipating that what he wanted to discuss wouldn't be good for her.

Draig sat in an Adirondack chair that gave him a view of Raptor Bay and the Atlantic Ocean beyond. Melissa ignored the empty chair across from him, preferring to stand. In case she needed to make a quick escape, she told herself. A habit, really, when she felt threatened. No more than that. Because she knew that making a quick escape from Draig likely wasn't possible.

"The kiss?"

"The kiss," Melissa prodded, crossing her arms. "Of course the kiss. Is that why you let her go?"

Draig ignored the accusation in her voice. "After what just

happened, Warlocks and a Sorceress coming for you, you want to focus on Callie kissing me?"

"It's as good a place as any to start," she grumbled. "You had Excalibur just inches from her throat. Yet still she got away from you."

"I could think of better places to start." Draig stared at Melissa, his eyes hardening as he ignored her insinuation.

She didn't flinch, tapping one foot, refusing to back down. "Who is Callie?"

"A friend."

"She seemed like more than just a friend," Melissa countered.

"Are you jealous?"

Draig's question took Melissa by surprise. "Of course not!" she replied vehemently when her breath returned.

Draig smiled at that, Melissa unable to interpret his mysterious expression. "For a time, she was more than just a friend."

"Was Hestia speaking truly?"

"Hestia always speaks the truth," Draig confirmed.

"Then Callie is ..."

"Calypso."

"The Calypso," Melissa murmured, not quite wanting to believe it. "A Sorceress on par with Hestia and a few others?"

"I would suggest that after this morning Hestia believes, and rightly so, that she is a stronger Sorceress than Calypso. Hestia is a goddess after all."

"Fine, I'll give you that." Melissa lifted her arms and rolled her eyes before placing her hands on her hips. "Still, the Calypso? You were involved with her? A Teg with her reputation?"

"Why does that seem so strange to you?"

"Because I thought you had better judgment."

Draig nodded, his smile becoming more predatory as he sensed an opportunity. "I chose to help you, didn't I?"

Melissa bit the inside of her mouth. He had her there. She refused to acknowledge his success, however. "Helping me doesn't compare to being involved with Calypso. Not after some of the stories I've heard about her."

"It was a long time ago." Draig waved it off, leaning back into his chair and crossing his legs.

"Not to her."

"She does have a long memory," Draig admitted.

"How did it happen?"

"Why are you curious?"

"Because I need to know what's going on," Melissa countered quickly, not wanting him to guess at what really was driving her. "All these new players are getting involved because of you. It's making for more challenges and complications than I anticipated."

"Every new player that has become a part of this engagement has done so because of you," Draig clarified. "Don't try to place the blame at my feet."

Melissa was about to offer a sharp reply, the words on the tip of her tongue. She held back instead. Because though she was reluctant to admit it to herself, Draig was right.

She sighed, realizing that she had lost the high ground. "How did you become involved with her?"

Melissa worked hard to keep her eyes on his as Draig stared at her for an uncomfortably long period of time. She wasn't certain if he was testing her or looking for her to break and reveal her real reason for questioning him.

"When I first met her, Callie enchanted me, or at least tried to." He shrugged. "I was working an assignment for my father, and she was a part of it, so it wasn't all that surprising."

"When you say enchant, you don't mean she had an enchanting personality. You mean she actually tried to enchant you with the Grym."

"Both," Draig replied, giving her a knowing grin and a wink that soured her expression and her stomach.

"You actually allowed her to enchant you?" Melissa couldn't believe it. She expected more from the Dragon.

"I said she tried to enchant me. It didn't work."

"And even after she tried to enchant you," Melissa drawled, her fingers making air quotes, "you became involved with her?"

"It's an on-again, off-again relationship," Draig clarified. "More off than on the last few decades." He shrugged. "It will never work between us, that much is clear. But when we're together, we have fun ... until we don't. A few days. Maybe a month. Rarely longer than that."

"And when was the last time you ... had fun with Calypso?" Melissa still couldn't believe Draig had become involved with a Sorceress of her reputation. Nor could she understand why it bothered her so much.

"A few months before I decided to die."

"She knew that you were going to do it? Fake your own death?"

"No one knew that I was going to do it. It wouldn't have worked otherwise."

"I still can't believe you got involved with her," Melissa grumbled, clearly disappointed in him, though still curious about the timing. Why did he decide to seemingly go to the other side while on a particular job that was uniquely important to Melissa and her family?

"It felt right at the time," Draig explained.

"Do you always do what feels right to you?" Once again, Melissa failed to keep her emotions in check, a spark of annoyance coloring her voice. A hint of jealousy as well.

Draig's expression clouded. Melissa realized that she might have pushed a bit too hard and too far on this topic. And why she did ... well, she didn't really want to delve into that. Just another of the several paths she wished to avoid.

"No, I don't." His eyes burned a little brighter as he caught her eyes. "Although I'm beginning to wonder whether I should."

"In terms of what?"

"In terms of you."

"Me?"

"The act you're putting on is getting a bit old."

"What act?" Melissa demanded, although her heart really wasn't in her protest. This time he had caught her, and she doubted that she'd be able to escape him.

Draig pushed himself out of his chair with a speed that made her gasp. She tried to take a quick step back, Draig standing just a finger away from her. The chair she refused to sit in stopped her.

"You're being hunted, and you're not telling me all that I need to know to help you."

Melissa didn't bother to deny the claim. "I told you that I didn't need your help."

"And if I didn't help you, then where would you be?"

"We've been through this before," Melissa replied, not wanting to admit the truth to him. "There's no reason to go through it again."

"You're right, there isn't," Draig confirmed. "Yet we are." He crossed his arms in front of him, the movement startling Melissa. For an instant, she thought he might actually be reaching for her. "Do you have any idea what you've done?"

"With respect to?"

Draig smiled then. It wasn't a pleasant expression.

He was beginning to wonder if it would just be better to let the Three Brothers take her. It would reduce his stress and remove any immediate threats to Kraken Cove and his friends.

He discarded the idea the moment it came to him. Allowing Tom and Harry to complete their assignment and take Melissa would make his life easier, but only for a time. Because even though she wasn't willing to explain all that was going on, he had a good view of the larger picture. Especially after what happened in the Circle.

He didn't think that she did. Rather, Draig believed that Melissa saw only what she needed to see. Her motivations her own. Those motivations blinding her to the greater danger.

And he doubted that he could do anything to broaden her perspective. Why that was the case, he couldn't say for certain. Nevertheless, Melissa was going to do what she needed to do, regardless of the broader potential consequences.

Draig couldn't think that way.

Well, actually he could. He'd been doing it for more than a decade.

But now, though he had little desire to involve himself more deeply in Teg affairs, having relished his time away, he understood what likely would happen if he simply stepped back and allowed events to play out on their own.

It was the easiest course to take. That was undeniable. But when had he ever taken the easiest course?

"Even after this morning, you don't feel like you can trust me." Draig didn't sound disappointed or sad. He was simply stating a fact.

Melissa closed her eyes and then dropped her head. "I can't tell you. I'm sorry. I wish I could. But I can't. There's too much at stake."

She really wanted to reveal to Draig all that was going on. Why she was acting as she was. Because she did trust him. Especially after this morning.

But her trust in him wouldn't help her do what she needed to do. Not with what she was up against.

She needed to solve the problem that was in large part one of her own making. No one else.

"Do what you need to do or she dies." Those words were

burned into Melissa's brain. *"Involve anyone else and she dies."* Those as well.

She trusted Draig. She also trusted the Teg who had put her in this untenable position to follow through on his threats.

Draig stood in front of her a few seconds more. She couldn't lift her eyes. She feared that if she did, she would finally break. And she couldn't. Not after she had come so far.

"I'll be back later today. You need to make a decision by then. Either you're with me or you're not. And if you're not ..."

6

TIME TO CATCH UP

"You have some nerve showing your face here."

"Good to see you too, father." Draig ignored the jibe as he pushed open the door, paying little attention to the view offered by the floor-to-ceiling windows, Central Park just below.

"If you were smart, Draig, you would have stayed dead. It would have been easier that way for both of us. Now you're forcing my hand."

"If I were smart, I would have figured out what you had in mind for me much sooner than I did."

Arthur Pendragon, King of the Teg, scowled at his son, marring his handsome features. He looked much the same as he did when he was proclaimed the King of Britain more than a thousand years before, his dark, wavy hair only carrying a light sprinkling of grey.

Although Arthur's eyes didn't burn brightly like Draig's did, they revealed a personality similar to that of his son. Strong of will. Strong of character. Certain in his decisions. Certain in himself. Always.

"Why are you here, Draig? I have an afternoon of meetings,

so I don't have a lot of time. Or should I call my Knights? The pressure of my kill order too much for you? Do you just want to be done with it?"

Draig ignored Arthur's jab as he walked slowly around the large table, his father sitting at the far end. He trailed a hand along the surface. He had always enjoyed the feel of the wood.

The Round Table.

Carved from the Llangernyw Yew, the oldest tree in Wales.

An artifact with a glorious history.

Draig was more than willing to give his father credit where credit was due. Upon becoming King of Britain, Arthur used the Round Table as a symbol that caught the hearts and minds of the people. A physical representation of the chivalric culture that he sought to infuse within the society he was creating. A reminder to his Knights that they were all of an equal rank since there was no head to the table.

The Knights of the Round Table as they were known when his father took the throne. Now simply the Knights of the Round.

Arthur had cut off the last word because a branding consultant recommended that he make the change. Merlin had laughed at Arthur when he went with the suggestion.

Whether Arthur agreed with the consultant's advice was of little concern. What mattered to Arthur was that he had spent a good bit of money on that branding review, so he felt the need to follow through on the proposal no matter how many of his veteran Knights disliked and argued against the change.

A small decision on Arthur's part in the larger scheme of things. Nevertheless, just one more example of how the former King of Britain had changed over time as the burdens on his shoulders and the dreams that he sought to make real became heavier.

His father had always been a dreamer. He had to be if he

was to have any chance at all of achieving the success that he desired.

And Draig was willing to acknowledge that the initial dream that had emerged from Camelot was a good one.

Unfortunately, it proved to be no more than a dream. There was never any real equality between Arthur and his Knights. Moreover, the ideal that Arthur and his Knights sought to emulate, perhaps something actually tangible when Camelot first took shape, became no more than rhetoric as the years passed, ripped apart by jealousy, malice, and betrayal. And it was that reality that slowly pushed Arthur down the road that had molded him into what he was now.

One of the most powerful of the Teg.

And, in his father's own mind, the glue that held the Teg together despite the constant and increasing pressure being placed upon those capable of employing the Power of the Ancients, both from within and without.

Draig stopped when he was no more than a few feet away from Arthur.

"I thought you might like to catch up since I've been away for so long."

"You thought wrong."

Draig nodded, expecting just such an answer. His father didn't like surprises.

Draig returning from the dead had shocked him like nothing had for quite some time. Not because Draig was still alive so much as Arthur had failed to kill him.

That put Arthur's mystique at risk. Because Arthur never failed at anything.

Worse, Draig had gotten in the way of his father's most important operation. And as Draig had learned time and time again, his father hated when someone threw a wrench into his plans more than he hated surprises.

"From what I can tell, business is good. You should be in a better mood."

His father actually smiled at the compliment. Draig wasn't surprised. His father always liked to crow about his successes.

"More than good. Excalibur Capital is up sixty-five percent year over year for the last ten years. No one can beat us on Wall Street. No one ever will now."

"The AI you were talking about before I left is working as you thought it would."

"With a few necessary tweaks from Merlin, yes." Arthur offered his son a self-satisfied grin. "Who would have thought the most powerful Sorcerer ever to walk the earth would have a head for numbers and the skill to merge artificial intelligence with the Grym?"

"You did," Draig replied, knowing that's exactly what his father wanted him to say.

"Damn right I did." Arthur pounded the table with his hand in pleasure.

The surface was polished to a high sheen. Draig had always liked the flash that blinded him when the sun going down in the west struck the tabletop. That and watching the darkness settle over the park as the lights of New York City fought against the night.

"What's next?"

Arthur's expression changed in an instant. Wary. Not viewing the conversation with his son as a discussion but rather as a type of combat. "Wouldn't you like to know."

Draig expected just such a response. His father rarely told him anything about his larger strategies. Except what he wanted his son to do.

He was disappointed when Merlin confirmed that for him. The Sorcerer had explained that when Arthur first pulled Excalibur from the Stone, he was open and honest. Not at all like what he had become by the time Draig was growing up.

Of course, that secrecy, though it hurt Arthur in other aspects of his life, certainly proved its value in the business world. His father adopted new strategies and innovations constantly, making decisions faster than anyone else, employing the knowledge that only Merlin could provide to him.

Together, they built a business empire that was so big that it dwarfed the GDP of almost every country in the world except for a handful. And Merlin had done it in a way so that most of their holdings were hidden and untraceable.

"I just thought you wanted me to ask," Draig said, not offended by his father's sharp reply, and more than willing to push like he had done so in the past, "so you can talk more about yourself and your victories."

Arthur smiled, though in amusement, condescension, anger, or a mixture of all three, Draig couldn't tell for certain. Probably all three. "This is why you're here? To judge me?"

"Never satisfied with what you have, always wanting more," Draig suggested with a wistful smile. "We hit the crux already."

"The crux?" Arthur's expression revealed his confusion. His displeasure as well. He never liked to be challenged. Particularly not by his son. "What are you talking about?"

"The crux of the matter between us."

"Back to this again?" Arthur growled. He should have assumed that this was where Draig would take the conversation. "I would think that you coming back into the Teg world, you might have a different perspective. In fact, I had hoped that you might have learned something during your absence."

"I did learn a few things, father," Draig replied as he sat on the table, one leg hanging off. He was provoking his father in a subtle way. Draig would be the first to admit that. But he had discovered that often the only way to get the truth from his father was to do just that. Arthur's temper often let slip what he wanted to keep to himself. "A great many things in fact."

"Will you be sharing this knowledge with me, Draig, or will you be keeping it to yourself?"

Draig smiled then, although there was not a hint of warmth to his reaction. "You're going to allow me to offer my viewpoint?"

Arthur's expression didn't change. His eyes did, however. Flashing dangerously. "Enlighten me. Tell me what I'm doing wrong. Tell me all my mistakes. You've been waiting to do that for quite some time, I'm sure."

Draig didn't reply right away, knowing his father was humoring him, also seeking to antagonize him, but what did he have to lose? "I won't go into what you're doing wrong. Neither of us have the time for that."

"Very magnanimous of you," Arthur replied with a mixture of scorn and sarcasm.

Draig ignored him. "I will talk about how you're doing too much."

"Too much? Explain." Arthur motioned for him to continue. Curious. Having expected Draig to return to the complaints and gripes that his son had pestered him with before their confrontation at Belvedere Castle, which wasn't very far away from where they were sitting now.

"You're trying to do too much, and that's going to cost you."

"Will it?" Arthur leaned toward his son, placing one forearm on the table, his other resting on his knee.

"It will," Draig confirmed, refusing to back down or back away.

"How will what I'm doing cost me?" Arthur asked in a dangerously quiet voice. He had never handled criticism well.

"With you being stretched so thin, it leaves you open to being challenged."

A tense silence descended between them. Arthur glared hard at his son, trying to judge his intentions. Enjoying no success, Arthur found Draig just as unreadable as he had been before …

Arthur preferred not to dredge up that unhappy meeting.

Arthur leaned back into his chair and crossed his legs, adopting a pose of cool indifference even as his insides churned. Because his son had spoken aloud the fears that had kept him up at night for the last few years.

"Are you one of those who's going to challenge me, Draig? Do you believe that you deserve to be the King of the Teg?"

Draig stared at his father. Not saying a word. The silence dragging on. The longer it did the more furious his father became.

"Have no fear, father. I have no desire to unseat you and assume your role among the Teg."

"Because you can't," Arthur stated with a confidence that he wasn't really feeling. "You cannot do what I do."

"Nor do I want to, father." Draig's tone revealed less his lack of interest and more his belief that his father wasn't doing what he should be doing as the leader of the Tylwyth Teg.

Arthur studied Draig for quite some time after that, not quite sure how to interpret Draig's reply. Then he nodded. He believed Draig. His son had betrayed him. That was a truth that Arthur would never forgive. But Draig had never lied to him.

"Tell me but do it quickly."

Draig nodded, feeling no reason to hold back. "From what I've learned from Merlin, Gaheris, and many of the other Knights who were with you at the start, you did well. Building the concept of Camelot and all the chivalric principles upon which it was to be based."

"Those principles were absolutely necessary," Arthur argued. "The times that we were living in demanded them. And they still apply today."

"I won't deny that," Draig agreed amiably, not feeling the need to work up his father any more than he already was.

"That's very kind of you."

Draig didn't miss his father's sarcasm. He simply chose to ignore it. "The problem wasn't to be found in the principles you were seeking to apply nor was it located in your vision. Both are to be admired."

"You're going to make me blush."

"I doubt that very much," Draig replied, not put off by his father's snide comment. "The problem was attempting to create the world that you wanted too quickly. Change is hard. It takes time. If you're lucky, it's two steps forward, one step back. You didn't demonstrate the necessary patience, and that's been costing you."

"You weren't there," Arthur spat. "Who are you to judge me?"

"I'm not judging you, father," Draig explained with a cool composure, unaffected by Arthur's outburst. "I'm simply providing you with my perspective based on what I learned firsthand from your friends and colleagues. You said you wanted to hear it. Is that still the case? Or am I making you uncomfortable since you've never been one to enjoy having your decisions picked apart?"

Arthur nodded reluctantly after taking a deep breath to calm himself.

"You got off to a good and fast start in Britain, but you weren't satisfied. Thus your decision to expand to the entire Teg world."

"It was the right decision. Order and structure were necessary, are still necessary, to our long-term success."

"I never said it wasn't. Policing the Tylwyth Teg and the other magical creatures touched by the Grym, and keeping the magical world separated from those not of the Teg, definitely are worthy and necessary causes. But the speed with which you did it and the methods employed created fractures among the Teg. Some anticipated, others not."

"It's all a common part of the growth process," Arthur argued, a hint of defensiveness in his tone.

"It is, you're right," Draig agreed. "But you faced an additional challenge. The Teg are a difficult people to rule without complicating matters by pushing for change in or elimination of age-old practices and customs. Seeking to adjust some of the foundational values of the Teg and remove or revise many of the core freedoms that had been in place for eons only made your efforts more difficult. How am I doing so far?"

"Continue," Arthur ordered, not feeling the need or the desire to contest or support his son's argument because it hit too close to the truth.

"Added to that was the challenge of having the resources and infrastructure to support what you were doing, because even among the Teg, finances are key."

"We're doing quite well," Arthur affirmed. "As you well know since you've been talking to Merlin behind my back."

"You are, yes," Draig agreed, once again not rising to the bait his father threw his way. "Merlin showed me how it all worked before I came here."

"He showed you?" Arthur wasn't pleased to learn that his longest advisor and friend was revealing information that was better kept secret.

"He did," Draig nodded, "and you have nothing to fear. Many of the Teg not with me at Kraken Cove want me dead, so who am I going to tell? Your sister?" He chuckled at the thought. "She and Mordred want me dead more than you do."

"You have a point," Arthur admitted.

"Thank you for that. And the other point I was trying to make was that yes, you are enjoying a good bit of financial success now thanks to Merlin merging the Grym with AI, but before that you were struggling. The return on your efforts wasn't as good as it should have been, nor was it as good as it needed to be. Because of that, you had to make some hard decisions that started pulling you off mission."

"You do what you can with what you have."

"I remember that lesson all too well, father."

"At least you remembered something I taught you."

Draig ignored the latest barb. "Many of the decisions you needed to make forced you to ignore long-term strategy in favor of short-term tactics. In essence, you had no choice but to put out fires."

Arthur didn't bother to deny Draig's claim. "You had some experience with that yourself."

"More than I cared to I will admit. But that only led to more challenges, because you lost track of your overarching strategy."

"Are you actually going somewhere with all this?" Arthur demanded, beginning to lose patience. Not needing a reminder regarding some of the errors that he had made.

Draig didn't bother to reply to the question, not feeling the need to rile up his father all the more. He simply continued. "Every time you put out a fire, another one appeared. Or more than one. You were dealing with so many issues, too many issues, that you didn't have the time to consider the full consequences of your decisions. You just did. You didn't think before doing. Ease became more important than effectiveness."

"It almost seems like you're giving me a pass. How gracious of you."

"Almost but not quite," Draig confirmed. "You focused on your successes and ignored the mistakes you made as much as you could. Your ego getting in the way, a common failing for someone in your position."

"Be careful, Draig."

Draig studied his father. He appeared to be calm. Composed. Seemingly at his ease.

But he could tell that Arthur was anything but. Draig

sensed the energy radiating out from him. The desire to act. To move. Without thinking. Exactly what Draig was touching on at that moment.

"If I'm making you uncomfortable, I can stop."

Arthur didn't reply right away. After he took a deep breath and let it out slowly, he nodded. "Go ahead. Just because you say something doesn't make it true."

Draig didn't allow his father to sidetrack him. "The demands being placed on you forced you to make some decisions that you might not have made otherwise. There are many that come to mind, but I'll touch on one with which I am intimately familiar."

"The Knights of the Round."

Draig nodded. "The Knights of the Round. What began as a disciplined organization with a long vetting process shifted over time because of the demands being placed upon it. You brought in recruits who should never have been invited to take part in the training."

"We addressed that," Arthur argued, once again not denying his son's charge. "That's no longer an issue."

"In part you did," Draig was willing to admit, "but only in part. As a result, some of the allure of serving as a Knight of the Round lost its luster as the need to expand our numbers took precedence over the quality of the applicant."

"*Our* numbers?" Arthur challenged. "*You* are no longer part of the Round. *You* are the Fallen Knight."

Draig nodded, not feeling the need to dispute his father's claim. "A title for which I am both proud and grateful."

"You truly are impossible," Arthur snorted, shaking his head in disappointment. "You have been ever since you were a child."

"Pushing all that to the side, because of the changes you made to the Round Table, many of the more experienced Knights, some of the founders in fact, retired."

"Gaheris is still here. I can name several more."

"Lancelot isn't, nor are several more who I can name."

"That fat fu …"

"Father, there is no need to argue your case. I'm simply stating facts."

"It's better that Lancelot left," Arthur grumbled. "After what he did to me. After he took Gwennie … if he had stayed, I would have killed him."

"I won't begrudge you that desire, I'm simply trying to point out that in the last few centuries, several of the founding Knights and many with hundreds of years of experience have left. Only a few remain. And, in turn, the quality of the several thousand Knights you've recruited from the Teg does not compare. That has affected your ability to rule as well."

"I won't deny it," Arthur grumbled, recognizing the futility of trying to argue his son's point. "Nevertheless, I did adjust how the Knights of the Round functions because of that and a few other weaknesses that you failed to mention."

"You did, and I got to experience it for myself. A more rigid approach to the code of chivalry that was so important to you. A perspective that was less understanding. More black and white that couldn't be applied effectively to the reality of a changing Teg world."

"There's nothing wrong with such an approach when the circumstances demand it."

"Maybe not, but there is a cost. Your efforts to ensure you remained on the Teg throne required a uniformity of thought and action that butted up against the diversity of the magical world. A diversity that even today is expanding. Your rigidity and recalcitrance created more fractures among the Teg. More antagonism. More anger. And that anger led to action." Draig held up his hands to ward off his father's protest, which was on the tip of his tongue. "I had to deal with that. So you can't tell me that it wasn't real."

"Maybe if you had dealt with it as I wanted you to, it never would have become such a problem."

"I didn't join the Knights of the Round to suppress thought or questions. I didn't join the Knights of the Round to eliminate those who might have a different perspective yet still abided by our laws."

"Tread carefully, Draig."

"Have no fear of that, father. I am simply trying to explain why I left you. Why I needed to disappear." Draig shook his head sadly, recognizing because of his father's expression that Arthur never would understand. That he would only view Draig's decision one way. "Employing more severe measures to ensure control was having the opposite effect. Your tactics increased the tension and anger building up among the Teg."

"Only within certain segments of the Teg, and at that those who only understand such methods. I did what I needed to do, Draig. I did what no one else wanted to do. Because it was necessary. That was something that you never learned. That is why you were never qualified to be my heir. You never had it in you to make the hard decisions. To do what needed to be done despite how hard it was."

"Thank you for another of your lessons, father," Draig said after taking a few seconds to ensure he had control over the anger percolating within him. He understood that this conversation was going to take this path, just as it had so many times before. His father was who he was for a reason. He didn't see the need to look at the world from a broader perspective. The only perspective that mattered was his own.

Still, Draig needed to try. If for no other reason than to confirm what he already suspected. "Believe what you want. All I'm trying to say is that your attempts to eliminate some of the confusion from a confusing world only served to make the fog thicker."

"This has been a great deal of fun, Draig. More for you than me, of course. Giving you the chance to try to make light of all my mistakes -- some real perhaps, most not -- feels like another error on my part. Now why are you really here? It's not just to restart the arguments of the past."

"That broad perspective of yours coming to the fore once again."

"Be careful, Draig." Arthur didn't appreciate his son's sarcasm. "Be very careful. I haven't lifted the death sentence from your head. And with more conversations like this, I don't know why I should."

"This conversation of ours applies directly to why I'm here."

"Really? Why is that?"

"Callie."

For the most part, Arthur's expression didn't change. He had mastered the art of never revealing anything unless he chose to do so. Yet for just a second, his mask slipped, his left eye twitching ever so slightly.

Draig knew his father's moods and his expressions better than anyone. This one surprised him.

Confusion.

"Callie? You mean Calypso? What about her?"

Clearly, Arthur hadn't anticipated Draig's interest in the Sorceress.

"Why did you send Callie to Kraken Cove? I thought we had reached an agreement, or at least a détente of sorts, in the Dragon Vault."

Arthur didn't reply right away, frowning. "I admit that I'm less than pleased by what happened in the Dragon Vault. Specifically, what you did to me in the Dragon Vault."

"Protecting one of the Teg from you?"

"Attempting to protect one of the Teg," Arthur corrected. "It seems that you've lost your touch since the Witch died. But that's only a part of it."

That admission told Draig everything that he needed to

know. He should have seen it right from the start, but past practice on his father's part had pushed his suspicions down a single path. The wrong path.

At least there was one positive that he could take away from his father's response, because he knew that he wasn't lying. Arthur still believed that Melissa was dead.

"*The Book of Whispers*."

"*The Book of Whispers*," Arthur repeated with a nod. "You kept that artifact from me. If I had obtained it, I could have ..."

"Exercised complete dominance over the Teg. You would have been all powerful or as close to it as you could possibly be."

Arthur shrugged. "A key benefit, yes, but I was going to say that with *The Book of Whispers*, I would be in a better position to defend against a threat that I thought long buried."

"You didn't send Callie to Kraken Cove?"

"You need to get that Sorceress out of your head," Arthur demanded, his patience beginning to wear thin, "or does she have you enchanted again? Of course I didn't send her. I haven't employed her since you two had that falling out."

Draig nodded. He had been wrong about his father. He hadn't wasted his time, however. Because he still gained the knowledge that he needed, just in a roundabout way.

If his father hadn't sent Callie to Kraken Cove to kidnap Melissa, then there was only one other player to blame.

His aunt.

"There had to be more to your decision not to work with Callie, regardless of our falling out. You liked her work."

Arthur nodded. He couldn't disagree. "I did. She did exactly as I ordered her to do, and she was almost as efficient and ruthless as you were."

"High praise coming from you."

"Maybe so, but she was playing both sides."

"She was working for Morgase as well?" Draig nodded. Further confirmation just as he wanted.

"She was, and she should have known better. All the other Teg understand that's a line that they should never cross."

That painted a much clearer picture for Draig. Callie had committed the cardinal sin in his father's eyes. She had gone behind Arthur's back to ally with his age-old enemy.

The fact that she was still alive revealed not only her skill at staying under the radar, but also her importance to Morgase, who was likely helping Callie navigate the darker recesses of the Teg world.

More concerning, however, was Draig's belief that Callie would make another try for Melissa. Much like Morgase, Callie was many things. Forgiving wasn't one of them. Nor was accepting defeat.

Morgase gave her an assignment, and Draig had no doubt that Callie would do everything in her power to complete it.

"One last question."

Arthur chuckled at that. "I told you before I have places to be, and you've taken up enough of my time. In fact, you're lucky I haven't called in the Knights to dispose of you." He began pushing himself out of his chair. "I'll give you five minutes to exit the building. After that, all bets are off."

"Typhon."

At the mention of the god, Arthur slid back down into his seat, his eyes sparking with his legendary shrewdness.

"Why do you want to know about Typhon?"

"Humor me."

Arthur did, because he saw a chance to gain some information himself. Merlin had hinted that there might be an unknown Teg making a play for his throne, and Arthur was beginning to take the claim more seriously.

Not the usual suspects, however. Perhaps his son had hit the nail on the head, and if he did, Arthur really would like to know how he did it.

And, of course, also because he couldn't resist talking about one of his many victories. "The legends say that Zeus was the one to send Typhon to Tartarus, the underworld created by his namesake father. But that's only part of the story."

"The other part?" Draig prodded.

"Zeus banished Typhon to Tartarus, but he couldn't keep him there. Typhon was too strong. In fact, Zeus won his battle against Typhon by no more than a hair, so much of what has been said about Zeus' victory is more false than true."

Draig didn't bother to point out that much the same could be said about his father's achievements, understanding how quickly that would sour the conversation between them.

"If Zeus couldn't keep Typhon in Tartarus, then why is he still there?"

"Me," Arthur replied, a broad smile replacing his usual frown.

"You? How so?"

"The protections that kept Typhon in Tartarus were weakening." Arthur leaned forward, relishing the opportunity to share a story with his son that few had heard. "This was before you were born. Merlin and I made a deal with the Druids."

It didn't take Draig long to understand. "They owed you after Caesar tried to wipe them out."

"Exactly. The Druids aided us in rebuilding the wards that prevent Typhon from touching the world beyond Tartarus. But they were clear that those wards wouldn't last forever. As I said, Typhon was too strong. Eventually, the protections would fade to the point where Typhon could make his escape."

"And because there are so few Druids left ..."

"We have few options for ensuring that Typhon remains where he is."

"Which is why you haven't called for the Knights to hunt

me with greater vigor. You knew the wards were weakening and wanted to know what I know."

"I know many things, Draig. Even when we were working together, I didn't tell you all."

"Perhaps if you had, things could have played out differently between us."

"I doubt that."

"Why would you say that?"

Arthur gave his son a sad smile. "Because we are too much alike."

Draig chose not to follow the trail of breadcrumbs that his father scattered before him. "Why should I believe you? It's not like you have a great history of being honest with me."

"There's no reason to disbelieve," Arthur argued. "Merlin would tell you the same if you asked him. The Druids are fewer in number, but their power is no less potent."

Draig thought about that. He never doubted what he had seen atop the Druid's Peak. He had just hoped that he might be able to find another solution to the dilemma other than the two possible paths that were revealed. He was beginning to realize, however, that his efforts to find some other way to address the challenge given to him would be a waste of time and effort.

He could either choose death or an almost absolute power that would make him into someone who he didn't want to be.

Recognizing that, he would prefer to choose death. But he knew as well that taking that route would sentence the Teg to an even worse fate.

"Would you know if the wards were no longer working?"

Arthur shook his head. "Merlin might. I wouldn't be surprised if he's already looking into it. But confirming it would require that he go to Tartarus."

Draig nodded. No one, not even the strongest Sorcerer among the Teg, went to Tartarus on his own. It was too risky.

Too dangerous. Because though he was imprisoned there, Typhon still owned the joint.

Better that Merlin go with those who could rebuild the weakening protections. However, after what his father had done to the Druids, none of those who were left would ever agree to aid Merlin.

"And what if Typhon is no longer in Tartarus?"

"We don't know that he is free from Tartarus," Arthur argued.

"We don't know that he isn't," Draig replied, ignoring his father's hurried claim. "If Typhon is free -- once he is free since the wards will fail at some point -- then he will have one objective and one objective only."

"He will seek to conquer the Teg," Arthur stated without an ounce of fear in his voice. It almost sounded like he relished the chance to stand against the god. "Now perhaps you understand why I relied on you so heavily. Why I made you into what you are. Why I must have my Knights do what is required, no matter how distasteful it might be to them."

"Nice try, father, but I'm not buying it." Draig leaned down, placing his hands on the Round Table and catching his father's eyes. "Have you ever considered that Typhon has been touching the Teg world for longer than you suspect? Have you ever considered the possibility that he has been taking advantage of the bad blood between you and your sister to weaken you and the Teg before he strikes?"

"That's impossible," Arthur hissed. "You'd be a fool to think that. The conflict between me and Morgase has nothing to do with the threat that Typhon presents."

"You keep telling yourself that, father," Draig allowed, pushing himself off the table. Under other circumstances he might have enjoyed the reaction that he had earned from Arthur. Not now, however. Not when so much was at stake.

"You're grasping at straws, Draig. You're looking for villains in the shadows when the real villains are standing right in front of you."

Several interesting and potentially satisfying rejoinders came to mind. Draig kept them to himself, certain that they would only antagonize his father and place Draig in an even more tenuous position. "You taught me to think like this. To look for pieces that didn't fit and find a way to put them together."

"It's still not possible," Arthur huffed.

"Why else would I see Typhon when I visited the Circle just a few days ago?" Draig demanded. He didn't want to tell his father the complete story, knowing how Arthur likely would respond. But he wanted to tell him enough so that Draig could gauge his reaction.

Arthur sat back, hands tightly gripping the armrests of his chair. "You speak the truth?"

Draig nodded, knowing that words weren't necessary. His father could read it in his eyes and in his face.

Arthur nodded as well, this new piece of information forcing him to reevaluate. Although not for very long. "Even if what you say is true, Typhon cannot defeat me. I beat him the last time he tried to break out of Tartarus. I'll beat him again, whether in Tartarus or in our world."

"That was long ago, father. Believe what you want, but there are no guarantees. In fact, that's the only guarantee you can count on with any certainty."

"Are you saying that I'm weak?" Arthur leaned forward in his chair as if he were about to launch himself at his son for the perceived slight.

"No, I'm saying that times have changed. The Teg are not what they were. We are more divided. More interested in what is best for each of us rather than in what is best for all. Typhon likely knows that. He's likely already been playing off those divisions, seeking to expand the fractures."

"That doesn't matter," Arthur growled. "I rule here. I will always rule. I am the one and only King of the Teg."

"And rightly so," Draig said, hoping to placate his father at least enough so that he didn't lose his temper. "But as I said, circumstances have changed. You face more pressures and competitors now than you did when you first dealt with Typhon. Perhaps most importantly, you have alienated the Druids, so you cannot rely on them to help you this time. Although they are fewer in number, they are still powerful and important allies."

"The Druids are of little concern."

"If not the Druids, then who else do you call on for assistance besides Merlin?" That question prevented his father from offering an immediate defense. "Your objective of maintaining order among the Teg, of ensuring the Teg's future, is quite admirable, but your methods have left you isolated."

"And you're the shining example of that. Fleeing my side when I had need of you the most."

"Father, I left your side because ..."

"Save your useless arguments for another time, Draig," Arthur ordered. "I made Camelot what it was. I made the Teg what they are. Me!"

"Father, please, you need to consider ..."

"When Typhon comes again, I'll do more than send him back to Tartarus," Arthur declared, his anger at Draig challenging him finally boiling over. "I'll destroy him once and for all. And then the Teg will know the cost of disobeying me."

Several responses to his father's tirade immediately came to mind. Draig chose to keep them to himself. They would do little good.

Much to his regret, he realized then that his father would never change. He couldn't. He had bought into the image that he had portrayed for so long that it had become a part of who he was. The very foundation of his identity.

The King of the Teg.

Infallible.

Omnipotent.

He could be nothing else but that now. And that meant making decisions that didn't conflict with that character. No matter the consequences of that flawed approach.

Arthur was who he was now. He couldn't be anyone else. Because he didn't know how to be anyone else.

If he tried to be, he would appear weak. And above all else, he could not appear to be weak.

There was nothing more to be said, Draig concluded. It was time for him to move on. He had visited his father hoping that there might be a chance for them to work together. He knew now that it wasn't possible.

"I'll take my five minutes now," Draig said quietly, walking toward the door that led out of the conference room.

"Or you could stay."

Draig stopped with his hand on the door, about to push it open. "I could stay?" He turned back toward his father, recognizing that calculating look of his that had set Draig on the path that almost destroyed him.

"If Typhon is free as you think he might be, then his Vipers are once again playing a larger role in the world as well," Arthur noted. "With you back at my side, we can ensure the Teg not only survive but thrive."

"Just like old times," Draig mused, never expecting a move such as this from his father. He was not the type to forgive and forget.

"Why not?" Arthur suggested. "Typhon needs to be dealt with. To do that, we need to clear the playing field and ensure that we can focus our full attention on him." Arthur leaned forward, seeking to use the power of his personality to strengthen his argument. "Morgase is a threat that needs to be removed. But there are others as well. More dangerous. Not yet revealed."

Draig closed his eyes and pinched the bridge of his nose between his thumb and his forefinger. "You're offering me a way back."

"I am," Arthur confirmed with a smile whose warmth never touched his eyes. "With stipulations, of course."

"I remove your enemies and any other threats you identify and then I'm at your side to fight Typhon. You remove the death sentence from my head." When he looked up, Draig shook his head in disappointment. Why he had hoped that his father could change, he didn't know.

"Exactly. Consider it a way for you to prove your loyalty to me once again."

"You want me to become once more the person who I don't want to be."

Arthur's eyes blazed with an almost frightening fervor. "I want you to become the person you were meant to be, Draig. I can defeat Typhon. I've done it before. I can do it again. But it will be that much easier for me to do that if you do for me as you did before. If you're dealing with these lesser threats as I know you can, I can focus my full attention on the greater peril. A fair deal, don't you think?"

Draig wanted to scream. To release the rage building within him. And he almost did. But he refused to give his father the satisfaction.

"You sound like you're trying to campaign for Congress, spouting words of doom and gloom, and you the only person who can save us."

"I am the only one who can save us!" Arthur roared, pushing himself out of his seat remarkably fast, his face a mask of rage.

"Do you truly believe that? That you can do what needs to be done all by yourself?"

"I've always believed that," Arthur hissed harshly. "That's the only reason I'm doing as I'm doing now. Giving all of myself, selflessly, at great cost, for the Teg. All that I do is for the Teg. Always."

Draig should have seen this coming. The emotional blackmail at which his father excelled.

And Draig could give in. It certainly would make things easier for him.

Working for his father again. Doing the deeds that only he could achieve. Committing the crimes that his father deemed necessary, not giving a single thought to the toll of his decisions.

It would be so easy. And it would cost Draig a lot less than it would to refuse and take the harder path.

Draig chuckled softly then. He should have known that it would come to this. When had he ever chosen the easier path?

"Thank you for the offer, but I think not. I'll deal with this challenge as I deem appropriate. I can't work with you. The cost is too high."

"You're betraying me again," Arthur charged in a deadly quiet voice.

"You're betraying yourself, father ... again." Draig placed his hand on the glass door and pushed it open. Before he could step through, his father's words caught him.

"You were a member of the Round Table. *You* gave that up! *You* betrayed us! And now *your* refusal to join me is more than just another betrayal of me. It is a betrayal of all the Teg, because I am the Teg." Arthur pounded the table to make his point. "I am the Teg!"

Draig ignored his father's emotion and theatrics. Instead, he asked his father a question without bothering to turn around. "Why did you select a round table? You told us all when we started in the Knights that we were equal. But that wasn't the case, was it? Just more of your PR. There was only you, well above the rest of us. Just as it's always been. You above all else. You above the Teg."

Arthur tamped down on an anger that he had not experienced since his duel with Draig more than a decade before, trying one last time to reason with his son even though he expected that his effort would fail.

"I did what I needed to do. I did what was necessary to protect the Teg and keep those who have twisted the Grym for their own purposes from taking over our world. If I hurt your feelings while I was doing that, I'm sorry. But this isn't about you. It's never been about you. It's always been about what's best for the Teg."

Draig nodded, seeing his father's reflection in the glass. There was a hint of sorrow there, but more desire. Hope that he could convince Draig to join him.

Draig struggled to control the emotions raging through him, because his father already had given himself away. "You can say whatever you need to help you sleep at night, but I know the truth. You turned me into a killer for your own purposes. Not for the good of the Teg. For you." Draig bit out each word slowly, venom dripping from every syllable.

"If you believe that then you're even more naïve than I thought, Axel," Arthur said with a deep sadness that appeared to be genuine. "You were a killer to begin with. Don't try to fool yourself. Don't try to deny it. I just gave you the means to fulfill your destiny. A little push, nothing more. After that tiny nudge, you did the rest all on your own."

7

SURPRISING QUESTION

"You heard?"

"How could I not?"

Merlin stepped out from the hidden alcove in the shadowy back corner of the conference room. He had watched the confrontation between Arthur and Draig as if he were a police lieutenant observing an interrogation through a two-way mirror.

Father and son playing around the edges for a time. Then biting at one another with greater ferocity. His own angst intensifying the longer the encounter played out.

Merlin had hoped for a better outcome, though he was not surprised by the result.

"And?"

Merlin had a great deal to say. Nevertheless, he decided to reply diplomatically, sensing Arthur's agitation and not yet ready to deal with that as it would only get in the way of what he needed to do. "It didn't go as badly as I expected. Even so, you probably could have handled it better."

Arthur's expression soured. "I thought I handled him pretty well."

"You asked for my opinion." Merlin's eyes flashed with anger, although Arthur missed it, too consumed by his own thoughts and worries.

The King of the Teg stared out the window, the sun dropping to the west and almost even with the skyscrapers standing sentinel at the far edge of the park. "And that was my mistake."

"At least this time the conversation between the two of you didn't come to blows," Merlin acknowledged, needing to massage Arthur's ego at least a little bit. "So a small victory."

"That last clash between us was his fault, Merlin, not mine. He should have known when to stop pushing. If he had, then it might not have come to that."

"Arthur, we don't need to relive the past. It never helps anyone."

"Fine, you could be right." Arthur shook his head slowly from side to side, tapping the fingers of his right hand on the table as if he was playing a piece of music on a piano. "The past is the past. Perhaps I could have handled the discussion better. But can you blame me for that? After what Draig did? After all that I did for him?"

Merlin needed to answer carefully. Arthur spoke with a deceptive calm while his rigid posture and sparking eyes gave away the agitation just beneath the surface. That and his fingers, now tapping out a much faster rhythm.

Arthur could claim that the past was the past. But for him, and particularly with respect to his son, it never would be. No matter what he might say. No matter how he might act.

Merlin took a seat just a few chairs down from Arthur, having no desire to get into another argument with him. "I'm just saying that a more delicate touch could have led to a more palatable conclusion for you both. That's all."

"Easier said than done," Arthur grumbled. "You know it just as well as I do."

"Perhaps," Merlin replied with a noncommittal shrug. Not

wanting to get stuck on a difficult topic, he tried to move the dialogue forward. "Was your offer real?"

Arthur finally shifted his gaze toward his friend, giving Merlin a slightly confused expression. He needed to go back and sift through the confrontation masquerading as a conversation so that he understood to what Merlin was referring. "You mean with respect to allowing Draig back within the fold?"

"Yes, exactly that."

It was Arthur's turn to shrug. "It seemed like it was worth taking the chance. I have little to lose by making the offer."

"That may be, but were you being truthful with him? Would you have forgiven Draig if he agreed?"

Arthur didn't respond right away, requiring some time to form his response. "I don't know. I'd like to think that I would have, but I don't know."

Merlin sat back into his chair, appreciating Arthur's honesty even while at the same time it disappointed him. "Then better that he didn't. You didn't gain anything from the conversation, but you didn't lose anything either."

"Maybe so," Arthur agreed reluctantly.

"Why did you give Draig the chance?" That was a question that Merlin wanted the answer to, knowing at the same time that it might push Arthur's agitation past the boiling point. A much-too-common occurrence ever since he had learned that his son was still alive.

However, instead of getting angry as Merlin thought he would, Arthur adopted a pensive expression before he responded. "Draig proved useful before he betrayed me. I thought he might prove useful again."

Merlin closed his eyes in dismay. He had been a fool to think that Arthur could change after all this time. He viewed his son as no more than a tool. He always would.

"What would you suggest that I do?"

Merlin lifted his chin, studying Arthur. If he was asking

about how to rebuild his relationship with his son, maybe there was still a chance. If he was asking about how to deal with him because Arthur perceived Draig as a threat …

That would place Merlin in an even more difficult position. It would sour his mood greatly, as well.

Merlin had viewed Draig coming to New York to speak with his father as a promising opportunity to begin mending the rift between them. Yet neither of them appeared to be in the mood to make the effort. Not without a gentle nudge in the right direction.

"You could give Draig some help. That might be a good first step."

"Help him how?"

"I've come upon some information," Merlin replied, a hint of mystery drifting into his voice just as it always did when he had some useful nuggets that he could put in play. "Regarding your sister."

That caught Arthur's attention. He nodded as he thought about what Merlin was offering him.

He didn't bother to ask Merlin his source. The Sorcerer rarely revealed his eyes and ears, citing the need for secrecy.

Arthur believed that it had more to do with the fact that Merlin felt that doing so offered him less control. Always better to keep things close to the vest.

And if Arthur had learned anything at all about Merlin during all the time that he had known him, it was that the Sorcerer preferred to be in control. Always.

"My sister and Draig?" There was an uncomfortable edge to Arthur's voice when he asked the question.

"It's not what you think, Arthur," Merlin said, concerned by how rapidly Arthur's features clouded with anger. "The bad blood between those two will never go away. Not after the mistake your sister made with him. What she did to him."

That memory mollified Arthur ... somewhat. If nothing else, reducing his fears to a more manageable level. "Tell me."

Merlin provided a barebones review of what he had learned.

"So she's trying to play her games again." That was so like his sister. Plots within plots within plots. Frequently so convoluted that she lost her way. Often with consequences that she never could have imagined.

"It seems so."

"Any idea why?"

Merlin shook his head, disappointed that he didn't have a better reply. "Only guesses. None of them worth sharing."

"Where has my sister focused her attention with respect to Draig?"

"Kraken Cove."

Arthur thought about that. "She's going to make a play in the Dragon's den? Gutsy."

"Stupid," Merlin corrected. In his opinion, the expression let sleeping dogs lie applied even more to Dragons.

"You want to warn Draig?"

"That was my thought." Merlin shrugged, trying to hide the tension building within him. This was a good opportunity for Arthur to bank some credit with Draig. He'd be a fool not to see it.

Arthur didn't reply right away, seemingly lost in thought before he smiled in a way that curdled Merlin's stomach. "Let's allow it to play out."

Merlin didn't bother to hide his disagreement, disappointed that Arthur would allow his stubbornness to get in the way of such a promising opportunity. "Arthur, we have the chance ..."

"Let it play out, Merlin. You can keep an eye on things, can you not?"

Merlin nodded reluctantly. Not saying anything. Worried that if he did he would let slip something that he would regret.

"Good. I want to see what Morgase has up her sleeve, and there's only one way to do that."

"Arthur, please think about this a little bit more. I understand why you want to handle it this way. But if we warn Draig, then we ..."

Arthur's gaze hardened. Merlin had seen it many times before, and he knew what it meant. There was no moving the King of the Teg. He would only dig in his heels all the more if Merlin continued to push.

"Let it play out, Merlin." Arthur's voice was cold, brooking no argument. "Watch, but do not engage. I want to see what Morgase has planned."

Still, Merlin felt the need to try one more time. He couldn't let it go. "Arthur ..."

"Enough, Merlin. Let's see what happens. You know Draig. What he's capable of. He doesn't want to work with me? Fine. I don't want to work with him. Besides, he might do us some unanticipated favors."

8

MORE BITE THAN BARK

"It's too bad he's not here."

Maxim gaped at Cassian, not quite sure what to make of the other Paladin. Then he shook his head in bewilderment. Probably just talking out of his ass again.

They had known each other for a long time. Decades. And during all that time, Maxim had never been able to pinpoint what it was that made him believe that his friend had a screw loose.

They were both rare individuals. Having joined the Knights of the Round at the same time, they switched their allegiance to Morgase and Mordred at the same time as well.

Few Knights did that, and for good reason. In the King Teg's mind, there was only one penalty for treason.

Nevertheless, neither felt that they had any choice. Not after the mistakes they had made and the dirt that their current employers had dug up on them.

"You want the Dragon to be here while we're searching his property?" Maxim hoped that he had misheard Cassian, but he doubted it. "You're serious? You want to come face to face with the Dragon again?"

Cassian snorted then smiled. "I'm not going to ignore what he can do, but I doubt that Draig could defeat two full squads of Paladins. Even he would struggle against so many of us."

"Are you sure that you're remembering correctly what the Dragon can do?"

"Of course I remember," Cassian replied, his lips twisted into that smirk of his that never failed to annoy Maxim. "I stand by what I said. Twenty Paladins can take him."

Maxim didn't bother to reply. He doubted that Draig would face much of a struggle against twenty Paladins. Not if he was in a bad mood. Which he tended to be.

As Cassian continued to spout crap about what the Paladins, and he in particular, would do to the Dragon if he had the guts to make an appearance, Maxim turned his mind toward the task they had been given.

When they beached their Zodiacs on the shore, none of them had died a horrible death as he thought would be the case, the information Mordred had provided proving accurate.

Draig wasn't there. Just as Mordred promised.

The Raptor Bay Lighthouse was dark except for the torch shining brightly atop it.

All was quiet, and the only movement that Maxim identified came from his men as they scouted the small island.

So far, so good.

Maybe they could complete their mission without being discovered.

Although he wasn't about to breathe easy. Not until the job was done and he was well away from the lighthouse.

"You have a very selective memory, Cassian."

"Why do you say that?" The Paladin scanned the beach one final time before trotting up the trail toward the lighthouse. The men with them spread out on both sides, screening him and Maxim.

"You seem to have forgotten what Draig was like when we

were both still a part of the Knights. Scary doesn't even begin to describe him. The man was a force of nature."

"Try not to jump at any shadows," Cassian laughed softly, refusing to allow his friend to dampen his mood. This assignment was one that could push both of them higher up the Paladin ranks. A gift to be savored. So long as they got the job done. "Draig isn't here. That much is obvious. Nothing is here. But if you're so worried, then let's pick up the pace and get this over with. If we have anything to worry about, the boys will let us know."

Maxim frowned as he watched Cassian jog up the trail to the backdoor of the lighthouse, seemingly unconcerned by what might be waiting for them.

Maybe Cassian had the right of it. Maybe there was nothing to worry about.

The Paladins with them knew their work. They were experienced. They were good at what they did. And they were alert and wary.

He couldn't ask for any more than that. Other than for Draig to stay away until he and his men completed their assignment.

Yet still he felt uncomfortable. This all seemed a little too easy to him.

They had invaded the Dragon's territory, after all.

The Dragon!

The most dangerous Teg of the last thousand years who had somehow convinced King Arthur and Morgase that he was dead and then had come back to life, defying them both.

The Dragon wouldn't leave his home undefended.

Maxim stepped onto the back porch, joining Cassian. Not too close to him, however. Staying back toward the steps, the alarm in the back of his head rang with greater fervor. "Do you know what you're doing?"

Cassian shrugged. "We have the incantation. Let's see if it works."

The Paladin put his hand just above the doorknob, making sure that he didn't touch the metal. Cassian was confident though still cautious, hoping to avoid any unwanted and potentially lethal surprises. Then he chanted a series of phrases just beneath his breath, a dim white light appearing at his fingertips and trickling down into the door's locking mechanism. The whole process took no more than a few seconds.

"What are you waiting for?" Maxim prodded. He was amused that his friend was hesitating, his hand still not grasping the handle. "I thought you said we had nothing to worry about from the Dragon."

"I did," Cassian grumbled. "Even so, we still need to worry about the Grym."

"Finally some caution. Will wonders never cease?"

"Instead of busting my balls, you can always try the door if you're in such a rush." Cassian stepped back, giving Maxim the chance to take his place.

"Thanks, but no," Maxim replied, not moving from his place a few feet behind his friend. "You started the spell. You need to be the one to complete it."

"Afraid?" Cassian teased, hoping that his taunt might prompt his friend into action since Mordred had taught them both the incantation that he had guaranteed would allow them to get past any of Draig's magical defenses.

"Aren't you?" Maxim challenged. "Besides, I can't get involved now that you worked the spell. It should offer you protection against the Grym. A protection that I don't have since you were in such a rush to be the one to do this."

"Convenient on your part."

"You're the one looking to get ahead, Cassian. You're the one who volunteered us for this assignment even though I told you it was a bad idea. You put us out in front, so you can stay there."

Cassian had no good reply to that since it was the truth. Still, he hesitated.

Maxim was right. Mordred had told him that if he performed the incantation correctly, it would offer him some protection from any wards the Dragon may have set around the lighthouse. He was hesitating because he was caught on the word *some*.

That bothered him. That and the fear that he hadn't performed the spell as he had been instructed.

He had never been as good with the Grym as Maxim was. He should have let his friend work the spell.

There was nothing for it now, however. He had begun the incantation and he needed to complete it.

Maxim was right as well that he had volunteered them for this assignment. He needed to see it through.

Taking a deep breath and then blowing it out through his nose, he turned his body to the side and closed his eyes, hoping that if there was a blast of some sort – although Maxim might think that Cassian had forgotten what the Dragon could do, he hadn't – he could avoid catching the full brunt of it. Then he placed his hand on the knob, cringing the second he touched the cold metal.

Nothing happened. No explosion. No blast of light or energy. Nothing at all.

The spell Mordred had given them had come good.

Cassian opened one eye, his fearful expression turning into a thankful grin. He had done it correctly. He was touching the doorknob and nothing had happened. He and the Paladins could enter the lighthouse without having to worry about a painful and likely fatal end.

"Are we going to stand here all day?" Maxim demanded now that it seemed like they were in the clear. "We're sitting ducks until we get inside."

"Just enjoying the moment," Cassian replied, giving his

friend a smile and a wink. He turned back toward the door and tried to twist the knob.

What the …

The door was locked. That wasn't possible.

Mordred said that with the spell he should be able to …

Cassian never had the chance to complete his thought.

A bright flash of light blinded him and then he was hurtling backward through the air as if he had been shot out of a cannon. Landing hard on his back, he lay there, gasping desperately for breath, the air knocked out of him.

"Cassian! Cassian, you good?"

Maxim was there, lifting Cassian's back off the ground so that he was sitting. Then his friend placed a hand under his elbow, helping him to his feet.

It was harder than either of them anticipated. Cassian couldn't stand straight. He could barely breathe, his lungs still struggling to work. And all he could see were the large black spots that danced in front of his eyes.

"Just give me a second," he rasped.

Hands on his knees, Cassian tried and failed to take several deep breaths, so he settled for a few shallow gasps. Finally getting the wind back into his lungs, he pushed himself up.

He couldn't decide what hurt more. His chest from the blast and the resulting lack of air or his back from where he hit the unforgiving ground.

Wait. What was wrong with the hand he had placed on the door handle?

He wheezed. And again. Then he moaned softly, the pain that had started as a pinprick intensifying.

He watched in horror as the skin on his hand turned a bright red, much like the shell of a scalded lobster. That burning heat swiftly traveled up his hand and into his arm.

"Ahhhhh!"

"Cassian, what's the matter?"

He ignored Maxim, having eyes only for what was happening to his arm, the pain becoming more and more unbearable as the scorching red enveloped his bicep and reached for his shoulder.

What was this?

This wasn't supposed to happen.

Mordred had promised him that all would be well if he did the spell correctly. Mordred had promised Cassian that since he was the son of Morgase he was stronger than Draig in the Grym.

Cassian groaned in a way that sounded more like a whine. The pain unbearable. Unable to pull his eyes away from his hand.

This shouldn't be happening.

It couldn't be happening.

But it was.

Cassian almost dropped to his knees as he clutched his burning hand and arm to his chest, tears forming in his eyes. His agony intensified. Close to sending him over the edge.

Now it felt like a thousand hornets were stinging him, all at the same time. Again and again and again. The spark of poison with each sting mixing with the scorching heat and almost driving him insane.

Hissing in pain, the torment making it too hard for him to even think clearly, he didn't know what to do. He had to stop the pain. But how? How could he stop the pain?

"Cassian, what's the ..."

Maxim reached out, trying to help his friend. Cassian shrugged him off.

Stumbling more than running back down the trail, the injured Paladin ignored the Zodiacs. He dropped to his knees in the surf and plunged his arm into the seawater. He didn't care that the rolling waves smacked against his face with an annoying repetitiveness. He needed to submerge his entire arm in the water. He needed to put out the fire. That's all he could think about.

Eyes widening in concern and fear as he watched Cassian stagger away, Maxim shifted his focus back toward the lighthouse. Except for that brief flash of energy that had forced him to turn away for just a heartbeat, the Dragon's lair appeared to be completely innocuous. Just an empty building.

What the hell had happened to Cassian?

He had unlocked the door, hadn't he? Was this some kind of residual magic? Or was it a delayed snare?

Before he could ponder his questions, several Paladins trotted up to him.

"What's the matter with Cassian?"

Maxim ignored the men clustered around him, whipping his head toward the far corner of the lighthouse. What was that?

He thought he caught a flash of movement there, but he could have been wrong. Distracted by Cassian's misery. Probably just the wind ruffling the sawgrass.

Maxim looked back down toward the beach. His brow furrowed.

Where was Cassian?

He had been kneeling right next to the Zodiac on the far right, and now he was gone. Maybe he went a little deeper into the surf or he shifted his position and was now blocked from view.

"He made the mistake of underestimating the Dragon," Maxim murmured quietly. He nodded toward one of the Paladins at the back of the increasingly nervous squad. His men had completed their circuit of the island and returned. Since they had nothing to report, he assumed that they had found little of concern. Except for Cassian. "Petra, head down to the boats. Check on Cassian for me."

Maxim turned back toward the lighthouse. Studying the building.

Clearly the Dragon's wards were a great deal stronger than Mordred had led them to believe. If that was the case, how were they supposed to break in and search for the artifact?

None of them had the strength in the Grym required to challenge the Dragon's natural magic without Mordred's assistance. Then again, Mordred's assistance had done little for them.

"Maxim."

The Paladin ignored Stefan. He needed a few seconds to think.

There had to be a way to get past the Dragon's magic and into the lighthouse. He couldn't leave empty-handed. Even if the artifact wasn't there, he still needed to complete his search. Mordred would expect nothing less.

"Maxim."

Stefan was more insistent this time, a hint of confusion and concern coloring his voice. Still, Maxim ignored him. Searching for some other way to enter the lighthouse without falling victim to the same fate as Cassian's.

"Maxim!"

"What?" Maxim pivoted to face Stefan, the vein on his forehead pulsing. He didn't have time for these interruptions. They needed to get to work. The sooner they were done and off this island the better.

Stefan didn't reply, nodding back toward the path that led to the beach.

"Where in all the hells did they come from?"

Stefan shrugged at his commander's question. "Don't know. None of us saw them on our sweep. One minute they weren't there. The next, they were."

"You didn't see them? None of you saw them?"

Stefan shrugged again. "They're not very big. And with that

black and brown fur of theirs, they blend in well with the darkness."

"I'll give you that," Maxim replied reluctantly. Where could they have come from? And were they Draig's?

Three small dogs sat on the trail, no more than ten yards away from the Paladins.

Stefan was right. With the moon sliding in and out of the clouds, it was devilishly hard to see the trio.

Except for the eyes. The eyes reminded him of Draig's.

They were a deep reddish orange that seemed out of place on three dogs that couldn't weigh more than thirty pounds apiece.

"Where did they come from?"

Stefan shrugged for a third time. "Don't know."

"Do you know anything at all?" With what had happened to Cassian and now these three mutts appearing out of nowhere, Maxim had a very difficult time controlling his temper. In large part because he was getting worried.

This was supposed to be an easy job. Yet this mission was proving to be anything but.

"Do you want me to get rid of them?" Stefan asked. Seeking some way to improve his commander's mood, he pulled the sword from the scabbard across his back. Several of the other Paladins standing around them did the same.

Maxim didn't reply, instead taking a step back toward the lighthouse.

The three dogs were no longer sitting on their haunches. They were standing. Apparently irritated by the drawn steel.

Their eyes burned like the flames of a bonfire, a low rumble escaping from deep within their throats. A rumble that small dogs shouldn't be able to make.

"Do you think you can manage that?" Maxim asked. He studied the dogs. Poodles of some sort? A mix? He didn't know. Based on the size, these three shouldn't be dangerous. Even so, those eyes of theirs made him uneasy. Why? They were no more than cute little furballs.

A conundrum that Maxim had no desire to deal with in that moment.

He took another involuntary half-step back toward the lighthouse when the trio of dogs took a step closer to the Paladins. Almost as if they already knew what he was going to say, and they were getting ready to make their move before his men could.

"Easy," Stefan replied, waving his sword at the dogs, although he didn't sound so sure of himself now. There was a slight crack in his voice, the Paladin staring into the eyes of the mutt that was standing right in front of him. Those eyes made him nervous, suggesting that the pooch saw him as nothing more than a piece of meat. He tried to laugh off the feeling of dread that swept through him. "Just give the word, Maxim. We'll clear them off."

"Do it," Maxim commanded. "Get rid of them."

Stefan nodded. But before he and the Paladins could do as ordered, the dogs were sprinting toward them.

Rumbles turned into growls turned into roars.

Bodies shifted and grew at a frightening rate.

Paws became talons.

Maws became snouts.

Teeth elongated.

Wings formed.

Scales replaced fur.

Reddish-orange eyes burned brighter than the sun.

Astonishment giving way to terror, Maxim and the other Paladins stumbled backward, trying to bring their swords to bear.

They were too slow.

Too shocked.

All they could do was scream as razor-sharp teeth and talons dug into their flesh.

"I should have known. Why hope that he could change after all these years?" Draig shook his head in both amusement and irritation. Mostly at himself for his error in judgment. "More than ten years away isn't an excuse for still not having learned."

Draig snorted out a disappointed laugh as he stepped through the Dragon Door, the frame flashing, the dark trails of Central Park's Ramble disappearing as the door closed behind him.

He was glad to be back home. Yet now he was talking to himself as well. Never a good sign.

Draig closed his eyes and gripped the metal railing that led down to the lower floors of the lighthouse. He could have handled the conversation better with his father. At least he thought he could have. He should have.

But he hadn't.

Maybe he was asking too much of himself.

Taking a deep breath and letting it out slowly, he remembered what Kassie had told him the last time he visited her. She said, several times in fact, that he was allowed to cut himself some slack. He was allowed to acknowledge that he wasn't going to succeed as he wanted to in every situation. That he couldn't control everything in his life and that trying to would not only drive him crazy, but also drive crazy the people around him. A hint there that he couldn't miss.

A smart young lady he was more than willing to admit. Wise beyond her years.

Of course, she had to be considering who her parents were.

Opening his eyes and taking one last deep breath, he sought to shift his focus.

Kassie was right. Doing as she suggested, giving himself permission to not always live up to the high standards he set for himself, helped him feel a little bit better about what had happened with his father.

Besides, although he hadn't succeeded as he wanted to, he hadn't failed entirely.

He had still gotten the information he needed, just not in the way he anticipated.

He should feel good about that.

A small win, and as Kassie liked to say, you took those whenever you could get them. Because small wins one after the other could lead to a big victory.

Keeping that advice in mind, rather than focus on what hadn't occurred, he needed to focus on what to do next. What he could do to earn the next small win. And then the one after that.

Because in addition to the reason he had visited his father, he suspected that the tensions roiling the Teg world that worried him even more were escalating faster than he originally suspected.

It was no more than a feeling. He didn't have any hard evidence to back it up yet. But he had learned to never ignore premonitions such as these. The sense of doom that chimed in the back of his head warning him that a reckoning was coming.

Added to that was the urgency intensifying within him. The feeling that he would need to act. Soon.

Draig feared that if he allowed this hidden adversary to continue to build his strength unchecked, working from the shadows, taking advantage of all the other distractions flowing through the Teg world, the real battle would be lost before it even began.

For just a heartbeat, his vision clouded, black spots appearing at the edge, the weight of what he was dealing with pressing down on his shoulders.

He hadn't experienced this sensation in quite a long time. Not since he was a Knight of the Round.

However, he was certain that it didn't resurface now because of what he believed was happening. Rather, he experienced it because he already had a good sense as to what was going to be required of him.

If he chose to follow a certain path. The right path. The one laid out in front of him when he visited the Circle atop the Druid's Peak.

A choice to make between two possible futures. Neither appealing. One more frightening than the other.

Draig cursed softly under his breath, a sense of resignation rushing through him. He should have known.

He had left his father and the Knights of the Round because he couldn't continue to be what Arthur wanted him to be. He couldn't continue to be the person who he was.

Now, however, he feared that if his suspicions were correct, and he had no reason to doubt them, for him to prove successful, he would need to once again be the person he hated. The version of himself that had almost destroyed him utterly, removing what little of his conscience remained.

To say nothing of the many other fears that threatened to immobilize him.

If he was right about the peril the Tylwyth Teg faced, he didn't know if he could stand against it alone.

How was he supposed to bring the Teg together to fight against this threat when they were so divided? How was he supposed to gain their trust after what he had done for his father? Worse, during a time when his father was steadily losing the trust of the Teg as he functioned more like a dictator rather than a wise ruler? And what of his aunt? Where and when would she attempt to take advantage?

Because he had no doubt that she would. She would sniff

out the opportunity and strike. She wouldn't be able to help herself.

The age-old battle between brother and sister may have become a hidden war. Nonetheless, it was still a war. Morgase sought to topple Arthur from power so that she could claim the throne for herself.

All the while with a more dangerous threat biding his time and preparing to strike at the moment of greatest weakness. A moment that his aunt might create on her own. Or his father on his own. Or, most likely, both brother and sister would have a hand in it because neither had the capacity to recognize just how destructive their competing goals and desires were to the Tylwyth Teg.

Definitely not the position he wanted to be in, Draig mused. Yet he was in this position – calling it being stuck between a rock and a hard place didn't do it justice -- for a reason.

He believed that. And though it didn't appeal to him, he knew that he couldn't escape what was being asked of him. He knew what he had to do.

There really wasn't a choice to be made, in fact. Because he had made his choice long ago.

He would do whatever was necessary to make up for what was demanded of him when he was the Dragon.

He would seek atonement from those he had wronged in the name of the King Teg.

He would give all that was necessary to protect the Teg, even if a large segment of the Teg had no use for him.

He would make the ultimate sacrifice if that was required of him, although he would do everything in his power to avoid that if he could.

His decision made, realizing that continuing to think about the challenges he faced was a waste of time, Draig pushed himself off the railing, eyes narrowing, expression flinty. He had been so captured by his own thoughts and concerns that he hadn't been paying attention to all that was going on around him.

Trotting down the steel steps that circled the inside of the lighthouse tower, he stopped in the kitchen and peered out the window.

He really needed to stay more in the present. Another piece of advice from Kassie. Not spending so much time concentrating on what he had just done and what he needed to do.

He had sensed them before he even walked through the Dragon Door, yet he had allowed himself to be distracted by his worries and fears.

There were intruders on the island who had tried and failed to breach the lighthouse.

But who?

Reaching out with the Grym, he found the answer in an instant.

Paladins.

He should have known after his conversation with his father. Further confirmation that Arthur spoke the truth. At least this time.

Draig smiled maliciously at the sight that greeted him, unfazed by the incursion.

Butch, Cassidy, and Sundance clearly were in control of the clash. In fact, not surprisingly, they were enjoying themselves.

More than a dozen Paladins lay on the rocky ground, dead or dying. The remainder fought with the manic energy of those desperate to stave off a bloody end.

The arrogant bastards likely never expected that what should have been a fairly simple burglary had instead turned into a battle for their lives against three dragons three times larger than draft horses who spent most of their time masquerading as cockerpoos.

The fight would end soon.

That much was apparent.

Cassidy had just removed two more Paladins from the clash and was spinning swiftly to assist Butch, who had just ripped a Paladin in half at the waist with a single swipe of his claw before spitting a stream of fire that consumed two more of Mordred's soldiers, the men dropping to the ground, rolling, hopelessly beating at the flames that couldn't be extinguished except by magical means.

With the battle almost over, Sundance already had begun to feast. With a lightning-fast swing of her tail, she knocked down three Paladins. She killed two before they could rise, stabbing each through the chest with a bloody claw. She took the third Paladin's head in her maw, crushing it before ripping it free from the dead man's shoulders, then chewing on the skull as if it were no more than an appetizer.

There was no need for Draig to make an appearance. Nevertheless, he decided that he should offer his friends some moral support from the porch.

Turning toward the back door, Draig stopped. He tightened his grip on his blackthorn shillelagh, a brief flash revealing the walking stick's true nature. The sword that had chosen him instead of his father.

"You have nothing to worry about, Dragon. I came alone. I am only the messenger. No more than that."

Draig, already slashing with the blade, halted Excalibur just a hair from his visitor's throat, holding the glowing steel in place. Illuminating his unwanted guest. "There are better ways to speak with me than to break into my home. Safer too."

"True," the visitor admitted. "But time is of the essence, and when I got here, with your wards focused on the men dying outside, I had a chance to slip through. So I took it."

"A weakness on my part that I'll correct as soon as we're done here."

"You're not going to banish me like you have so many of my brothers and sisters?" The visitor tilted his head down, gazing at the glowing steel that with a single flick of the Dragon's wrist would send him back to his native realm.

Draig didn't reply immediately, studying his visitor.

The soulless black eyes gave him away. That and his vague human shape, which was a misty black at the edges.

Daemon.

Not fully formed in the lighthouse. Probably because though the Daemon had made it through his exterior defenses, the creature wasn't strong enough to challenge all of Draig's magical protections.

"Not today," Draig replied. He pulled Excalibur back from the Daemon's throat, resting the blade on his shoulder, two hands on the hilt as if the blade was a bat.

"Thank you for that." The Daemon stepped out of the shadows. He looked like anyone else Draig could meet on the streets of Kraken Cove. A nondescript man who would leave no impression unless you knew what you were looking for. The only feature his visitor couldn't change to blend in his pure black eyes. The tell-tale sign that the creature had been summoned from the Daemon Realm.

"Why are you here? I have business to attend to outside."

"From what I saw your dragons do not require your assistance."

"True," Draig agreed with a nod. "Even so, I was hoping to join in the fun. So let's get to it."

"You haven't replied to my Master."

"I've been busy."

"Obviously you have," the Daemon agreed. "Still, I must ask. Will you meet with him?"

Draig didn't respond right away. An uneasy feeling rolled through him. His past interactions with the Daemon King had not gone well, at least not for the Daemon King. And the Master of the Daemon Realm was known to hold onto his grudges for an eternity.

However, all those other instances involved Draig hunting Daemons that were sowing mayhem in the Natural World. He had never taken action against the Daemon King for any other reason than that. And Draig had shown him some leniency when leniency was not required.

Besides, with the task that he had set for himself, he needed help. From anyone able and willing to provide it. Even from those who might like nothing more than to stab him through his heart with his own blade if the opportunity presented itself.

"I will."

"That is good," the Daemon sighed, surprised that the Dragon had agreed so readily. "I will let him know. He will be expecting you."

A shriek from just outside the lighthouse drew their gazes. Draig shook his head, disappointed in the Paladins' efforts. These elite fighters molded into form by Morgase and Mordred were not doing well.

With almost all their number slaughtered, the handful of survivors, gathered together in a small group, were attempting to hold off Butch, Cassidy, and Sundance.

The dragons towered over the Paladins, obviously indifferent to the weapons the men brandished before them. It was only a matter of time before the end came. Despite all their training, these Paladins were no better than the Weres who visited the lighthouse uninvited just a few days before.

"Mordred's work, I assume?"

"What makes you say that?" Draig asked, giving the Daemon a more thoughtful expression. This Daemon was not like all the others he had met. Which only made sense since the Daemon King had given him this assignment.

"Morgase would attack you out of the shadows, a knife in the back, avoiding a direct confrontation. She's the more devious of the pair."

"I'll grant you that."

"On the other hand, your half-brother is not the smartest of the lot. He prefers to wield blunt instruments." The Daemon's eyes widened, and he lifted his hands in apology as he caught the flash of anger in the Dragon's reddish-orange eyes. "My apologies. I hope I do not offend."

Draig hated the fact that he shared a father with Mordred, but there was nothing that he could do about it. And there was no reason to push his own displeasure at that unfortunate reality onto his visitor. "No offense has been given. With respect to Mordred, I agree with you. If he sees a nail, his only desire is to hit it with a hammer."

The Daemon nodded, understanding. "I have over a thousand brothers and sisters. Most I can deal with. Some ... I'd rather we were not related."

"Any of them as bad as Mordred?"

The Daemon took his time before responding, obviously needing to work through that very long list. "No."

"Then you have me there." Draig wanted to smile, but he didn't. Because he knew after his many encounters with Daemons that what this one had said wasn't a joke. He was speaking the truth. Simply answering his question.

"I will wait to hear from the Daemon King." Draig felt the need to end this conversation.

A strange uneasiness had come over him. A hint of warning. He thought it might be because of his visitor, but on closer inspection he didn't believe the source of his apprehension resulted from the close proximity of the Daemon. No, there was another cause. He just needed to identify it.

"Thank you." The Daemon slowly faded into a black mist. Before he disappeared completely, he nodded at something just over Draig's shoulder. "Watch your back."

Draig didn't bother to think. He moved. Allowing his instincts to guide him, he spun around.

His foreboding took shape as a new threat appeared.

The thin steel links of a whip with a barbed end streaked toward his face.

SWORDS HELD SHAKILY OUT to their front, their fear threatening to consume them, the last of the Paladins had formed into a wedge, slowly stepping back down the beach.

They gave no thought whatsoever to their dead and dying comrades. They thought only of themselves. Seeking to escape this hellhole of an island and three monstrous dragons that stalked toward them on all fours. Tails swishing from side to side. Gusts of steam erupting from their nostrils.

They had seen what these beasts could do, killing several of their friends with pinpoint swipes of their claws and streams of fire that were still burning.

They knew that these dragons could kill them whenever they wanted.

It would take very little effort.

A single blast from any of the three would do it.

Yet the dragons restrained themselves. They had something else in mind, and the Paladins knew what, several of them unashamed by the trickles of piss that ran down their legs as a result.

The dragons were hungry, and the Paladins were on the menu.

Thurston, the Paladin on the far right, yelped when the green dragon lunged at him. Stumbling back, he only kept his feet because he ran into Chase, who stood next to him.

"Stand strong, Paladin!" Rufus ordered. He was positioned at the point of the wedge, assuming command when no one else would. "We are almost to the Zodiacs. Be ready."

Rufus' order infused the other Paladins with a brief moment of clarity and mental strength.

It didn't last long.

The red dragon on the left side lunged with a shocking speed, clamping down on Bernard's blade and tearing it from his grip. The dragon appeared to smirk as the beast threw the steel into the ocean.

Rufus gulped. The dragons were playing with them now.

He knew then that they were never going to make it off the island as the trio of monsters continued their slow, inexorable advance. Still, they had to try.

"We're here," Chase called out. He had just bumped into the inflated hull of one of the Zodiacs.

None of the other Paladins looked over their shoulders. They only had eyes for the dragons that continued to snap at them. In sport now, it seemed, the predators not in a rush to take the last of their prey.

"When I give the order, get the Zodiac into the water. As fast as you can."

None of the other Paladins responded, tensing, preparing themselves, understanding that turning their backs on the dragons was nothing more than an open invitation to strike. Yet they had no other choice.

"Now!" Rufus bellowed.

As one, the Paladins turned, trying to forget for the next few seconds the terrible threat at their backs.

Chase and Thurston got to their positions first, Erich and Julio joining them.

With a strength born of desperation, they pushed the Zodiac into the water, not bothering to turn around when the horrible scream ripped through the air.

Rufus.

They were certain.

He was dead. Joining their many comrades.

One of the dragons had gotten him.

Maybe more than one.

They didn't care.

They only cared about getting away.

They didn't want to die.

Clambering over the hull, Chase went directly to the engine and hit the ignition. The powerful outboards started on the first try.

Breathing a sigh of relief, he took the wheel and increased the power, the three other Paladins gripping the rope on the bow and pulling themselves out of the surf.

They were going to make it.

Chase was certain of it.

Rufus had distracted the dragons. Giving his life for theirs.

The beasts were probably pulling him apart right then, enjoying their meal.

A terrifying and disgusting possibility, but one that played in his favor.

Maybe, just maybe, the dragons' desire to feast would give him and the last of his unit time to get away.

He swung the bow around with a quick spin of the wheel, the ocean beckoning to him. The Zodiac quickly gained speed as it raced away from the shore, Chase finally letting go of his almost paralyzing anxiety. Then he laughed.

They had done it!

They had survived!

The last of his laugh died in his throat when he heard a sound that chilled his heart.

A loud pop over the roar of the engine.

And then another.

Followed by the shriek of air escaping.

His spirit broke when the back of the boat began to sag into the ocean.

When he felt the first touch of water at his heels, the waves rushing over the deflating tubes, Chase didn't turn around.

He couldn't.

He was too terrified.

Then he whimpered, feeling the hot puff of breath on the back of his neck.

DRAIG DODGED TO THE LEFT, the barbed tip of the whip slicing right past his cheek. So close that he could see the poison drops on the inch-long spikes of the metal head. One touch from any of those and he was dead.

As the chain slid back by his side, Draig dropped to the floor and rolled, anticipating his attacker's next move.

Just in time.

With a flick of the assassin's wrist, the chain curled in the air right above Draig's head. If he hadn't known what to expect, the steel links would have wrapped themselves around Draig's chest, the barbed head finishing him.

He had not fought a Viper for more than a century. But he had not forgotten what it had taken to defeat the last one who sought to kill him.

"Your luck will run out, Dragon," hissed the Viper, his split tongue giving Draig's attacker a permanent lisp. "You will not escape me."

"I don't plan on escaping you," Draig replied. His voice was calm, controlled, his eyes blazing brightly, matching the blazing fire running along the length of his steel. "I plan on killing you."

Although Draig understood full well that was going to be a difficult task. Vipers were created by one of the Ancients. One of those who was there when the world of the Tylwyth Teg first came into being. An almost all-powerful god. An Ancient who exercised an immense potency against which little could stand.

Most of the Ancients had crafted proxies to complete tasks

in the Teg world that the Ancient could not or would not be bothered with.

Typhon had made the Vipers with the assistance of his wife Echidna.

His assassin confirmation as to what Draig truly was up against. The threat in the shadows finally revealing himself.

When Typhon was imprisoned in Tartarus, it was said that the Vipers had continued their work, shifting their loyalty to one of Typhon's daughters while their master was locked away.

Draig had never believed the story completely. Yes, that the daughter played a big part in deciding what assassination contracts the Vipers accepted. But he had no doubt as well that Typhon continued to exercise some influence over the Vipers despite his imprisonment. Much like a mob boss still running his empire from the inside.

"Dream while you can, Dragon. When I am finished with you, you will dream no more. You will become a part of the never-ending sleep."

The Viper flicked his wrist, the whip snaking out toward Draig.

This time he didn't dodge out of the way. This time Draig stood his ground.

Knocking the barbed tip out of the way with Excalibur, at the same time he crafted a small buckler out of the Grym and affixed it to his forearm, protecting against the poison that threatened to splatter him as the Viper attacked with even greater ferocity.

The assassin's whip snapped through the air. Time after time. A seemingly unending assault, the Viper moved Draig around his living room with ease.

Yet Draig blocked every attack, catching the whip with either sword or buckler. He kept his movements precise, understanding the risk of allowing the whip to wrap around Excalibur. Not wanting to lose his sword. If he did, his death was ensured.

As he moved around the large open space of the bottom floor, never giving the Viper the chance to corner him, as he had done when he first arrived back at the lighthouse, he decided to give himself the leeway to forgive himself for not sensing the Viper's presence straightaway.

Actually, Draig should consider himself lucky. Most Teg never knew that a Viper was there until they felt the bite of the whip or the creature's sharp fangs, either one guaranteeing a slow, horrible death as the poison ravaged their insides, melting organs and flesh until there was nothing left but a bloody pile of steaming bones.

The Paladins on the beach were a convenient distraction. The Daemon as well.

Catching that brief hint of warning thanks to his finely honed instincts was more than most Teg could ask for and likely had saved him from an agonizing and gruesome death. And the Daemon helped by providing him with the evidence that he couldn't see with his own eyes.

At least not at first. Because that was the trick when it came to Vipers.

Typhon's servants were such excellent assassins because they were so rarely seen. Infused with some of their master's unique abilities, a Viper used the Twisted Grym to blend into his environment. Unlike a Warlock who could disappear from one moment to the next, a Viper functioned more like a chameleon.

Now that Draig knew what he was up against, he used the Grym to latch onto the assassin, refusing to let him go. Certain that if he allowed the Viper to slip away, if only for a heartbeat, that could mean the end for him. That split-second of extra work to find his attacker again ceding the advantage to the assassin who would not hesitate to make use of it.

Whip continuing to snap through the air with an irritating frequency, Draig saw the Viper clear as day. Pale green eyes matched the pale green cast of his skin, his hair a blackish green. Scales grew where his eyebrows were, working their way up his forehead to the crown of his head. A reminder of the animal Typhon had used to create his very skilled killers.

Draig lifted his forearm, blocking the barbed head of the whip with his buckler. Then he dove to the right, rolling, coming back to his feet instantly. The dagger the Viper had thrown at him with his free hand missed by just a hair. Lodging itself in the wall, the poison on the blade sizzled as it scorched the wood.

This wasn't working. Doing nothing but defending.

The strategy chafed and went against every one of Draig's instincts. It likely ensured his death as well if he didn't adopt a more aggressive approach.

Seeking to take the initiative, he rolled back to the left when the whip shot through the space where his head had been just a heartbeat before. At the same time, he sent a blast of the Grym toward the Viper.

Draig didn't expect to hit the assassin with his magic. The Viper was too fast.

But that was all right with him. All he wanted to do was force the Viper to hesitate. To slow his attack just enough so that Draig could close with the assassin.

Covering the distance between them in three long strides, Draig succeeded. Slashing with Excalibur, he forced the Viper to dodge, the assassin having no good way to defend against his steel, the dagger that appeared in his clawed hand of little use. His whip even less so without the space needed to extend the chain.

Draig kept up his attack. Forcing the Viper around the common room, he refused to allow the assassin to gain the distance that he wanted so that he could get away from Draig's gleaming blade and once again make use of his preferred weapon.

Yet though Draig had stolen the momentum of the clash from the Viper that didn't mean his victory was assured.

Draig lifted his buckler just in time, protecting his eyes from the venom the Viper spat at him from the fangs that hung down over his lower lip. Then again. And once more. One drop of the poison in his eye or on his skin enough to kill him.

Draig pivoted to his right, the Viper's dagger missing his ribs by just a hair, Draig unable to get his buckler down to his side in time after blocking the latest splash of poison aimed at his eyes.

Most Teg would be pleased. He was holding his own. But he wasn't most Teg.

He needed to try something new.

He needed to take a risk.

Draig rushed forward. Catching the Viper in the chest with his shield and shoulder, he smashed the assassin back against the wall. Rather than continuing his assault as the Viper anticipated, he stepped back instead.

Putting ten feet between them, he could tell by the murderous expression on the Viper's face what was going to happen next. Just as Draig wanted.

When the whip shot out toward Draig, he shifted the shape of his buckler with barely a thought and grabbed the poisoned length of chain with the magical gauntlet he now wore on his hand.

Twisting his body and taking a few steps in the direction the whip was going, he yanked hard, pulling the Viper off balance.

Before the assassin knew what was happening, Draig had wrapped the chain around the Viper's chest, crushing his arms to the side of his body and eliminating the assassin's ability to use his whip or dagger.

Hissing in rage, the Viper still had a chance. No more than a foot separating him from Draig, the assassin lunged, seeking to bite Draig's shoulder, drops of poison dripping from the tips of his fangs.

A good idea, Draig had to admit.

Unfortunately for the Viper, once again that was exactly what he wanted the assassin to do.

The Viper's neck extended, Draig didn't hesitate. With a wickedly fast slash, he severed the assassin's head from his shoulders.

Releasing his grip on the whip, Draig allowed the body to collapse to the ground. He then kicked the head against the far wall. The spray of poison from the Viper's fangs would continue until the creature's brain realized that the body was dead.

Draig took a deep breath then, settling himself. Pleased with his victory. But not yet certain that the combat was complete.

It had been a long time since he fought a Viper, but he had not forgotten one key detail. When there was one Viper about, there tended to be another. The assassins worked in pairs usually, which helped to guarantee fast and effective kills.

That concern running through his mind, Draig spun swiftly, sensing another presence at his back that had moved out of the shadows as soon as he killed the first Viper.

He was ready, about to block the whip screaming toward his throat with the magical buckler once again fixed to his right forearm.

Draig didn't have to. The Viper's lash lost its energy right before it struck, Draig knocking it to the side with a surprising ease.

"You certainly are a popular fellow these days," a craggy voice said from just behind the Viper, who remained in place just a second more before dropping to the floor.

Seamus stood there in his fisherman's sweater and work pants, giving Draig his best shit-eating grin.

"It's not the kind of popularity I'm looking for."

"I can understand that," Seamus replied with a nod. He knelt down, wiping the blood from the fish fillet knife that he had driven into the back of the Viper's neck.

"Thanks for the help," Draig said with a nod. Releasing his hold on the Grym, the buckler faded away and Excalibur once again looked like a blackthorn shillelagh.

"I figured I owed you," Seamus responded with a shrug, the knife disappearing in his pocket. The crusty mariner jumped back from the door when a large, green, tooth-filled snout poked its way through the opening. "A curse upon the Ancients! Could you please control your mutts?"

Butch, Cassidy, and Sundance stalked around the outside the lighthouse, Cassidy poking his nose through the door and ready to crash through the entrance and join in the fight. The trio growled, the deep rumble making the lighthouse shake ever so slightly. They smelled the blood of the Vipers, and they didn't like it in the least.

"They're just here to help," Draig replied. "You know how they are."

"Unfortunately I do. Could you get those three mongrels to shift back please. They always make me nervous when they're like this. I don't like feeling as if I can be ripped apart in a single bite."

"I can't imagine why," Draig replied, unable to miss the bloody streaks along their snouts and the bits of gore stuck between their teeth.

"Any Paladins left for Seamus and me?" he asked. Silence greeted his question. "I thought not. Could you stop scaring Seamus, please?"

Draig ignored the several reluctant growls as the dragons did as he asked and shifted to their other form.

The three cockerpoos raced into the lighthouse, sniffing around the inside to ensure that there were no more Vipers to worry about before wandering over to the two dead assassins. Sniffing the bodies and the blood, they stayed well away from the puddles of poison, Butch actually making his distaste clear by peeing on the Viper that lay dead at Seamus' feet.

The mariner smiled at the display. The mutts made him uncomfortable, that was true, but there were times when he appreciated their attitudes.

"What brought you out here, Seamus? I know it wasn't the Vipers."

"That was just lucky happenstance," he replied. "Your problems keep multiplying, and they're getting nastier."

"That's one way to put it," Draig murmured.

"Probably the best way. I came out here to get you. You've got another issue that requires your attention."

"Worse than two Vipers in my home?"

"Unfortunately, yes," Seamus sighed.

"Tell me."

"An old friend just came into Kraken Cove."

"An old friend?"

"Well, one of my old friends. And not really a friend. More like an enemy, actually. Maybe a frenemy because there was this one time that ..."

"Seamus ..."

"Sorry, I'm just not used to all the excitement of the last few days. Come on. I'll take you to where I think she might be lurking."

9

A JINX UPON YOU

"He's been living here all this time? Seriously?"

"That's what your father told us, Jinx." The Viper shrugged. He didn't quite understand it himself.

It was a small town. Or appeared to be. In Jinx's opinion, it was too quiet here. No one was on the streets on what should be a busy time of the day. Almost as if a warning had been issued when the thirteen Vipers appeared on the town green, striding through the portal crafted by their boss.

"There's no reason to doubt him because he's rarely wrong," Jinx murmured as she spun around slowly. Taking in the crag and then the ocean to the east. The church and the fire station to the south and north respectively. The main drag just ahead, which really wasn't much of a main drag. No more than a couple blocks. "Knowing the Dragon, he came here for a reason."

"To hide away from us?" wondered the Viper, the assassin gripping his poisoned whip and anxious to make use of it.

"I doubt it." Jinx swept her long green dreadlocks to the side and back over her shoulders. "Like I said, he came here for a reason. And not to hide away from us, you can be sure of that. Little frightens the Dragon. Don't forget that."

"Jinx, I still think ..."

"Shut it, Cyrus." Her eyes flashed a dark green that was almost black as she turned her full attention on her second in command. "There's a reason father has let the Dragon be for so long. Best to remember that as well."

"Because he eliminated so many of our comrades," the Viper sighed, embarrassed by the admission. "I know. We all know. That's why we're looking forward to this. The Dragon has much to account for."

"In part, yes. In part because there was no need to alert the Dragon to our plans. Until now." She ran her gaze over the green once more, reaching out with the Twisted Grym, allowing the corrupted strands of energy to spread and probe the center of the small town. She couldn't help but notice the magic that radiated throughout Kraken Cove. Even more, where it was strongest.

"Will he face us?" Cyrus' voice contained an excitement that he could barely contain.

He and his comrades had heard a great deal about the Dragon. They knew the quality of his work thanks to the stories about him that circulated among the Vipers, yet none who accompanied Jinx had ever gone up against him. And all hoped to be the one to earn the glory and the reward their master promised for his head, assuming the Dragon didn't agree to their master's terms.

"We'll give him little choice," Jinx replied. "Tell the Vipers to get into position so that they're not easy targets. Tell them also to be ready for anything. I don't want us to be taken by surprise."

"Do you really believe all this is necessary? We are thirteen Vipers, you as well. An unheard-of number to take on a single Teg."

Jinx's eyes flashed dangerously, having little tolerance for second guessing. She didn't understand why these Vipers couldn't comprehend just how lethal the Dragon was. "Cyrus, who gave us this mission?"

"Your father, of course."

"Who decided how many Vipers would go on this mission?"

"Your father, of course."

"Do you know something that my father doesn't?"

That question stopped the Viper right in his tracks, forcing him to think rather than offer the response that was on the tip of his forked tongue. He answered cautiously, realizing that he had wandered into perilous territory. "No, I don't."

"If my father sent thirteen Vipers to kill the Dragon – and he's the Dragon, Cyrus, not just a Teg, but the Dragon – then he believed we would need that many Vipers to complete this job. Do you understand?" The Viper nodded, telling himself that he would stop challenging his commander and just get on with it, not wanting to risk her wrath. "Good, now tell the Vipers to spread out and be ready. The show is about to start."

Jinx snorted in disgust as Cyrus hustled away to relay her orders. Too many questions, not enough thinking on her subordinate's part.

Once she completed this mission, she would identify a new second in command. She didn't have any time or energy to waste on a Viper who didn't obey without question. Thinking too much rather than doing could put all that they were working toward at risk.

Glancing over her shoulder, satisfied that her nest of Vipers had done as ordered, she turned toward the building giving off one of the strongest signatures of the Grym.

The bakery.

The dossier her father gave her confirmed that the Dragon owned the bakery and several other businesses just off the town square. She would start there.

Wisps of green and black drifted up from her palms. Holding her arms down toward the ground, she allowed those wisps to spin faster, taking the shape of a small tornado that grew in size and strength as more of the Twisted Grym answered her call.

Then, in a whiplike motion reminiscent of a cobra's strike, she flung the whirlwind of energy directly toward the bakery.

She wasn't surprised by what happened next.

Nothing at all.

Her strike slammed into an invisible barrier of energy that shimmered a golden white. The tainted power played along the surface for several seconds, seeking a way through, failing, fading slowly as the protective magic consumed the Twisted Grym.

Jinx looked back over her shoulder at Cyrus. "Do you understand now?"

She didn't bother to wait for his reply, shifting her focus back toward the storefront. Jinx sent several more tornados crafted of the Twisted Grym streaking toward the bakery. Each time the magical defenses set around the store prevented her attack from breaking through, though not only repelling the corrupt power, but also cleansing it. A rare skill that was almost unheard of among the Teg.

That was all right with Jinx. She had assumed that it was a possibility, because it confirmed the intel given to her. Besides, she wasn't interested in destroying the bakery. Not yet anyway.

She just wanted to get the Dragon's attention. Force him to come out and play.

When the door opened a moment later, she smiled with a cold menace. Now the fun was finally going to begin.

"Where is he?" Jinx demanded, disappointed that the Dragon hadn't emerged.

"Where is who?"

Cerridwen stepped out onto the sidewalk, still wearing her

baking apron, wiping flour from her hands. Ragnar, Urs, and Thorsen followed, spreading out behind her, clearly not pleased to have their meal interrupted as they licked the last of the cinnamon rolls they were eating from their fingers.

"The Dragon, Sorceress. We are here for the Dragon."

Jinx's face twisted into a scowl, interpreting the expression that the woman gave her as scorn with a strong pinch of disbelief. A look of disrespect, obviously, one that she never received and only served to get her blood boiling that much more.

"Are you sure you want to wake the Dragon? He's not known for being all that forgiving when someone decides to visit him unannounced and with poor intentions. And since you decided to attack his bakery, I have no doubt that he's going to be in a very bad mood when he arrives. Better just to hop onto the sea horse you rode in on and get out while you can."

"You dare to challenge me, Sorceress." Jinx sensed the potent magic the woman controlled. A deep well of power. One of the stronger of the Tegs. Based on the information her father had given her about the town, she assumed it was Cerridwen, the Dragon's second. "I have no time to waste on you. Bring us the Dragon so that we can be done with this business. Then we will be gone."

Cerridwen stared at Jinx, her expression shifting to one of amusement. Then she chuckled softly, which rankled Jinx all the more. "The Dragon does as he wants. Not what others tell him to do."

"The Dragon is here," Jinx growled. She knew that he was. She was certain of it. Though she couldn't say where he might be in this seaside enclave. "Give him to us and we will leave you be. You can get on with your miserable lives with nothing and no one the worse for wear."

"And if we don't?"

"Then I will release my Vipers and you can test yourselves

against my finest assassins. I will not waste my time on you and your friends. You are beneath me."

"You dare to invade our home and insult us," Ragnar demanded, his face red with rage. He and his brothers stood behind Cerridwen completely at ease. Though their expressions were thunderclouds as their fingertips brushed the steel bars holstered on their thighs. They knew a fight was coming. They could smell it. A clash that couldn't be avoided. A clash they desired, relishing the chance to take on an opponent they had never faced before. Quick to anger, Berserkers were even quicker to fight when the opportunity presented itself. "You will pay with your lives for your slight."

Ragnar took a step past Cerridwen, Urs and Thorsen about to follow. That was as far as the giant got, Cerridwen grasping his forearm and holding him in place.

She whispered to him quietly and patiently, making sure that only the Three Little Bears heard what she said.

"Ragnar, I ask that you and your brothers wait just a little while longer."

"Cerridwen, the woman has insulted you. She has insulted us. We must defend your honor and ours. It is our way."

Cerridwen smiled at that. These three big, burly, blonde behemoths with beards that ran down to their belts – usually; they would have if Draig hadn't given the long whiskers a crispy trim when they first met -- had grown on her in just a matter of days. She loved their attitudes. But they needed to control their tempers for now. They needed to wait until the time was right.

"And you will gain your chance, Ragnar. Have no fear."

"Cerridwen, please ..."

"Too afraid to allow your three puppies off the leash," taunted the green-haired woman.

Cerridwen ignored her. She remembered who she was now. She should have seen the resemblance sooner. The green dreadlocks a dead giveaway.

Jinx.

Daughter of one of the Ancients. She had to give credit where credit was due. Draig was right to be concerned now that the enemy hidden in the shadows had revealed his hand.

Ragnar tried to pull free from Cerridwen's grasp at the latest insult, but gently. He didn't want to show his new friend any disrespect.

It didn't work. Cerridwen's grip was as strong as iron and held him in place.

"I have no doubt that you can manage these monsters," Cerridwen explained in a very composed voice, sensing that the three brothers were preparing to shift. Once they did, all hell would break loose. That didn't bother her. She just didn't want it to happen yet. "Still, better to have more friends with us when we give our unwanted visitors the welcome they deserve."

"Who are we waiting for?" Ragnar whispered, his eyes sparking with excitement when he realized that this chafing restraint wouldn't be required for much longer.

Cerridwen smiled evilly, then nodded behind Jinx and the Vipers. Ragnar and his brothers followed her gaze.

"Peggy Rose, of course, and Pinkie. It would have been rude to keep them out of the fun." Taking hold of the Grym, Cerridwen stared daggers at Jinx, who had yet to notice what was coming at her from behind. "Have at them, boys."

Ragnar, Urs, and Thorsen already were on the move. Sprinting across the street, they shifted in a heartbeat, monstrous blonde bears taking their place, jaws snapping, claws swiping as they raced toward the Vipers with a rabid ferocity.

Pinkie came from the other direction. Shifting as he roared across the green like a freight train, having eyes only for the Vipers, the already large dog grew bigger than a draft horse. His canines lengthened into fangs and a dozen sharp spikes appeared on his tail that was now as long as a Viper's whip.

The St. Bernard was gone. In its place charged one of the dreaded offspring of Cerberus.

The Vipers didn't know what hit them, crushed between two distinct, almost unstoppable forces.

THE URGE TO join the fight that erupted on the town green was almost too much to resist. Yet Cerridwen controlled herself, holding back despite the pull growing more insistent with each slash, snap, and bite.

She had little doubt that the Three Little Bears and Pinkie could stand against the Vipers. Do more than stand, in fact.

The initial charge of the Werebears had knocked four of the Vipers from the fight in just as many seconds.

But the danger remained. Those Vipers were eliminated before they could bring their poisoned weapons to bear.

To allow her friends to fight freely, Cerridwen remained where she was, using the Grym to protect the Berserkers and Pinkie from the Vipers' venom.

So far, so good.

Despite the Vipers' many attempts, whether with their fangs, their whips, or the streams of venom they spit at their adversaries, none had yet to strike any of the Teg she guarded.

Still, her need to defend grated on her.

She preferred to attack first. Whenever she could. Hating to cede the momentum to an opponent.

That's how she had been trained.

Then she saw her chance.

A Viper had drifted to the edge of the fight, circling around the battle, seeking to take from behind one of the Three Little Bears – she couldn't tell which one was which once they shifted.

The Viper brought his whip hand over his shoulder, about

to send the steel chain and barb cutting into the back of the massive blonde bear who fought with a manic energy as he forced two other Vipers to duck and dodge. The assassins only were able to focus on how to keep themselves alive, and doing that with a great deal of frantic desperation as they had no other options against the shifter's unceasing and vicious assault.

Before the Viper could flick his whip forward, he grunted. Then he looked down, not quite understanding what he was seeing. A hole had appeared in his chest, a sphere of energy ripping through him from behind, the edges of the wound charred and smoking. A second later, he collapsed to the grass, never knowing who killed him.

Cerridwen grunted with satisfaction.

Not at the killing, but rather at aiding one of her new friends.

More than pleased with her work, she returned to her original task. Doing all that she could to ensure a fair fight against the Vipers so foolishly trying to infest the Dragon's home.

RAGNAR ROSE on his hind legs, roaring in triumph, his maw covered by bits of greenish flesh and blood.

The Viper had underestimated him, never believing that the Werebear that was three times his size could move with such speed. A mistake that cost the assassin his life.

A snake could kill the largest animal, but only if given the chance to bite.

Ragnar used the brief pause he had earned to survey the clash. He roared again, delighted by what he saw.

The spawn of Cerberus was a terror, ripping through the Vipers as if they were no more than tiny serpents just out of the nest. And his brothers were not far behind with their own efforts.

With all of the surviving Vipers occupied, Ragnar sensed his chance.

The leader of the Vipers remained at the rear of the fight. Not engaging. Just watching. Directing. Clearly not believing that she needed to dirty herself against such lowly challengers.

It was time for Ragnar to demonstrate the error in her judgment. To show her that she should never have come here.

About to leap toward the green-haired woman, a petite older woman with multicolored hair and wearing a sundress stepped in his way.

"Leave Jinx to me," Peggy Rose ordered. "We're old friends."

Ragnar fought against his instincts to ignore the Sorceress' command, calming himself when he glimpsed the power behind her eyes. The promise of what was to come if he didn't get in her way.

Offering Peggy Rose a nod of respect, Ragnar crashed back into the fight, roaring, swiping with his claws, aiding Thorsen who fought against two Vipers trying to circle around him so that one of the assassins could attack from behind.

A smart tactic. Useless now.

The Viper turning too late, Ragnar trampled him. Holding him against the ground with one massive paw, Ragnar bit down into the fallen assassin's shoulder, crushing bone, tearing through flesh and muscle, and ensuring that the assassin could no longer use his whip.

Ragnar stepped back then and began to circle the wounded Viper, who slowly pushed himself to his feet. The pain of his injury almost too much for him.

A fairer fight now in Ragnar's opinion, who huffed and growled, pawing at the ground as he stalked his prey.

The combat having only one possible end.

A dead Viper at his feet.

~

"I FORGOT how much fun it was to argue with you, Peggy Rose."

Jinx laughed as she glided and spun away from the spikes of energy that shot from the Sorceress' palms. Jinx was always a split-second ahead of her, avoiding Peggy Rose's attacks by no more than a hair. Clearly relishing every second of the encounter as she demonstrated her skill and adroitness.

Peggy Rose growled, maintaining her attack all the while. Knowing from experience just how dangerous it was to give this particular adversary any opportunity to breathe.

"It would be much more fun for me if you'd stop dancing around. Don't have it in you for a real fight, Jinx? Is that the problem?"

"Why would I want to do that?" Jinx demanded. Green dreadlocks whipping through the air, she laughed, unconcerned and unaffected by the taunt masked as a challenge. "It's much more satisfying to see you this way. Angry at yourself." Jinx laughed again, pleased to have gotten under her opponent's skin so easily. "You're losing your touch, Peggy Rose. Slowing down. Losing a step."

"Lost a step you say?" Peggy Rose's eyes burned with a brighter fire, her voice taking on a menacing tone. She hadn't lost a step. She had lost what little of her patience remained.

Not wanting to give free rein to her anger, she decided that she needed to change the dynamic of this combat. Now was the time to show Typhon's daughter that she had only gotten stronger with age. Reaching for more of the Grym, she prepared for the next stage in their clash. The final stage.

A callused hand on her shoulder stopped her.

"Do you mind if I cut in?" Seamus asked, a wicked gleam in his eye.

Peggy Rose studied him for a moment. "Are you certain, dear? I know what she did to you?"

"More than certain," Seamus confirmed with a nod. "It's time."

"Then have at it," Peggy Rose replied, stepping back so that Seamus would have more room with which to work.

"Hello lover," Jinx called from the green, a space in the clash opening naturally around her.

"That was a long time ago, Jinx."

"True, but you can't tell me it wasn't fun." Jinx offered Seamus a seductive grin that sent several pleasant, and just as many unpleasant, memories rushing through his brain ... and to certain parts of his body.

"It was fun," Seamus replied. "For a time. Then it became one of the worst mistakes I ever made."

"You're calling me a mistake," Jinx hissed, her mercurial anger almost palpable.

Seamus smiled. He thought it would be harder to rev her up. It seemed that some things hadn't changed since last he saw her. "I just did, lover. Biggest mistake of my life."

Jinx glowered at Seamus, the mariner standing there as if he didn't have a care in the world despite the battle raging around him.

"Your biggest mistake wasn't falling for me, Seamus. It was coming here now and giving me the chance to wipe that smirk from your face."

In a blur, Jinx appeared right in front of Seamus, her right hand now a claw that slashed toward his throat.

DRAIG STOOD at the far edge of the green, ocean at his back, keen eyes tracking the battle.

He had held back at Seamus' request. His friend wanted to reintroduce himself to his former lover before Draig became involved.

And quite an introduction it was that Seamus made.

Whatever the salty mariner said to Jinx had really gotten her goat, the woman attacking with a vindictive savagery.

Seamus didn't really fight back, allowing Jinx to expend her energy in useless attacks. He focused solely on defending himself, crafting shields of swirling water that he threw in place time after time rather than seeking to penetrate Jinx's defenses. That lack of aggression on his part only served to provoke Jinx all the more.

Draig wasn't really surprised by Seamus' approach. It was much like the dance Seamus and Jinx engaged in when they were together. The romance between them more a combat than anything else. One of them the hunter. The other the prey. Depending on the day ... and the mood.

"Sorry, but this isn't your fight." Draig directed his words toward Butch, Cassidy, and Sundance, the trio of cockerpoos standing at his feet eager to join the clash. "You already had your fun with the Paladins today."

All three dogs huffed, snorted, and grumbled, unhappy with Draig's decision. Still, they remained where they were. Although Butch did nudge Draig in the leg with his nose. Big eyes sad, he hoped to change Draig's mind by applying a little emotional pressure.

Draig bent down, scratching the fur on Butch's back. "Yes, if the clash goes sideways, you can tag in. But it looks like all is under control for now."

Butch growled, acknowledging the truth. Thirteen Vipers had started the combat on the town green. Only three remained. And they wouldn't last for much longer.

Surrounded by the Three Little Bears and Pinkie, it was only a matter of time before they met the same fate as their dead and dying comrades.

Certain in that knowledge, Draig concluded that he couldn't wait any longer. Striding across the green, Butch,

Cassidy, and Sundance at his heels, he had eyes only for Typhon's daughter.

Seamus lost himself in the combat. Calling on the power of the ocean, he flowed around the green more than strode, shields of seawater forming with scarcely a thought, strands of water snapping at Jinx, either trying to keep her back or seeking to wrap around her, irritate her, harass her, prevent her from pressing any advantage she might attempt to exploit.

He had not had so much fun as this in quite some time, the angry look Jinx gave him as she failed time after time to get past his magic only making it that much more enjoyable. Claws that failed to penetrate the water that turned to rock-hard ice in an instant then returned to its original form just as fast. Blasts of the Twisted Grym that slid off or were deflected by the waves and spouts of seawater that appeared at the very last second. It had been too long since he and Jinx had danced in this way, and he didn't realize just how much he missed it.

"Done with your fun, Seamus?" Draig asked.

Seamus stumbled ever so slightly, almost as if he had been fighting in a trance. And perhaps he had been, caught up in the past, his eyes never leaving Jinx as she tried and failed to kill him. Just as she had done so many times before when they were together. That thought curled his lip ever so slightly into a wistful smile.

Draig's words snapped him out of it, although it took a few seconds for him to come back to himself. "Sorry, couldn't help it. With Jinx here ... it just brought me back to my younger days, and I didn't want to let go."

"I can understand that. I'll let you back at it if you can give me a moment with her."

"She's all yours," Seamus grumbled, stepping back with a

bigger smile on his face. Clearly pleased with himself. Exhilarated by the duel.

"The prodigal son lives. How unfortunate."

"Sorry to disappoint," Draig replied, turning to face Jinx.

"No matter. You're the reason I'm here."

"Not to rekindle your romance with Seamus?" Draig asked, a hint of disappointment in his voice. "Back in the day you two made quite the couple."

"Unfortunately not," Jinx sighed. "And you're right, we did make quite the couple. Until that chowderhead went and ruined it."

Her first instinct was to attack the Dragon. She was fast. Very fast.

She might even have a chance. Snatch him and be done with it. Get him away from here before he could defend himself and before his friends could break away from the last of her Vipers and come to his aid.

She threw out that idea with scarcely a second thought, understanding now why the Dragon stood there calmly, his sword still appearing as a blackthorn shillelagh.

All of her Vipers were dead. That's why he was so at ease.

She hadn't expected that result. Then again, she hadn't anticipated coming up against two of the Teg's strongest Sorceress' in this tiny town along with three Werebears, the spawn of Cerberus, three little dogs that clearly weren't just dogs, and a former lover, all of whom were now arrayed against her.

"Why are you here for me, Jinx? I take it that your father is free from his prison, and he wants to have a chat before he kills me."

"So sure of yourself?" Jinx laughed, although it sounded more forced than real, even in her own ears.

"In this instance, yes. I am."

How could the Dragon have known? No one else among the Teg did. She was sure of that. She had made sure of that.

"Yes, he would like to speak with you," she admitted grudgingly. "He would like to make you an offer."

"I'm sure he would," Draig replied, although he made no move toward her. "How is your father? Is he enjoying his time out of Tartarus?"

"How couldn't he? Who would want to stay in that hellhole of a netherworld any longer than necessary?"

"A fair point. Although from what I understand, he deserved to be there."

"He deserved no such thing," Jinx spat. "He was betrayed by those who were jealous of him. They did not understand what my father would bring to the Teg. They locked him away because they feared him. Your father made sure he stayed locked away because he knew that if he didn't, he would lose his throne."

"You're entitled to your perspective, Jinx. Clearly, there's no point in arguing the matter. What's done is done."

"No, but there is cause to discuss another matter. I understand you have little love for your father."

Draig shrugged. "Many Teg have little love for my father. That doesn't mean we would turn our backs on him and side with an Ancient who has stated explicitly what he plans to do to the Teg if he ever takes the throne."

"Those are nothing but lies," Jinx challenged. "Rhetoric at best, no more than that, to sway the weak-minded."

"Your father has said it enough for it to sound more like a plan than just rhetoric. He seeks to enslave the Teg. That's his goal. To turn us into thralls who exist only to serve him."

Jinx took a breath to calm herself, her anger rising within her once again. Although it didn't work very well. Her fury wrapped in her voice. "Regardless of your perspective, misguided though it may be, he requests your presence. He believes that a conversation with the Dragon is long overdue. I will take you to him. Safe passage guaranteed so long as you behave yourself."

She offered him a solicitous smile, expecting him to acquiesce, because who in their right mind would deny a summons from her father with full knowledge of the consequences of doing so?

"No."

"No?" Jinx couldn't quite believe her ears. No one refused her father. No one dared to stand against an Ancient.

"No," Draig repeated. "You expect me to trust you?"

"You will come with me one way or another, Dragon. It will be to your benefit to listen to what my father has to say. He believes that you and he have common cause. As I said, he seeks only to make a deal with you."

"You mean like Monty Hall?"

"Who?" Jinx asked, confused by the reference, her face reddening because it drew a snigger from Seamus, who stood at Draig's back.

"Never mind," Draig replied, not having the desire or the energy to explain. "Why should I trust your father? He's not known for keeping his word."

"You shouldn't. But he sees something in you. Something that reminds him of himself."

"I don't know if I care for that comparison."

"You should be proud. Typhon stands alone among the Ancients."

"He stands alone for a reason," Draig countered.

Jinx growled softly, realizing that her efforts to persuade were proving fruitless. "Come with me now, Dragon. You can discuss your concerns with him. I'm sure that you can come to a meeting of the minds. He can be flexible when it serves his purposes."

Draig smiled at that, knowing exactly what would happen when he came face to face with Typhon. The Ancient would offer an ultimatum. He would try to convince Draig to kill Arthur and Morgase, offering the Teg throne to him in return, so long as he swore his obedience.

Then, when the time was right – meaning when Draig had outlived his usefulness -- Typhon would kill him. And, if Draig refused outright, Typhon would kill him. Neither result appealed to him.

If he went with Jinx, he'd never return to Kraken Cove.

"And if I still say no?"

"You will come, Dragon." Jinx's green eyes flashed, her dreadlocks beginning to swirl slowly around her head as she prepared herself to compel her recalcitrant quarry to her will. "What my father wants my father gets. You of all Teg should know that."

"Even without your Vipers? You think you can still force me to do what you want?"

Jinx's dreadlocks swirled with even greater speed, whipping through the air like the snakes of a many-headed Hydra. "We don't want to disappoint my father, Dragon. You of all people should know something of that."

"If you want to test your luck, feel free, Jinx."

The coldness of his voice was like a slap in the face. She studied Draig from a new perspective. She saw how his reddish-orange eyes glowed brightly. How he now held Excalibur in his hands. How he appeared to be eager for a fight.

What convinced her to restrain her instincts was the aura of energy that framed him, bright sparks flaring across his body, revealing just a hint of the power that he contained. Just a hint of the power that he could bring to bear against her if he so chose.

"I will leave you be this time, Dragon." Jinx gave him a nod, as if she were offering him a favor. "But the business between us is not yet done. Remember that. We will meet again, and when we do, you will not be able to refuse me."

In a flash, Jinx vanished, stepping back through a portal that flashed green and white and disappeared just as quickly as it appeared, so fast that it didn't reveal where Typhon's daughter had gone.

"You need to deal with this, Draig," Peggy Rose said, stepping up to him on his left side, patting him on his arm. "And you know what I'm really talking about. We haven't had a problem for more than ten years, and then in a matter of days we've got Werewolves hunting around Kraken Cove. We've got Vipers coming into town. And Jinx? That devilish monster rarely emerges into the light. For her to come here ... you need to do what you do best."

"Even if I don't want to?" Draig asked, although he already knew the answer. Because he already had made his decision.

"Even if you don't want to," Peggy Rose confirmed, offering him one more comforting pat on the arm before walking toward the bakery, famished after her duel. "But at least you know after what just happened that you won't be all on your own like you were last time."

That comment offered Draig some solace. Peggy Rose was right about that.

Seamus sidled up to him then, patting him on the back. Draig shook his head, not really surprised to find the usually cantankerous mariner in a good mood. Clearly, he had enjoyed sparring with Jinx. "Like I said, you're getting way too popular. And Peggy Rose is right. It used to be nice and quiet here."

"I preferred the quiet myself."

"Well, you know what they say."

"Say about what?" Draig asked, confused.

"That sometimes if you want the quiet to return, you need to make a little noise first."

10

A LUCKY DISTRACTION

Melissa pushed closed the front door of the Safe Haven, then trotted halfway down the walkway in her running gear.

Tom and Harry were probably right. After what had happened with Draig's former girlfriend showing up with five Warlocks, the smartest move was to stay at the inn.

It was the safest place for her to be. Hestia had strengthened the protections around the Safe Haven, ensuring that nothing and no one of the Teg could enter without her permission.

Even so, Melissa couldn't stay cooped up in her attic room, hiding away, even though Hestia had repaired the damage in just minutes.

She needed to get out for a few hours. Get some exercise. Clear her head. Figure out her next step.

Because her last conversation with Draig kept running through her head.

He kept pushing her. Not as hard as he could have. Not as hard as he probably would have when he had worked for his father.

Still, she knew that he wouldn't stop. He would continue to press until he got the truth from her.

He wouldn't be satisfied with just the pieces he'd already chiseled free or worked out on his own. He wanted all of the truth.

She'd be standing in front of him in her knickers. Figuratively, of course. Although based on how she envisioned that conversation going, she believed that she would be a great deal more comfortable doing so literally.

That's what worried her.

She wanted to trust him. She needed to trust him. She did trust him.

But with all that she was dealing with, all that was in play, was it fair to pull him in even farther?

Melissa was certain that Draig had figured out a great deal, especially after that morning's excitement. Callie's appearance likely helped to fill in a great many gaps for him.

He might even know it all and he was just waiting for her to trust him. To tell him what he already knew. So that he could trust her.

And he did want to help. She believed that. Despite his reputation.

He was the Dragon. She had heard the stories. She knew why she should be afraid of him. Terrified, actually. Especially after seeing with her own eyes exactly what he could do.

But she wasn't afraid. Not after what he had done for her. Not after what he had done for her mother and her sisters.

Well, that wasn't quite true.

She was still a little afraid of him. For several reasons, in fact. A few that she didn't want to admit to herself.

And she did trust him.

To do what he thought was right.

The problem was that his doing what was right might not be what was right for her. It might harm her chances of extricating herself from the almost impossible situation in which she had allowed herself to be trapped.

The almost impossible situation from which she had yet to find a path to freedom. For her and the person whose life was in her hands. A person who meant more to her than anyone else in the world.

Melissa needed to make a decision. And to do that she needed to move.

She would go no farther than the trails that snaked around the town. She would be safe there. Hestia had told her that Draig had added protections to the paths. She couldn't be harmed so long as she stayed on them.

Yet she had taken only a few steps toward the street when she stopped abruptly, tilting her head toward the center of town.

She heard the growls and roars that made her think of the Three Little Bears. Then the clash of steel and curses drifting on the wind. Followed by several small explosions and flashes of light that were visible just above the houses that blocked her view.

The skin on her arms tingled, hair sticking on end. She sensed it then.

The Grym.

Melissa hesitated. Was what was happening just a few blocks away because of her?

She didn't know. But she wouldn't be surprised if it was, because it seemed like everything that occurred in Kraken Cove the last few days happened because of her.

She should probably heed Tom and Harry's warning and head back to the inn. Stay somewhere safe.

She could go for a run later. Think and decide then. Once she knew what was going on.

But she couldn't help herself. Melissa needed to know what was happening. She needed to help if she could.

Draig and his friends had done so much for her already. She couldn't allow them to continue to fight her battles for her.

Melissa made it only a few feet down the walkway before she stopped, the hair on the back of her neck prickling, and not because of the use of the Power of the Ancients just a few blocks away.

All the gnomes positioned around Hestia's property had been facing toward the commotion in town. Not anymore. Every single one of them turned on a dime.

Identifying a new threat. A closer peril.

One coming from the direction of the side garden.

Right behind her.

Melissa was almost afraid to look.

"Hello, darling. Did you think I would allow you to slip away? After all that I invested in you?"

The cold sweat that dripped down Melissa's back seemed an appropriate response to the frigid voice that threatened to set her teeth chattering.

Melissa didn't want to face the woman who terrified her. She wanted to run. But she knew that would be a useless effort.

Tightening her fingers into fists, arms held straight down by her sides to ensure that she could control the shivering that she feared would break out, Melissa forced herself to turn around.

Even so, she kept one foot in front of the other. The instinct to run still strong in her. Still an option if an opportunity presented itself.

A natural reaction based on the predator who stepped out from the gate that led into the side garden.

Morgase.

Sister to the King Teg. Claimant to his throne. The real power behind the Paladins.

And someone to whom Melissa owed a debt.

A debt that she wasn't certain that she could pay. And that even if she could whether she should.

"Running is probably the best option," Morgase murmured in the high society drawl that was expected of her as part of her work with her foundation in New York City. A good cover, and a way to keep an eye on her brother and adversary from afar, though not too far. "But why bother? You have no way to escape me."

Morgase smiled briefly as she took a few steps closer to Melissa. "I can see as well that you're thinking about putting up a fight. I'd advise against that. In my current mood, I might lose my temper." Her expression shifted for just a flash, becoming menacing, almost inhuman. "You wouldn't want to see that."

"You're the cause of what's happening on the town green?" Melissa asked. She hoped to buy some time. She needed a few seconds to think. To figure out some way to get away from Morgase.

"No, dear, not me," Morgase replied in an amused chuckle. "It seems that your successes and failures have stirred up quite a hornet's nest. I assume that what's happening now is caused by another of the parties seeking to obtain from you what you owe me. An unanticipated distraction that I'm more than happy to make use of."

Melissa swallowed, almost choking, her throat dry. The look that Morgase offered her was that of a cat about to pounce on a mouse. "I can't give you what you want. Not yet."

"Of course you can, dear. And you will."

Morgase smiled, although it didn't reach her cold, black eyes. She seemed no more than an older, elegant woman dressed in an expensive blood-red pantsuit that appeared almost black. Her dark, silky hair was carefully configured with a fiery red hair pin that flashed whenever touched by the sunlight. But she was so much more than that.

Melissa realized that she only had one choice, and a poor one at that. Still, she needed to try. She stopped before she took more than two steps back toward the inn.

"Trying to escape me is a waste of time, dear," Morgase advised in a lethally quiet voice, continuing to advance on her prey. "Best to just go quietly so we can have a talk and work out this messy business between us. You don't want to make me angry, now do you?"

"Morgase, I'm telling you the truth," Melissa replied in as strong a voice as she could muster, hoping that it didn't sound as if she were pleading. "I don't have what you seek. Not yet. I just need more time. Once I have it, I'll give it to you."

Morgase chuckled softly at the claim. "My dear, the one thing I've learned after watching your work is that you're always running more than one game."

"That isn't true."

"Isn't it?" Morgase challenged. "Then how do you explain the other party who has come to town just for you?"

"I don't know what party you're talking about?"

"Of course you do, dear. Is not this other party affiliated with Tweedledee and Tweedledum over there?"

Melissa's eyes flicked toward the left. Tom and Harry stood on the top steps of the Safe Haven in their freshly ironed suits, shiny black shoes, and fedoras. Neither seemed to mind Morgase's mocking words.

"Insults will do you little good, Morgase," Tom replied, showing not a hint of emotion.

"A pleasure to see you again, Morgase," Harry offered with a respectful nod.

Morgase stared at the Three Brothers with a hint of scorn. "Where's the other one? Hiding in the shadows thinking he can take me from behind? He never was the smartest of the bunch."

"Dead," Tom replied quietly.

Morgase smiled at that. "Probably deserved. You're better off without him."

"Thank you for your support, Morgase, we do appreciate it." The sarcasm in Harry's tone couldn't be missed.

"But we must ask you to leave," Tom said. "We can't allow you to interfere in our business."

Morgase's expression hardened in an instant, mixing with an obvious anticipation. Almost as if she relished the opportunity to test her skills against these two relics from the 1950s.

"You think you can stop me, boys?" Her tone contained an obvious challenge.

"Perhaps not, but we need to try," Harry confirmed.

"Because of who sent you?" Morgase nodded, putting together the few pieces of the puzzle yet to be made clear that had been bothering her.

She knew Arthur had been in play. Finding the Three Brothers here, and the Witch clearly not worried or fearful of their presence, along with what was happening in town, confirmed that these two were not working for her brother. Of course, why would they after the way Arthur treated them the last time they did a job for him?

Nevertheless, that didn't mean they might not be willing to work with her rather than against her. They had always been sensible boys, probably even more so now with the psychotic third one off the table for good.

"We do have a contract to honor," Tom admitted.

"Contracts are made to be broken when they don't suit the purposes of all parties," Morgase explained. "Both of you should know that after your dealings with the King Teg." She smiled mischievously when she caught their minute reactions. Just a quick twist of their lips in disgust that just as quickly disappeared. "As you know, I am not my brother. When I say something will be done, it is done. And exactly how I want it done. Knowing that, I'm sure that we can make an arrangement that works for both of us."

Morgase nodded toward Melissa. "We have one chip in play. We can cut her in half if necessary."

"A kind offer, Morgase, but not one that we can accept," Tom said, never seriously considering the proposal.

"Standard rules," Harry explained. "I'm sure that you understand."

Morgase snorted out a laugh. She should have assumed as much. "Already fallen under the Dragon's spell? How sad. You two were always much too honorable for your own good."

"That being said, we must ask you to leave, Morgase," Tom said in an apologetic tone. He walked down the steps, his brother right beside him. The magical spikes they preferred now gripped firmly in both hands.

"For your own good," Harry added.

Morgase shook her head slowly from side to side. "And here I was hoping that we could be friends."

Her black eyes flashed, an aura of energy rippling along her arms, white flames burning just above her palms.

Sensing the danger, Tom and Harry sprinted toward her. Certain that they needed to get in the first blow if they were to have any chance of surviving a duel against one of the strongest of the Teg.

Their eyes widening in anticipation -- their distance from the Sorceress decreasing rapidly, with each step they took the time for Morgase to act disappearing -- the only outward sign that demonstrated their belief that they might actually succeed.

Spikes pulled back over their shoulders, they sought to disable Morgase before she could attack. Just a step away now. Small hammers on the back end of the spikes coming down.

Just a hair away from striking Morgase's hands, ending her use of the Grym would place the combat on more even terms.

The clarion call that rang out when Tom and Harry's hammers struck the thin shield of energy that formed around Morgase at the very last breath sounded like the clang of Big Ben.

Melissa watched it all in disbelief and horror. The bright

flash of light that followed. Spikes crafted of the Grym shattering into thousands of pieces. Tom and Harry flying backward through the air. Slamming against the wall of the Safe Haven. Sliding down to the ground. Not moving. Unconscious or dead, Melissa didn't know.

And it seemed that Morgase didn't know either. She walked slowly toward the bodies crumpled in the pachysandra that ran along the base of the inn, white flames still dancing above her palms.

Melissa's first thought was to flee while she had the chance. She probably wouldn't get away. But if she was going to make the attempt, the time was now.

Although it proved incredibly difficult, she ignored that initial impulse.

Tom and Harry already had saved her life once, and now this. They didn't deserve what happened to them.

She couldn't leave them. Helpless. Already on the other side or on their way there didn't matter.

She needed to aid them if she could, before Morgase decided to make sure that the brothers were well and truly dead.

Grasping the Grym, Melissa sent a blast of energy streaking toward Morgase.

She hoped to catch the Sorceress by surprise. Morgase still having eyes only for Tom and Harry.

Sadly, she was mistaken. With a disdainful flick of her wrist, a swirling cloud of power spun from Morgase's hand, not only blocking the energy that Melissa shot toward her, but taking it in, making it her own, confirming that no matter what she might try, Melissa didn't stand a chance against her.

Yet instead of being terrified by her discovery, by how easily Morgase had defended against her attack, Melissa tried again, giving in to her anger, pulling in as much of the Grym as she could safely manage. Her arms reaching out to the side, she was about to slam her hands together and launch a stream of power toward Morgase that she was certain would throw the Sorceress off her game at least for a few seconds.

That's as far as she got. The energy surging through Melissa died in an instant, her connection to the Power of the Ancients cut as a thin shield of the Grym formed around her and froze her in place.

"A valiant effort, Witch, and one that I certainly didn't expect from you of all Teg."

Morgase stepped right in front of Melissa, who struggled to break free from the magic that held her.

A futile attempt.

She was stuck fast. She couldn't move. She couldn't do anything other than stare into Morgase's frightening eyes, which revealed pools of never-ending black that promised a terrible end.

"It didn't have to come to this, Witch," Morgase murmured quietly, refusing to allow her anger at the young woman who had dared to challenge her to break through her calm façade. "I came for the book. Give me the book as you owe me, and we will be done here."

Melissa gasped, a spark of pain burning at the very center of her back. Her body wanted to move, to escape the agony, but it couldn't. She could only moan as the spark struck again and slowly became a fiery burn that erupted up and down her spine.

"You're not made for such torture, are you, Witch? Give me the book and I will put you out of your misery."

Tears flowed from Melissa's eyes as the fiery agony ravaged her, moving from her spine into her arms and legs. Then it was gone in a flash, as if it had never been there. Replaced by a wonderful cool that Melissa was certain would become a painful and terrible iciness if she did not do as Morgase required.

"I don't have the book here. But I can get it for you. I will get it for you." Melissa incorporated a heavy dose of desperation in her voice that she hoped Morgase interpreted as the truth.

Morgase offered Melissa's pleading a snort of disgust. She knew the Witch was lying. But that didn't bother her, because she had no doubt that she could get to the truth.

Just not at that moment. And not there.

The sounds of the battle just a few blocks away had faded. It seemed that her unanticipated but welcome distraction had come to an end.

"You will indeed give me what I want, Melissa. Of that, have no doubt."

With a quick slash of her hand through the air, a rip in reality appeared right behind Melissa. Then, with a flick of Morgase's index finger, Melissa drifted back through the portal.

Morgase followed the thief, her eyes burning brightly with the promise of what was to come.

Morgase would obtain *The Book of Whispers*. There was no question about that.

Then the Witch would get what was owed to her.

The reckoning that she was due.

For her failure.

For her betrayal.

And because Morgase felt the need to have a little fun after having to waste her time visiting a nothing town like Kraken Cove.

11

DECISION ALREADY MADE

Draig stood on the walkway, arms crossed, watching as Cerridwen and Hestia used the Grym to heal Tom and Harry.

The Three Brothers were lucky they hadn't joined Dick on the other side. Most other Teg struck with that much of the Power of the Ancients would have died in an instant.

But not them. Apparently, they were too stubborn to know when to let go and move on.

Draig had several questions about the combat. But there was no point in asking them anything. They were still too groggy, just coming out of unconsciousness, to tell him what he needed to know.

How Melissa had been taken.

Therefore, Draig called upon a rare talent that he used infrequently, speaking with several of the spirits linked to the garden gnomes. They had seen and heard all and been more than willing to share.

Their narratives confirmed what he had sensed shortly after Jinx disappeared.

"Will they be all right?"

Cerridwen was guiding the dazed Tom and Harry into the inn and back to their room.

"They will be in a few days," Hestia replied, her voice laced with the anger that mirrored the savage look on Draig's face. "They took quite a blow."

"There's a lot to be said for hard heads."

"True," Hestia agreed, "and you should know. I take it you already have something in mind?"

Draig's eyes narrowed. Hestia knew him too well. "A few possibilities."

"Don't take any unnecessary risks."

"Do I ever?"

"When do you not?" she replied, her eyes blazing with a challenge as she started up the steps. "I've got a special guest arriving in a few minutes. I need to make sure her room is ready."

Draig nodded, watching one of his oldest friends go until the door closed behind her. Staring a few seconds more at the mermaid carved into the glass door that appeared to have a life of its own.

He was angry. More at himself than anyone else.

He liked to be in control of the world around him. And he had been.

Until Melissa appeared in Kraken Cove.

He smiled thinly.

"Beware the Witch."

Riga had told him that, and she had been right to do so.

But it was more than just being wary of the Witch. It was being wary of what came with her.

Because Melissa was just the catalyst. The flashpoint. There was a great deal more going on among the Tylwyth Teg than just what was obvious.

And that in itself wasn't unique. That didn't bother him so

much as all the unnecessary clutter piled around the larger concern that he needed to address.

What he had learned in the Circle confirmed just how dire the situation was, and it was becoming much too complicated.

There were too many players involved who could and would affect the game in unexpected and dangerous ways. Because every player acted in their own self-interest and believing that they would act rationally was a mistake.

As he considered that, one thought kept playing through Draig's mind. A lesson learned from his father, in fact.

And though he tended to balk at any advice his father gave him, in this instance Arthur was right on the mark.

When there were too many players and you didn't know how the game was being played, when you weren't even sure what game you were playing, it was best to remove as many players as possible.

Simplify the game.

Observe how the game plays out after that.

Then make your move.

Draig knew why Melissa was taken and what Morgase wanted from her.

He knew as well that despite her best efforts, Morgase had no chance of obtaining the artifact from Melissa.

That meant that Melissa was just a distraction now. He couldn't ignore that fact. If he chose to put his father's advice to use, he should leave her to her fate. Allow one critical piece to be removed.

That would be the easiest decision to make. Leave Melissa with Morgase and allow his aunt to do what she wanted with her.

That would waste Morgase's time and give Draig a chance to get ahead of her.

He frowned at that strategy, however. It was the most

sensible thing to do. That was undeniable. And perhaps in the past he would have done that.

Who was he kidding?

In the past, while he was working for his father, he would have definitely done that.

But now ...

That was no longer who he was. Despite all that was at stake, he couldn't leave Melissa to her fate.

Besides, taking the last few minutes to re-examine the larger picture, he was beginning to see how helping Melissa would help him as well.

His aiding Melissa might clear the board that much faster of some aggravating and unneeded obstacles who had been pestering him for much too long.

Melissa first, though, because she would set the smaller game that he wanted to play into motion.

And if circumstances worked out as he hoped they would, he could improve his odds of success in the longer game that was in play.

"You look no different than last I saw you in Central Park."

Drawn from his thoughts, Draig turned slowly, a welcome smile curling his lips. "It's been too long, Medusa."

Running her hand through her thick curls that seemed to move on their own when the light struck in a certain way, she offered Draig a warm smile in return.

"I can see it in your eyes. You're wondering why I'm here."

"I was, but I see the resemblance."

"That obvious?"

"She's the spitting image. Same bullheadedness as well."

Medusa laughed at that. Only for a second, though, a cough striking that bent her at the waist. She pulled a tissue and wiped her lips.

Draig frowned at the specks of blood. However, he didn't ask her what was ailing her. "I'm glad to see you."

"But the timing seems a bit convenient," Medusa nodded. "Yes, I know. I'm looking for a new place to live, and I thought I might spend a few days here. Check out any available property."

"And check on your daughter as well."

"Yes, that too," Medusa admitted. "I just missed her, I believe."

"You sensed it?" Draig asked, even though he knew that she would have. Not only because of her strength in the Grym, but also because of the bond that she had with her daughters.

Medusa nodded, tears in the corners of her eyes, clearly distraught though she refused to show it. Worse, she knew that there was little that she could do to remedy what was a terrible and frightening situation. "I did. I was still an hour away."

She turned her sad eyes toward Draig. He looked at her without a hint of fear.

The myths spoke of Medusa's magic. Her hair made of snakes exercising a mesmerizing power from which her victim couldn't look away. Her gleaming eyes turning that victim into stone.

A useful story to keep people away when you wanted your privacy, but a story, no more than that. Just like many of the other ancient myths. Though not all.

Sometimes no more than stories. Sometimes much more. The risk being not knowing the difference until it was too late.

"I'm sorry," Medusa sighed.

Draig nodded. He could see that she was tired. That she needed to rest. "Let me get you into the inn."

He offered her his arm, which she took gladly. He helped her up the steps and then opened the door, walking her into the foyer.

When Draig aided Medusa during her escape from his father and his Knights more than a decade before, she had been full of vim and vinegar. No more. Now she was just a shadow of herself. Frail. And weakening fast.

He eased her down onto the couch in the living room. "I'll find Hestia. She'll get you settled."

"You've done so much for me and my daughters, yet I seem to have inadvertently gotten you mixed up with Melissa's trouble."

Draig turned back before he reached the foyer. "You sent her here." It wasn't a question.

"I thought it was the wisest course," Medusa sighed miserably. "Obviously I was wrong."

"You're not going to ask me to find your daughter?"

"No, I'm not." Medusa fought to hold back her tears.

"Why?" He knew from experience just how fiercely Medusa protected all of her daughters. That obstinance had almost gotten them caught while they were fleeing through New York City. Her demand that Draig help not only her, but her daughters as well.

She would have stayed and fought against the Knights sent after them if Draig couldn't promise to keep her and her brood safe. That was an attitude that he could understand, and one that he admired.

Medusa smiled, giving him a mysterious look that suggested she didn't need to answer his question, but that she would anyway. "Because no matter how much you might not want to, you always do the right thing, Draig. You always have. And if not for that, my daughters and I wouldn't have made it."

Draig stared at Medusa for several heartbeats, hearing the truth in her words. Seeing as well what had really brought her to Kraken Cove.

Medusa wanted to save her daughter. But she was too late. And she couldn't go after her. Not in her current condition. He could, however.

"I can't make you any promises."

"I wouldn't believe you if you did."

Draig nodded. "I'll do the best I can. That's all I can offer you."

"That's all I ask for," Medusa replied. Then she reached quickly into her purse and pulled out a fresh tissue, bringing it to her lips as another coughing fit struck.

A shock of sadness running through him, Draig stepped out into the foyer where Hestia waited for him.

"You sensed it?"

Draig nodded. "I did. How long does she have?"

Hestia shrugged. "It's hard to tell with curses such as these. With what she's experiencing now ..." She didn't feel the need to complete her answer.

"Is there any way to lift it?"

Hestia considered Draig's question for a time. "With a curse like this, there's only one way to do it."

"Can you?"

"No, I don't have the strength." She gave Draig an incisive look. "But you do."

12

A TASTE OF RED

"You've got some nerve."

"No more than most." Five very large figures who resembled an all-pro offensive line stood in front of him, putting him in shadow. Draig offered the quintet a smile, although it didn't contain a hint of warmth. "I believe I'm on the guest list."

He should have expected just such a greeting, but he had been distracted after all that had happened that morning in Kraken Cove.

Even though he tried to ensure that there was no doubt as to his intentions when he walked through the Dragon Door, emerging by the front entrance to the steel and glass mansion situated atop the hill, row upon row of vines and ripening grapes leading down the slope, several heavies all with grudges to bear sought to intimidate him.

Understandably so, Draig had to admit. He recognized three of them. Two he had returned to their own realm a decade or more before. The third he had been about to banish until he had been rudely interrupted.

The fist of Daemons glowered intently, pure black eyes

pulsing with a deep hatred. A promise of coiled violence in their stances.

Perhaps these five sensed an opportunity. That didn't bother Draig. If they wanted to take a chance, get in the first strike, he was more than happy to engage with them despite the peril of his circumstances.

After the battle on the Kraken Cove green, he was still edgy. He would embrace the opportunity to release the energy that continued to surge within his veins. The energy that he had locked away despite every instinct urging him to let go. To be who he truly was no matter the cost.

"I've been looking forward to this," the largest of the five said. The man stood well over seven feet tall, and he was built like a brick wall. Nothing but muscle on even more muscle.

He took a step closer to Draig, cracking his knuckles, limbering up his shoulders and his arms, as if he was preparing for a boxing match.

"Be careful, big man. You know what they say."

That stopped the Daemon in his tracks. "Who says what?"

Draig didn't reply immediately, not expecting the question. Instead studying the Daemon. Brow furrowing. Big. Strong. Likely an excellent fighter. But not all there between the ears. "Does it matter who said it?"

The Daemon and his comrades scowled as they considered Draig's question. "I guess not," the leader of the group said finally after gaining nods of support from his ilk.

"There you go, big man. It's not who said it but what was said that matters."

The towering Daemon nodded. "You're right ... little man." Clearly, he was pleased with his jibe, as were his friends, who chuckled softly at his back.

"I'm glad you agree."

"So what do they say?"

Draig smiled again, tensing. Knowing where the conversation was headed and ready for it. Welcoming it. The energy surging through him demanding to be freed. "Escape the bear and fall to the lion. Or in this case, the Dragon."

The Daemon's frown deepened as he slowly comprehended Draig's meaning. "Is that a threat?"

Draig's smile disappeared, his expression hardening in an instant, his voice as cold as a frozen river. "I don't make threats, big man. You should know that. I make promises. And I keep them."

Draig stepped in close to the Daemon, unconcerned by the difference in size. In fact, based on the aura that resonated from him, the faint hint of energy dancing along his frame, the power that he could access surging and flaring, Draig appeared to be even bigger than the Daemon. A fact that pushed the other Daemons a few steps away from him, leaving the leader isolated.

Try as they might to ignore their instincts, they couldn't. The Daemons did not like being so close to him. These supposedly fearless creatures from the Daemon Realm were nervous. Perhaps even slightly afraid.

A truth that Draig could use to his advantage if he felt the need. But he didn't have any desire to push. Not then.

He never shied away from a fight. Nevertheless, giving in to that desire now would only slow him down.

So Draig decided on a different approach that might get him where he wanted to go a little bit faster than a combat against a fist of creatures from the Daemon Realm.

Draig offered the Daemon leader a wink. He sensed it in the creature. Not so much the hunger for a fight the Daemon sought to project upon confronting him.

No, Draig sensed instead concern. Masked. But still there and unmistakable.

The Daemon wasn't the smartest of the bunch. Though he had a strong survival instinct. And that instinct was telling the

Daemon that to continue to push would lead only to one inevitable result. Draig meant to play on that.

"If you want to return to the Daemon Realm, I'm happy to oblige." Draig's reddish-orange eyes flashed, making the large Daemon and his friends take a few more steps backward. "And we can get right to it. But I'm not here for you. I'm here at the request of your master."

Draig tapped his blackthorn shillelagh slowly on the tile of the entryway, working the illusion as he did so. Every time the walking stick struck the stone, its true essence appeared, the concern among the Daemons becoming a palpable fear that they struggled to control. "Please let him know that I'm here so we can get past this crap and move on to more important matters."

"You're not the Dragon here, little man," the Daemon growled, although it sounded more forced. As if he needed to put on a brave face that he couldn't let go just yet. "Here you're ..."

"He's still the Dragon, Frenchie," a deep but soft voice said from behind the gathered Daemons. A voice that earned not only widened eyes from the giant Daemon trying and failing to maintain his composure, but also a gulp of concern. "He'll always be the Dragon. Maybe you keep forgetting that since he kicks your asses so frequently. Doesn't leave you as sharp as you need to be."

A short man with tightly cropped salt and pepper hair stepped out of the mansion, the front door opening on silent hinges. As he made his way down the steps in his leather sandals, wearing khaki shorts and a Hawaiian shirt of green vines and red grapes, his servants bowed their heads in respect as they cleared out of his way.

"Go find someone else to bother, Frenchie." The man gripped the Daemon's shoulder. Not warmly, however. Sparks of energy trailed from his fingertips, the shocks making the towering figure flinch. A lesson for next time. "We'll talk about this later."

The Daemon stepped away quickly, nodding and bowing. The obsequiousness a strange thing to observe from such a hulking figure. "Yes, Master, as you wish."

In a flash, all five Daemons vanished in a cloud of black. Whether at their own instigation or because of the man who now stood alone at the front of the mansion, Draig didn't know.

"You didn't come here to pay your respects."

"Not entirely, no," Draig admitted.

"The Dragon," the Daemon King chuckled softly, nodding slowly as he took in his nemesis. "It's been a long time." His pure black eyes flashed for just a second before they returned to their regular smolder. "And still honest to a fault. I should be disappointed by that, but I'm not."

"Why is that?"

"Because I usually have to put in a great deal more effort to hear the truth from those I work with. It can be exhausting."

"I can imagine," Draig replied. He didn't miss the Daemon King's word choice. *Work with.* The Daemon King and the Dragon working together. A concept foreign to him until just recently. Though perhaps not for much longer.

"So besides paying me a visit as I requested, you came here for another reason."

"I did."

"Care to share?"

"I get the feeling that you already know."

"Perhaps I do," the Daemon King admitted with a broad smile, enjoying the game they were playing. "You hunt for the thief."

It was Draig's turn to smile. "And I thought that I had a good network of sources."

"Information trumps all else. You know that better than anyone."

"That I do," Draig agreed, "which is why you wanted to meet with me."

"Really? How do you come to that?"

"You're less interested in the thief and more interested in what she took."

"Why am I not surprised?" the Daemon King mused. "Not only honest, but also right to the point. Just as always." He nodded toward his right. "Walk with me."

The Daemon King headed down the path that led along the side of the house. Once around the corner, they walked shoulder to shoulder toward a large grange, its open doors beckoning.

"Are you enjoying working on your own?" the Daemon King asked right before they entered the welcome shade of the barn. "Or are you looking for a partner of sorts? I could use someone like you at my side. It might shift the balance in a necessary direction."

Draig didn't respond right away, understanding that he needed to be careful. The Daemon King wasn't known for dealing with rejection well. "A kind offer, but you know how it is with family."

"Even when your family wants you dead?" the Daemon King asked with a lifted eyebrow.

"Even so. Blood is blood, even when you would prefer that it was no more than wine."

The Daemon King nodded, laughing softly, valuing the reference as he led Draig toward the back of the barn. Lifting a trapdoor in the floor, he motioned for him to take the ladder down. "I've been there, so I can certainly understand."

The Daemon King led Draig down the large tunnel, casks lining both sides, placed carefully on shelves three stories high and leading off into the shadowy distance.

He stopped when he reached a cask atop which sat two empty glasses. He remedied the lack of wine just a moment later. Not needing a dipper. Instead, drawing the drink from the cask with a thin stream of the Grym.

Nodding in thanks, Draig took a sip after smelling the wine. He took his time, savoring the flavor, wanting to give a considered opinion. Knowing that the Daemon King expected no less.

"Too fruity."

"Too fruity?" the Daemon King snorted, not expecting Draig's comment. Not insulted, just surprised. And amused. "I kind of like the taste."

"You would."

The Daemon King glared at Draig, his black eyes burning brighter than the gloom surrounding them. Then he laughed. His dark eyes sparkling with delight.

"After all the harm you've caused me, I don't know why I like you so much."

"Yes you do."

"Yes I do," the Daemon King admitted with a sigh.

"Can you give me what I need?" Draig asked. He didn't feel the need to explain what was required. The Daemon King already understood. Draig wouldn't have been there otherwise.

"I can, yes."

"Along with the intelligence that I require?"

The Daemon King confirmed it all with a nod. "You know what I require in return?"

Draig nodded. "I do."

The Daemon King studied Draig for several seconds. More out of habit than anything else, having already made up his mind. "Honest and always to the point. If this was how most of my other business was conducted, life would be so much easier."

"I don't doubt it," Draig agreed.

"You understand that you're asking for quite a lot?"

Draig's expression remained as flinty as ever, hearing the veiled warning just beneath. "I do."

"And you're willing to work with me after what happened in Williamsburg?"

"You're the only one who can help me," Draig replied with a shrug. "I try not to hold grudges. It cuts down on my options."

"You're right about that. Even so, it took some guts to come here. Walking into my lair."

Draig kept a straight face until he couldn't, breaking out into a gentle laugh that the Daemon King joined him in. "Your lair?"

"Sorry, it's been a slow day."

"Even here ..."

"I know, I know," the Daemon King admitted. "No need to remind me. It's too embarrassing."

"That wasn't my intention." Draig had no choice but to imprison the Daemon King, demonstrating a surprising and appreciated leniency by granting him what was essentially house arrest here at his winery rather than what his father demanded of him.

As a result, the Daemon King exercised full control over his environment, except that he couldn't leave. And the fact that even here, he didn't have the strength or the skill to challenge the Dragon. A reality that they both understood and framed their interaction.

"I just want to make sure you understand that Williamsburg was a mistake," the Daemon King explained. "My Daemons exceeded their authority."

Draig's eyes hardened for just a flash. "You allow them to do that?"

The Daemon King didn't reply immediately, realizing that he had just walked onto dangerous ground. He needed to be careful about how he answered. "No, I don't. The ones you didn't return to the Daemon Realm, I did."

"Then water under the bridge."

"Good," the Daemon King said with a thankful sigh. "My

therapist said that it's always good to get everything out into the open. Surprisingly, she's right. Who knew? I thought holding it in was the best way to go. Build your rage and all that until you explode."

"Your therapist?"

"My therapist," the Daemon King sighed. "After ending up here, I was nothing but angry. It wasn't working. It was hurting. I needed to find some way to deal with it."

"Anger at me, you mean."

The Daemon King shrugged. "In large part, yes. If it wasn't for you, I wouldn't be here."

"If it wasn't for me, you might no longer exist."

"True," the Daemon King admitted, "which is why I sought therapy rather than revenge."

"Very enlightened of you."

"I like to think so."

"And are you making progress?"

"I am," the Daemon King replied, and pleased that he could say so. "But I worry about a backslide."

Draig nodded sagely, understanding. "You're worried that if I break the deal ..."

"Exactly."

"You have nothing to fear in that regard," Draig replied with a voice as solid as the wooden timbers at his back.

"Even if it's a choice between the Witch and the artifact?"

"Even so."

The Daemon King thought about that, caught by the Dragon's eyes, which glowed brightly in the gloom. "I get you the information you need ..."

"And I make sure that you have nothing to fear from *The Book of Whispers*."

Draig held out his hand. Waiting. Knowing what the Daemon King was thinking.

Was making this compromise worth the risk?

If the Daemon King could obtain *The Book of Whispers* on his own, there was no need to do the deal with him.

Draig didn't push. He simply observed as all that played across his prospective partner's face. The Daemon King was correct. Information was the key. But the Daemon King was beginning to realize something just as important.

When it came to *The Book of Whispers*, Draig had the necessary knowledge. Not him. That decided it.

The Daemon King reached out and shook Draig's hand. "You're putting me in a dangerous position."

"And I'm putting myself in your hands. So we're in the same boat."

"A fair trade," the Daemon King nodded.

"A fair trade."

"And once you have the thief?"

"Then you will have nothing to fear from *The Book of Whispers*. On that, you have my word."

"I'm glad to hear it." The Daemon King shook his head slowly in amusement. "You know, if we could have come to an arrangement like this before that unfortunate incident from so many years ago, I wouldn't be locked away here."

"True," Draig replied, "but you were seeking to dominate the Teg, were you not? I really didn't have much choice."

The Daemon King's eyes sparked with pleasure, then he chuckled softly. "That was part of it. But only a part."

He didn't offer any more than that, waiting for Draig to catch up. Having little doubt that he would.

"My father needed an enemy."

The Daemon King nodded, almost proud that Draig had figured it out so quickly. "He did, and your aunt wasn't available at the time."

"So he used the threat of the Daemon Horde instead."

"He did," the Daemon King replied. "Very Machiavellian of

him. And, admittedly, I went right along with him. I allowed him to play me. I'm still not happy about that."

"That doesn't sound like you at all."

The Daemon King shrugged. Normally, he wouldn't admit to such an error in judgment, but he wanted to stay true to what he was learning about himself during his private sessions. "I was going through a difficult time. Not fully focused."

"Your breakup with Lilith?"

The Daemon King smiled at the memory, although not entirely in joy. "That was the one. Your father took advantage of my weakness."

"I learned myself that he's quite good at that."

"He is. But we're only chumps if we allow him to do it more than once." The Daemon King waved away the sourness in his tone. Clearly, he still had a long way to go. He couldn't allow his failures and mistakes to stay with him. Better to let them go and move on, or so his therapist liked to say. "As you said before, water under the bridge. We don't have time for these age-old animosities anymore."

"Why do you say that?" Draig asked, intrigued.

"As you can see, business is going well. I'm enjoying this life more than I had anticipated."

"Less stress."

"Exactly."

"Because you're not trying to conquer the world."

The Daemon King pointed at Draig, then touched the tip of his nose with his index finger. "I'm just trying to protect what's mine in the world. That makes life a lot simpler."

"Definitely a more enlightened approach."

"I like to think so. And you?" asked the Daemon King.

"Me?"

"When you left your father, I knew that I could trust you. And I do. That's the only reason I adhered to our original deal."

"I appreciate you doing that." Draig nodded, seeing the truth in the Daemon King's eyes. "You're still concerned."

"I am," the Daemon King admitted. "As I said, I'm trying to build something new here, and it's going well. But if you don't keep *The Book of Whispers* from your father and your aunt, it will destroy not only the Teg world, but also me and my world."

"I understand. Have no fear of that, however."

"Why shouldn't I?"

"Because *The Book of Whispers* is in the Dragon Vault."

The Daemon King gave Draig a hard look. "Is it now?" Clearly, he didn't believe him.

"It is. I can promise you that neither my father nor my aunt will lay a finger on *The Book of Whispers*. Not even when I go to the other side."

The Daemon King stared even longer at Draig, then nodded. He believed him. "I'll get you the information that you need. While we're waiting, I'll show you how to work with shadows."

13

TESTY ENCOUNTER

"Is this how you treat all the women you bring here? Lock them in because they won't stay otherwise?" Melissa shook her head slowly as if she wasn't surprised in the least. "How very, very sad. Though not unexpected."

"Only the ones I fear will bite."

Mordred chuckled as he walked into the small suite on the upper floor of his mansion.

Melissa snorted, not bothering to turn around from where she stood in front of the windows, looking past the long green lawn that ran to the cliffs and focusing on the Atlantic Ocean that extended off to the horizon. At that moment, she wished that she was back where this all had started. Treading water in the small bay below the cliffs, on the outside looking in rather than the other way around. "You're afraid I'm going to bite?"

"I know your mother," Mordred replied.

Melissa's eyes narrowed, glimpsing his beautiful reflection in the glass. And beautiful was the only way to describe him. If Michelangelo needed another example of a Greek God for his sculptures and paintings, Mordred would have been the perfect selection.

Long wavy hair. Dazzling smile. Powerful physique. Confident stride. As if the world moved around him instead of him moving through the world.

The only visible weakness was the sneer that curled his lip whenever events weren't playing out as he wanted. Or if he wasn't being treated as he believed that he deserved to be.

What she said next confirmed that for her, making her smile slightly, pleased that she could get under his skin without even having to try.

"Your mother is letting you off the leash?" Melissa nodded, as if she were seriously contemplating that decision. Questioning it. "Risky on her part, don't you think?"

Mordred stopped when he was no more than ten feet away, tightening his fingers into fists, the color on his cheeks flaring ever so slightly at the insult. "You got lucky. You know it just as well as I do."

"Luck had nothing to do with it," Melissa replied, finally turning.

Her smile broadened when she saw his expression. Almost murderous. Good.

She assumed that she had some protection from him until he regained what she had stolen from him, besides his dignity of course. That would forever be lost. So she could play off his rashness, at least for now.

"Such arrogance," Mordred replied with a forced chuckle, seeking to take control of the conversation. "Lie to yourself all you want. You would never have left here alive otherwise."

"Not arrogance, far from it. Just as luck had little to do with my initial success." Melissa crossed her arms, studying her captor. "Just a belief that you would make a mistake." She shrugged. "And you did."

"Tell yourself whatever you want, Witch," Mordred snorted. "You're not going to get lucky during your latest visit to my home ... unless you want to."

Melissa ignored Mordred's insinuation and accompanying leer, deciding to press on a sore point and see what she could gain for her effort. "If you hadn't made a mistake, I wouldn't have succeeded at breaking in here and stealing the artifact in the first place."

Mordred took a lightning-fast step toward her, the red on his face turning a slight purple before he regained control. Although the struggle within him continued, his knuckles white. "What mistake would that be?"

Melissa studied him, not bothering to reply right away. Not needing to. Rather, learning all that she could by his tone, his expression, the minute details that he couldn't hide, just as her mother had taught her. Taking in all the information that Mordred inadvertently revealed to her without having to say a word. "Where would be the fun in sharing that?"

In a blur, Mordred stood right in front of her. Staring down at her. Right hand gripping her arm. Too tightly, making her whimper. Making her angry. At him, promising herself that she would inflict a similar pain. Even more so at herself for not staying in character.

"You will tell me all that I need to know, Witch. I promise you that."

"Promises aren't worth much, Mordred. You should know that ... what with your father and all."

For just a heartbeat, Melissa's world disappeared. Then she felt Mordred's strong grip on her arm again. He was pulling her back to her feet.

She tried to reach for her cheek, but she couldn't, even though the ache pulsing in her skull demanded it. Melissa tried to work her jaw free, running her tongue inside the left side of her mouth.

All her teeth were still there. That was a good thing. But the pain was getting worse.

Through watery eyes, she looked down. Already starting to swell.

Rather than being afraid, she allowed her anger to build, her resolve strengthening.

The Greek Adonis liked to hit women. She couldn't wait until she had the chance to return the favor.

"My promises are worth more than gold," he hissed, his lips just a hair away from her bruised cheek. "Because my promises are fact. Always. When I say that something is going to happen, it does. Always."

Despite the pain that pulsed in her jaw, Melissa couldn't stop herself from laughing. Even though she knew it might be a mistake. That it might provoke Mordred even more.

Instead of hitting her again as she thought he would, Mordred shook her as if she were no more than a doll. Then he pushed her back against the window, pressing himself against her to hold her in place.

"A fool twice over," he murmured, his lips now right up against her ear. His breath warm against her skin. "Steal from me. And now you laugh at me." Mordred chuckled then, a sickly sound. As if he wasn't really all there. "I will enjoy breaking you, Witch. It is what you deserve after all."

"Promises, promises, Mordred," Melissa whispered, finding it difficult to speak as her jaw and lip swelled.

Growling in rage, Mordred stepped back. Hand raised, preparing to strike her once more. Then he dropped his hand, instead grasping her arms in a painful grip. "You don't seem to understand the situation you're in, Witch. Do you think the Dragon is coming to get you? That he cares about you?" Mordred more cackled than laughed, a strange sound from such a large man. "I might hate my half-brother, but I do know him. Much better than you do."

"What do you know about him?" Melissa wanted to keep

Mordred talking. The more he spoke, the more she could learn. And if he was talking, then he wasn't shaking or hitting her.

"I know that we are much the same in how we look at the world," Mordred hissed.

"I doubt that very much."

"Believe what you want, Witch. It doesn't matter. He can't get to you here. And he likely has no desire to help you. He does what he does for himself and no one else. Just as I do."

Melissa chuckled softly then, unable to ignore the irony. Mordred thought he knew so much, when in fact he knew so little.

"What the hell are you laughing at?"

"You," Melissa replied softly, a small trickle of blood and saliva working its way out of her swollen jaw and down her chin. "You're jealous of the Dragon." She chuckled but had to stop. The pain too much for her. "You have all this, but you're jealous of the Dragon. That is so ridiculously sad."

Mordred's expression changed in a flash, becoming surprisingly thoughtful. He had visited the Witch for a specific reason. To remind her of her place in the world. His world to be more specific. But it seemed that he had gotten sidetracked.

Just as always was the case when talk of the Dragon came up.

His half-brother.

His most hated enemy.

In fact, Mordred hated Draig more than he hated his father, and that was saying quite a lot.

Draig didn't belong with the Teg. He didn't belong with the Draca.

Mordred knew that. Anyone with any intelligence knew that.

Yet somehow, despite being a part of two different worlds, Draig had not only survived but thrived. And in ways that were quite unexpected and, from Mordred's perspective, quite disconcerting.

If he didn't hate Draig with such a vengeance, he would have given him the credit he deserved. But he couldn't.

Because Draig had taken from him the one thing that he desired most. The only thing that he truly desired in the world.

His rage building into a white-hot fury, Mordred reached back with his hand, ready to smack the Witch again. At the very last second, he restrained himself, changing his mind.

Hand shooting forward, ignoring her grunt of pain, he gripped her jaw tightly.

"Don't test me, Witch," he growled. "I don't need you alive to get what I want from you. I can take you in the afterworld if necessary. Don't ever forget that. You're mine. You will always be mine."

"Really?" Melissa wheezed through her clenched, throbbing jaw, not knowing from where her added burst of inner strength came from. "I doubt that."

"Doubt what?"

"Doubt that you could take me anywhere. Because you didn't take me in Kraken Cove, now did you?"

Mordred leaned back then, not quite understanding why the Witch continued to push him. Continued to challenge him. Despite making her hurt. Almost like she wanted him to hurt her more. "What are you talking about?"

Melissa smiled as best as she could, pleased by how her patience and perseverance were paying off.

"Your mother."

"What?" Mordred demanded, not understanding.

"Your mother."

"My mother?"

"Yes, your mother. You're jealous of the Dragon, that's undeniable. But that's another matter entirely. What's truly sad is that you can't do anything without your mother. You didn't take me in Kraken Cove. Your mother did. Without her, you never would have taken me. Your Berserkers couldn't do it. Your Weres couldn't do it. It was your mother, not you. Only your mother could capture me."

"That may be one possible truth, but ..."

"That must feel very emasculating," Melissa continued, ignoring her worry that she may have overstepped, pushing forward as fast as she could, hoping that doing so knocked Mordred off balance. "Does your mother still tuck you in at night and read you a bedtime story before turning out the light?"

Melissa realized that she was taking a risk by challenging Mordred in such a way. Nevertheless, she gave in to the impulse. In part because she was curious. She wanted to find out how far she could go. In part because she was in so much pain, his grip on her swollen jaw tightening, sending a fiery bolt into the back of her scalp. A small part of her hoping that if Mordred hit her again, she would pass out. "Does she still make your meals for you? Tie your shoes? Maybe wash your ..."

"You filthy Witch," Mordred snarled. Eyes crazed, hand raised, he was about to strike her again with a power that might do more than send her into a blissful unconsciousness.

"Mordred, please don't play with your food."

The quiet but commanding voice froze Mordred in place, a silence descending. The only sound to be heard was Melissa's ragged breathing.

After taking several deep breaths, a shudder surged through Mordred, his body spasming. Only then did his eyes regain their clarity.

He had lost himself for a moment, demonstrating a weakness that he hated. He had allowed the Witch to push him to a dark place that he didn't want to go.

He stepped back then, releasing his hold on her. "We will talk again soon, Witch." Straightening his neatly pressed shirt,

Mordred returned to himself in an instant. The deranged abuser replaced by the successful businessman. Swiping his curly hair out of his eyes, his arrogant smile returned. He gave Melissa a wink that was more a promise of what was to come before he stepped past his mother and out of the room.

"Clever, dear, but not clever enough," Morgase said from the doorway. "I could even say what you did was brave, but I won't. It was foolish. You underestimate my son, just as everyone does." Morgase turned away, slowly closing the door behind her. "Enjoy your evening as best as you can. My son and I will deal with you later."

Too tired to push herself back up, when the door closed Melissa slid down the window and sat on the floor, back against the glass. Wiping blood from her mouth, she teased the bruise on her cheek with her fingers. Barely able to touch it without hissing in pain.

Definitely going to leave a mark, she mused.

The thought made her chuckle ever so slightly, though not enough to increase the pain that she was already experiencing.

A hard way to learn about Mordred. That was undeniable. But it had proven useful.

She had identified several of the buttons that she could push while she sought some way to escape her prison.

Because, unfortunately, Mordred was right at least in one respect.

No one knew who took her.

No one was coming to save her.

She was on her own.

Just as she usually was.

If she was going to survive, much less escape, she was going to need to do it on her own.

14

A QUICK VISIT

"Why in all the hells are we doing this?"

"What are you talking about?" Raza whispered. She was more spirit than substance. Scarcely there. Her features hazy at best, fading into the gloom of the hallway. A shadow to all but the most discerning eyes, as was her partner. Exactly the way it needed to be. "You know exactly why we're doing this."

"I know, I know, it just doesn't make sense," Resin complained. He shook his head from side to side, the wispy black folds of his features hanging at the edges before coming back into focus. He was barely visible in the dim light, no more than a faint outline. There, but not really there.

Shadows.

Daemons.

Creatures of shade and mist who could take flesh when the circumstances demanded it. When there were victims available for their use.

"Does it need to make sense? We were given a job, so we do the job. It's that simple, Resin. Get it together."

Raza shifted her gaze slowly from side to side. She wanted to muzzle her larger companion – throttle was more like; he had been complaining nonstop ever since they employed the magic of the Daemon Realm to pass through shadow -- so that she could get a better feel for the mansion they had entered uninvited, unannounced, and undiscovered ... she hoped.

She didn't see anything that gave her any cause for concern. Nothing except for the gloom that she relished so much.

But she couldn't hear what might be lurking around them because her partner's voice was in her ear.

"Yes, but the Dragon?" Resin whined. "Seriously? We're working for him?"

"Why does that seem so strange to you? The Dragon showed leniency when leniency was not required. A debt, even if it remains unsaid. There is a respect there now as well. It's to be valued, appreciated, built upon if possible."

"That's all well and good," Resin grumbled, his pure-black eyes pulsing in the darkness. "But do you know how many of our kind the Dragon has sent back to our Realm?"

"No." Raza shifted her focus to her left. She drifted toward the corner where the hallway met another. There she waited. Patient. Unmoving. No more than a darker darkness within the darkness.

Hearing voices, she considered preparing herself, then decided against it. The voices were moving away from them. Nothing to worry about.

"Too many," her partner replied, the larger shadow gliding up right next to her and speaking into her ear once again. "Too damned many. So many I don't know how many. That's how many."

"It doesn't matter," she replied in a harsh murmur. "We're doing this for the Dragon because our King commands it. Do you want to go against our King knowing what he does to those who fail at the tasks given to them? What the Dragon could do to us doesn't even come close. The Dragon can banish us to our Realm. The Daemon King can make sure that we stay there for eternity."

Raza turned her head briefly, locking eyes with her partner who seemed more a plaintive child. "Is that what you want? To be condemned to the Daemon Realm forever?"

"No, definitely not," Resin replied meekly. He hated being in his natural Realm. There, it was nothing but work. A dreary monotony that continued until you knew nothing else. All sense of time lost. And absolutely no fun to be had. No, he didn't want to experience that again.

"Then shut your trap and let's get down to business," she ordered, about to step out into the hallway.

"Watch it," he warned ever so quietly, reaching out and grasping her shadowy arm, pulling her back into the gloom with him.

Right after Resin did, three large men dressed in matching khakis and black Polo shirts stomped by, oblivious to two intruders hiding in the darkness of the corridor.

"Thanks," Raza murmured.

She shouldn't have allowed herself to be distracted by Resin's complaints. She and her partner had been selected specifically for this assignment by the Daemon King himself. They were the best at what they did. Infiltration. And she had no desire to face the dire repercussions if they didn't achieve the objective their master set for them.

Peeking around the corner, Raza didn't see anyone coming from either direction. They could begin their reconnaissance.

Staying in the shadows of the long hallways, they glided silently down several corridors, sneaking into each room along the way. Mapping out in their minds the exact layout of the mansion that was more a castle.

Just as they had been instructed, they kept well clear of the doorway crafted of an ancient wood warded with runes that led into the central turret.

The Daemon King had told them what would happen if they got too close, much less tried to break through. They wanted no part of that.

Raza and Resin were uniquely good at their work because they took their time. Never feeling the need to rush. Even in the brightly lit rooms they employed their unique ability to fade away into the slightest of shadows when one or more of the musclebound Paladins who spent all their free time in the gym trudged by, their heavy footfalls always giving them away well before they reached the Daemons.

So long as Raza and Resin didn't move and the Paladins, sometimes no more than a few feet away, didn't look at them directly -- more importantly, not knowing to look for them -- they had little to fear.

Because of their caution and thoroughness, it took the pair more than an hour to finish their survey of the lower floor. Confirming the placement of the guards, their routines, and their routes through the mansion in that time.

Not only avoiding the turret, they stayed clear of the kitchen as well. They snuck a glimpse when a Paladin swept open the swinging door as he hustled to his post but did no more than that. Even with their distinctive skills, there was too much activity there. Paladins moving in and out. Always a handful of men sitting at the table or the counter or cooking at the stove.

The likelihood of discovery was too much of a risk. Besides, they doubted the Dragon planned to stop in the kitchen for a quick bite before tweaking the nose of the mansion's owner.

Heading back through the main dining room, sliding along the wall, savoring the touch of the shadows that lengthened as the sun descended, the mansion's lights slow to come on, it was Raza's turn to prevent Resin from being discovered.

Her partner was about to glide around the corner into the foyer right when she heard a light step on the main staircase that curled up from two different directions to the second floor.

Almost realizing his mistake too late, he allowed Raza to pull him backward with her tight grip on his arm. Resin nodded his thanks. Then they settled in to wait. Better to stay in place than to move, having no desire to give the residents of the castle any hint as to their presence.

Just seconds later, a sense of tremendous power struck them. Almost pushing them back into the wall. Drawing closer. The sound of footsteps grew louder.

Neither could help themselves, peeking around the corner at the same time.

"I will return later this evening," an elegantly dressed woman said in a commanding voice, her high heels clicking on the Italian tile floor. "Make sure our guest is fed and well cared for. We have much to discuss later tonight. I want her ready for when I return."

"Of course, Mistress," a Paladin replied. The hulking muscular figure who barely fit into his clothes draped a fur coat on the woman's back, then opened the front door for her.

Raza and Resin pulled back from the edge as quietly and surreptitiously as they could.

"Morgase!" they both mouthed to one another at the same time. Her being there had been referenced as a possibility, though they never thought to actually come across her, assuming she had better things to do with her time. But apparently not. Apparently the Witch was her current priority.

They remained where they were for several minutes after the door closed and the Paladin stalked off toward the kitchen.

When there had been nothing except silence for quite some time, Raza and Resin both certain that they were once again alone, they sighed with relief.

"That's not someone we want to deal with," whispered Resin.

"On that, I agree with you," Raza murmured. She nodded toward the foyer. "Let's take care of the second floor. I don't want to be here when she gets back."

Resin nodded and then slipped around the corner, Raza right on his heels. Even with the light of the chandelier illuminating the large, open space, both Daemons still appeared to be no more than a flash at the corner of the eye as they glided up the steps.

When they reached the top of the stairs, they waited several seconds to get a better feel for the space. Empty for the most part, they believed.

They started in the southern wing. Moving from one room to the next as they had done on the lower level. Confirming what they suspected.

There was little of interest on this side of the mansion. Bedrooms for guests that weren't in use. Nothing else.

When they made their way back to the steps, they caught a brief hint of movement in the northern wing, a flash of black disappearing around the corner at the end of the hallway.

It was as they suspected. They had followed the residue of Morgase's power up the staircase. That trail continued into the northern wing.

They needed to be exceedingly careful now.

Having learned during their search of the southern wing that the rooms were all connected by interior doorways, they slipped into the first room, sliding through the narrow space above the carpet.

Just in time. Right before a few low voices became audible coming up the stairs behind them.

Once the Paladins passed by the closed door, Raza and Resin began their search of the rooms on that side of the mansion, moving so quietly that they couldn't be heard above the murmur of the draft that snuck through the old windows.

Once again, they found little of interest in any of the unoccupied bedrooms and the small fitness center that clearly was reserved for the lord of the castle.

That was until they reached the last room on the far southern side. Knowing that just beyond the closed doorway the hallway took a sharp right, without saying a word, Raza and Resin nodded to one another.

Raza turned the knob, opening the door, glad for the silence of the well-oiled hinges. Needing to check in case the Dragon chose to use their current path as a point of access. After she and Resin stepped into the dark hallway, she shut the door just as quietly.

The murmur of deep voices could he heard right around the corner.

"Just a peek," Raza murmured.

Resin nodded, agreeing. Pushing himself back against the wall, the shape of his wispy body slowly changed, lengthening, becoming thinner, almost melting into the wall. He tilted his head until only one pure-black eye extended around the corner.

He wasn't worried about being discovered. Even if one of the Paladins looked in his direction, they would assume that his discerning orb was no more than a black spot on the wall.

He didn't need long to scope out what blocked their way.

"How many?"

"Ten." Resin didn't reply until all of him was back around the corner and his form had regained some thickness. "We could take that many."

"We could," Raza whispered, "but that's not the issue. The issue is whether we should."

"You think the Witch is here?"

"It's the only place she could be," Raza replied. "Why else station so many neanderthals in front of a bedroom door?"

"We should probably check. Just to make sure. They won't have any idea what hit them."

Resin began to change again, this time in a more terrifying way, his hands transforming into razor-sharp claws.

"You can't be serious?" Raza hissed.

Resin stared at her for a second, eyes glowing in anticipation of the slaughter to come, then he smiled. "I'm not." He laughed softly, unable to maintain the ruse any longer. "Sorry, just wanted to see the reaction I could get from you."

"You son of a demon dog. I can't believe you would ..."

The carpet had hidden the sound of approaching footsteps until whoever was coming was almost upon them. They didn't have a chance to slip back into the bedroom. Therefore, they did the only thing that they could, dissolving swiftly into a wispy black mist that drifted into the corner of the corridor where the light was the worst, adding themselves to the shadow that already stretched down the wall there.

And just in time as a fist of Paladins pounded by. Probably the change in guard.

Raza and Resin took advantage of their good luck, the men sworn to Mordred not noticing them as they went by. More focused on taking up their position.

Still in the form of two wispy clouds of black, the Daemons slid along the wall, back along the hallway, and then down the stairs, not taking their human shape until they were once again in the small study at the front of the mansion where they had appeared originally, sliding into Mordred's home through the many shadows that as the hours slipped by had only grown larger in front of the floor to ceiling bookcases.

"We didn't get into the bedroom," Resin whispered. "The boss won't like it."

"He would like it even less if we were caught or we gave ourselves away by killing some of the Paladins."

"Good point. They would move the Witch for sure."

"Now you're finally thinking, Resin." Raza nodded as she considered the situation, deciding that they had done all that they could. "Back to the boss. If the Dragon hits the place soon, the Witch will still be here."

"But what if there are surprises we haven't identified?"

"He's the Dragon, Resin. Nothing ever surprises the Dragon."

15

DOWN THE COAST

"You should have killed him when you had the chance," huffed Seamus.

The salty mariner who wore his preferred fisherman's sweater kept a steady hand on the wheel of the *Kraken* as she powered through the five-foot swells. More habit than anything else. He didn't need navigation equipment or the moon and the stars to see where he was or where he was going when he sailed on the ocean.

He could sense all that was around him. Any perils or concerns, anything of interest, both above the waves and below.

Seamus was pleased with their progress since leaving Kraken Cove, running at a steady pace south about a mile off the eastern seaboard. Having just passed Block Island, soon they would head into Long Island Sound, Montauk not too far off on their west. Then it would be no more than another hour before they reached the small cove that was their ultimate destination.

"You're probably right about that," Draig agreed.

"There's no probably about it," Seamus cut in quickly, his cantankerous nature on full display. He had a point to make, and he was going to make it. "Mordred has been nothing but one problem after another since you had him under your blade."

"Again, you're right, Seamus," Draig replied evenly, knowing that this was just the way it was with Seamus. Usually complaining. More sour than sweet. Yet never failing to protect his back. Just as his ornery friend had demonstrated with respect to the second Viper lurking in Draig's lighthouse. "And I would have killed him – it certainly would have made my life easier, but my father required mercy from me instead. I wasn't in a position to deny him back then."

"What in blazes was your father thinking?" Seamus demanded, not understanding the logic of that decision. "That half-brother of yours is one of the two primary hemorrhoids the King Teg has had to deal with during his rule. And that father of yours isn't known for his mercy. A sudden burst of guilt get in the way of clear thinking? Memories of all his poor parenting giving him a brain fart?"

"Something like that," Draig admitted, a small smile playing across his grim expression. "There was an extenuating circumstance that affected his reasoning."

"Extenuating circumstance?" Seamus challenged. "What could have possibly gotten in the way of your father getting rid of that turd when he had the chance?"

"Gwennie."

Seamus didn't reply for several seconds, his usual grimace twisting up into a bemused smile as he nodded his head slowly. "Figures. That woman has caused more trouble than she's worth."

"You're singing to the choir, Seamus."

Seamus couldn't quite understand how the King of the Teg had allowed anyone, woman or no, to tame him. It just didn't make sense. He understood what love could do to a person, having experienced it himself. But to give up so much of yourself for one person? That wasn't right. "And she put you in a few pickles as well because of your father being smitten with her."

"All too true, Seamus."

"Why did Gwennie want your father to show mercy to Mordred? He's not her son. And that boy hated her guts from the beginning."

"That's when Gwennie was first getting into meditation, homeopathy, living a life of gratitude and forgiveness." Draig shrugged, as if to convey that he really didn't understand why his former stepmother did what she did. "My father was still more than just smitten with her. He hadn't realized yet that she was having an affair."

"His infamous best friend."

"One and the same."

"Now it all makes sense," Seamus sighed. "Poor timing on her part. Still, she deserves some of the blame. She mucked things up more than she helped."

"I certainly won't deny that." Draig smiled sadly. His father had enjoyed a great many paramours over the centuries. The only one Draig really liked and cared about was Gwennie. Perhaps it was because she was willing to listen when Draig was going through some difficult times. Not giving advice. Not telling him what to do. Just being there for him, having faith that he would figure things out on his own. "Of course, right after that Mordred made a play for my father's throne. He had wised up by then, beginning to wonder about Gwennie and Lance. So my father's previous thoughts on gratitude and forgiveness had withered on the vine. He was less than tolerant to those challenging him."

"The beginning of the end for Gwennie."

"That time, yes, and none too soon."

"Until your father fell in with Gwennie again," Seamus offered.

"He always seems to think that each time he connects with

her, it will turn out differently. But it doesn't." Draig shrugged. "She is his Kryptonite."

"His what?" Seamus didn't understand the reference.

"His Kryptonite." Draig gave Seamus a quizzical expression, not quite believing that he had stumped his friend. "You don't know who Superman is?"

"Super who?"

"Super ..." Draig stopped himself. "What about Aquaman? You've got to know who Aquaman is. He's right in your bailiwick."

Seamus shook his head, his expression of confusion only deepening. "Sorry, neither ring a bell."

Thinking about it, Draig couldn't say that he was all that surprised. Seamus wasn't a big follower of pop culture, and he didn't watch television. He preferred to read. Usually dusty tomes of history or academic works focused on oceanography and marine science, primarily so that he could laugh at all the mistakes.

And when he wanted to relax, he liked to work jigsaw puzzles. Never fewer than one thousand pieces.

In fact, down below in the main cabin Seamus had three laid out that he had not yet completed. The thousands that he had finished were carefully preserved in a storage unit in Kraken Cove. Actually more than one storage unit. Seamus could solve a puzzle in a day when he wasn't out on the water.

"Never mind," Draig said, not wanting to waste time on an explanation. "As you said, Gwennie had an effect on my father that no one else ever did or likely could. She's probably his greatest weakness."

"An excellent segue," Seamus grumbled. "All that being said, why are we wasting time on the Witch?"

Draig began to reply. He stopped himself. Then he smiled, looking at his friend in a new light.

Clever. Very clever indeed. Seamus usually wasn't so

patient. But he had taken his time, maneuvering their conversation to the topic that he really wanted to discuss by starting with an example that proved his point.

"You think that Melissa is just like Gwennie?"

"Not entirely, no," Seamus replied. "Besides, you're not like your father. Your father could never do that with Gwennie. He started thinking with a different part of his body when she smiled at him. I know that you see her for who she really is."

"And who do you think Melissa is?" Draig's eyes flashed. Not in anger. More in warning.

Seamus snorted, not caring if he told Draig something that he didn't want to hear. That's why they got along. They were honest with one another. Brutally so when required. "I haven't decided yet. I'm just concerned."

"Concerned why?"

"Because it's been a long time since you've demonstrated so much patience and allowed someone so much leeway despite the challenges and complications she's brought into your life." Seamus challenged Draig with a lift of his eyebrows. "In just a matter of days no less."

Draig nodded. "You think I'm going soft?"

"The Dragon going soft?" chuckled Seamus. "Far from it. Although I do think that you're sweet on her."

"I beg to differ."

Seamus chuckled again, then started laughing.

"What? You still think I'm sweet on her?"

"Yes, but I'm not laughing because of that," Seamus said.

"Care to enlighten me?"

"I said much the same as you just did when those mangy wolves tried to hijack my boat. It took some effort to help them understand the meaning of the phrase and that I wasn't actually begging."

Draig's rising temper diffused swiftly as the image filled his mind of Seamus trying to explain the multiple meanings of beg to the Weres so foolish as to step aboard the *Kraken* without his friend's leave. "They weren't the smartest of the pack, now were they?"

"Far from it," Seamus confirmed, "which worked in my favor." Seamus gave Draig a quick glance, wanting to make sure that his friend wasn't angry with him because he intended to push him a bit harder, before returning his attention to the ocean. They were passing Montauk on their port side. "Look, I'm not trying to twist your knickers in a knot. And maybe you're not sweet on the Witch. I'm just concerned."

"Concerned why?"

"Because from where I'm standing, it looks to me as if you're trying to be her knight in shining armor."

Draig scoffed at the idea. "Far from it."

"Maybe, maybe not," Seamus replied, refusing to give up his argument. "I've known you for a long time, and you've always had a soft heart when it comes to those in need."

"You really know where to hit a guy so it hurts."

Seamus ignored Draig's attempt at humor. "I've got news for you, my friend. Your armor is rusted. It has been for quite a long time. That's why you're the Fallen Knight, after all. You trying to help every stray kitten stuck in a tree puts you at risk, just as is the case now. It also puts what we're trying to build at Kraken Cove at risk."

"I'm well aware of that, but thanks for the reminder," Draig growled. He was irritated, although he didn't really have any right to be. Because every word that Seamus spoke was true. And his concerns were legitimate. In fact, Draig was having many of the same concerns.

"I'm just saying that your attempts to make good are worth the effort. However, there are some things that you can't undo. And as you are well aware, there are consequences that must be dealt with based on the decisions you make. Consequences not just for you, but for all of us."

"I'm well aware, Seamus, but thanks for the reminder," Draig replied again, this time through gritted teeth.

Seamus was exactly right. Draig understood that any decision he made could have ramifications for his friends in Kraken Cove. In this instance, though, after all that had transpired, and after learning the possible paths in the Circle atop the Druid's Peak, he believed that he had no choice except to insert himself into the schemes currently in play among the Teg. Because his not doing so put himself and his friends in Kraken Cove at even greater risk.

"Saving Melissa won't save you, Draig," Seamus continued, trying to get his point across without belaboring it. "I hope you understand that. No matter how much you might hope for that to be the case, helping her won't absolve you of your past sins."

"Have no fear of that, Seamus," Draig sighed, his irritation draining out of him. Seamus was just trying to help him, something that Draig appreciated. "I'm well aware that what I do in the present won't allow me to escape my past. There are still debts to be paid that can never be paid. And have no fear. I'm still the person who almost killed you. Although I didn't."

"And for that I'm thankful."

Draig saw an opportunity, in part because Seamus seemed to have finished with his lesson, so he decided to make use of it. "Did you ever wonder why I didn't kill you?"

"I have such a fun and engaging personality?" Seamus mused with a raised eyebrow.

"There is that," Draig chuckled, "but try again."

"You were tired of killing and you were tired of being made to kill. That much was obvious. You had me dead to rights. Nevertheless, you refused to do the deed."

"That was only part of it, Seamus. Try a little harder."

"Because not killing me ..." Seamus didn't complete what he was going to say. He didn't need to. His deep blue eyes that often appeared grey, much like a stormy sea, widened as the realization came to him. In all the time that he and Draig had been friends, he had never really considered this possibility.

Draig nodded when the lightbulb appeared above Seamus' head. "I didn't want to kill you, that's true. You certainly didn't deserve to die at my hand. But there was an added benefit. Not killing you gave me a chance to go after someone higher up the food chain. Leaving you alive was the only way to make that happen."

"So the Witch is bait," Seamus snorted, never anticipating that Draig could still make such a cold, hard decision when someone else's life was at stake.

Or perhaps it was more that Draig hadn't had to make such a decision since he had moved to Kraken Cove, so Seamus had forgotten just how calculating his friend could be.

Draig was still the same Draig. He was still the Dragon. It was just that the circumstances of his current life hadn't required him to act as he had before. Until now.

"She is, but she put herself in this position, not me," Draig clarified, although he saw from Seamus' admiring expression that his friend gave little credence to the distinction that he tried to make. "I'm just going to make use of her if I can."

"That's very callous of you," Seamus stated, although his voice contained a hint of respect and pride ... even admiration.

"I prefer realistic."

"And here I was worried that you were going soft. More interested in your baking and books than anything else."

"I didn't want to get involved in Teg affairs again, that much is true, but I don't have much choice. And as I said, the situation is much the same as when I was sent after you. There are bigger fish to fry. One in particular. Melissa is just the minnow. Even so, she's the catalyst. She's the one who has allowed me to start tugging on the line. Eventually, if I tug hard enough, I'll be able to pull that fisherman into the water with me."

Seamus had to give his friend credit. He certainly knew

what he was doing. And he certainly hadn't lost his touch ... or his devious mind. "Do you trust her?"

"Only not to tell me the entire truth."

"Good, then you're not as bad off as your father was with Gwennie."

"I'll take that as a compliment."

Seamus took a few seconds to think, enjoying the strong breeze that gusted off the water. "Still, you don't think that you can yank that fisherman in without her? I'm not questioning the legitimacy of your strategy. It's a good one. But it's risky."

"I can't deny that."

"Then why not do what you need to do without her? Why is this woman so important? She's just a Witch. Why go to all this effort just for her? There's got to be a way to climb higher up the ladder without having to go after her."

"You don't like her?" Draig asked.

"Actually, I do like her," Seamus admitted. "She's got spunk, and she doesn't take a lot of crap. Moreover, you and some of the other Teg don't scare her."

"Even so ..."

Seamus shrugged. "You know it as well as I do. It's quite obvious that she's hiding something. You just admitted it yourself."

"One of her unique skills it seems."

Seamus nodded, pleased that Draig wasn't so taken by the Witch that he missed the obvious. "I just haven't seen you do something like this in quite some time. You haven't cared so much about something, or someone, since you had that minor altercation with your father."

"Minor altercation?" Draig didn't remember the encounter with his father at Belvedere Castle that way at all, the combat giving him the chance to escape his previous life.

Seamus smiled, then corrected himself. "My apologies. Major conflagration."

"Maybe it's because I haven't had to care for a while," Draig mused. "Maybe it's because I thought I could withdraw from the Teg world and not have to worry about what could happen if I did."

Not wanting to go down what would quickly become a depressing road, Draig stepped to the railing, gazing at the shadowy coastline lit up now and then by the lights of the small towns that ran along the coast on this far eastern section of Long Island. "Ragnar, Urs, Thorsen. Come on up. We're getting close, and we need to talk."

The three blonde giants nodded as one, then began to make their way from the bow toward the staircase in the cabin that would bring them up to the helm.

"You don't call them the Three Little Bears as do Cerridwen and Peggy Rose?"

Draig shook his head. "No, although they do seem to like the name Cerridwen gave them. I haven't asked them why yet."

Seamus was curious about the answer to that puzzle, but it could wait. "Will those blonde behemoths do what's required of them?"

"They're Berserkers, Seamus. They've been hungry for a fight ever since we left Kraken Cove. And, we're going to give them a fight that they're going to write stories about. What's not to like about that?"

16

PAINFUL CONVERSATION

"Are you going to hit me again, Mordred?" Melissa leaned forward, placing her forearms on the metal table separating them.

The small room into which four Paladins had marched her had the feel of an interrogation chamber. Concrete walls and nothing but a small table and two chairs, as well as a two-way mirror that extended across the wall at Mordred's back.

There were shadows in each of the corners, the only good light coming from the small halogen lamp set on the table. Thus her decision to lean closer to the man she despised. She wanted to make sure that her captor could see clearly every inch of her bruised and battered face.

"The thought had crossed my mind," he murmured. "Is that what you want? You want to feel the touch of my hand again?"

Mordred leaned away from the table, legs crossed, seemingly at his ease. His eyes told a different story.

He was restless, almost on edge, as if he was only a heartbeat away from the violence that lurked just below the surface. And the spark in the back suggested that he was getting tired of their circular conversation of the last hour.

Her interrogator kept asking the same questions, though in a slightly different way each time.

Melissa provided the same responses. Every time. Refusing to reveal a single opening. Despite knowing what her continued recalcitrance likely meant.

Another beating ... or worse.

"Then why don't you do just that, Mordred? Why don't you give in? You didn't have any trouble giving in just a few hours ago." Melissa pointed to the bruising and swelling along her jaw and cheek. "You don't want to prove to me what a big man you are? You don't want to touch me? Make yourself feel powerful again?"

Mordred pursed his lips as he studied his captive, tapping the fingers of his left hand on the table as he did so.

"Maybe I will," he replied finally, nodding his head slowly as he contemplated that possibility. His right lip curled ever so slightly when Melissa flinched at his response and then pulled back from him. Uncomfortable being so close to him despite her brave words.

She had pushed his buttons with consummate skill earlier. No longer. He would have his fun with the Witch, but not until he got the information that he wanted.

She owed him, after all. And she would pay what she owed.

No one embarrassed him like she had and got away with it.

No one. Not even the Dragon.

"If it proves necessary," Mordred continued. "If you continue to ask me to because you like how my touch makes you feel." He smiled more broadly then, pleased at how she drew within herself just a bit, shoulders coming together ever so slightly.

He knew what she was trying to do. It wouldn't work this time. She was tough. He was willing to admit that. But she wasn't tough enough to hold out on him forever.

Pain – emotional, physical, psychic – had a way of making a

person see the world and the hopelessness of their circumstances in a new light.

"But we can avoid all that," he explained in a kindly voice. "Quite easily, in fact." He leaned forward then, placing his forearms on the table. At the same time Melissa withdrew her arms and sat back, clearly having no interest in being so close to him despite her goading. "All you need to do is give me what I want."

"I already told you I don't have it."

"You did. Time after time. But I keep asking you for it. Why is that?"

"I can't give you what I don't have. I've already told you that. More times than I care to remember."

"Of course you can't," Mordred agreed amiably, "but you did have *The Book of Whispers* in your possession."

"I did." Melissa gave him a sardonic grin. Another attempt to push him closer to the edge. "Right after I stole it from you."

Mordred ignored the barb, continuing to smile, even though his primary instinct right at that moment was to leap up from his seat and slam a fist across her jaw.

The audacity of the Witch!

To steal back the item that she had stolen for him. He would have been impressed if he had not been the victim of her betrayal.

"I know that you no longer have the artifact."

"Then why are we wasting so much time here? Why did your mother kidnap me? If I can't give you what you want, why am I here?"

"You gave Draig the book."

"I didn't give him the book. I didn't have a choice. He took it from me."

"Of course he did," Mordred murmured. "Because that's what Draig does. He takes what he wants when he wants."

Mordred failed to keep the hate from his voice. There were gallons of bad blood between him and his half-brother. Eventually, Mordred would have the chance to settle the score between them. Just not yet.

"Then why are you bothering me now? Draig has the book. If you still want the book, then take it from him. You and your mother should be able to manage that much."

"As you say, we would do that quite easily," Mordred replied calmly, although the fact that once again Draig had gotten the better of him continued to gnaw at his gut. "But we need to know where he's hiding it before we can obtain it. He's not as easy a nut to crack as you are."

"I am not an easy ..."

"I didn't say you were. I said he wasn't as easy a nut as you are. A compliment, you would know, if you spent more time listening and less time instigating. Because I must admit I like your fire. In fact, I'm looking forward to seeing a little more of that fire once we're done here."

"You would dare to ..."

Melissa's breath caught when Mordred rose up from his chair, lightning fast, and slammed his fist down onto the table. She feared he might try to reach for her, his nostrils flaring, eyes red with rage. "I dare to do whatever I want, Witch! Don't forget it. Now tell me where Draig is hiding *The Book of Whispers!*"

Melissa was out of her seat in a flash, stepping back toward the far wall, placing the chair between them. "I told you I don't know! And I don't! He took the book from me. The last time I saw it in his possession was when we were in the Dragon Vault. I haven't seen it since. I don't know what he did with it. I assume it's still in the Dragon Vault."

"So you've said," Mordred murmured as he slowly stepped around the table.

Melissa shifted her positioning as he did so, keeping the chair between them. She stood little chance against him, particularly since the wards in the room prevented her from using the Grym.

She would put up a fight. For as long as she could. But she couldn't beat him.

"This is going to be fun, Witch." Mordred cackled more than laughed. "Since you're proving to be so difficult, it looks like I *will* need to crack you like a nut."

He was about to lunge for her when an unyielding voice froze him in place.

"Stop toying with her, Mordred. We don't have time for this."

Morgase stepped into the room, leaving the door behind her open. Back from wherever she had gone.

"I don't have it. I already told your son that. And I can't get it. He's not listening."

"No, listening was never one of Mordred's strengths," Morgase agreed. "You had *The Book of Whispers*, though. You took it from my son, and then it was taken from you."

"That's what I've been telling him," Melissa almost pleaded, although she succeeded in keeping the whininess she feared might leak into her voice from doing so. "I don't have it anymore. I don't know where it is. And I have absolutely no idea how to obtain it."

"I believe you," Morgase said in an equitable tone.

It was then that understanding dawned for Melissa, the fuzzy picture finally gaining some clarity. Her expression became shrewd, forgetting at least for a moment the threat that Mordred presented. "You already knew that. Before your son hit me. Before I was brought down here."

Morgase nodded. "I did."

The cold truth was like another slap in the face, just as stinging as the one that Mordred had given her.

There was only one thing that Morgase really wanted from her, and it wasn't the book.

The rest of it was all just a game.

"What if Draig doesn't come?" She doubted that he would. She doubted that he even cared enough about her to make the effort. And even if he did, he had no idea where she was.

"Then you die."

"WE'VE TALKED ABOUT THIS, Mordred. You need to do a better job of controlling your urges."

"I don't have the patience for this now, mother," Mordred replied tightly, needing to force out the words through his teeth. "I did what I thought was necessary."

"Yes, your standard argument, isn't it?" Morgase tsked, shaking her head from side to side as she frowned in disappointment. "Patience does seem to be your weakness ... among your many other faults."

Mordred bit back the response that was at the very tip of his tongue, angry but not foolish enough to allow his temper to rule him. Understanding what could happen if he did.

He had hoped that his mother would leave him alone after he left the Witch. He needed time to relieve the stress flowing through him, and he had the perfect solution for doing that. Assuming that Candy was still available.

But just as always his mother refused to let him go, following him to his office in the central turret of his mansion. Once again feeling the need to make the same points that she had been belaboring him with since he was a child.

Her very presence ensured that the peace he sought remained just beyond his grasp. Even here. In this, his private space, where he felt most in control. Most in command. Of himself and others.

He had placed symbols and artifacts from his many victories around the room, every one a strategic decision, so that any visitors he permitted to join him here would have no choice but to acknowledge just exactly who they were dealing with. The power he wielded. The power that he could wield over them.

The son of Morgase, greatest Sorceress of the Teg.

The son of Arthur Pendragon, the greatest Teg of them all.

And the heir to the Teg throne.

Yet none of that mattered in the least when it was his mother who sat across from him.

She dwarfed him, emasculated him, in a way that no one else, not even his father, ever could.

"I told you to leave her be, but you didn't. You couldn't." Morgase's expression shifted quickly into the flinty mask with which Mordred was so familiar, her deep violet eyes sparkling in a way that was almost mesmerizing. She was less than pleased. That much was obvious.

"I wanted to find out if she knew anything else that would be of interest to us and our efforts," Mordred explained with a shrug, as if his disobeying her was a small matter at best.

"You wanted to break her because you wanted to use her against Draig." Morgase's eyes flashed, the only hint that his giving her anger short shrift would be a perilous decision. "And before that you wanted to use her for yourself. Did you not? Not satisfied with your latest conquest? The one in finance if I recall correctly?"

"And what's the matter with that?" Mordred demanded, the heat rising in his voice. "Did you not teach me to take the aggressive path? Did you not teach me to never back away when an opportunity presented itself? I saw an opportunity with the Witch, so I chose to make use of her. And yes, you're right, I hoped to have a little fun with her as well. But not until I got what we needed from her."

Morgase didn't reply right away, her eyes narrowing. Her gaze somehow becoming even more unyielding and unsympathetic. "Don't make me take you over my knee, Mordred. I know how much you enjoyed that when you were younger."

"You wouldn't dare," Mordred almost choked.

"Try me, Mordred." Sparks of energy flashed in the back of her eyes, mirroring those that now danced across her fingertips and began to skip from one hand to the other.

Mordred's anger faded to a low simmer in a flash. There were few Teg who could have such an impact on him. Cow him so swiftly. His mother was one of them. Because though he was powerful in the Grym, he had learned quickly and quite painfully that he was no match for his mother.

"I'm sorry, mother. You're right. I lost myself for a time." Mordred nodded to her in respect as way of an apology. "It wasn't my intention for that to happen. It's just that ..."

"Save your excuses and apologies, Mordred. We don't have time for them and as we both know they have little meaning." Morgase kept her hard gaze on her son for a few seconds more, not tempering her displeasure until she was certain that he had his own anger under control. "We still need to acquire the book. The contract remains in play and our own plans depend upon it."

"And how are we supposed to do that if the Witch gave it to ..."

"Do we really need to go through all this again, Mordred. It's getting quite tedious."

Mordred smiled thinly. "My apologies, mother. It seems my emotions are still a little raw. An unfortunate occurrence whenever the subject of my half-brother comes up."

"A weakness more like. Don't bother trying to hide from the truth, Mordred. It's never worked for you before."

"Be that as it may," Mordred started, not wanting to give his mother more ammunition to use against him in what was an age-old argument between them, "just because we can dangle the Witch as bait doesn't mean we'll get Draig to bite."

"That's the most intelligent thing you've said since I brought the Witch to you."

Mordred's cheeks flamed a bright red. Gritting his teeth, he held back the expletive that threatened to break free. He wanted to avoid the likely result if he allowed that to happen, the sparks of energy continuing to flash in the back of his mother's eyes impossible to ignore.

She still held the Grym. She was still angry with him. Knowing that, he had no desire to test what little of her patience remained. So he chose a different question than the one that originally had come to mind.

"Why would Draig even think to come here?" Mordred asked, lifting his arms to demonstrate his skepticism. "I have dozens of properties all around the world. And I wasn't the one who took the Witch. You did."

"He's the Dragon, Mordred. You know that better than most."

"That may be, mother, but I ..."

He never had the chance to complete his argument, Morgase running right over him. "Don't forget that he is the Dragon. Ever. Not you, even though you should be. But him." She almost spat out the last, the cutting edge of her disdain and disappointment in her own son threatening to slice into his flesh.

"I never forget that, mother," Mordred replied in a deathly quiet voice, his face a bright red to match the flash of rage in his eyes. "Have no fear of that."

Morgase nodded. Pleased to learn that her son wasn't a complete fool, she continued with her explanation. "Draig might not be working for your father any longer, but he remains the same pain in the ass that he's always been. He still has resources that are only available to him. If he wants to find out where the Witch is, he will. The only question is whether he will choose to come for her."

"And there's the rub for us," Mordred scoffed. "If he's smart, he wouldn't waste his time." He leaned forward then, placing his forearms on his desk. "Why even bother? He has what we want. Why would he assume the risk of coming here?"

"Other than the chance to kill you?" Morgase replied in barely a whisper.

"I don't find that joke funny, mother," Mordred hissed. Angry. Mostly at himself because of the bolt of fear that shot down his spine at her suggestion.

Mordred hated Draig. Yet, try as he might, and though he refused to acknowledge it, in the very deepest recesses of his heart, he feared the Dragon. He had seen firsthand what his half-brother truly could do when the situation demanded it of him. The power that he could bring to bear. A power that Mordred only could dream of.

"It wasn't a joke, Mordred. Maybe the bad blood between you two is enough to draw him out from his hiding place. Perhaps he's grown bored of the quiet life and the thought of gaining his vengeance upon you appeals to him."

"I doubt that."

"You hope that, you mean."

"I doubt that," Mordred repeated with greater strength. "He died for a reason. He came back to life for a reason."

"You don't believe that you were reason enough for him to do that?" Morgase felt the need to poke her son just a little bit more, although she was gratified that despite Mordred's often overarching arrogance, he was not so proud to think that he was worthy of the Dragon's attention.

"No, mother, I am not as much the fool that you believe I am." Mordred smiled thinly. "Then again, if Draig does choose to come here, and I kill him ... I can become the Dragon." He said the last in a barely perceptible whisper, as if the very concept of that happening was beyond his imagining.

Morgase stared at her son, studying him, looking at him as she had done so many times before when he was younger. Measuring him. Trying to identify his strengths and weaknesses. His chances of success. And, just as important, his chances for failure.

Once again, after her latest perusal, she determined that not much had changed for Mordred. He was the same as he had always been. That was neither good nor bad. It just meant that she needed to plan accordingly.

"Draig is the Dragon for a reason, my son. As I said, never forget that. Your life likely depends on it. We don't want a repeat of the last time you two met. We don't want to depend on luck to ensure you remain among the living."

A flash of shame raced through Mordred. He did not like thinking about that last encounter with his half-brother. The mortification and terror that had set his entire body shaking as Draig held Excalibur to his throat. Not wanting to relive that experience, he attempted to turn the conversation back to its original track.

"I doubt that Draig has any interest in coming for me in one of my homes. He knows that I would hold the advantage here. That there is no way that he could even get onto the property without revealing himself. So besides his desire to kill me, what other reason could there be for him to take such a risk?"

"The Witch is still alive, Mordred. Draig revealed himself to his father because of her."

Mordred thought about what his mother hinted at. It was a theory he had not considered. "If he had been smart, he would have just killed her and been done with it. In fact, before he died a decade past, he would have killed her."

"Correct," Morgase agreed with a malicious smile. "So perhaps our Dragon isn't entirely the Dragon of old. He has revealed a weakness to us. If we play this right, we kill the Dragon, take the book ..."

"Then kill Arthur," Mordred finished for her.

"Exactly, my son. Then we rule the Teg and the Daemon King can kiss my ass."

17

STORMING THE BEACH

"That is our objective?" Ragnar stood at the bow of the *Kraken* with his two younger brothers.

Seamus had cut the engines before they passed from Long Island Sound into the cove, allowing the current to push them toward the shore. When they were about a mile from the beach, he dropped the anchor. Certain that no one who might be watching from the cliffs knew that they were there.

"It is," Draig confirmed. "At the top of the precipice you'll find the lawn that extends all the way up to the mansion. Take a few steps out into the light and you won't have to worry about hunting for anyone looking for a fight. They'll come to you."

"Music to my ears," Ragnar rumbled. The Berserker stood several heads taller and a few hundred pounds heavier than Draig, as did his two brothers.

In the world in which the Three Little Bears grew up, size, strength, and skill determined their place on the pecking order. Yet despite the physical differences between them, they treated Draig with a deference and respect that they reserved for few others.

And not just because he was the Dragon.

Draig had given them a gift that they had never anticipated receiving. The opportunity to break away from their old life and start anew. Beholden to no one other than themselves. Making their own decisions. A dream with which Draig was quite familiar.

The Three Little Bears doubted that they could ever repay him. Although they would try. Honor demanded it.

"You and your brothers don't have to do this."

Ragnar smiled upon hearing that. Yes, it felt good being able to make his own decisions. He turned and looked down at Draig. "We know that, Dragon. And you acknowledging that is why we are here now."

Draig offered Ragnar a nod, understanding the true importance of what the Berserker shared.

"Give me a minute and then we'll get started."

Draig reached for the Grym, welcoming the Power of the Ancients as it filled him. A familiar and energizing feeling. One that offered him a confidence and belief that he could achieve in no other way.

With the energy coursing through him, it felt like he stood in the center of a lightning storm. His skin prickling. His closely cropped hair standing on end.

Yet even his ability to use the Grym couldn't help him with what he wanted to do now. He needed some additional assistance. A unique skill for which he could thank his mother.

Extending his senses toward the shore, he identified the many distinct magical wards that protected the beach, the staircase, and even the lawn that led toward the mansion.

He could disarm those magical defenses. But that would take too much effort and too much time. And the latter he didn't have, because this was only the first step in a larger, more complex plan.

Worse, if he made a single mistake while attempting to

render the protections harmless, then Mordred and his Paladins would know in an instant.

Instead of taking that risk, he employed a different approach, one that was only available to him. His birthright.

He merged with the Grym a primordial power that was unique to his mother's Draca. Then he sent out stream after stream of energy that was thinner than a fishing line. Each one snaked toward the shore of its own volition, along the way hooking a magical protection that barred Draig's way.

As soon as a line latched onto a ward, it functioned like a siphon, draining away the power used to construct the protective device.

In seconds, it was done. Every single ward removed rather than disarmed. That energy becoming a part of the power that Draig controlled.

Then, to prevent discovery of his work, in the place of those missing wards, he set a thin layer of the Grym. No more than an illusion, really. But enough of the Power of the Ancients to suggest that the property's defenses remained in place.

For just a heartbeat, Draig considered doing the same to the wards guarding the mansion.

He decided against the idea just as quickly.

He wasn't concerned about Mordred. He had faced his half-brother in combat several times in the past, and he had little doubt that he could defeat him just as he had done every time before.

He reserved his concern for one of the other Teg who might be in the castle.

Morgase.

More powerful in the Grym than all but maybe two or three other Teg.

He had never faced her in a combat before. He really wasn't quite sure that he wanted to, having seen what happened to those foolish enough to challenge her.

That thought guiding him, he left the mansion's wards alone. He preferred to keep Morgase in the dark for as long as he could.

Besides, he had done enough. The Berserkers should have little problem reaching the top of the cliff and then engaging in the practice in which they excelled.

Causing havoc.

"You'll need to make some noise." Draig released his hold on the Grym and turned his reddish-orange eyes to Ragnar. "You and your brothers up for that?"

"Does a fish like to swim?" the blonde, bearded giant chuckled.

"Then off you go and try not to have too much fun."

"No promises, Dragon," Ragnar replied, his two brothers giving Draig the same expression as Ragnar did, revealing an almost insatiable hunger to test their skills against those foolish enough to place themselves in their way.

Draig stepped back, giving the Berserkers a half-salute that was more a wave and allowing Seamus to take his place. The captain of the *Kraken* nodded to Draig, his eyes gleaming with the anticipation of what he was about to do.

"You can swim, can't you?" Seamus asked.

"Like fish," Ragnar promised. He dove off the bow, sliding gracefully into the water. Urs and Thorsen followed right behind him.

"Good to know," Seamus mused. One less thing for him to worry about.

Then with another nod to Draig he dove right after them. He had been looking forward to this ever since Draig had asked him for his help.

Life had been a little staid until the last few days, and he was enjoying the adrenaline that was coursing through his veins as a result of his endeavors on behalf of his friend.

He felt more alive than he had in years, and he planned to

make the most of it. Truth be told, he always enjoyed tweaking the nose of a Teg like Mordred.

A little humility every now and then never hurt anyone. And he was more than happy to dole it out to the uppity Teg who always seemed to believe that he was owed more from life than what he could earn himself.

As soon as Seamus slid beneath the surface, the water felt wrong to him.

He was used to sharks in this section of the Long Island Sound. Great whites often swam in from the Atlantic Ocean, those animals regularly patrolling from Montauk Point to Block Island all the way up to Cape Cod Bay.

Sharks stayed away from him when he went for a swim, and for good reason.

But this was a different feeling entirely. As if there might be a more virulent presence lurking nearby. Several, in fact.

Seeing that the Three Little Bears were making good progress toward the beach, Seamus dove down until he was forty feet below the surface. Where it was cold and dark, the moon unable to pierce the watery gloom.

He had little trouble penetrating the darkness, his vision actually improving compared to what it was like when he wasn't in the water, picking out everything around him for hundreds of yards in every direction.

Beyond that distance, he sensed rather than saw all that was with him in the water. An innate form of sonar, he liked to joke. A gift that came from who he was.

He hovered there beneath the waves for a few seconds, allowing the water to speak to him.

The sense that he and the Berserkers weren't alone became stronger.

Seamus reminded himself that he needed to remain calm despite the excitement that urged him to act.

If he could stay patient, then the trouble he sensed would come to him.

Thankfully, he didn't have long to wait.

A few hundred yards to his front, streaking in from the shore.

They circled just ten feet below the Berserkers. The three brothers completely unaware of what tracked them.

Seals in appearance.

Although unfortunately much more than that.

With a powerful kick that churned the water behind him, arms extended to his front, Seamus shot forward.

"WHAT IS IT?" Urs had stopped and was now treading water, having almost swum into his older brother.

"Something touched my leg," Ragnar complained.

"Your leg?" Thorsen asked. He tread water right next to Urs, the beach still several hundred yards distant. "A fish perhaps? Maybe a jellyfish?"

Ragnar shook his head, slightly confused. "It felt like a hand."

"A hand? How is that ..."

"What do we have here?" asked a melodic voice.

All three Berserkers spun quickly, using their hands and legs to push themselves around in the water. They couldn't quite believe what greeted them.

A beautiful woman with hair the color of seaweed tread water just a few yards away from them, her arms moving gracefully in the gentle water just as much keeping her head above the surface as beckoning to the trio of brothers. Her pixie-like face with a button nose and her green eyes that flashed in the darkness not only entranced them, but also sent a surge of heat to the very tips of their fingers and toes. Other parts of their bodies as well.

"Yes, what do we have here?"

The three brothers shifted their position quickly, looking behind them. Another woman.

"Three very handsome young men swimming with us?" The Berserkers glanced to their left. A third woman. Her voice just as melodic. Her features just as beautiful as the first two.

"Who could ask for anything more than that?"

The brothers looked to their right. A fourth woman appeared, her head poking above the surface.

All of them gazed at the brothers with mesmerizing almost incapacitating green eyes. All of them spoke with voices that talked to the Berserkers' souls and tugged at their hearts.

The first woman to appear swam slowly toward Ragnar, reaching out a hand and stroking his face, scratching softly beneath his wet beard.

He flushed and almost groaned, but he caught himself in time. Nevertheless, he doubted that he could control his enjoyable agony for long. Her warm hand radiated a heat that reached into every part of his body ... focusing on one in particular.

"Tell me, big boy, where have you been all my life?"

"I'm sorry, what?" Ragnar mumbled, not quite understanding what was happening. Still trying to figure out why four women were swimming off the coast at that time of the morning. Even more so, why this beautiful creature had taken such an interest in him.

The woman drew herself even closer to the Berserker until she was holding onto Ragnar with both hands, using him to keep her head above water. Her eyes flashed even more brightly, spinning and flashing like a kaleidoscope. Her lips curled into a more than welcoming smile. A smile promising

Ragnar things that he could only dream of. That he had dreamed of more frequently than he thought healthy.

The other three women swam closer as well. Within touching distance of Urs and Thorsen, although the two Berserkers didn't realize it. Their eyes were drawn to what was happening to their brother, a faint hint of jealousy rising up in both of them.

"I've been looking for you, silly," the woman laughed softly.

"You have?" Ragnar didn't understand why that would be the case, although he was quite pleased to hear it.

He grunted, more in pleasure than in discomfort, when the woman wrapped her legs around his waist. One hand now on his arm, the other on his cheek, Ragnar thought – hoped – that she was about to kiss him, and he had no intention of putting up a fight.

The woman nodded. "Yes, I have. I've been looking for the love of my life for quite some time. I've been looking for you, big boy. Only you."

"You have?" Ragnar could barely get the words out, and he couldn't pull his eyes away from the woman's. He remained happily trapped in those softly glowing green orbs, even as the woman's fingers, at first rubbing gently along his forearm, began to dig into his flesh, her sharp nails slicing into his skin.

Pinching, then hooking.

Ragnar ignored the discomfort and then the pain, completely entranced by those wondrous green eyes that seemed to offer a window into the woman's very soul. He didn't notice how the woman's hand slowly changed. Becoming a claw. The fingers lengthening. The fingernails sharpening.

"I have, big boy. I've been looking for you." The green-haired woman laughed softly, clearly amused, which made Ragnar smile, pleased that he could have such an effect on her. "And now that I've found you, I will never let you go."

"You won't?" Ragnar asked. The woman's grip on his arm

began to hurt, five trickles of blood mixing with the sea. But he didn't care, the pain barely registering in his consciousness.

He only cared about staring into those softly glowing green orbs that filled him with an enjoyable, seductive warmth.

"Yes, silly. You. I found you." She pulled on his hair so that their foreheads were touching. "You and I will be together forever, big boy. I will never let you go. Ever."

"Release him!"

The harsh voice just beyond the four women broke the spell that had captured the three Berserkers.

The woman's head whipped around, and as soon as her hypnotic orbs turned away, Ragnar and his brothers were released from the magic that had been cast upon them.

Growling in surprise and anger, he tried to push the woman off him. But he couldn't.

She wouldn't budge. Her grip was too strong, her legs like iron around his waist.

"Leave us be, old man," the woman ordered. "You have no place here. And this business certainly isn't yours."

Seamus smiled mockingly at that. He swam a little closer, and as he did so, he appeared to grow in size, a nimbus of energy framing his figure.

Perhaps it was an illusion, perhaps it wasn't, but it certainly had an impact on the four women. The three yet to latch themselves onto the Berserkers paddled a few feet farther away. Their eyes nervous now instead of hypnotic.

"The ocean belongs to me, Selkie. Best you remember that." The water began to bubble and then churn around Seamus, until a small whirlpool swirled slowly around him. "You will leave my friends alone, or you will deal with me. And I am not in a very forgiving mood this morning."

The woman's eyes narrowed, her beautiful face now marred by an angry scowl. "We have a contract, McCracken. As I said, this is our business, not yours."

Seamus nodded. Although his expression never changed, his eyes did, shifting from a clear blue to a stormy grey. He didn't care much about the woman's argument. "Break the contract."

The woman snorted at that. "We can't break the contract. Not without paying a penalty that we do not want to pay. Besides, there are four of us. Despite what you might think, you cannot stop us all."

Seamus shrugged. "Perhaps, though I will enjoy trying." His voice hardened until it grated like steel across stone. "Break the contract, or you will pay a price worse than the one that you do not want to pay. I promise you that."

"I told you that I cannot break the contract. It is binding. I will not put myself and my sisters at odds with the Sorceress and her son. I don't care what threats or promises you make, McCracken. None among the Teg are foolish enough to anger the Sorceress."

"Break the contract, Selkie, or you will face not only my wrath, but that of the Dragon."

"The Dragon?" The woman's already pale complexion became even whiter. Few among the Teg had the power to strike fear into a heart with just a name. Morgase was one, thus the Selkie's reluctance to accede to Seamus' demand. And one of the others was the Dragon.

"I do not use his name lightly. You know that he does not look kindly on those who do."

"The Dragon is dead. Everyone knows that."

"Miracle of miracles the Dragon lives again." Seamus glided a few feet closer, the whirlpool gaining speed, lifting him out of the water. Within touching distance of the Selkie. Ready to seize the woman if she tried to pull Ragnar below the surface, just as she had been preparing to do.

"There is no way that the Dragon could still ..."

"The Dragon is the Dragon. Do you really believe that he could die so easily?"

That question cut short the response the woman had been ready to offer. "If you are lying to me, McCracken, we will find you."

Seamus nodded, accepting the threat, although clearly he was not concerned. "If it comes to that, Selkie, I look forward to it. What's life without a few good challenges."

The woman stared at Seamus for several seconds, then nodded, more to herself than to him. Unwrapping her legs from around Ragnar, she gave him a slight peck on his cheek. "It would have been fun, big boy. Maybe next time." Then she slipped beneath the surface, disappearing just as quickly as she had appeared, her sisters already gone.

"Those were Selkies?" Ragnar asked, a shiver of cold running through him at the thought.

He had heard of Selkies and what they could do. The thought that a creature such as that had gained control over him with such ease terrified him in a way that nothing else ever had. It also filled him with the immediate desire to get out of the water.

Seamus nodded. "Yes, quite effective in the use of their natural talents, aren't they?"

"Quite beautiful as well," Urs offered from just a few feet behind Ragnar.

"Yes, very comely," Thorsen agreed.

Seamus snorted at that. "And exceedingly dangerous as you were about to find out."

"What do you mean?"

"They were about to pull you and your brothers below. Once they did, you were done for."

The coldness that shivered through Ragnar only intensified, the chill of the water having nothing to do with it. Because he heard the truth in Seamus' words. He had been about to be pulled to his death, and in his own mind he knew that if the Selkie dragged him beneath the waves, he wouldn't have put up a fight. "But they seemed like such nice girls."

"Come on," Seamus said, not surprised by the Berserker's response, the glamour of the Selkies still affecting him. "Let's get you and your brothers to the beach before you three lotharios decide to go after them."

SEAMUS KNELT IN THE SURF, fingers digging into the sand, enjoying the rush of the waves cascading over him. The three Berserkers crouched next to him.

"Thank you again," Ragnar rumbled, more than just a little embarrassed that he and his brothers had fallen prey to the Selkies without putting up a fight. Promising himself that he would more than make up for it now that he was once again on land. "Without your assistance, we would have been taken to our doom. With barely a whimper."

Seamus shrugged, as if to say that he had done very little for the Berserker and his two brothers. "There's no reason to thank me. It might have been fun for you until the very end. Selkies do like to play with their food before eating it."

Ragnar gave Seamus a confused look, one that suggested that he didn't quite know whether to interpret his response literally. Seamus didn't care. He had moved on, staring intently at the beach.

He watched as two pairs of Paladins met almost right in front of them, just thirty yards farther up the beach and closer to the sand dunes, then continued on their way toward the far ends of the crescent-shaped shoreline. The guards would meet again in the same place after completing their circuit.

That was good. Routine worked in Seamus' and the Berserkers' favor. As did the fact that Draig had done exactly as he said he would, eliminating the magical traps and snares that protected the beach and crag.

"I don't know if you're being serious or making fun."

Seamus chuckled softly, keeping his gaze fixed on the Paladins until they were lost in the gloom. The full moon slipping back behind the clouds that drifted out toward the ocean would make what the Berserkers needed to do next that much easier.

"A little of both. I used to spend some time with a Selkie. It was quite an experience. Until she decided that she didn't want to spend time with me anymore."

The edge in his voice hinted that the end of that relationship had not been a pleasant experience for him. "You will have to tell me about it."

Seamus grinned at both the request and the memories that flooded up in him. Most of them pleasant. A few bringing some heat to his cheeks. The last few reminding him why he broke it off with the Selkie. "So long as you're buying."

"Done," Ragnar agreed, offering Seamus a smile in return.

"Now off with you," Seamus urged. "You have seven minutes to get to the top."

In a flash, Ragnar, Urs, and Thorsen were up from their crouches and sprinting across the beach.

Seamus was impressed. Despite their hulking size, the three blonde behemoths as he liked to think of them – not as the Three Little Bears as Cerridwen had named them, were fast and quite nimble on their feet, already climbing up and over the sand dunes.

The Berserkers disappeared for just a second then appeared once more on the staircase. They raced up the crag at a rapid clip, fearing that if they didn't keep the pace, the Paladins on the beach would see them. The brothers disappeared over the crest in four minutes flat with no one the wiser but Seamus.

Very impressive indeed.

And one less thing for Seamus to worry about. Now he could focus on what he was supposed to do.

He glanced to his left and then to his right.

His smile became more menacing.

It looked like he wouldn't have to wait for very long.

The two pairs of Paladins were coming back in his direction. Right on time.

Pushing himself up to his feet, he walked out of the surf and up the beach, placing himself in the path of the approaching Paladins.

WITH SEAMUS and the three Berserkers swimming toward the shore, Draig entered the darkness of the *Kraken's* main cabin.

He decided on the shadows at the very back. The ones that seemed to be darker than all the others, the few rays of moonlight streaking through the windows only illuminating the front of the living space.

"I thought I had an agreement with your Master."

Draig frowned, holding his walking stick in front of him like a baseball bat. He didn't remove the magic hiding his sword, however. Not yet. Not until he needed to.

Because he did trust the Daemon King. Or rather he would until he had cause not to.

"You do have an agreement with our Master. That has not changed." A petite older woman dressed like a hiker stepped out of the gloom. "Our Master thought you might be able to use our assistance. So we offer our services to you."

"For a fee, of course."

"There is always a fee, Dragon. You know that better than most. However, our Master told us that if you succeed, that would be favor enough to him. All debts paid. The contract completed."

Draig thought about the offer being made. He had to admit, he was having a hard time turning it down. "So you want to come along and have a little fun."

"With your permission, of course. We would not intrude otherwise."

"You understand what I need to do?"

"We do. Our Master was quite explicit."

"You'll stay away from where I'm working?"

"We will. We will provide a distraction as you require, and then we will leave you to your work. You need not worry about us."

Draig studied the five Daemons. They didn't look like much. Three women and two men who appeared to be no different than anyone else he might see walking down the street of a small town on the Long Island coast. All of them dressed as if they were getting ready to head down a trail to do some birdwatching.

Yet all of them with the pure-black eyes that gave away their true essence and the power that they could bring to bear.

Draig knew quite well exactly what Daemons could do. What they would do if given the chance.

They were vicious fighters. They never surrendered. And Draig had no doubt that they would cause a great many problems for anyone unfortunate and unlucky enough to face them in a combat.

He almost felt sorry for the Paladins. Though not quite.

"Come on," Draig said, making use of the Grym exactly as the Daemon King had instructed and stepping into the larger shadow running along the back of the cabin. "The more chaos the better."

18

PLAYING ON THE LAWN

"**W**hy is it so quiet?"

Urs and his two brothers stood atop the crest, gazing out across the manicured lawn that extended all the way to the castle. They had expected an attack as soon as they stepped on the gravel path along the crag, three-foot-long magical bars stronger than steel gripped in their meaty paws, but there wasn't a hint of movement. Not even on the shadowy, tree-lined paths on both sides of the lawn that ran right up to both corner towers.

"I do not know," Thorsen replied, just as perplexed as his brother. "It is quite disappointing."

"Although not all that surprising," Ragnar rumbled. "The Dragon warned that this might happen. That our enemies might be so reliant and trusting in the Grym used to defend this castle that they have little fear of attack."

"Then we must show them the error of their ways," growled Urs, smacking the bar held in his right hand into the palm of his left.

"Yes, we must," Ragnar agreed. "The Dragon said that we must make some noise. It is time for us to do that."

The eldest of the three stepped onto the grass, his younger brothers right behind him, one on each side. If they had made their appearance only minutes before, not only would alarms have sounded, but a variety of magical traps would have snapped closed, several with a lethal finality.

Ragnar almost wished that challenge remained. It would have made what they were doing that much more interesting. Because this incursion into enemy territory was proving to be much too easy.

Case in point, he and his brothers almost made it all the way to the castle before they were challenged.

"Halt!"

A black-clad Paladin carrying a mace infused with the Grym sprinted down from the back porch, rushing to confront the intruders. Another Paladin emerged from the other side of the portico. Then a handful more. They arrayed themselves in front of the three brothers in a line that curled toward them from the edges, preventing the intruders from proceeding any further.

"What in all the hells do you think you're doing here?" the Paladin who had arrived first on the scene demanded.

"Going for a stroll," Ragnar replied. He didn't feel the need to rush the confrontation, although he certainly did look forward to it. Draig had asked that he and his brothers keep the Paladins occupied for a good amount of time. They would do just that.

"A stroll?" The Paladin appeared to be dumbfounded by the giant's response.

Ragnar nodded. "Yes, it seems a lovely night for a stroll. Does it not?"

The Paladin frowned, not quite sure what to make of the three massive men who stood before him. He glanced at his comrades, looking for some help. Yet they were at just as much of a loss as he was.

"Do you know who owns this property?"

"We do," Ragnar replied with a confident nod.

The Paladin waited for more of an answer, his frown becoming a scowl as the seconds ticked by. He was scheduled to go off shift. If another ten minutes had passed, he could have avoided this headache.

"Then who lives here, big man?"

"The would-be usurper." Ragnar gave the Paladin a smile and a wink meant to increase the level of the man's ire.

It did, the Paladin's tone sharp. "You dare to call the Lord Mordred a usurper?"

"I did not call him a usurper, Paladin."

The Paladin stared at the blonde giant, his confusion plain. "You just said he was a usurper."

Ragnar grinned, enjoying the game he was playing. "I said he was a would-be usurper. That is different."

"How is that different?" demanded the Paladin.

"A usurper is assumed to have achieved his or her objective, usually taking a throne. A would-be usurper has that objective yet has not achieved that objective. A would-be usurper is a failure. A fraud."

"You're mincing words," the red-faced Paladin replied, "and you insulted Lord Mordred."

"How so?" Ragnar wondered mildly. "Mordred seeks the Teg throne, everyone knows it, and he has gone after that seat of power many times. Yet Arthur Pendragon remains the King Teg. That suggests failure, does it not?"

The Paladin studied the giant who smiled at him pleasantly. He was finding it difficult to argue against him. And he had little desire to continue down that path.

He glanced at the men with him, seeking their support and assistance.

Once again, none of them had anything to offer other than

a few shrugs, as if they had a hard time disagreeing with the giant conversing with him.

Not wanting to remain stuck in a circular argument, he shifted to another topic, hoping to push the matter before them forward at a faster pace. "How did you get past our defenses?"

"What defenses?" Ragnar asked, giving the Paladin a shrug that suggested he didn't know what the soldier was talking about.

The Paladin thought about that response, then turned to one of the men at his back. "Check it. And bring a few more squads."

The soldier nodded, then sprinted toward the northwest corner of the castle where the Paladins' barracks was located.

"You're on restricted property. You shouldn't be here."

"Yet here we are."

The Paladin frowned again at the huge man who appeared to be completely at his ease even though a half-dozen well-armed and well-trained Paladins were ranged against him. "Are you always so difficult?"

"I am not being difficult."

"You're not being difficult?" The Paladin's temper flared. He was done with this giant. He just wanted his bed. But he couldn't return to the barracks until these three were taken into custody.

He could deal with them later after they had been locked in a cell for most of the day. That would soften them up and make for an easier interrogation.

"I am not trying to be difficult. Not yet. But you will find out soon enough just how difficult I and my brothers can be."

"Your brothers," murmured the Paladin. The resemblance between the three was unmistakable.

Shaking his head, he decided that continuing this conversation was a waste of time. When a few more squads appeared, he would lock the trio away and be done with them. The three brothers were starting to make him more than just a little uneasy. "Who are you?"

Ragnar gave the man a disappointed look, pursing his lips and shaking his head slightly from side to side. He took his time before deigning to reply. "We are Berserkers, Paladin, sworn in service to the Dragon."

That stopped the low murmurs that had begun among the Paladins, several of them snorting in disbelief. The leader of the group laughed softly, now certain that these three weren't quite right in the head.

"Berserkers?" the Paladin snorted. "Berserkers are exceedingly rare."

"We are indeed," Ragnar confirmed, not feeling the need to offer the man the more detailed explanation that he so obviously wanted.

Tired of waiting, the Paladin moved on. "You serve the Dragon?"

"We do."

"The Dragon is dead. He has been for more than ten years."

"The Dragon has risen from the ashes," Ragnar replied, "just like the phoenix." With his free hand down by his side, he flicked his fingers. The secret language of the Berserkers, his brothers reading it easily. "Ware to all those who oppose him."

The Paladins stared in silence, then burst out laughing. Several seconds passed before the leader of the group spoke again.

"The Dragon is dead, boyo," the Paladin stated with complete confidence. "Clearly you're mistaken."

"Actually, the only mistake is the one that you made."

"And what mistake would that be?" the Paladin asked right before he saw the giant's eyes change, narrowing, sharpening, next his body tensing, a barely contained violence radiating from him.

"Believing that you could stand against Berserkers without consequence."

In just a heartbeat, two of the Paladins, one on each side of the leader, lay on the ground. Knocked senseless.

Urs and Thorsen moved so swiftly that they appeared to be no more than blurs, the Paladins' brains having a great deal of difficulty keeping up with what their eyes were telling them.

The leader of the Paladins met the same fate just an instant later, Ragnar bringing his bar down in a short, sharp blow.

To the credit of the remaining Paladins, they attempted to fight rather than flee. But their efforts did them little good. Only one of the men was able to actually swing his mace before joining his comrades on the tightly cut grass. The others weren't so lucky, falling before they could even engage their attackers.

"I was hoping for more of a challenge," grumbled Urs.

"As was I," admitted Thorsen.

Just then, an alarm sounded, a shrill screech that pierced the quiet of the night. With it came a rush of Paladins from the northwest side of the castle.

Ten men.

Then twelve.

Then twenty.

Until there were twenty-eight in all.

Ragnar grinned. Now this was more like it. "Let us demonstrate what happens to those seeking to challenge Berserkers sworn to the Dragon."

Ragnar sprinted toward the Paladins rushing at him, Urs and Thorsen at his heels. As they ate up the ground, they shifted.

Three blonde bears almost twice as big as the Berserkers took their place, sharp claws digging up the turf and roars of rage splitting the night as they raced toward the combat they relished.

19

WAKE-UP CALL

"What's going on, Desmond?"

The Paladin popped up from his bunk, half asleep, almost knocking his head on the bottom of the one above him. His friend, who had gotten off his shift a few hours before just like he did, was already out of his sheets and pulling on his combat boots.

"I don't know, Lucas, but we need to report. Now. So get going."

Lucas nodded, still groggy as he pushed himself out of his cot and reached for his boots. He had learned upon joining the Paladins that it was always best to sleep in his uniform so that he could be prepared for situations just like this one.

The alarm, which was a rare occurrence, had woken him and the several dozen other Paladins who had been sleeping in their bunks. Many of them already hustling toward the command center at the front of the building with their Grym-infused maces in hand. Others were struggling just as Lucas was to get their bearings.

The boss had changed the schedule just a few days before. Requiring more men on shift and longer shifts. And since there were only a hundred Paladins stationed at this property on Long Island Sound, the greater demands already were affecting them.

"I thought that the estate was impregnable," Lucas muttered, struggling with one boot. "Lord Mordred crows about it all the time."

"If that was the case, then how do you explain the alarm?" Desmond demanded. Strapping on his utility vest, he reached for his mace. "Now hurry up. I don't want to be the last one out of the barracks."

Turning to go, Desmond stopped, a hint of movement in the corner of his eye holding him in place. Frowning, he squared up to the back wall that was only a few feet away from him.

He and Lucas had selected these bunks at the very end of the long row because the air-conditioning units were right above them. A must for the hot and muggy summers.

However, he was questioning that decision now. Because despite all the men getting dressed and gathering their gear just a dozen yards away from him he felt isolated. In his own little world where a cry for help wouldn't be heard. The closest Paladins ten bunks farther up in the barracks.

That realization sent a flutter of concern through him. One he didn't quite understand.

Maybe it was because of what had caught his eye. The shadows that played along the wall and moved to a rhythm that made him think that they were alive.

And why were there shadows covering the entirety of the wall to begin with?

The overhead lights in the barracks failed on occasion. But never an entire section that put where Desmond and Lucas slept into an unnatural dusk.

Desmond's flutter of concern shifted into a tremor of fear as the shadows covering the wall shifted and flowed. It was almost as if they were responding to Desmond's rapidly changing emotions, feeding off them.

"What is it, Desmond?"

Lucas finally was up from his cot, wiping his eyes to clear the last of the fog of sleep from them, ready to go. Yet his friend remained frozen in place, staring into the gloom.

"I don't know." Desmond frowned. What was bothering him? They were just shadows, after all. And there was a simple explanation. There had to be shadows back here because the lights had failed. An infrequent occurrence, but not unheard of. Still, that niggling of doubt burrowed deeper within him. "Do those shadows look wrong to you?"

"The shadows?" Lucas didn't understand why Desmond asked him that question. Still, he looked in the direction that Desmond nodded, frowning as he did so. "It's just because the lights aren't working." Lucas snorted, trying to brighten his friend's somber mood. "I didn't know that you were afraid of the dark."

Desmond shook his head, ignoring the well-intentioned barb. "It's not that there are shadows. There should be. I don't deny that."

"Then what's the problem?"

Desmond started to reply, then stopped himself. Worried about how he was going to sound. Then he realized that his friend wouldn't see what concerned him if he wasn't completely honest. "The shadows look alive."

"Alive? How could shadows be alive?"

"I don't know," Desmond replied. "But they're moving in ways that aren't right. Like they've got a life of their own."

"Aren't right?" Lucas wanted to laugh, but he couldn't. Desmond was the most grounded of his friends. Never getting too high or too low. Yet now, Desmond appeared to be not just frightened but terrified. Of shadows, no less. What was that about? "They're just shadows, Desmond. It's just because we haven't been sleeping much the last few days. Come on. We need to get going before Sergeant Preston comes looking for us. You know how he can be."

"The shadows, Lucas," Desmond hissed with a surprising intensity. Still frozen in place. He wasn't concerned in the least about Sergeant Preston. What bothered him more and more were the shadows that, if he looked closely enough, appeared to be taking on shapes, solidifying, transforming into figures that resembled humans.

"Lucas, you need to look closer. Shadows can move, but not how they're moving now." Desmond looked back over his shoulder at his friend, a plea in his eyes. "These shadows are alive, Lucas. Actually, they're not so much alive as they're coming to life. That's not right. That shouldn't be possible."

Lucas opened his mouth to reply, then closed it just as quickly. He shook his head then, not knowing what to say. Worried about Desmond. He hoped it was just the lack of sleep that was making his friend act this way.

He stepped up next to his friend and stared into the gloom just as Desmond was doing. Even squinting, hoping to see whatever it was that Desmond saw. "I don't see anything that …"

"There!" Desmond almost shouted as he pointed toward the far corner of the wall.

Lucas focused on the gloom where Desmond pointed. His eyes widened. He wanted to tell his friend that he was just seeing things, but he couldn't. Because now he saw them, too.

What looked to be a shimmer in the black. A fold in the gloom and then another, as if the shadows were building one upon the other, for what purpose he couldn't say. Wait, was that …

It couldn't be.

Lucas grunted in shock, then looked down slowly.

A long spear of misty black extended out from the wall and

through his chest, slicing right through his ribs. Probably out his back, but he couldn't look behind him to confirm.

Requiring Desmond's assistance, Lucas turned his eyes to his right, pleading. He recognized his own horror mirrored in Desmond's expression, his friend's lips moving like a fish out of water but saying nothing.

Then he watched in shock as a second shadowy spike shot forward, sliding through Desmond's chest and then out his back. At the very end of the spear, it seemed to be more a claw than a blade.

His friend grunted just as he had, eyes widening as Desmond looked down at the wispy black spear that retained the solidity of steel.

Just an instant later, those streaks of black disappeared, pulled back into the larger shadow that moved along the back wall with a life of its own.

Lucas and Desmond stared at one another, unable to speak, unable to breathe, a sheet of blood spreading down their broken chests, then their legs, finally pooling on the floor by their feet. They collapsed at the same time, their eyes glazing over. Never getting the opportunity to learn what killed them.

"Do you always have to be so dramatic?"

A grandmotherly woman who looked like she was dressed for a morning hike and maybe a little birdwatching stepped out of the shadows, her pure-black eyes gleaming brighter than the darkness surrounding her as she took in all the activity taking place at the front of the barracks.

Twenty or so Paladins remained in various states of undress. But they were farther up the bunk rows, and they had neither seen nor heard what had happened to the men who lay dead at her feet.

The tall man who stepped out of the shadow-covered wall shrugged. "I wasn't being dramatic. I was just clearing our path. That was the easiest way to do it."

The woman didn't bother to argue with her companion. There was no point. They had known each other for millennia, and if she had learned nothing else during that time, it was that trying to argue with him was wasted effort, because he never bit.

Two more women and another man emerged from the shadows, taking in all that was occurring in the barracks with a single glance.

Their pure-black eyes gleamed as well.

In anticipation.

"Shall we get started?" the older woman suggested.

She knelt down, touching the still warm body of one of the Paladins. The change occurred in seconds.

The grandmotherly woman no longer looked like a bird-watcher. She looked like the soldier she killed. The same facial features. The same clothes and gear. The same physique and size.

There was only one difference. The color of her eyes remained, scleras and irises pure black.

The transformation complete, she stepped out of the way, allowing her four companions to do as she had just done.

In less than a minute, five new Paladins stood in the back of the barracks, hidden in the shadows. Three were exact replicas of the dead man on the left, two of the dead man on the right.

"The Dragon asked that we create some chaos," the one who had appeared as the grandmotherly woman said. "Let's get to it."

One of the Daemons who now was the carbon copy of Desmond stalked up the aisle, hands shifting in an instant into razor-sharp claws.

The Paladins hustling to respond to the alarm still were unaware of the terrible danger that approached them from behind.

20

WATER SHOW

"I've always got to do the hard work," Seamus muttered when he finally reached the top of the crest.

He stood there for a moment, one hand on the wooden railing, the other on a knee, bent over, as he tried to catch his breath. It's a good thing Draig wasn't there to see him in his current state.

His friend had been nagging him that he needed to get more exercise. Just go for a walk every once in a while, he'd tell him.

Draig's nudging had grown tiresome, so Seamus had tuned him out. But now, after huffing and puffing his way up the staircases that switch backed along the cliff, he realized that his friend might have been right.

A little cardio work would have done him some good. Although he had little desire to admit that truth to Draig. His friend wouldn't say anything, of course. He'd just give him that condescending look of his with the raised eyebrow that always irritated Seamus.

Of course, Seamus wouldn't have had to make the effort to

climb the crag if the Paladins had done as they were supposed to.

Seamus had assumed that as soon as he confronted the first few patrols on the beach, more of those thugs would come streaming down the staircase to join the fight.

He wouldn't have to leave the beach.

But no such luck.

As soon as he dispatched the four Paladins who had rushed at him, maces raised, ready to pound him into the sand, they in turn finding themselves buried beneath the beach after just a quick motion of Seamus' hand, sinkholes opening right beneath their feet and closing just as rapidly, that had been it.

Neither hide nor hair of another Paladin. Not even one of those bastards taking a peek down from the top of the precipice to goggle at his handiwork.

It was all quite disappointing.

And it was probably his own fault, Seamus mused. He had been too thorough, too quick, in his work. He didn't give the Paladins time to call for assistance before he finished them.

That had been his mistake.

He was just too good at this kind of task.

He probably should blame the Three Little Bears as well. Finally able to breathe again, he pushed himself back up.

Seamus had to give those blonde behemoths credit where credit was due. The gargantuan Werebears had ripped through a score of Paladins with ease and now, after demonstrating the extent of their abilities, they were playing with the soldiers seeking to tame them. The Paladins not realizing that they were willing accomplices to the Werebears, who were happy to occupy Mordred's defenders for as long as they could.

Good work on their part, but it left Seamus with very little to do.

Taking a deep breath, finally catching his wind, he walked away from the lawn toward the tree-lined path to his left. He would begin again closer to the mansion. Maybe he could cause a commotion out in front of the property and create a two-flank dilemma for the Paladins.

The Berserkers had done an excellent job of drawing most of the attention from the Paladins, and he didn't want to get in their way. So he would try to make life even more difficult for Mordred's soldiers by dividing their forces.

A few broken windows at the front of the house and perhaps even a little structural damage should be enough to pull Paladins his way so that he could get in on the fun again.

"What in all the hells do you think you're doing, old man?"

Seamus stopped abruptly. He had been watching the fight on the lawn, peeking through the tree branches, not paying as much attention to where he was going as he should have.

Glancing up, he smiled. It looked like he was going to get what he wanted sooner than he anticipated.

The Paladin stood well over seven feet tall, his uniform barely fitting him. His short-sleeved Polo shirt and tactical pants strained to contain the man's bulging muscles. Clearly, the Paladin spent too much time in the gym.

Seamus' smile grew even wider when a fist of Paladins stepped out from between the trees, joining their comrade and blocking the trail.

Now this was more like it.

A roar from the Werebears drowning out the shouts and screams from the battle taking place on the lawn only got Seamus' blood boiling all the more.

Still, he faced only six opponents. He had been hoping for more, because six didn't seem like much of a challenge. Not compared to the Berserkers.

"I'm looking for a fight."

"A fight?" the soldier snickered, his voice strangely high for such a big man. "Really?"

"A fight, Arnold," Seamus confirmed, shaking his head at having to repeat himself.

"Who the hell is Arnold?" demanded the Paladin.

"Your name isn't Arnold?" Seamus asked innocently, waiting to see if it would click for the musclebound soldier.

"Arnold Schwarzenegger?" Seamus continued upon receiving blank stares from the giant and the men with him. "You haven't heard of him? Bodybuilder? Movie star? Former governor?"

"I know who he is. What of it?"

Seamus motioned to the giant, urging him to look a bit more closely at himself. Still nothing from the Paladin, his confused expression only deepening. Clearly Seamus' attempt at humor was lost on the man.

Seamus sighed, not wanting to have to continue to do the work of trying to explain. "Never mind."

"Why do you think you'd stand a chance against us in a fight?"

"Why not?" Seamus replied.

The man laughed then, the unexpectedly high-pitched noise making Seamus cringe. It sounded much like fingernails scratching against a blackboard "As you'll find out soon enough, you stand no chance against me, old man."

Just then another squad of Paladins appeared, five men joining those already arrayed around the giant.

Seamus smiled. Now this was more like it. Almost like pins lined up in a bowling alley ready to be knocked down.

"I beg to differ," Seamus replied, then regretted his words as soon as he said them. Because he saw the confusion on the giant's face become bewilderment, just as had been the case when he had said the same to Derek, the now deceased Renegade.

Not wanting to get stuck in a conversation with no end, before the giant could ask Seamus what he was talking about, he acted. Spreading his feet so that he was firmly grounded on the path, he lifted his arms then motioned with his hands.

A surge of water erupted from Seamus' palms, rolling like a monstrous wave down the path and washing away the giant and the other Paladins.

Seamus grinned as he examined his handiwork. The drenched and drowned Paladins were scattered for thirty or more yards, several knocked back in among the trees. A few wouldn't rise again, hitting the trunks with such force that they broke their backs, necks, or both.

Now that's the way it was supposed to be, Seamus nodded to himself.

Exceedingly pleased with his accomplishment, Seamus started walking down the sodden path toward the mansion, every few steps sending blasts of water shooting from his hands. Knocking back down to the ground any of the Paladins who were trying to get to their feet with a power that was strong enough to crush chests and bones.

For the giant, wanting to make a point, Seamus had something else in mind. Bringing his hands together, he knelt and pounded his fists into the mud.

The response was startling and instantaneous. A geyser of water shot up and out of the ground right where the giant had regained his feet, throwing the Paladin into the air well above the tree line, then leaving him there to hang for a second before he fell, screaming, floundering, back to the earth with a resounding and very final thud.

Seamus' eyes flashed with delight. That was definitely more like it.

"Stop!"

Seamus didn't stop. He kept going, striding crisply toward the Paladin who had jumped out from between the trees to block his way, several more of the soldier's comrades racing down the muddy trail to join him.

He didn't focus his attention on these new challengers first, however. Instead, Seamus fired quick blasts of water to both sides of the trail much as if he was working his way through a shooting gallery.

Seamus had sensed the movement along both his flanks, the Paladin on the trail attempting to hold his focus so that more of his men working their way through the trees could blindside him.

A good strategy, Seamus admitted.

But it didn't work.

And it didn't slow him down.

Only two men creeping among the trees actually made it out onto the trail. The rest Seamus smashed backward with a childlike glee. Those who didn't smack against the unforgiving tree trunks with a bone-crunching force were sent flying back through the wood, fighting against the rush of water that threatened to drown them.

The pair that managed to reach the path at the same time charged Seamus, one from each side.

He wasn't worried. Turning his palms so that they faced the sky, watery ropes sprouted, twisting and turning, snapping to the left and right, wrapping around the two Paladins, who struggled vainly to break free.

Seamus gave the Paladin blocking his way a wink, enjoying how the man gulped. Then he flicked his wrists.

The coils of water shot toward the Paladin and his squad, the two men, now unconscious, faces blue, shot toward their comrades in the grips of their watery bonds.

The Paladins tumbled to the ground, rolling backward, the two men trapped in the watery coils slamming into their compatriots much like a wrecking ball crashing through a brick wall.

Seamus waited then. Wanting to see how many adversaries remained.

Five in all.

The two soldiers he sent toward the others as bowling balls, flipping uncontrollably through the air, slammed into the leader of the squad. Those three would not be rising again. The first two asphyxiated, the third's neck bent at a terrible angle.

The soldiers still breathing groaned as they pushed themselves to their feet. Waterlogged. Bruised and battered. A few with broken bones. All of them spitting out the seawater that had come close to drowning them.

Their eyes widened in alarm when they saw that Seamus stood there waiting for them.

Lifting a hand to just below his lips, he blew softly, his breath frosting. The watery spikes that appeared on his palm froze at his touch then streaked toward the Paladins.

The attack was so swift and so unexpected that the men didn't even have the time to dodge out of the way, the barbs no more than blurs. It was over in less than a second.

Seamus nodded to himself in appreciation. Now this was most certainly more like it.

He hadn't felt this alive since ... he couldn't really recall when. It had been a long time since he had put some of his more unique skills to use.

A cold, almost bored voice brought him out of his reverie.

"You should have stayed on the boat, McCracken. Here you're in my domain."

"It's been a long time, Morgase," Seamus said to the elegantly dressed woman who stepped out onto the trail. He hadn't expected to find the Sorceress here, assuming that she would stay in the mansion. Yet that was the way of it, wasn't it? Nothing ever went according to plan. "Although I was hoping for even longer before I had to see you again."

"You should get used to disappointment, McCracken," Morgase warned. "Do you really think that you can challenge me? Have you not learned your lesson after the last time you decided to test your luck?"

"I tend not to listen very well. Too much water in the ears. So you know how that goes." Seamus offered his response with a smile. At the same time his mind worked frantically for a solution. Because Morgase was right. On land, he wasn't a match for her.

"Hardheaded as always."

Seamus shrugged, taking what she meant as a criticism as a compliment instead. "That's why I'm still alive."

"Or is it because you are living under the Dragon's protection?" Morgase mused, lifting an eyebrow to stress her point.

"That could be part of the reason as well," Seamus admitted, all the while seeking to draw out the conversation as he searched furiously for some way to extricate himself from this increasingly dangerous dilemma.

"Unfortunately, he's not here to save you like the last time."

Seamus smiled, unable to forget. He had been hired to locate and retrieve several magical artifacts believed to be lost in a shipwreck off the coast of Nova Scotia. A simple job and one that he had conducted under similar circumstances several times in the past.

Simple until he had come face to face with his real employer.

He hadn't known that he was working for Morgase until she tried to kill him once he acquired the items she required. He had held his own against her -- for a time -- yet even while on the water she proved too strong for him.

Seamus had put on a good show, but not good enough.

He had lost his boat, Morgase setting it on fire. He would have lost his life if Draig hadn't appeared out of the blue, getting him away before Morgase could set fire to him as well.

Literally.

The fireball streaking toward him. Seamus having nowhere

to go. Draig appearing right in front of him, Excalibur in hand to deflect the energy and then take him through a Dragon Door before Morgase could attack them both.

A disheartening encounter, to say the least.

Seamus had lived, but he had loved that boat almost as much as he loved his current one.

He grumbled to himself then, completely out of ideas. He would defend himself as best as he could. Maybe throw a few distractions at Morgase and hope that he could get back into Long Island Sound before the Sorceress killed him.

Because she would kill him.

He couldn't beat her.

He knew that.

He might be arrogant on occasion, but he was never a fool.

And Draig wasn't coming to rescue him this time. The Dragon had his own mission to complete.

The cold reality of his situation filling him with a newfound energy, Seamus burst forward.

A flood of water blasted from his hands as he charged down the path, the crest of the wave rising around him well above twenty feet in height.

Seamus skated more than sprinted atop the surf right behind the breaker, shifting as he went.

Various mythologies spoke of the Kraken. In some, the monster was a giant sea crab or a leviathan. In others, a many-horned fish. Still others referenced a many-headed, many-clawed creature.

It could be one of those or all or something else entirely. Because the truth was that the Kraken was whatever Seamus wanted to be. He could transform into any sea creature he chose or take the best features of several all at one time.

And then, as he battled the most powerful Teg Sorceress, he selected the form that he believed gave him the greatest chance of survival.

Retaining his human shape, he grew in size to twice his current height. Spiky shells like those on a lobster formed on his chest, shoulders, arms, and legs, becoming a flexible armor that was stronger than titanium. And in his hand he grasped a harpoon made of the bone of a sperm whale.

The wave about to crash down on his adversary, Seamus leapt into the air, harpoon poised at his shoulder as he prepared to thrust, hoping that the rush of water would distract Morgase just enough so that he could strike the one and hopefully only blow of the combat.

His eyes snapped shut in disappointment, cursing in frustration, when the crashing wave didn't strike as he desired, instead parting around Morgase.

The Grym streamed from Morgase's hands, encasing Seamus, freezing him in place a few feet above her, the sharp tip of his harpoon less than a foot from her smirking gaze.

So close, yet not close enough.

He should have assumed that this was going to happen.

His frustration increased a hundredfold when he felt himself shifting back to his human form despite his making no effort to do so.

Morgase had cut him off from the Grym, something that only a handful of the Teg could do. Without access to the Power of the Ancients, he didn't stand a chance against her.

Of course, his chances against her even with the Grym had been slim to begin with.

"You should have taken the offer," Morgase purred. "You were foolish to ignore my entreaties."

"As you said, hardheaded and all that," Seamus grumbled, still unable to move a muscle, only able to speak and flick his eyes from side to side.

"I told you long ago that I could use the services of the Kraken."

"You did, but I didn't like you then." Seamus wanted to shrug to emphasize his point, but he couldn't.

"And now?"

"Now I like you even less."

"A pity," Morgase clucked. "Still, it will be fun trying to crack the Kraken. Now come along. We need to have a conversation, and then I have bigger fish to fry."

21

UNEXPECTED VISIT

Draig welcomed the silence that greeted him as he stepped through the shadows along the back wall of the small office on the lower floor of the mansion. The same shadows, in fact, that the two Daemon scouts had used as their entry point.

He had feared that several dozen Paladins would be waiting for him here. Fighting them not so much a concern as giving up the element of surprise.

Yet he had no cause to worry. His decision to trust the Daemon King proved to be a good one.

He owed a debt to the Daemon King. If he had used the Grym to craft a portal to enter the estate, Mordred and his mother would have known in an instant.

Those two couldn't sense what Draig had just done, however, because this was a different type of magic altogether. A type that Draig had never used before though certainly would in the future if the circumstances warranted it.

Convinced that he was alone, Draig stepped quietly toward the corner windows. He glanced through the glass. Not a soul to be seen. Nothing was happening at the front of the mansion.

On the northwest side, all was quiet as well. The only sign that a battle had taken place at the barracks the body of a dead Paladin that prevented the doors from closing. Another debt owed to the Daemon King. His servants had done exactly as they promised.

The only noise that he heard, and at that only faintly, came from the back of the estate. From the roars, it sounded like the Berserkers were having a great deal of fun with their assignment. Hopefully Seamus was as well down on the beach.

Pleased that all was going as he hoped, Draig smiled, his expression resembling that of a predatory beast just about to strike.

Now it was his turn.

Turning the knob, he pushed the door open just enough to peek out. Not a soul to be seen. Although that didn't surprise him. He doubted that many Paladins remained in the mansion, most of them ordered to deal with the intruders on the grounds.

Stepping out into the hallway, he closed the door behind him. He started moving through the mansion, following the path the Daemons suggested, thereby easily avoiding the lone Paladin who sprinted through the living room and then into the kitchen, slamming the door behind him.

When Draig reached the main staircase, he waited just around the corner. Another recommendation from the Daemons.

A good thing that he did, too. No more than a minute passed before several Paladins rushed down the stairs and then curled around the banister toward the back of the mansion.

Then silence again.

He controlled his urge to step out from around the corner and sprint up the staircase.

Draig could employ the Grym to search around him, but he didn't. Assuming that any use of the Power of the Ancients would be registered, especially with Mordred and his Paladins on a high state of alert, he didn't want to take the risk.

He'd have to do this the old-fashioned way.

Peeking around the corner, not hearing a sound, not glimpsing any hint of movement, he snuck across the foyer and then up the staircase, staying close to the wall to ensure that any squeaky floorboard didn't give him away.

When he reached the top, he turned to the left just as the Daemons directed, glad that Mordred had installed such a thick, expensive carpet. It deadened his footfalls, ensuring that he didn't make any noise. Of course, that would apply to anyone coming toward him as well, so he needed to stay sharp and rely on his senses.

He glided down the hallway only a few yards when his instincts saved him, Draig feeling the movement in the air in front of him even though he didn't hear a sound.

The Paladin coming around the corner at the end of the hallway wasn't ready.

Draig was.

Eyes widening in shock at finding an intruder on the top floor of the mansion, before the soldier could yell out a warning or reach for his mace, Draig punched him hard in the throat with a knuckle.

Choking, the Paladin reached for his trachea. There was nothing that he could do other than gasp for breath. That problem no longer a problem when Draig punched him in the jaw, sending him to a less-than-blissful slumber.

The man's muscles giving out, Draig eased him down the wall. Draig left him there, sensing the air shifting on the other side of the corner before he heard the second Paladin coming in his direction.

"Joshua, what's going on?"

By the tone of his voice, Draig assumed the second soldier

believed that something was wrong. Rather than wait for him to approach, Draig stepped forward.

A good decision on his part. Because just as Draig suspected the Paladin had assumed the worst, Grym-infused mace in his hand and above his shoulder. The instant he saw him, the Paladin swung his mace down toward Draig's head.

Wanting to avoid the clash of steel striking steel sounding throughout the mansion, Draig kept Excalibur against his side. Instead, he reached up with his left hand and caught the Paladin's right.

The man grunted in anger and shock, not quite believing that Draig had the strength to stop his strike cold and lock his arm in place. The mace was fixed, unmoving, a foot above Draig's scalp.

Straining to break free, the Paladin's eyes widened in fear when he caught the reddish-orange flash of Draig's orbs. It couldn't be. He was supposed to be ...

The Paladin groaned, eyes fluttering when Draig brought his knee up hard into his crotch. His left hand naturally going to his injured groin. Still, the Paladin kept his feet and struggled to free his hand from Draig's, knowing that using his mace still was the best option for ending this clash.

Or rather he continued to resist until Draig brought his right hand up, smashing the hilt of his sword against the Paladin's scalp.

The Paladin's eyes rolling up into his head, Draig grabbed the man's shirt and slid him down along the wall.

Then he waited for almost a minute, curious as to whether a phalanx of the Paladin's friends would rush out from the bedroom suite at the far end of the hallway.

Thankfully, the larger fight that Draig anticipated didn't materialize. There was nothing except for silence once more.

Feeling a new sense of urgency as the sounds of the battle raging in the back of the mansion quieted, deciding that now wasn't the time for stealth, Draig stalked forward, Excalibur held at the ready. Decisive action was his best friend now, Draig believing that he could eliminate any Paladins in the suite before they could bring their weapons to bear.

Yet when he pushed open the door with his shoulder, the knob slamming through the drywall behind it, no one was there.

The suite Mordred had been using to hold Melissa was empty.

It hadn't been empty for long, however. He was sure of that.

He sensed the faint signature of the Grym here. Not because Melissa used it, but rather the use of the Grym to ensure that she couldn't touch the Power of the Ancients. Morgase's work. Of that he had no doubt.

So where had Mordred taken her?

Before he began his hunt anew, he went back into the hallway and dragged the two Paladins across the carpet and into the room, shutting the door quietly behind him. That done, he headed back toward the main staircase.

Not sensing anyone else on the top floor, Draig was about to trot down the stairs when the tingle of warning in the back of his brain stopped him. His right foot in the air, about to touch the first step leading down, he pulled back his leg and slipped around the corner, the whole time his eyes glued to the foyer below.

He didn't have long to wait, hearing the click of high heels on the tile growing louder.

"Where would you like him put?" a deep voice asked.

Morgase stepped into the entrance hall, not bothering to slow. Coming right behind her was a giant of a Paladin and then four more of Mordred's soldiers. Two of the men were dragging Seamus across the floor.

"I don't like being manhandled," Seamus growled.

"Shut your trap," the Paladin holding him up under his right arm barked, "or we'll beat you until you're blue."

Draig knew Seamus would have little trouble against the Paladins. Morgase was another matter entirely. As evidenced by her use of the Grym to prevent him from employing the Grym himself, because that was the only possible way to tame the Kraken.

"Just wait until I get out of this, smart ass," Seamus grumbled. "When I do, I'll ..."

He never got the chance to spit out the rest of his threat. The Paladin punched him hard in the side of his head, earning a string of muttered curses from the bloodied mariner.

Morgase ignored the interaction between her prisoner and the Paladin.

"Bring him to the main turret," she ordered. "Mordred is there with the Witch. I can deal with both of them at the same time."

Draig considered leaping down from the top of the steps. He could remove the Paladins with little difficulty. He was more concerned about Morgase.

He wasn't afraid to challenge her. In fact, Draig welcomed the contest. But taking her on now might make what he needed to do that much more difficult since Melissa wasn't here as well.

Now that he needed to aid Seamus and Melissa, he had to adjust his approach. So he stayed where he was, watching as Seamus was dragged through the foyer.

Draig knew exactly where the Paladins were taking his friend. Just as important, now he knew exactly where Melissa was.

Seamus being captured could be a complication. Particularly since Draig hadn't anticipated that happening.

Then again, this could be an opportunity.

Two birds with one stone if he played it right.

22

KNOCK AT THE DOOR

"You keep asking the same questions, Mordred. You're like a broken record."

Mordred ignored Melissa. He leaned back in his finely crafted leather chair, his feet up on the overlarge antique desk that separated them.

Two Paladins had taken Melissa from her room and deposited her in the straight-backed chair just across from Mordred only a few minutes before. Now they stood along the wall near the doorway that led into the turret.

"Because I know that you're lying to me," he replied breezily. "Say what you want, deny all you want, but I will get the truth from you."

With a flick of his wrist a spark of energy shot from his palm, Melissa unable to move out of the way in time.

When the spark landed on her arm, she flinched, then cursed. The magic didn't singe her flesh as she thought it would. Instead, it stayed there even when she tried to wipe it off with her hand. Until it fizzled out a few seconds later, though not before the spark sent what felt like an electric charge through her entire body.

Seeing that a few more of those painful sparks were dancing around Mordred's fingertips, Melissa tried to push herself out of the chair. She wanted to get behind it and use it as a shield. But she couldn't.

The two Paladins behind her were faster than she was. Each one bolted forward and placed a meaty paw on a shoulder, holding her in place.

Acknowledging the futility of fighting back with the Grym since Morgase's block remained in place, Melissa unable to touch the Power of the Ancients, she continued to resist the only way she could. "You think I'm lying because you don't want to hear the truth. But I am telling you the truth. I've told you all that you want to know."

Mordred chuckled softly at that. With another flick of his wrist, several more sparks shot forward, each one landing on Melissa, each on a different place on her body, each sending a surge of sizzling energy through her that continued until the spark fizzled out.

"Maybe, maybe not, Witch," Mordred replied. "Regardless, you did break our agreement."

He was disappointed. He had expected the Witch to show some fear, at least, after what he had just done to her. Maybe even remorse.

Every other Teg who had experienced this unique use of the Grym had folded quickly. Yet not her.

Admirable in a way. Although foolish on her part. It just ensured that the Witch was going to hurt a great deal more before he broke her.

Slightly frustrating for Mordred. Yet even more ... exciting.

Because he always enjoyed breaking Teg who needed to be broken. And he would break her. No one had yet been able to resist him, as the Witch would find out soon enough.

"Our contract was completed to the letter," Melissa hissed, her breath short and fast. The pain Mordred inflicted upon her lingered, and she had no choice but to suffer through whatever Mordred wanted to do to her.

"And after that you stole from me, Witch," Mordred clarified. "Poor form on your part and a very bad decision."

A cloud of sparks streaked through the space between them. When each one hit her, Melissa grunted, straining not to reveal her agony. Keeping her teeth locked together. Refusing to cry out and give Mordred the satisfaction of listening to what he wanted to hear.

Of course, Melissa had no good argument against her captor's claim. Still, that didn't stop her from trying to shift his focus in another direction, seeking to gain a little time to recover and think of some way to get herself out of this mess. "You know who has *The Book of Whispers*."

"Draig," Mordred nodded, "as you've said."

"You can get it from him," Melissa growled, taking deep breaths as she shuddered through the last of the scorching sparks of pain that made it feel like every cell in her body was on fire.

"Or perhaps I should have you get it back for me." Mordred snorted out a laugh at the thought. "A shame that I can't trust you."

Melissa couldn't prevent a bark of her own laughter from escaping.

"What's so funny?" Mordred demanded.

Melissa didn't respond, shaking her head, her amusement helping to dampen the pain that still danced across her body.

"What is so funny, Witch?" Mordred repeated, biting out the words slowly, his previously calm demeanor replaced by a red-faced fury.

"You keep talking about what you're going to do when next you come face to face with Draig." She wanted to lean forward then to press her point. She couldn't. The two Paladins behind her remained in place. Holding her back. "I told you that Draig has what you want. You know where he is. You say that you look forward to your next combat with him, because then you will finally kill him. Yet here you are, sitting behind your desk, having nothing better to do than torture me."

Melissa chuckled softly, enjoying how a vein began to pulse on Mordred's forehead, because of that knowing that she was pushing him closer to the edge. Closer to not thinking clearly, which might give her an opportunity. "But you don't want to face him yourself. Do you? You like to talk big, but you act small."

"Watch what you say to ..."

Melissa cut him off with another laugh. This one harsher. More ragged. Mordred was going to torture her regardless of what she said. So she might as well say what she wanted to say while she could and see what if anything it gained her.

"You're afraid of Draig, Mordred. It's as simple as that." Melissa lifted her eyes then, latching onto Mordred's. Her expression revealed her complete lack of respect for the man sitting in front of her whose calm had wavered and then broken after just a few of her well-placed barbs. "What are you going to do? Send your mommy after the Dragon so that she can fight your battle for you? Is that what she's done in the past? Always there to save your sorry ass?"

Mordred shot up out of his chair at Melissa's last insult, which struck a little too close to home. Hands pounding on the top of his desk, eyes burning with a maniacal fury, he reached for even more of the Grym, the sparks of energy dancing around his fingertips forming into a long spike that hovered just above the tabletop.

That spike aimed right at Melissa.

"I tire of you, Witch. You will regret that slight."

"Leave her be, Mordred. We're not done with her yet, so you'll need to require penance from the Witch later."

Mordred jumped slightly, startled to see his mother striding into his office and taking a seat on the edge of his desk. Recognizing the look on her face, one that promised a very painful and likely humiliating punishment if he didn't do exactly as she said, Mordred released his hold on the Grym and sat back down in his chair with what little dignity he could manage.

"Mother, I didn't expect you ..." Mordred stared in shock at the figure a pair of his Paladins were dragging across his extremely expensive medieval carpet. "What in all the hells is he doing here?"

Seamus slumped into the chair next to Melissa, giving Mordred a tired wink and seeming to enjoy the opportunity to get off his feet for a time.

"You don't know what's going on outside?"

"How would I know what's going on outside?" Mordred demanded. He tempered his tone when his mother's eyes flared dangerously. "I've been here with the Witch. Besides, this space is protected and soundproofed with the Grym."

Morgase shook her head in disappointment and disbelief. The more time she spent with her son, the more she wasn't certain if his mistakes were made in a good faith attempt to do what she required of him, or they simply resulted from a stupidity that he had learned to mask over the years.

A fair concern, she believed, considering the future she had laid out for him, although not one that could be addressed now.

"The Witch is the cause of all the commotion outside."

"What commotion?"

"A rescue attempt."

Mordred stared at his mother, still trying to understand. "A rescue attempt by the Kraken? What was he doing? Trying to kill us with boredom by performing water ballet in the cove?"

"Funny, little man," Seamus grumbled. Mordred had little respect for him, though he chose to ignore the scorn for now. Seamus believed his time would come soon enough, so he might as well do what he did so well. Aggravate and annoy. "When I try to kill you, pretty boy, you'll know. And it won't be when you're hiding behind your mother's skirts."

❧

DRAIG DIDN'T FOLLOW Morgase toward the central turret. He didn't need to.

He remembered the map the Daemons provided him. Besides, he wanted to think about his strategy before he challenged her.

Taking his time, he worked his way through the lower floor of the mansion. Clearing the space so that he wouldn't have any unwanted visitors coming at him from behind when he implemented the plan that came to mind.

Along the way, he ran across three Paladins. Each one stationed where Morgase left them along the path that led to the tower that rose above the center of the mansion. Each one shocked to find himself confronting the Dragon. Each one knocked senseless before they could raise the alarm and give away Draig's intrusion.

And now he stood just around the corner from his objective, which was ten yards down the corridor that intersected with the one that he hid in.

Draig knew exactly what Morgase meant by her comment about having Seamus and Melissa together. Once they had outlived their usefulness, she would take care of them. Permanently. Just as she took care of any Teg who crossed her.

It was time for him to seize the initiative.

He was losing patience. He was losing time as well. And he was tired of sneaking around an ostentatious, over-the-top mansion meant to assuage the ego of a Teg Draig would like nothing more than to kill.

He needed to speed events along, so he did.

Draig infused Excalibur with the Grym, the steel blade gleaming brightly with a white-hot energy.

Curling around the corner, he strode toward the two guards with an impenetrable confidence and implacable glare.

"Halt! This is a restricted area!" the Paladin standing to the right of the door shouted.

His partner didn't bother to yell. He was already in motion, pulling his mace from the holster on his back, stepping forward to meet this new threat.

Draig had to give the Paladin credit. The man was fast, and he was aggressive.

Neither attribute did him any good.

Draig charged faster than the Paladin's eyes could follow, Excalibur sweeping through the space in front of him. The blazing steel sliced through the Grym-infused mace as if it were no more than a roll of paper then cut just as cleanly through the man's neck.

The Paladin's body stumbled a few feet further down the hallway and past Draig, not yet understanding what had happened, the Paladin's head rolling to a stop several feet beyond where the body finally fell.

Draig didn't see it happen, having eyes only for the last, unfortunate Paladin.

The final guard to Mordred's inner domain was so scared that he was having trouble pulling his mace free from its holster. Struggling desperately to bring his weapon to bear.

Draig didn't feel an ounce of sympathy for him.

When the Paladin looked up, having finally released his mace, Draig's steel already was singing right through the space where his head was.

There was a momentary gasp from the Paladin and then a sickening understanding as his body crumpled to the ground, his head rolling down the hallway and coming to a stop not too far away from that of his partner.

Draig nudged the Paladin's body out of the way with his foot, then stared at the ancient door that blocked his way. He had no doubt that the wood was harvested from the time that his father ruled in Britain. The runes and sigils carved into it gave the door its strength while also serving to defend against those who might try to enter without the requisite invitation.

An impressive display by Mordred. Yet it offered little protection against someone like him.

He just needed to decide what kind of entrance he wanted to make.

Draig could use shadows to sneak into the turret as he did the mansion.

A simple approach that offered little fuss.

He decided against that as soon as the idea popped into his mind.

The time for subtlety and subterfuge had come to an end.

Now was the time for a little drama.

Mordred swung a heavy fist right toward Seamus' cheek.

Tired of getting hit in the same place, and unable to get out of his seat because of the Paladins holding him in place, Seamus tilted his head down just enough to absorb the punch on his brow.

It still hurt, though not as much as it did with Mordred working him over on the right side of his jaw ever since the laird of the mansion stepped around his desk and began to beat on him, Morgase allowing her son to release some of his rage upon her revealing that a few of the Teg had the temerity to infiltrate his estate.

Despite the pulsing pain, Seamus smiled and even snickered softly when he heard Mordred wince and then grunt.

Clearly, his captor disliked crunching his knuckles on Seamus's bony forehead.

"How did you get onto my property?" Mordred demanded, stepping back, shaking his hand and then holding it, rubbing his knuckles and fingers, wincing as he did so, refusing to look down, not wanting to confirm the telltale bruising of a broken bone. Refusing to show any weakness to his captives and, more importantly, to his mother.

"I told you, Mordred, I swam. Simple as that."

"He has a tendency to ask the same questions over and over," Melissa murmured. She had thought of going to Seamus' aid, or at least trying to, but his brief, barely perceptible shake of his head held her in place. Besides, there was little that she could do with the two Paladins still standing right behind her, ready to push her back into her seat if she attempted to leave it.

"So I've learned," Seamus grumbled. "Very, very tiresome. You'd think he could just get on with it."

"Shut up!" Mordred warned. "Both of you!"

Once Mordred began to work over McCracken, Morgase slipped off the desk and sat in the chair behind it. She doubted that her son would get any information of use out of the mariner. But she did know that her son needed to let off a little steam and demonstrate who was in charge.

There were other ways to do that without having to beat on a man. Mordred was who he was, however.

Sad, really, her son had never grasped one of the key lessons she had tried to teach him so many times before, one for which Theodore Roosevelt was known.

"Speak softly and carry a big stick."

A West African adage that the former President had made his own and employed again and again while governing and making decisions.

In fact, much to her chagrin, Mordred had reversed the

saying. He preferred to wield the big stick first, as he was doing now, before even thinking about speaking softly.

She could intervene and put a stop to this drubbing since they would gain little of value from Mordred's attempt to display his dominance.

But what was the point?

Neither the Witch nor the Kraken would be leaving this room alive.

That truth sending a flush of warmth through her body, Morgase resolved to sit back and allow her son to have his fun. Once he spent his rage, he would be more amenable to the topic that they really needed to discuss.

She had captured the Kraken. Even so, the Three Berserkers who had torn through more Paladins than she could count had vanished. And she had yet to determine what had slaughtered the Paladins in the barracks, although she would.

First, she had needed to rebuild the estate's defenses. How they had been disabled, she didn't know. But she would learn the answer to that as well.

And no real harm done, actually, other than the loss of almost a hundred Paladins. In the larger scheme of things, those deaths mattered little. There were more than a thousand Paladins after all with another company already on its way to the seaside mansion.

What really disappointed Morgase was that though his friends had attempted to rescue the Witch, Draig hadn't.

That's who she really wanted since he was the key to unlocking all of her schemes.

Morgase had searched the property several times with the Grym and couldn't find him.

Either he had never come here, or he had decided that after his initial success he would cut his losses.

Remembering the Dragon before he died, she assumed that he had taken the latter course. Draig had been clinical in his thinking back then, taking calculated gambits as needed, and never, ever allowing a hint of emotion to color his decisions.

A trait to be admired and to be expected of the man given the responsibility by his father to eliminate anyone who threatened his throne. Arthur liked to claim that the Dragon worked for all the Teg. But that was a fallacy. Nothing more than a little public relations to hide his real purpose.

She could respect that even as it annoyed her to no end since the Dragon was the one who threw a wrench in her plans time and again.

Still, though she had little doubt that the Dragon remained no different than before his supposed demise, there was something about this incursion that bothered her.

Who or what had snuck into the barracks?

With all the men there, one of them should have been able to escape and at least shout a warning. None of them had, however.

Was that the work of a hidden ally or was that Draig doing what he did best?

Morgase was pulled from her musings when the Kraken spoke again.

"You've made a mistake, Mordred," Seamus said quietly after working his tongue along both jaws, confirming that he hadn't lost any teeth. "A big mistake."

Mordred's eyes narrowed as he considered what he would do next to crack the Kraken. It really shouldn't be this difficult since the Teg was nothing more than an old man out of the water. His mother making sure of that by shielding him from the Grym.

"You talk too much, McCracken. It's going to be the death of you."

"That's not the first time I've been told that," he replied in a soft chuckle.

"Then maybe you should shut up like I told you."

Seamus' chuckle turned into a soft laugh, then a hacking cough. His stomach still hurt. That's where Mordred had started in on him. The bastard might have broken a few of his ribs. Probably did since it hurt to draw a full breath. He would have liked nothing more than to return the favor, but in his current state he couldn't.

"What is it to be, Mordred? You want me to talk? You want me to tell you whatever you want to hear? Yet when I do talk, you tell me to shut up. You can't have it both ways, boy. You need to decide."

"I've had enough of you, old man. The Teg world, *my* world, will be a better place without you."

"You sound just like your father, boy," Seamus spat.

Enraged by the comparison, Mordred stepped forward again, flexing his fingers, deciding to use his other hand this time as he prepared to continue with the beating.

"Please, just leave him alone," Melissa pleaded. She didn't know Seamus very well. She only knew that he was Draig's friend and that he had helped him when the Werewolves came for her at Raptor Bay Lighthouse. Yet that was enough for her.

"Then give me what I want, Witch," Mordred hissed, stopping just a few feet in front of Seamus, his eyes revealing his sadistic delight at what he was about to do.

"I can't. I told you that." Melissa was more angry now than scared, tired of the same questions and the same useless demands. Concluding that Mordred asked them only because it gave him a chance to indulge his crueler impulses. "I don't have the artifact. I can't be any clearer now than I have been. I took *The Book of Whispers* from you after I gave it to you. I won't deny it. But I lost it to Draig. I don't have it. I don't know where it is. Hurting me or Seamus doesn't help you in any way."

"When I'm done with the old man, you're next, Witch. If you can't help me, then I have no use for you."

Mordred stepped toward Seamus again, murder in his eyes.

"As I said, you're making a mistake, Mordred."

"Shut it, old man. You're no better than the Witch. Not a single piece of actionable information. Just lies and confusion."

"I'm just trying to warn you, you stupid whelp," Seamus growled. He had tired of the games as well. It was time to move the encounter along, and he had no doubt that insulting the man who viewed himself as the heir to the Teg throne would do the job. "Better just to let me go. Then you can go back to hiding behind your mother's apron."

"Why would I let you go, old man?" Mordred demanded, placing both hands on the arms of Seamus' chair and leaning in close. Their noses almost touching. "And after you've insulted me?" Mordred shook his head, angry, amused, bloodthirsty. "No, I'm not done with you yet. I've got a great deal more pain to inflict upon you before I'm done with you."

"If you want to live, boy, you'll let us go. This is the only time I'm making this offer. Don't be as stupid as you usually are. Let us go. Before it's too late for you."

Seamus watched as Mordred's expression turned to stone at his latest insult. There was no reasoning with him. Mordred had decided on his course, surrendering to the need to defend his warped sense of honor.

But that was all right, because Seamus believed that with his taunts he had earned all the additional time that he required.

"Stop talking, old man. Your end approaches. Try to demonstrate just a little bit of courage while facing it."

Seamus shook his head sadly from side to side, even though doing so made the room begin to spin. Broken ribs and likely a concussion, Seamus decided. Not surprising after so many blows to the gut and the head.

"You had your chance, Mordred. He's here."

Mordred laughed at that, believing that his captive was becoming delusional. "Who's here. The Big Bad Wolf?"

Mordred leaned in closer. Foreheads touching. "Is the Big Bad Wolf going to huff and puff and blow my house down?"

"No, not the Big Bad Wolf, dumbass," Seamus snorted. "The Big Bad Dragon."

At exactly that moment, the ancient door to the turret exploded inward, thousands of splinters flying through the air, many of them embedding themselves in the backsides of the Paladins who bore the brunt of the blast, a ball of fire rushing into the chamber as the entire structure rumbled and shook.

23

QUITE AN ENTRANCE

Draig strode through the shattered doorway, Excalibur gleaming brightly in one hand. With the other he motioned from left to right.

A gust of air blasted into the chamber, clearing the swirling cloud of smoke and grit to reveal the results of his entrance into Mordred's private sanctuary.

Four Paladins lay crumpled against the far wall, their backs shredded by long splinters of wood and shards of stone. None of them would be getting up any time soon. Unbeknownst to them, they had served a useful purpose, shielding Seamus and Melissa from the worst of the blast.

Seamus, sensing what was about to happen, knocked Melissa from her chair and took her to the ground just in time. He had already helped her back to her feet and was pulling her gently toward the doorway, taking both of them out of the line of fire.

"Just couldn't help yourself, could you?" he accused, though the sparkle in his eye suggested that Seamus was far from annoyed by Draig's dramatic display.

Draig nodded to Seamus, receiving a pleased grin in return.

Despite his rough appearance, his face battered and bruised, Seamus appeared to be in a very good mood. As if all that he had suffered to reach this point had been well worth it.

Draig could understand why. Seamus had little love for Mordred and Morgase, who were just then emerging from behind Mordred's overturned desk.

Mordred, usually impeccably dressed and accoutered, was anything but. His black Armani suit, smoking and covered in soot, was torn in a dozen or more places. His face covered in ash, his usually perfectly styled hair was sticking up in all directions, a good bit of his wild coif singed.

Morgase appeared to be little worse for the wear, not a hint of dirt on her expensive pantsuit, the kaleidoscope of jewels around her neck and on her fingers gleaming brightly. She stood calmly in front of Draig, lips pursed, giving him the look he had seen from her so many times before, as if she were staring at a rabid dog that needed to be put down.

She had shielded herself with the Grym, the power of the explosion washing over her barrier. The four Paladins at her back who sprinted toward Draig out of the last wisps of grey that still swirled in the chamber had benefited from her protection.

Maces glowing with faint traces of the Twisted Grym, the sickly black threads of energy infecting the bright white of the Power of the Ancients, the Paladins sought to take down Draig before he could do any more damage.

They misjudged him badly.

There were few Teg stronger in the Grym than he was, even Morgase reluctant to challenge him directly. Especially now.

The Sorceress closed her eyes briefly and shook her head in resignation, not needing to watch, already knowing how the encounter was going to play out.

Because at that moment Draig called upon not only the Power of the Ancients, but also the Power of the Draca.

The magic innate and unique to his mother's people. A potent force that set Draig apart and made him who he truly was no matter how much he might try to fight it.

The gift made him a part of two ancient bloodlines, yet at the same time ensured that he remained an outsider to both as well. Of the Teg and of the Draca, yet only in part. A half-blood. An oddity. When seeking to wound, some had even said a mongrel.

When he was younger, such comments struck deep, filling him with anger and shame. They still did in a way.

Yet he had learned that being different was only a definition imprinted upon him by others.

Draig was who he was. He couldn't escape it, nor would he try. He would use the gifts granted to him, because not to do so would deny the potential of who he could be.

The tremendous power that radiated from him – reddish-orange eyes blazing brightly and hinting at what it was like to look at the very gates of Hel's underworld, hair standing on end, charges of energy sparking along his body, fiery nimbus surrounding him -- was almost too much for the circular chamber to contain. The skylights ringing the ceiling above shattered outward, releasing the building pressure of which he was the source.

His face set in a grim, implacable mask, Draig seized the initiative before the four Paladins could even think about halting their progress.

With a casual swipe of his free hand, a wave of energy slammed into them, sending the soldiers flying back against the wall. Knocking them senseless if they were lucky. Killing them if they were not.

"You son of a ..."

Draig didn't waste his time listening to the expletive Mordred flung at him. He was used to his half-brother's threats and insults.

He focused instead on Morgase.

No matter how hard he tried to appear otherwise, Mordred was no more than a blunt instrument. He lacked creativity in his thinking.

His aunt was a different animal altogether. She always preferred to strike from the shadows.

Unless she was cornered, as she was now.

Streams of fire shot from both her hands, sizzling through the air, swirling around Draig, wrapping around him, encasing him in flames, devouring him.

The strength of the blaze was so strong and so violent that it forced Mordred, Seamus, and Melissa to turn away.

Unable to look at the fire.

Unable to stand the heat.

Unable to see Draig.

Unable to believe that he could survive such a swift, vicious attack.

Nevertheless, Morgase set more and more of the Grym to the task of burning Draig to a crisp. With every pulse of energy that joined the blaze, the flames exploded, burning savagely, erupting into an uncontrollable inferno that reached for where the skylights had been far above.

Morgase's eyes widened in cautious expectation. She couldn't see Draig in the fire. She couldn't see anything other than the hungry flames of the conflagration.

Draig had been visible at the beginning, a vague shape, but no more.

Had she caught him by surprise?

Had she turned the Dragon into a pile of ash?

That thought sent a thrill of pleasure through her.

She certainly hoped so, and she was more than willing to pay the price of not acquiring *The Book of Whispers* if it came at the demise of the Dragon.

Growing more and more confident of her success, she

poured several more waves of the Grym into the task. Needing to ensure that Draig was well and truly dead. Then, nodding to herself, certain that even the Dragon couldn't survive her attack, she released her hold on the Grym.

The fire continued to burn, sizzling and crackling, razing ...

Morgase frowned.

Why did the fire still rage if there was nothing left to burn?

By all rights, Draig should be dead. The fire should have burned itself out the instant she stopped feeding it, the blaze having nothing more to consume.

Yet it hadn't.

The fire sizzled and roared as if it had taken on a life of its own. As if it ...

A horrible realization hit her like a punch in the gut.

Her fear was confirmed just a moment later when the flames began to move as if they were being guided. Their controlled chaos shifting into a slow swirl that moved in a clockwise direction.

With each rotation, the fire spun faster and faster, the motion so intense that a heated gust blasted out from the whirlwind, forcing Morgase, Mordred, Seamus, and Melissa to turn away and shield their eyes.

Having no choice but to crouch as the potency of the fiery whirlwind intensified, Morgase caught a glimpse of what stood before her. Shocked. Appalled. Worse, an emotion that she believed that she had suppressed long ago rose up from where she had buried it.

A crippling emotion.

Fear.

She had seen in the center of the spinning flames an image that she had not thought possible.

As the fire swirled with even greater velocity, the gusts knocking the furniture back against the walls, Morgase and those with her barely able to keep their feet, the flames began to diminish in size and then disappear entirely as if they were being sucked into a whirlwind.

With a bright flash and resounding crack, the fiery tornado vanished, the last of the flames surging into the man who stood before them.

The man Morgase had failed to kill, and not for the first time.

The Dragon.

Yet even though the frustration of having failed threatened to crush her, she couldn't help but wonder with her analytical mind how her nephew had survived her attack. And, more important, how he had taken the Grym that she used and made it his own.

She had never heard of any of the Teg having such a capability. Yet her deliberation on that matter would have to wait.

Because Draig's flashing eyes were filled with the promise of retribution ... and something worse.

"Of all the Teg, Morgase, you should know that you can't kill a Dragon with fire."

Glancing over his shoulder and seeing that Seamus had gotten Melissa out of harm's way, he returned his focus to his aunt and his half-brother, the smile he gave them colder than the grave.

"And then there were two."

"Did you know that Draig could do that?" whispered Melissa, astounded by what he had just accomplished and more than just a little awed.

She stood right next to Seamus, ready to help him if he started to falter. Even though he smiled broadly and clearly relished how Draig had eclipsed Morgase, she could tell that the crusty old man was in pain.

"No, but that doesn't mean all that much," he grumbled through clenched teeth, his aching jaw making it difficult for him to speak. "He keeps a lot to himself. And if you haven't noticed, he's even better at keeping secrets than you are."

"Fair enough," Melissa murmured, recognizing his gentle dig and choosing to ignore it.

With the conflict in the center of the turret drawing everyone's attention, Melissa glanced behind her. There was nothing to stop them from escaping the tower, the stone cracked and charred along the frame, the door shattered and broken, most of it in pieces embedded in the backs of the Paladins lying at the other end of the chamber.

She suppressed the urge to make a break for it, however. Draig had come here for her when he didn't have to. He could have left her to her fate, and she wouldn't have blamed him in the least if he did.

Yet he hadn't. He had put himself at risk. For her. Again.

She understood the concept of altruism. Of choosing to put the interests of another person before your own. Even at the threat of losing your own life.

But she had never seen that concept put into practice. She was more familiar with the Teg who would look the other way when assistance was required or run as swiftly as they could in the opposite direction, not wanting to get involved.

Much to her surprise, Melissa was experiencing an uncommon emotion as the man who had come to her aid fought for his life against the strongest Sorceress of the Teg.

The desire to help Draig.

Seamus sensed it. He reached out and gripped her arm gently, holding her in place. "We'd only get in the way. So long as Morgase is keeping us from touching the Grym, we'd be more hindrance than help to him."

"Then what are we supposed to do?"

"Stay ready," Seamus warned. "I don't know what Draig has

planned, but he always has a trick or two up his sleeve. We need to be prepared for whatever it is."

"The Dragon risen again," Mordred mused, studying Draig as if he were an oddity at a circus. Seemingly oblivious to the tremendous power that his nemesis employed. A power that Mordred could not call upon himself. "I've been waiting for you, brother. Finally, you have the courage to poke your head out of the sand."

"Say what you want, Mordred. You should know by now that your words have little meaning to me. No more than an annoying buzz in the ear."

"You underestimate me at your own risk," Mordred hissed, viewing Draig's response as an insult.

"I've never underestimated you, Mordred. That's why you've never defeated me. That's also why you never will."

"You arrogant jackass." Mordred's face turned bright red, his rage rushing to the surface once again. The long sword that he kept next to his desk appeared in his hand, already infused with the Grym. "I'll make you eat your words. Have no ..."

"Don't do it." Draig's voice had gone deadly quiet, his focus shifting to Morgase, who stood a few yards away from her son. Even with his weapon at the ready, Mordred was no more than an afterthought for Draig.

He had sensed what his aunt was contemplating, the air around them becoming brittle, much as it did before an electrical storm struck. Morgase pulling in as much of the Grym as she could safely hold, which, based on her previous though failed demonstration, was quite a lot.

Fingers of her right hand moving as if they were playing a piano, Morgase's eyes narrowed. Draig shouldn't be able to know what she was doing. No Teg, not even Merlin, could sense when she was calling upon the Grym. She had mastered how to mask her use of the Power of the Ancients long before.

"What are you talking about?" she asked, suffusing her voice with a touch of surprise as she sought to diffuse the building tension long enough for her to decide on what her next play should be since she had lost the element of surprise.

Morgase glanced at Mordred, realizing from his confused expression that he had no idea what was really going on and would be of little use. He wasn't prepared to attack Draig with the Grym. She had hoped that he would be, believing that if he caught on they would be able to eliminate Draig with little risk to themselves by working together. But apparently not. Her son too consumed by his anger and shame.

"Do you really want to try again, Morgase?" Draig challenged. "Do you really think the second time will be different from the first?"

"You're getting ahead of yourself, Draig," Morgase chuckled, trying to make him think that he was mistaken, her reaction forced rather than real.

"Think carefully," Draig warned, "because if you have another go at me, I will not hold back as I did during our first engagement."

"Leave him be, mother," Mordred interrupted, finally realizing what Morgase had in mind. "He's mine. When Draig leaves us for whatever Hell he belongs in, it's going to be because of me."

"You seem quite confident in yourself, Mordred." Draig didn't bother to look at his half-brother until he sensed that Morgase had reduced the amount of the Grym that she was holding. That didn't mean that she wouldn't attack him. It just meant that she was beginning to doubt her tactics, which gave Draig a little time to deal with her son.

"No more confident than usual," Mordred replied casually,

as if Draig's recent display held little meaning. "I've been looking forward to this for quite some time."

"Looking forward to what exactly?" Draig didn't quite believe that Mordred desired to relive the embarrassment he had inflicted upon him the last time they had stood across from one another, although he wouldn't put it past his brother, who had a very selective memory.

"Finishing the combat we started before you decided to slink away to that town of yours, hiding from your father and everyone else."

Draig ignored the jab, knowing that offering any response was a waste of time. "We did finish that combat, Mordred. It seems that you've forgotten that I had my blade at your throat."

"That may be, but I never surrendered to you, Draig. If our father had not interfered when he did, the combat would have ended differently."

"Would it have?" Draig wondered with a hint of amusement, working hard to contain the snort of disbelief that threatened to break free.

"Indeed it would have. I was about to get out from under your steel, but our father never gave me the chance."

"If our father hadn't intervened, we wouldn't be having this conversation now. I would have sent you to the pit of Tartarus."

"You don't know that!" Mordred shouted, his roiling emotions threatening to get the better of him. The vein on his forehead pulsed even more violently, his already red face turning a shade of purple at Draig's insult.

"I do know that, Mordred, although clearly you've been unable or unwilling to admit that to yourself." More certain that Morgase would not be attacking him with the Grym, he squared up to Mordred, only a few feet separating them now. "Why shouldn't I kill you now with the Grym? We both know you can't stand against the power I can bring to bear." Draig shrugged. "You're no more than the undercard after all. Your mother is the real prize fighter."

"You ignore and insult me at your own risk," Mordred hissed, his face scrunching up, marring his handsome features.

"Ignore you?" Draig scoffed. "I barely think about you."

Mordred could scarcely contain himself. Draig wasn't truly of the Teg. He had no right to the throne. He had no legitimate claim on Mordred's birthright.

Yet Mordred needed to be careful. He needed to stay focused. He needed to control his rage.

Mongrel Draig may be. But he was still a dangerous opponent.

"Where's the sport in a combat with the Grym?" Mordred couldn't deny no matter how much he wanted to that Draig spoke the truth with respect to the Power of the Ancients. Still, he would not put that truth into words. "Besides, our rivalry is centuries old, brother. Better blades than the Grym for us to reach a resolution after all that time."

"It's not a rivalry," Draig corrected, "although you might see it that way. This competition between us is a burden of your own creation. It comes from your hatred and nothing more than that."

Mordred growled, a spark of psychotic anger flashing in the back of his eyes when he realized that Draig didn't view him as a competitor. That Draig looked down upon him. An admission that Mordred took as the greatest of slights. He had no patience for insults, whether real or imagined, and particularly not those that impugned his honor or challenged his courage or skill.

"I know you want to kill me, Draig," Mordred hissed, trying to give some substance to the claim that Draig challenged. Attempting to imbue their confrontation with more meaning than Draig was willing to give it. "Just as I want to kill you. Blades it must be."

Before Draig could accept the challenge, Mordred rushed forward, longsword leading the way with a wickedly fast slice from shoulder to hip.

Draig pivoted, allowing the steel to slide right by his side. Mordred coming in closer than he wanted because of his miss, Draig took full advantage, slamming his shoulder into Mordred's gut and knocking him onto his back.

"Are you sure you want to do this, Mordred? Our father isn't here to save you this time."

"Fight me, you freak!" Mordred demanded, angry that Draig didn't even bother to taunt him, his half-brother's voice devoid of any real emotion. He surged up from the thick carpet and charged Draig once again, allowing his rage to drive him.

Draig would have dodged out of the way if Seamus and Melissa weren't right behind him. Knowing that neither could use the Grym and that they would both be vulnerable if Mordred took a swing at them, he lifted Excalibur in a blur, the sound of steel meeting steel echoing around the turret.

Before Mordred could pull his blade back and slash again, Draig slammed his forehead against Mordred's nose. Breaking it with a nasty crunch, a gush of blood ran down his half-brother's grime-covered tailored dress shirt.

Groaning in pain, slightly unsteady on his feet, his eyes watering as black spots formed at the very edge of his vision, still Mordred sought to continue the combat. Stumbling back a few feet, Mordred slashed wildly at Draig from right to left, trusting more in fate than skill.

Draig deflected the steel with a quick swipe of his wrist. Then he spun around, avoiding Mordred's counterstroke. The sword hissing through the air right by his ear before he kicked forward, his right boot caught Mordred in the chest and sent him backward, Mordred's arms windmilling in the air as he tried to brace himself for the ground that was rising up to meet him.

"You sure you want to keep doing this, Mordred? Perhaps it would be best if you went back to hiding behind your mother. That way, life would be much easier for you. Safer as well."

Gasping for breath after landing heavily on his back for the second time in just a few seconds, he pushed himself up. Draig's insult ringing in his ears, he gave little thought to strategy. Mordred wanted only to crush Draig. Destroy him.

Grasping the hilt of his sword with both hands and bringing it down from behind his head with a fury-fueled rage, instead of splitting Draig's skull he found himself face to face with his half-brother, blade locked against blade, Draig positioned no more than a foot away from him.

As Mordred strained, pouring every ounce of strength into forcing his blade down, desperate to feel his steel slice into Draig's flesh, his half-brother stood there calmly, scarcely having to exert himself to prevent Mordred from doing as he wished.

Mordred growled, raged, and grunted, yet he couldn't move Excalibur a hair.

Draig's question caught him by surprise, although it didn't hinder his effort to break the stalemate.

"You call them Paladins? Really?"

"What's wrong with that?" Mordred grunted, not understanding the purpose of the query or why Draig would ask it in the midst of a life-or-death struggle.

"There's nothing wrong with it." Draig smiled then. A smile intended to work its way deep beneath Mordred's skin and fester there. "It's just that the name suggests that you spend too much of your free time playing Dungeons and Dragons."

"You son of a ..." Draig's comment bit deeper than Mordred should have allowed. His rage breaking free, Mordred stepped back as he scraped his steel along Excalibur's length. He prepared to lunge again, imagining himself striking faster than a coiled snake and finishing Draig once and for all.

Mordred never got the chance, shocked to find himself down on one knee, Draig's boot pressing his sword into the carpet.

So consumed with his desire to kill Draig, so focused on his next move, Mordred lost his grip on the larger combat. Right leg swept out from beneath him, he was more than just vulnerable now.

Excalibur pressed against his throat, Mordred was at Draig's mercy. Again.

Mordred searched frantically for some means of escape, but nothing came to mind. His own blade pressed against the floor, he could try to take Draig down to the ground with him by tackling him around the legs, perhaps gaining the upper hand while wrestling.

That was quite risky, however, especially with Draig staring down at him with his merciless eyes, clearly having no compunction at all about slicing his throat, which would require nothing more than a flick of his wrist.

He looked up, catching his mother's eyes with his own. Pleading with her for assistance.

She shook her head ever so slightly, confirming that there was nothing that she could do for him. Draig would know if she reached for the Grym and kill him before she could attack.

He was on his own.

"This seems to be a common ending to our combats," Draig murmured, the glowing steel of Excalibur a hair away from slicing across Mordred's throat.

Draig found it quite ironic though not surprising that he and Mordred were back where they had been the last time they crossed blades. Draig could kill him. Just a small slice across Mordred's carotid artery would do the trick.

Nevertheless, he restrained his desire to do just that even though no one would have taken issue with him if he had succumbed to the temptation.

Draig kept himself in check because killing Mordred then didn't feel right. He couldn't explain the decision he made, even to himself. He just sensed that Mordred had a larger role to play at some point in the future and that killing him now would affect that future in a negative way.

"Do you yield?" Draig asked.

Mordred didn't reply right away, sweat pouring down his brow as he continued to struggle for a solution to what seemed like an unsolvable problem.

Draig repeated himself. "Do you yield?"

"Mordred ..." Morgase pleaded, concern plain in her voice. She might look down upon her son more frequently than she would have preferred. Still, he was her son.

Lifting his gaze, catching Draig's reddish-orange eyes blazing with the intensity of the sun, he realized that this was his one and only chance for clemency. "Yes."

"Yes what?"

Mordred attempted to push away the shame that coursed through him. He failed miserably as that shame burrowed into his gut, bringing back all the memories of his previous failures against Draig.

"I yield." His words tasted bitter in his mouth.

Draig stepped back then, removing his sword from Mordred's throat. Although he remained ready, on his toes, prepared to move. Because though Mordred said what he needed to say to gain his freedom, Draig didn't believe that Mordred would do what he had agreed to do and stand down.

Mordred proved Draig correct just a heartbeat later. Rising up with a roar of fury, Mordred swung his blade lightning-fast from above his head down to his feet, dreaming of splitting Draig in two.

Unfortunately for him, it proved to be no more than a dream.

Leaving Excalibur against his side, Draig lifted his arm, catching the blade in his left hand.

Mordred's eyes widened in disbelief. His steel should have separated Draig's fingers from his hand and then continued right down into his skull, killing him instantly.

But Draig was alive and well, and he held Mordred's sword locked in place just as he had done moments before with Excalibur.

Mordred didn't understand what was happening. That was until he tore his eyes free from Draig's hand, which remained clasped around his blade, and saw the energy sparking across his brother's body, eyes flaring, fiery nimbus surrounding him, Draig's expression colder than ice.

Mordred's entire body went cold when the realization struck him.

At that same moment, a flash of energy erupted from Draig's palm. Not just melting Mordred's blade, although that was the first step, but rather dissolving the steel into its elemental components, making it seem as if the blade never really existed at all.

Before Mordred could even comprehend his failure and what Draig had just done, a feat that should have been impossible, he was thrown backward. Flying across the room, he grunted in pain. His breath punched out of him when he hit the wall, the back of his head smacked the stone, almost knocking him out.

Though dazed, he still had the awareness to try to wriggle free, but he couldn't move an inch. Held in place against the turret wall ten feet above the floor. Shackled by the Grym.

"You think you can play with me like a toy!" Mordred raged, his mouth the only part of his body that he could move. "I'll gut you like the pig you ..."

Mordred's eyes bulged out of their sockets. He could speak.

He could feel his lips moving. He could shout at the top of his lungs just as he was doing. But no sound emerged.

A quick movement of Draig's fingers had stolen his voice from him.

"Your father will mourn your death, Draig," Morgase warned, still trying to wrap her mind around the power that Draig was displaying. A power that she had never come up against before. A power that she craved for her own. "Not for long, however, because soon after I kill you, I will kill him."

"You've been trying to kill my father for centuries, Auntie M," Draig replied with a shake of his head, knowing exactly how his sarcastic words were going to affect her. "How's that been going for you?"

The first crack in Morgase's armor finally appeared. Her lips curling into a rictus of rage, with a scream reminiscent of a Banshee she sent spikes of energy shooting toward Draig.

A shield crafted of the Grym and no larger than a buckler appeared on Draig's forearm. With a consummate skill, he deflected each bolt, the errant bursts of energy smashing into the turret walls and the ceiling. Scorching the stone. Setting tapestries and bookcases on fire. Destroying medieval suits of armor. Melting swords and daggers. Setting the tower shaking as several large sections of the circular wall crumbled and bulged.

Hissing in frustration, Morgase changed her strategy on the fly. Still relying on spikes constructed of the Grym, she targeted her former prisoners instead.

Neither Seamus nor Melissa stood a chance. The bolts of energy flashing toward them with a blinding speed, they couldn't get out of the way, having nowhere to go, and they couldn't defend themselves with the Grym.

Much to their relief, they didn't have to. A barrier of energy shot up from the floor with a blinding flash, the spikes smashing futilely against the shield.

The reverberations set the tower shaking even more violently. Several stones near the ceiling tumbled down, a few barely missing Mordred by no more than a knuckle, who remained pinned against the wall.

Understanding the reality of her circumstances, unlike her son who preferred to delude himself whenever he so foolishly challenged Draig, Morgase halted her attack. Staring daggers at her nephew rather than throwing them.

"You are the Dragon, are you not? Don't you have the courage to fight me?" Morgase had little doubt that Draig could defend against anything she might throw at him. She hoped that with a little prodding she could push him into a mistake.

"Why bother fighting you when I don't have to?" Draig replied, offering her a shrug that set her temper blazing once again.

Angry at herself for allowing him to antagonize her so easily. Even more so because she ignored the urge for self-control and instead chose to yield to the desire that rose up within her.

She reached out for even more of the Grym ...

Her eyes widened, a paralyzing chill racing through her.

The cold reality of what happened threatened to break her.

The Power of the Ancients was gone.

What was happening?

Where was it?

She couldn't sense the Grym.

She couldn't touch the Grym.

She couldn't use it because she couldn't even feel it, and she had always felt it. Ever since she was born.

Always there.

Always available to her.

Always filling her with a gentle, comfortable warmth.

Until now.

"As I said, why bother fighting you if I don't have to."

Morgase's furious expression shifted immediately to horror, realizing what he must have done. "You ..."

She couldn't say it, not after glimpsing the hint of pleasure in the back of his burning orbs. "How could you ..."

She still couldn't get a grip on Draig's display of power. He wasn't just blocking her from reaching for the Grym. He had taken the Grym from her. But to do that, he had to have made use of ...

"*The Book of Whispers*, yes," Draig confirmed with a nod. "You should have listened to Melissa. I took it from her, that was true. I also never returned it to the Dragon Vault."

"That may be, but it still doesn't make sense," Morgase almost whined, knocked off balance by this discovery. "To do what you've done, you would need to master the ..."

She realized then that she had been a fool. No one had ever found the primer that provided access to *The Book of Whispers*. And there was a reason for that.

Draig.

Draig had the primer.

Draig had the capacity to use *The Book of Whispers*.

The only way to take that singular ability from him, to claim the primer and the most sought-after artifact of the Teg, was to kill him.

But she couldn't do that. Because he had stolen from her the ability to use the Grym.

He had neutered her without her even realizing it.

With that kind of power and skill, she stood no chance against him. She had no hope of defeating him much less killing him.

Draig smiled thinly, pulling out from a pocket along his thigh what looked to be a book that was an inch larger than a paperback both in length and width, a beautifully scrolled leather cover protecting its contents. "I see that you understand now. I have the primer, of course. I will return the primer and the book to the Dragon Vault not long after we are done here."

Morgase truly had been a fool. She had never believed it possible that Draig possessed both artifacts. And she had never believed that he would actually bring *The Book of Whispers* here where, if she had played the whole situation with more skill, and not allowed her fool of a son to distract her, she might be the one holding the artifact now rather than him.

Draig's smile broadened upon seeing all that pass across his aunt's face, her failure a harsh blow. He saw another emotion there as well. One that didn't surprise him in the least.

Greed.

Just like most any other Teg who came so close to *The Book of Whispers*, Morgase desperately wanted the artifact for herself. She would do whatever was necessary to obtain it from him. Because if she could take it, she could do more than rule.

She could dominate the Teg.

Forever.

"It's been fun, Morgase, but it's time for us to go." Draig motioned with his hand, the Dragon Door appearing at his back and right next to Seamus and Melissa.

Before he turned away, Morgase sought to keep him there just a little while longer, desperate for a few seconds more, hoping to find some way to bring him to her side before she lost this chance.

"Think of what we could accomplish, Draig," Morgase purred. "We have not seen eye to eye, I will be the first to admit that. But you have not seen eye to eye with your father as well. And he felt the need to give his Knights a kill order."

She took a step closer to him, her mood shifting in a flash, becoming conciliatory. Trying to demonstrate an understanding and compassion that usually was foreign to her. "With me by your side, I could help you become whatever you chose to be. I could help you master *The Book of Whispers*, and by doing that you could live whatever life you wanted. You would answer to no one but yourself. Think of it. Think of the power that you could wield."

Mordred tried to protest his mother's offer, understanding exactly what she was doing.

She was cutting him out entirely.

Putting her own desires above his own.

Choosing Draig over him.

But Mordred couldn't as he thrashed uselessly against the wall, still unable to speak.

"You mean the power that I already wield," Draig replied, a question in his smirk.

That stopped Morgase cold, realizing that he was correct. She was wasting her time and making herself look like a fool.

"I am tired of you and my father competing for power and tearing the Teg apart. As I said, I will be returning the book to the Dragon Vault so that neither you nor he need worry about it again."

Turning on his heel, Draig strode toward the Dragon Door, which upon opening revealed a wind-swept beach made more of rocks than sand.

"This isn't over, Draig," Morgase called.

"Isn't it though?" Draig replied over his shoulder as he stepped through the door.

Melissa followed him, glad to have finally made her escape.

Before he followed Melissa, Seamus couldn't resist a final barb. "Wonderful to see you again, Morgase. It's always a plea-sure." He chuckled when he gave Mordred, trussed up on the wall with the Grym, a final look of grim satisfaction. "You too, kiddo. Can't wait to see you again. You can come out on the water with me, and we can have some real fun."

The instant Seamus walked through the door, the portal vanished.

At the same time Mordred dropped from the wall, the Grym holding him in place removed.

Morgase ignored his yelp and the many complaints that erupted from him. She didn't have time for his whining and useless threats.

Reaching for the Grym, she sighed with relief. She had felt empty when Draig stole her power from her. Incomplete.

She would never allow him to do that to her again.

She would be ready the next time they met.

Soon, in fact.

The Dragon was much too overconfident. But that was all right. Because she was going to make him pay for that.

She was going to use him just like she used every other Teg.

24

BATTLE ROYALE

There was so much to see, one priceless item after another, extending for row upon row until they were lost in the darkness of the cavern. How many there could be in the Dragon Vault, artifacts that made up the lore and the history of the Teg, the Draca, the Daemons ... he couldn't say.

Yet of all the items that tempted him, the Daemon King couldn't take his eyes away from one display in particular.

Muramasa katanas.

Swords cursed with Daemonic powers.

Once there had been twelve.

Now ... he didn't know how many remained, although he did recall watching them being crafted, several of his Daemons aiding Muramasa. He remembered as well when he lost the cursed blades to the man standing next to him.

"How many treasures do you have here?" The Daemon King nodded appreciatively as he studied the gleaming blades streaked with black, runes carved into the steel to protect the bearer against the Grym.

Draig shrugged. "I don't know. You'd need to ask Fafnir. He

knows all that's contained within the Dragon Vault and exactly where each artifact is located."

"A librarian, then, this Fafnir?"

Draig chuckled at that. "I wouldn't call him that no matter how much fun that might be. He can be a bit testy. He's known as the Keeper of the Vault."

The Daemon King grunted. He would take Draig's advice, having had too many run-ins with short-tempered Draca to push his luck by insulting the one responsible for maintaining the Dragon Vault and the artifacts held within it. He had no desire to leave this remarkable strongroom until the show was over and it hadn't even begun yet.

"Do you know the story of these?" the Daemon King asked. "Did your father tell you about them before he sent you to kill me and steal two of them?" He spoke in a mild tone, although his pure-black eyes flashed at the memory.

The Daemon King motioned toward the swords lying on the stone pedestal. A thin barrier of the Grym mixed with the Power of the Draca encased the artifacts, ensuring that they could not be removed except by one of the Draca, and even then not without the permission of the Keeper. Any thief seeking to steal the blades or any other item from the Dragon Vault would experience a slow and painful death.

"You mean acquired for safekeeping so as to ensure you wouldn't be tempted to make use of them during your confine-ment," Draig corrected.

"You're just parsing words," the Daemon King grumbled.

"Perhaps." Draig shrugged. "Then again, to the victor go the spoils, and I could have killed you just like my father demanded, but I didn't."

"Fair enough." The Daemon King nodded reluctantly. Draig had him there. "Do you know the rest?"

"How those blades, each infused with the spirits of one hundred of your Daemons, hunger for blood and are said to compel the bearer to commit murder or suicide?" Draig replied. He wanted to move the conversation along with greater speed, knowing that the real engagement of that morning was fast approaching.

"Exactly that," the Daemon King confirmed.

"Then yes."

The Daemon King gave Draig an appraising look, a smile cracking his usually stern visage. "And I thought you were just a warrior. That you knew nothing more than how to sharpen your blade and fight. Yet I find you're an educated Teg as well."

"That's just one of many surprises that Draig has revealed to me," Melissa offered. She stood next to the Daemon King, not studying the katanas with as much interest as he was. Rather, her eyes flitted about, taking in as many of the treasures and artifacts as she could. The last time she was here, she didn't have the chance, her concerns on more pressing matters, such as the need to die a convincing death. "In fact, he seems to take a deep pleasure from keeping as much of himself hidden as possible, only revealing small pieces of who he truly is as circumstances require."

"Much the same could be said of you," Draig replied in turn. Not in an irritated tone. Instead just stating a fact.

"Children," the Daemon King admonished before Melissa could argue against Draig's perspective. "Please, there is no need. We are who we are. Better to accept it rather than fight it." He tilted his head toward Draig. "I would really like to get my hands on one of those blades. Just so I can feel the steel once again."

"I'm sure you would," Draig nodded amiably, "but I'm sorry. I can't allow it."

He knew what the Daemon King could do if he touched that blade. Even for just a second. Even with just a finger.

Although the Daemon King was his ally – at that moment -- there was nothing to suggest that would continue to be the case, especially if he was allowed to wrap his fingers around the hilt of one of the weapons also known as a Death Whisperer.

"You will not touch any of those blades," Fafnir confirmed. The Keeper of the Dragon Vault stepped forward out of the gloom, his reddish-orange eyes that were so similar to Draig's glowing brightly. "You won't be touching anything."

He stopped right next to the case with the Daemon-made katanas almost as if he felt the need to not only stress his point, but also ensure that none of his visitors made a play for them. "No one will be touching any of the artifacts under my guard." When he said the last, he had eyes only for Melissa.

The Daemon King studied Fafnir for a time, seeing several similarities with respect to Draig. Several very obvious distinctions as well. The power radiating from the both of them strong and intense, yet where Fafnir blazed like a fire, Draig blazed like an inferno. Of course that certainly made sense knowing who and what Draig was.

Not wanting to cause a ruckus that might hinder his real purpose for being there, he nodded. "Have no fear, Keeper. I understand what is required of me as well as what's expected."

Fafnir nodded, pleased to hear the words, though his severe expression hinted that he was more interested in the Daemon King's actions.

Turning back to Draig, the Daemon King offered him a raised eyebrow. "Any chance that if I behave you might be able to reduce my sentence?"

Draig had anticipated the question, actually expecting it sooner rather than after they had entered the Dragon Vault. "No promises, but I'll consider it."

"Fair enough," the Daemon King said. "Do you believe that the guests of honor will come? I'd hate to waste my time."

"You have nothing but time," Draig countered.

"Harshly said, yet true. Still, you know how it is."

Draig smiled thinly. He understood what the Daemon King was saying.

He needed to keep moving. Keep doing. Standing still bothered him. Just like it did Draig. A failing, some would argue, the sign of someone unable or unwilling to relax. Draig disagreed. He believed that it was a strength.

"They will," he confirmed. "They won't be able to help themselves." Just a heartbeat later his smile became wolfish as he looked toward the entrance. "Speak of one of the devils, here comes my father now."

Arthur Pendragon pushed through the shimmering stone at the far end of the cavern, ignoring the help provided by his guide and striding toward Draig as if he owned the Dragon Vault.

Eris watched him go, snorting not in disbelief at his rude behavior but rather amusement, having expected no less from Draig's father. She had accepted enough contracts from the King Teg to know that there were few he deemed worthy of his attention.

He cared less about who you were and more about what you could do for him. And when you were done doing something for him, he was done with you. Until the next time he needed you.

Nodding to Draig, she stepped back through the shimmering stone, having one more task to complete.

"No Merlin?" the Daemon King whispered. "I've never known your father not to have the Sorcerer by his side."

"Merlin being here would simply complicate matters. He agreed to stay away so that we could conduct our business without any distractions."

"He does have a habit of doing that," the Daemon King agreed. "I'm curious, though. How did you convince him?"

Draig gave the Daemon King a mysterious expression tinted with menace. "I made sure that he understood the consequences if he chose to insert himself in the negotiation that I need to conduct."

"Negotiation? It seems more a verbal duel to me. Perhaps even a beat down."

"Negotiation. Discussion. Dialogue. Duel. A moment where I explain that the ground rules have changed ..." Draig shrugged. "Merlin understood that this couldn't be avoided and better that he not be here when it happens."

The Daemon King nodded, looking at Draig in a new light. The Dragon was a force to be reckoned with. But clearly he had misjudged the scale of his influence and the extent of his nuance in navigating a more than challenging environment.

"You've got a lot of nerve summoning me," Arthur growled, stopping when he was no more than a few feet away from Draig.

"I didn't summon you. I invited you here."

Arthur studied his son, though not in the way expected of a father. There was little love to be seen there. A fact that had bothered Draig when he was younger, though not any longer. At least not as much as it had when he didn't really understand who his father was and why he did what he did.

He had gotten used to being evaluated in this way. Understanding that it was all calculation on Arthur's part.

His father was less interested in the fact that his son stood before him and more interested in what his son could do for him.

"I'm only here because Merlin suggested that I come. Don't try to make more out of this than what it really is."

"Have no fear of that," Draig replied evenly. "I didn't think you'd be interested in making another appearance here without a nudge."

His father was lying. Of that there was no doubt. Arthur could say what he wanted to make himself feel better, but Draig discerned the truth from his father's tone and expression.

Arthur would have done anything to be where he was now knowing what Draig held in his possession.

"Merlin said you had it."

"I do."

Arthur's eyes flashed, his anticipation quickening. "Prove it."

Draig's eyes narrowed. If he wanted to be difficult, just to irritate his father a little more, he could draw this out.

It might actually be fun.

It certainly was deserved.

He decided against it, however, because Eris would be back shortly.

Reaching into the pocket of his hiking pants, he pulled out the artifact.

The Book of Whispers.

Arthur smiled upon seeing the relic he had set so many Teg hunting for, including the thief ...

What in blazes was the thief doing here?

He had watched her die in this very chamber only days before. There was no way that she ...

Arthur's smile quickly turned into a scowl.

Draig, of course.

Likely doing just as he had done to escape him in Central Park more than a decade before.

Feigning his own death.

His eyes widened upon recognizing who was standing next to the thief.

What in all the hells was the Daemon King doing here?

There was only one way that ungrateful wretch could leave his confinement.

Draig.

His son was playing a game. Arthur was certain of it.

But that didn't matter. What mattered was that *The Book of Whispers* was almost within his grasp.

Arthur would deal with the thief and the Daemon King once he had the artifact in hand.

His eyes returned to the reason he was there, failing to hide the greed that passed across his face, there for a flash then gone just as fast. With *The Book of Whispers* he could accomplish the one objective that had been eluding him since he first became King of the Teg.

Protect his people from all threats.

Protect his people even from themselves.

"You're making the right decision, Draig," Arthur said approvingly, giving his son a warm smile, realizing as he did so that it was harder than anticipated to pull his eyes away from the artifact that had dominated his thoughts for so long. "Giving me the book will allow me to defend the Teg from those seeking to destroy us."

Arthur nodded to himself, seemingly already plotting his strategy for doing just that. "And you giving this to me now will allow you to return to the fold. Return to my side so you can do what you were meant to do."

"Keep dreaming, brother dear," a melodic voice mixed with a poisonous venom called from behind them.

Morgase's high heels clicked on the stone of the cavern floor as she stepped through the magical barrier. Eris was right behind her, though she chose not to follow her guest any farther into the cavern.

"What are you doing here?" Arthur demanded.

He could barely contain his rage. He had not seen his half-sister for quite some time.

Centuries, in fact. Yet she looked no different. Still beautiful. And by the tilt of her eye and ever-present smirk, still scheming.

"I'm here for *The Book of Whispers* just as you are, brother," Morgase replied, coming to a stop just a few feet away from him.

"You look a fool coming here, sister dear," Arthur scoffed. "Draig won't give you the book. Not after what you did to him. He's giving it to me."

"I don't care who Draig gives the book to. I'm not leaving here without the book."

Arthur laughed then, a touch of scorn in his voice. "You think you can defeat me? Still? After all these years?"

It was Morgase's turn to laugh. "I know I can defeat you, Arthur. The last time we fought, the only reason I lost was because Merlin fought beside you."

She made a show of looking around the Dragon Vault. "I don't see him here unless he's skulking about in the shadows as he so enjoys." Morgase smiled. A vicious expression. As if she had been waiting for this moment for quite a long time. And, truth be told, she had been.

"I don't need Merlin to fight my battles for me," Arthur growled, his anger escalating at the insult.

"That remains to be seen," Morgase replied sweetly, "although clearly he needs to do your thinking for you."

"What do you mean by that?" Arthur hissed, Morgase's next slight striking a little too close to home.

"You know exactly what I mean, Arthur. Haven't you figured it out? Or are you still stuck in your dreams of domination that I promise will never come to fruition?"

Arthur's eyes flashed dangerously, a cutting reply on the tip of his tongue. Yet he managed to hold it back. Thinking a little more. Not reaching the conclusion that his sister expected him to, and that fact irritating him in a way that her several insults had failed. "Speak plainly, Morgase. I don't have time for your games and taunts."

"How you've remained the King Teg for so long I still don't understand," Morgase chuckled softly, enjoying how Arthur's face reddened with rage. "For that I only have myself to blame." Probably a touch of shame as well, she realized. "Your son brought us both here not because he was going to give us the book. He brought us here to tell us that he wasn't going to give us the book, just as he made clear to me only a few hours ago."

"What the ..." Arthur turned on Draig quickly. "Is this true? Did you lie to me?"

"You've got the nerve to say something like that to me?" Draig asked in a shockingly quiet voice that hinted that violence was only a breath away. "I never told you why I wanted you here, father, you simply assumed. I can't take responsibility for your greed."

"You should have realized sooner, Arthur," Morgase chided, feeling the need to stick the needle in as far as she could. "Did you not suspect based on who allowed you entry here?"

Arthur looked behind them. Eris stood by the magical barrier, grinning broadly. "But you ..."

"Please, Arthur, this is growing tiresome," Morgase sighed, turning toward the Draca by the entrance. "You weren't helping me or my brother who is ridiculously slow on the uptake. You were helping him." She nodded toward Draig.

"Actually, I was helping myself," Eris replied with a deep satisfaction. "Draig gave me an offer that I couldn't refuse. Pleasure doing business with you, brother." Then, with a wave to Draig, Eris slipped back out of the cavern, having no desire to be a part of the confrontation that was brewing and would soon come to a boil.

"Brother?" Melissa whispered.

"A story for another time," Draig replied.

"Hello, Morgase." The Daemon King stared intently at the Teg Sorceress. "A pleasure to have you here with us. Surprising as well since you're so difficult to get a hold of when debts come due."

Morgase had eyes only for her brother upon striding into the Dragon Vault. Until the cold, soft voice set her teeth on edge. "What are you doing here?"

"I was invited," the Daemon King replied, "while you were led."

"That still doesn't explain why you're here." Morgase tried hard not to show it, but clearly she was nervous. More than nervous. She was worried as well.

She believed that she had some protection against the Daemon King while he was confined to his winery. With him standing just a few feet away, she realized that was an illusion that she had convinced herself of. She had not mitigated the danger, she couldn't, and it was all too real.

The Daemon King smiled then, although it wasn't a smile that Morgase wanted to see. Predatorial in nature. "We had an agreement, Morgase. You were to provide me with *The Book of Whispers*."

"That's not entirely true. As you can see ..."

"You have not met the requirements of our agreement, Morgase," the Daemon King continued, ignoring her. "Therefore, according to the terms of that agreement, I found a new supplier."

"You can't be serious?" Morgase demanded. She understood full well what that meant for her and her son for failing to meet the requirements of their contract.

Also what it meant for all Teg if the Daemon King acquired the artifact, which was why she never intended to give it to him once she obtained it. Of course, the solution to her dilemma was quite obvious.

Once she gained *The Book of Whispers*, she wouldn't have to give it to him. She could renege on the deal between them without consequence, because with the most powerful artifact ever created with the Grym, she could do whatever she damned well pleased.

"You're working with the Dragon? You trust him after all that he's done to you and your kind? He's the one who put you in your jail cell. You're where you are now because of him!" She pointed at Arthur. "You can't trust either of them. You can only trust me."

"Not a jail cell, home arrest," the Daemon King clarified. He ignored her argument, understanding that there was little substance to it, having assumed that she would try to extricate herself from what was a very sticky situation by blaming others. "We might not see eye to eye all that often, but Draig and I do look one another in the eye. We tell each other where we stand even if the other doesn't want to hear it. Most important, we trust that the other will hold up his end of the bargain."

"You turned on me so quickly?" Morgase shook her head as if she had been betrayed, feigning shock at what he had done to her, choosing to ignore the fact that she had planned to turn on the Daemon King as soon as she could.

"You missed the deadline, Morgase, and you weren't returning my calls. You would have done the same in my position. In fact, your failure to meet the terms of our contract suggests to me that you were playing your own game." The Daemon's King's eyes flashed a blood red, his voice taking on a menacing tone. "Playing me, actually. I don't like being played, Morgase."

"Have you ever considered that having you here now was a part of my plan?" Morgase asked with as much confidence as she could imbue within her voice, seeking some way to get ahead of a situation in which she had yet to exercise the control she was so accustomed to and needed. "Getting you here in the Dragon Vault so that you and I working together would allow *us* to take *The Book of Whispers* from Draig."

Arthur snorted at her suggestion, unable to help himself. "Fat chance that."

"Are you enjoying this, brother?" Morgase demanded.

"I am indeed ... *sister*." He spat out the word. "I've always enjoyed watching you dig yourself a hole, and not knowing what was good for you, seeing just how deep it got. You might want to stop, because the hole you're in now is quite deep, and I doubt you'll be able to climb out of it."

"You mistake the situation, Arthur. Know that once the Daemon King and I acquire the artifact and dispose of your son, you will be next." She turned her attention back to the Daemon King. "We are here now. Even with my upstart brother in the way, we can take what we want. The terms of the deal we made will be met. But only if we act together now."

The Daemon King did not respond right away, giving her a hard look that also revealed a hint of disbelief. He knew that she was treacherous, yet he had never expected to see that aspect of her personality put on full display. "As I said, Morgase, I have done my deal."

"We can still …"

"Enough, Morgase," the Daemon King said sharply, having lost what little tolerance he had left. "Our agreement has been concluded except for one clause. The penalties you must pay. Yet it goes beyond even that because I don't like being scammed. We will deal with those issues later, however." He nodded to Draig. "Shall we get this done? This crowd tries my patience."

"I completely understand," Draig replied. Even he, who usually enjoyed watching his aunt squirm since it was so rare, had grown tired of her false promises and wheedling. "This is what you both want, is it not?"

Draig threw *The Book of Whispers* onto the floor equidistant to Arthur and Morgase.

And there it sat.

The blood-red cover gleaming brightly thanks to the glowing orbs that hovered near the ceiling of the cavern.

Arthur Pendragon stared at his greatest desire. Easily within reach. Unable to take his eyes from it.

Morgase also stared at her greatest desire. Easily within reach. Unable to take her eyes from it.

At the exact same time, they lifted their gazes.

Arthur and Morgase glared at one another. Hundreds of years of slights, insults, and hatreds passed between them, their expressions hardening. Both desperate for revenge. Both wanting blood and a pound of flesh from the other.

Yet neither made a move for the book.

Neither wanted to appear desperate.

Neither wanted to make the first move.

Neither wanted to fail.

The Daemon King enjoyed the spectacle even more than he enjoyed beheading the rattlesnakes that infested his winery. The struggle that Arthur and Morgase took up to maintain their composure was captivating.

The question was how long they could maintain that self-possession.

Because it was quite obvious that it was becoming more and more difficult for them both.

Arthur and Morgase were spending just as much time staring at each other as they were looking down at the book.

It wouldn't be long now.

The Daemon King was proven correct just a few heartbeats later. At the same time, Morgase and Arthur reached down with the speed of a stinging wasp, seeking to snatch the artifact before the other could grasp it.

Neither gained what they desired though both got a hand on the artifact.

Just as fast as their fingers grazed the cover, they pulled back, letting the artifact fall back to the cavern floor.

Cursing.

Shaking their singed and tingling fingers.

Eyes tearing from the painful shock that started in their fingertips and traveled all the way up their arms.

The Daemon King laughed loudly, unable and unwilling to

contain himself. This really was quite good theater. More than just entertaining for him.

He had battled both the King Teg and his sister for more than a thousand years. To see this happen to them was a moment to be savored.

Believing that his point had been made, Draig stepped in between his father and his aunt and reached down, grasping the book without consequence.

"Just a little extra protection from thieving fingers," he explained, "and a little fun for me with my two favorite Teg."

The Daemon King laughed again, enjoying himself quite a bit at the expense of his two primary adversaries. He took a few steps closer so that he could better see what Draig held in his hands.

"Perhaps you'd like to take a look," Draig offered. He flipped open the cover, carefully of course because of the age of the text, and then turned a few pages with the same care.

"I don't understand," Arthur said in confusion. "It looks just like ..."

"A recipe book." Morgase's brow furrowed as she considered this shocking discovery, rubbing her fingers together as the tingling and pain lingered. "It must be another ward. You can't read it without ..."

Morgase's eyes shot up from the text. She noted Draig's grin. So consumed by achieving her greatest desire, her nephew had played her for a fool. "To read the book you must have the primer. Where is it?"

"I don't have the primer," Draig replied calmly, clearly enjoying his aunt's rising irritation and his father's continuing bewilderment.

"You must have the primer if you're making use of the book," Morgase argued, certain in her belief. "There is no other way."

"Quite right," Draig confirmed, "but as I said, I don't have the primer in my possession."

Morgase considered her nephew's words, trying to make sense as much of what he was not saying as what he was saying. Then she understood, speaking softly, unable to comprehend how it could have happened. "Draig is the primer."

"Draig? What are you talking about?" Arthur was still trying to grasp what Morgase was explaining.

"Your listening skills clearly have not improved with time, brother. Draig is the primer. That is why he can use *The Book of Whispers*. That is why we cannot."

"Morgase is correct," Draig replied, though he focused his words on the King Teg.

His father's confusion faded slowly. When it did, his expression hardened into one in which Draig was all too familiar. Once again, Arthur viewed his son as nothing more than an obstacle that needed to be overcome.

No, that wasn't entirely correct. His father's perspective was colored by a new finding.

Arthur saw him as more than just an obstacle. He perceived Draig as a threat.

"I am the primer," Draig confirmed. "I can make use of the book. So long as that is the case, no one else can."

"How is this possible?" Morgase couldn't quite comprehend how Draig could become the primer. With all that she knew of the Grym, any time an artifact required some additional piece to make it work, a key of sorts or a catalyst, it was either another physical object or words, such as was the case with a spell, those words spoken or chanted.

Draig ignored her question. He didn't feel the need to educate his father or his aunt on how he had gained the power to use *The Book of Whispers*. Telling them that the primer had been imprinted upon him, thereby giving him the ability to translate the most powerful Teg artifact in existence, would only lead to more questions that he had no desire to answer.

While Morgase tried to will Draig to tell her more, Arthur's frown narrowed into his trademark shrewdness.

"When did this happen?" he asked.

Draig didn't reply immediately, trying to determine if it would be best if he kept that information to himself. Contemplating it some more, he decided that revealing when might actually prove beneficial.

"When I was much younger."

"How could I have not known?" Arthur demanded.

"There's a lot you don't know, brother."

Arthur ignored his sister, the knowledge coming slowly. But it did come to him.

"Tia!" Arthur cursed. He let a few more expletives fly, needing some outlet for his building rage.

"Yes, it was my mother's doing."

"Why would she do this to me?"

Draig shook his head. Everything was always about his father. No one else. The world revolved around him and only him. A perspective that had worked well for him over time, yet grated in a way that created problems that could have been avoided if he had demonstrated even an ounce of understanding or empathy.

Which in large part was why his mother had imprinted the primer within Draig by employing the Power of the Draca.

When Draig began spending time with his mother during the summers, Tia saw what his father was doing to him. What Arthur wanted Draig to become.

She tried to prevent it, and upon realizing that she couldn't, she attempted to at least temper Arthur's influence.

There was only so much that she could do, however.

That's what his mother had explained to him when she believed that the time was right and he was best positioned to understand what she was gifting him, and that was her reasoning for teaching him not only how to employ the tremendous power contained within *The Book of Whispers*, but also how he needed to think and function as a result.

Because his mother had been quite clear. She gave him control over the most powerful magical artifact in the Teg world. But just like a sword, the potency that she granted him could cut both ways. Deeply and irreversibly.

Her decision provided Draig with a greater chance of surviving in the lethal environment in which he functioned, what Arthur had done placing a target on Draig's back that remained to this day. All of that complicated by the fact that he was of the Teg as well as of the Draca. A difficult position to be in, part but also apart, both at the same time.

The Daemon Lord burst out into a laugh then, no longer able to contain himself, all eyes turning toward him as the bubble of tension that had been forming around the small group popped.

"What's so funny?" Arthur growled.

"You really don't see it?" Their expressions made him laugh even harder.

"Enlighten us," Arthur ordered through clenched teeth.

"Both brother and sister are desperate to obtain the most powerful artifact in the Teg world so that they can use it against the other and then their enemies. However, each of you can only access the power contained within *The Book of Whispers* through Draig. Even better, if you get your hands on the book, you can't touch it – that fact was just proven – and you can't make use of it because the primer is Draig." The Daemon King clapped his hands together, clearly relishing the dilemma Arthur and Morgase now faced. "Oh, this is delicious. It's got the makings of Shakespeare. I had no idea that I was going to have so much fun today at this show."

He directed his next question to Fafnir. "Could you tell

them what happens if they kill Draig? Based on their expressions, and knowing them as I do, I can see that's where their thoughts have taken them. They believe that if they kill Draig, it will release the primer and then they can gain access to the knowledge contained within the book."

Fafnir shook his head, putting a pin in that hope. "If either seek to kill Draig, then they will answer to the Queen of the Draca. So she has said." Fafnir's stony gaze suggested they would answer to him as well. "Besides, killing Draig would do neither of them any good. If either of you kill Draig, either on your own or one of your many servants, the knowledge in *The Book of Whispers* dies with Draig. The primer was unmade and made a part of the Dragon. It cannot be made again. Lose Draig and you lose the primer. Lose the primer and you lose *The Book of Whispers*. It's as simple as that."

"A delicious play indeed. Your mother puts the rest of us to shame." The Daemon King clapped his hands again and shouted with pleasure, truly appreciating how the mind of Draig's mother worked. Arthur and Morgase desperately wanted the artifact. They needed to kill Draig to do it. But if they killed Draig they had no chance whatsoever of obtaining it.

That just having been confirmed, naturally, the Daemon King assumed that Arthur and Morgase's next thoughts were that they could enslave Draig and force him to do as they wanted. But, with Draig able to call upon the knowledge contained within *The Book of Whispers*, they had no chance of doing that either. He was too strong. Too skilled. Too suspicious.

Checkmate.

Truly a marvelous maneuver.

And he saw now by their sour expressions that Arthur and Morgase had just reached that conclusion as well.

"You're right about that," Fafnir confirmed with a nod. "Our

Queen has a cunning that few can match. Something that perhaps the King Teg knows better than most."

"Perhaps when next the opportunity presents itself, you would introduce me to your mother?" the Daemon King asked Draig, nodding to him in respect. Draig's mother had achieved a master stroke, providing Draig with the ultimate protection. "I have always wanted to meet her, even more so now after learning how she neutered these two." He nodded toward Arthur and Morgase.

"I'm sure that can be arranged," Draig replied.

"Wonderful!" the Daemon King exclaimed. "I must say, you two are in quite a pickle!"

Despite their hate for one another and the fact that Draig had just shattered one of their oldest dreams, Arthur and Morgase still heard the truth in the Daemon King's words. They couldn't deny it. Yet they couldn't give up so easily. It wasn't in their nature. There had to be some way around the snare laid for them.

Needing more time to consider his next step, Arthur turned to Fafnir. The Keeper had tried to watch dispassionately as the drama played out. However, the small smile that curled his lips confirmed the difficulty of doing so.

"You allowed this to happen."

Fafnir straightened, his reddish-orange eyes shifting from a slow burn to a flash of flame. He did not like the challenge in the King Teg's voice. Matching his dislike of the King Teg himself. "I do not have the authority nor the skill you imply. Only my Queen can do so. She has the authority and the skill, no one else among the Draca."

"Why would she do this to me?"

Fafnir did not answer Arthur's question, even though several replies came to mind. He didn't believe that it was his place to say anything even though he knew the history between his Queen and the King Teg. "You'll need to ask her that. She may or may not choose to respond."

Clearly, from Arthur's bitter expression, he had no desire to assume that risk. So he took a different approach, one that irked him, yet he couldn't avoid. Gaining the power of *The Book of Whispers* was more important than anything else.

"The offer still stands, son. Return to my side. We did a great deal of good for the Teg. There is a great deal of good that we can do still for the Teg. Together, you and me."

"Don't listen to that pompous fool," Morgase warned. "You've seen his true colors. My offer still stands, nephew. Think of what we could do together. Think of what you could do to your father."

"Tempting as your promises are," Draig replied, not surprised either by his father or his aunt, "I think not."

Before Arthur or Morgase could protest, he lifted his hand. "You have both demonstrated for centuries that you can't work together. You each have your own objectives and those objectives are juxtaposed against those of the other."

"Son ..."

"Enough ... father." Draig's eyes flashed dangerously, his scorn obvious. His father had never called him *son* before. Ever. It was almost embarrassing that he was doing so now, Arthur's compulsion to do whatever was required to achieve his objective revealed for all to see. "You two refuse to work together, so I certainly won't work with you. Because of your constant failures, you will listen and you will do as I say."

"You insolent pup. Do you have any idea ..."

"I know exactly who you are, Auntie M," Draig replied with a strong dose of derision, what he called her stopping her short once again. "The rules are simple. Break them at your own peril."

He stepped in closer then, the illusion hiding his walking stick disappearing, Excalibur within his grasp. A fact that his father couldn't ignore. "You will leave me alone. Are we clear?"

Arthur and Morgase stared at him with loathing in their eyes, still not quite sure how Draig could have put them in this position of ... subservience. Just thinking about it made them sick to their stomachs.

"Am I clear?" he repeated, the words sharp, brooking no argument.

Reluctantly, they both nodded, having no other option.

"You will also leave each other alone. No more seeking to displace the other. No more proxy wars. Nothing. You and your Knights and Paladins will stay away from one another."

"Do you really believe that you can require us to do as you wish?" Morgase offered Draig a lifted eyebrow to emphasize her skepticism.

"Yes, I can," he said simply. "Penalties will be incurred for failing to do so. And as you both know, because of my service to my father, I'm quite good at ensuring that penalties owed are penalties paid."

Neither could deny that. Despite some grumbling, both his father and aunt agreed, neither having any other choice.

Draig was not naïve enough to believe that they would adhere to their promise. Still, he had to try. If for no other reason his hope that they would at least wait a short while before they returned to their hidden war that made life for all the Teg more difficult than it needed to be.

And that was time that he could use. Instead of worrying about them, he could worry about the larger threat the Teg faced. The threat that neither his father nor aunt knew about or if they did didn't care to acknowledge, their focus solely on themselves.

"Anything else?" Arthur demanded, his face red with rage, Morgase's little better.

"That's all ... for now."

Silence descended then, Morgase and Arthur glaring at Draig with an undisguised hatred. The Daemon King watching the scene playing out before him, understanding that the culmination was coming soon.

Because he could see that even with all that the two had learned and having no good cause to question it, perhaps because of their own failures, both brother and sister were contemplating a path that would have been anathema just moments before.

Working together.

They were mulling what would happen if they attacked Draig then and there.

The Daemon King was certain of it. Their expressions and stances suggested as much. He could tell that Draig saw it as well, and the fact that two of the strongest Teg wanted him dead didn't appear to faze him.

Draig stood across from them the perfect reflection of calm and composure, sword point balanced on the ground, hilt beneath his palms. Clearly expecting a battle of more than wills to begin. Clearly wanting it to happen. And ready for whatever Arthur and Morgase decided to throw at him.

Which was why they continued to hesitate.

When Arthur flexed his fingers, the Daemon King stepped up next to Draig.

Arthur scoffed. "You're siding with your jailer."

"Draig did what he did at your order, yet he didn't do all that you wanted him to do."

"What are you talking about?"

"You wanted to destroy me, Arthur," the Daemon King stated with a cold clarity. "Draig refused to do as you commanded. He showed me a mercy that I probably don't deserve, but I certainly welcomed it. A mercy that you never showed me."

"Be careful of the allies you select," Arthur warned. "They can stab you in the back just as easily as they can the front."

"Of that I am well aware. Isn't that correct, Morgase?"

Morgase ignored the jab, the standoff continuing. Arthur and Morgase squaring up to Draig and the Daemon King. Fafnir standing back near the first row of artifacts, his expression impassive although his eyes told a different story.

Melissa, who stood next to him, tried to mimic the Draca, but her face revealed the host of emotions running through her. Shock. Fear. Wonder. Curiosity. And so many more.

It was almost as if she had a front-row seat at one of the movies her mother had made her watch when she was younger. An old Western. *Gunfight at the O.K. Corral.* The tension building with each passing second.

If Arthur and Morgase were thinking rationally, they would realize that they had no choice but to back down. They could accomplish nothing now. Draig had won this battle.

Even so, there was still more to come.

They weren't thinking rationally. They were making their decisions based on emotion and not logic.

Both were touching the Grym. Both believed that if they acted with the speed with which they knew they could, they could seize Draig.

Doing so would earn them some time to consider how they might be able to turn the tables on him and make use of the power that he controlled.

Draig saw all that as clear as day, because he knew both better than they knew him.

They were who they were.

They weren't going to change now.

They weren't going to give in.

However, there was a great deal that Draig had not revealed to them, understanding the value of keeping certain information to himself. Such as the fact that only one with the

Power of the Draca could unlock the secrets of *The Book of Whispers*, a truth that had been lost to history thanks to his mother.

Also unknown to Arthur and Morgase was another important tidbit. Ever since his mother told him what she had done for him, he had worked with her to learn how to use *The Book of Whispers*. And since then, he had practiced ... a lot.

Before his father and aunt could do as they truly desired, Draig did what he knew he must because he believed that it was a necessary lesson. There was no way around it.

He made use of the power that only he could control.

He needed to give his father and his aunt a true taste of what they faced if they chose to challenge him. A spanking of sorts.

Arthur and Morgase dropped to their knees, pressed down by the Grym. Yet what truly terrified them was that Draig wasn't doing it to them.

Or rather he was.

But not with the Grym. Or at least not the Grym that he could call upon.

He was using the Grym contained within *The Book of Whispers*.

And that power was manipulating the tremendous reservoir of the Grym that each of them could tap into.

Draig was employing that damnable artifact to use their own power against them. Calling upon the Grym that they could control and applying it against them despite their desperate and useless efforts to prevent that.

Groaning and gasping, they felt as if they had been struck by a sledgehammer. But they had no time to focus on that, because they found themselves back on their feet in an instant, facing one another much like the gunfighters of the Wild West.

Their eyes widened in fear when they realized that they had seized the Grym, although not of their own volition. Draig had seized it for them and was forcing them to pull in even more of the Power of the Ancients.

Most terrifying for the both of them, they could do nothing to stop it.

They could feel what he was doing to them. They could see it with their own eyes as small spheres of energy formed atop their palms and grew steadily larger and blindingly bright.

Both recognized what he had in mind, and that sent a chill down their spines that they had never experienced before.

Both demanded absolute control. Over themselves. Over others. They had never been placed in a position where they had to answer to someone else, where they had to obey someone else.

That concept horrified them.

Their eyes widened in shock when they realized what Draig was going to do.

He was going to force them to fight one another.

Destroy one another.

Because with Draig controlling their use of the Grym, they had no way to defend themselves.

How ridiculously ironic and poetic, and there was nothing that they could do.

They were helpless.

No more than marionettes at the mercy of the puppeteer.

"You see now what I can do," Draig said. Not proud of what he was doing. Only believing that he had to do it. "There's more to *The Book of Whispers* than just using the potency of another Teg. The real power comes from a harsh reality. I can make any Teg do whatever I want." Draig frowned slightly, though he didn't balk at what he just said or what he said next. "Distasteful as that is, there is still a logic behind it. And as you both know, I will do whatever is necessary to get the job done."

The spheres of energy flickering atop Arthur and Morgase's palms became even larger, gaining strength and brightness until they blazed as bright as the sun. Draig forcing two of the most powerful Teg to do as he required. Demanding that they pull in even more of the Grym.

"Because I am tired of the both of you, just as so many of the Teg are."

"Son ..." Arthur pleaded, barely able to get the word out. He felt like his insides were being ripped apart, the reservoir of the Grym Draig was forcing him to call upon too much for him to manage, the energy slowly destroying him. The gasp from his sister confirmed that she was experiencing much the same as he was.

Draig ignored his father, forcing them both to pull in even more of the Grym. The pain excruciating, Draig seeing it on their faces and in their quickly weakening posture. Enlightening as well, he hoped. He brought them right to the edge of burning themselves out, not needing to have them fight one another to show that he could force them to destroy themselves, before he released them.

Gasping for breath, shaking feverishly from the power that had surged through them just a second before, Draig allowed Arthur and Morgase a moment to regain control of themselves.

"I wanted you both to come here so that you understood where matters stand between us now. I could have had you destroy yourselves. Completely and utterly. And you could do nothing to prevent it. But I did not. Although that might have been the easiest solution, I am no longer who I was. I must warn you, however. Do not mistake that for a weakness that you can exploit. If you do, you will do so at your own peril."

"You underestimate me," Morgase hissed, still struggling to breathe, the pain that she experienced as Draig manipulated the Grym that she controlled still more than just a memory for her.

"I don't think I do," Draig replied calmly. "You can both leave now. Today's lesson is over."

Morgase wanted to wait. To show her nephew that he had not cowed her. Yet she found herself taking a few wobbly steps toward the barrier on the far side of the cavern. Somehow, Arthur held his ground.

Refusing to show any weakness, especially to his son, he pushed himself up to his full height, ignoring the waves of pain that still wracked him.

"I challenge you to a duel."

Draig did not reply right away, staring at his father. His expression indecipherable. Although rather than being angry at the King Teg's demand, Melissa believed that Draig might actually feel sorry for him.

Her belief was confirmed when Draig shook his head. His look not one of surprise, but rather resignation mixed with a heavy dose of disappointment. Much like a teacher who had failed to teach his student.

"No."

Arthur couldn't quite believe how Draig responded. Surrendering to his rage, despite the agony it cost him, he reached for the Grym, needing to push his son to fight him. Believing that it was the only way that he could remind Draig of his place in Arthur's world. Still unwilling to acknowledge that Draig had just knocked Arthur's world, in which he was the center of all things, off its axis, and that it would remain that way ... forever.

"There will be no combats here," Fafnir said, stepping out from the shadows. With him came several more Draca only Draig had been aware were in the Vault with them.

"I am the King of the Teg!" Arthur roared. "I can challenge anyone I desire!"

"You may, King Teg," Fafnir agreed with a nod, "but not here. If you persist, you risk war with the Draca."

"I don't give a damn about the Draca. I want to fight the traitor who stands before me!"

"Then fight him somewhere else," Fafnir said, his tone even, unemotional. "You will not do so here." He nodded toward the barrier just a few dozen yards behind Arthur. "Best that you leave now before you do something that you regret. You have seen what Draig can do. I don't think you want to see what five Draca can do."

Arthur held his ground, his fury plain at the refusal and the veiled threat. Yet he was still rational enough to realize that there was nothing that he could do.

Desiring to maintain what little dignity remained to him after one humiliating experience right after the other, he stumbled more than strode toward the illusion that would allow him to exit the Dragon Vault.

"You're smarter than I ever gave you credit for," Morgase said to Draig as she followed after her brother, wiping her disheveled hair from her eyes.

"That's the nicest thing you've ever said to me," Draig replied, succeeding in keeping under wraps the smile he wanted to offer her, knowing that revealing it would only serve to set her off.

The Daemon King stepped up to Draig once the two Teg left, letting out the breath that he had been holding. He was amused. Concerned as well.

"They both want you dead."

"They both wanted me dead before this," Draig shrugged. "Now they're really going to have to think about whether making an attempt on my life is worth it."

"You certainly do like to play with fire, don't you?"

Draig turned to his new ally then, offering him a smile. "I am half Draca after all. Fafnir, do you have what I asked for?"

Fafnir stepped forward, the other Draca already having faded back into the darkness now that the fun was over. He placed a large tome in Draig's hands. "The Queen has agreed to your request."

"That was very kind of her," Draig acknowledged. "Please thank her for me."

"I will," Fafnir replied, "but the Queen has attached a requirement to this gift."

"I'm afraid to ask," Draig murmured.

"She requests your presence. That you thank her in person. She understands that you have larger matters to attend to. As soon as those other responsibilities are met, she asks that you visit with her."

"That's very gracious of her," Draig replied, knowing that a request from his mother was anything but a request.

"Our Queen is nothing if not gracious." Fafnir left him then, following the other Draca. "You know your way out. And don't forget the Queen. She does not take rejection well."

"That's an understatement," Draig said under his breath.

He then handed the large tome to the Daemon King.

"What's this?"

"A small gift of thanks for what you have done for me."

The Daemon King frowned as he looked down at the large, heavy book. "You can't be ..." He opened the cover made with cured human skin, then began to page through the tome. "This was taken from me centuries ago. How did you find it?"

"I own a bookstore, remember?"

"Yes, but *The Infernal Dictionary*?" The Daemon King couldn't believe it.

The text he held in his hands exercised a power over him and his ilk that nothing else could. The book was a living document, continually updating itself when he created a new Daemon or one was destroyed, listing their true names.

A dangerous proposition, because if one of the Teg knew a Daemon's real name, then the Teg could exercise control over that Daemon. Even over the Daemon King. It had happened in the past, and he had been searching for the tome ever since, fearful of what would occur if the text and the power it contained got into the wrong hands.

"I have a few other resources to call upon, including a truly excellent librarian."

For a moment, the Daemon King was speechless. Not quite believing what was happening. More than just curious about how Draig had achieved this coup.

"With this, you could enslave any of my servants. You could enslave me."

"I could," Draig admitted.

"But you won't."

Draig shook his head. "No, that's not for me."

"You do understand the power and opportunity that you're giving up by returning this to me?"

Draig shrugged. "After what I just did to Arthur and Morgase, do your really think I need it?"

25

THE FULL DRAGON

"That wasn't you going all full Dragon in Mordred's office?" Melissa asked with a lift of her eyebrows, her head tilting to the right when he shook his head. "Even so, it was quite impressive. I could not only see but I could feel the electricity coming off of you."

She sat at the counter in Draig's kitchen drinking the Arnold Palmer he made for her. Seamus was on his way back to the mainland, deciding to forgo Draig taking him across Raptor Bay in his cabin cruiser, swimming instead and seeking the restorative effects of the water that would help him heal.

"No, I didn't let go," Draig replied. He stood in front of her, hands on the counter. "I was almost there but decided to hold back."

"That seems to be one of your specialties," Melissa said in a joking tone.

"I'm sorry?" Draig didn't understand. It could be because he was tired, the encounter with his father and his aunt draining him. It could also be because his mind was elsewhere, thinking about what more he had to do, his guest being one of the variables that would determine just how much would be required of him.

Melissa gave him a mischievous smile. "Holding back. Not always taking advantage of the opportunity when you have it."

Draig didn't respond right away, not sure that he wanted to. The smile that Melissa offered him was both enticing and slightly concerning. He selected the cautious approach. "In some matters I don't like to rush. In the past I've been bitten in the ass more than just a few times and I'd like to avoid it in the future."

Melissa nodded. "Really? Care to explain when you were bitten in the ass?" She leaned forward on the counter, her hands almost touching his. "Remember that details matter. The more the better."

Rather than shying away, Draig leaned in farther, his nose just a few inches from hers. "Some things are better shown than explained." His tone was serious, quiet, his eyes revealing a captivating fire that Melissa had not seen before and found difficult to ignore.

For several seconds they remained as they were, the tension building. Her nerves threatening to get the better of her, never expecting this response from Draig, Melissa started to laugh softly, both pulling back at the same time, the simmering heat between them fading, though only slightly.

"Sorry, I know that you've got a lot on your mind, but I couldn't resist." She chose not to say that she would have welcomed him continuing to push, because if he had ... well, now wasn't the time for her thoughts to drift in that direction. She needed to stay on task. "It's been a very long last few days and a little fun helps to relieve the stress."

"It does," Draig agreed. "As do other activities."

Melissa gave a start, caught off guard. She looked away briefly, not wanting to risk getting caught by his powerful gaze. Swallowing, she sought to bring the conversation back to where it started. Having no doubt what could happen – what would happen – if she pursued Draig's comment any further.

"You said you didn't go full Dragon," Melissa prompted. She realized that she was reaching for the top of her shirt to pull it away from her chest and made herself stop, flicking a stray hair out of her eyes instead, the slight trickle of sweat running down between her breasts not something she wanted to reveal.

Draig smiled. He understood what Melissa was dealing with. He was as well. Did he want to take that risk? No, that wasn't the right question. Should he take the risk knowing where it had gotten him before?

Pushing off the counter abruptly, he crossed his arms and leaned back on the sink. "There was a key part missing."

"What?"

"The shift."

"The shift?" Melissa frowned. "What do you mean by the shift?"

"Going full dragon means becoming a dragon. One of the unique gifts of being of the Draca." He shrugged, as if shifting into a full-sized dragon, a creature that could be larger than a house, wasn't that big a deal. "I haven't had to do it for a while, although when I was losing patience in the Dragon Vault, I almost let go."

"How does that work? Like a Werewolf?" Melissa knew that there were many different types of Shifters among the Teg, although Werewolves seemed to be the most common. Or perhaps they were simply the most prolific and top of mind for her after her experience with the Renegades during her stay in Kraken Cove.

"It's similar. A special form of magic common to all Draca."

"How did you acquire this ability?" She knew that some Shifters were created by other Shifters, Werewolves the most obvious example in that respect. Others came to it innately. Draig seemed to be suggesting the latter.

"My father had an affair with Tiamat."

"Tiamat? You mean ..." Melissa's eyes widened with a mix of disbelief and fear. "You mean when Fafnir referenced the Queen wanting to see you ..."

Draig nodded. "Yes, Tiamat, the Queen of the Draca and my mother."

Melissa allowed that revelation to percolate. She couldn't really say that she was surprised. Not when it came to Draig.

Although once again she found it difficult to contain her curiosity, not knowing if she should be a little bit more grossed out rather than inordinately intrigued. It didn't take her long to give in to the latter urge.

"How does that work?" she asked in a light-hearted tone. "A man and a dragon? I've got so many questions."

"I'm sure you do," Draig replied in an amused tone. He should have expected this.

"To start, when they're romantic with one another ..." There was a devilish gleam in her eye.

Draig held up his hands, stopping her right there. "Let me take the fun out of it for you. My mother was in her human form when she was with my father."

"That makes more sense than where my mind was taking me," Melissa murmured. "Takes the yuck out of it." She wasn't done, however. "Another question."

"It'll have to wait."

"What?" Melissa was disappointed. She saw this as an opportunity to do some more digging, and she was still thinking about the offer that she had seen in the back of Draig's eyes. The offer that she found quite appealing despite all that remained for her to do. "Why?"

"I need to meet an old friend," Draig replied, "and I can't put it off any longer. I shouldn't be gone for more than a few hours."

He gripped her shoulder warmly as he passed by, heading

up the circular staircase that ran along the inside of the light-house and toward the Dragon Door on the third floor.

"I'll be waiting for you." Melissa offered Draig a smile that was more than warm.

Draig looked back over his shoulder. He gave her a smile that mimicked her own. Understanding what the next step between them would be. If he allowed it. "I'm glad to hear it."

MELISSA WATCHED Draig walk through the Dragon Door, the runes carved into the wood flashing brightly for a few seconds more after he closed the portal behind him before blinking out.

She wondered where he was going but had known better than to ask.

She nodded to herself. Having access to one of those portals certainly would come in handy, she mused. It would lower the level of difficulty on the jobs she usually took.

A wasted thought, however. Only the Draca could use a Dragon Door.

With Draig gone, the fire between them fading, Melissa felt the urge to get moving. She had enjoyed a great deal of success during the last few days, thanks in large part to Draig and his unexpected though quite timely assistance. Even so, the clock was still ticking, and she didn't know how much longer she had before it struck midnight.

Nevertheless, she sat on her stool for several more minutes and stared at the Dragon Door covered in shadows two floors above. Strangely torn. Worried that he might return right away. A small part of her hoping that he would.

Wondering if what she hoped for could be.

Realizing that she needed to crush her own desires, at least for a little while longer.

Her thoughts on the steel shield fixed to the wall just

behind her upon which three red Welsh dragons seemed to take on a life of their own when she looked at them a certain way and in a certain light.

She had watched him place *The Book of Whispers* in the safe behind the shield when they arrived back from the Dragon Vault.

She had tested the ward the first time she had visited him here, and she didn't think she could open the safe. Also, she was worried about what might happen if she somehow succeeded and touched the artifact, not forgetting and not wanting to experience what Arthur and Morgase did because of their own greed.

She didn't necessarily want to take possession of the arti-fact. Doing that would put her on a road that made her more than nervous.

Nonetheless, she did want to see if she could crack the safe. The challenge appealed to her as a professional, an impulse she had a hard time denying.

Melissa shook her head ever so slightly, trying to convince herself to let the desire go.

To turn her desires in a more amorous direction. If Draig returned soon ...

It wasn't working. Her fingers were getting itchy.

Still, she was conflicted.

Draig had given her more than she expected. More than she deserved, in fact.

Moreover, he had proven that he could and would help her against Arthur and Morgase, going so far as to risk his life for hers. Several times, in fact.

Was that enough for her, however?

Because Arthur and Morgase, though major worries, were, in fact, the least of her concerns.

Slowly, she pulled her eyes away from the Dragon Door, turning on her stool and shifting her focus to the shield.

Draig had said that he would return *The Book of Whispers* to the Dragon Vault when he was done with it. Once he did, she'd never get her hands on it. And there was little to suggest that if she tried to obtain it now she stood any chance of success.

Besides, she felt like she might have a chance with Draig. A good chance, in fact.

And he might actually be good for her.

He might even be able to help her with her primary dilemma.

Did she want to risk that?

Could she?

After thinking about it, she realized much to her surprise that she wanted to risk it. A sign of maturity at a time like this threatened to throw her for a loop.

But what she wanted wasn't as important as what she needed.

Because she couldn't just think about Draig and what might grow between them. She needed to put someone else's interests before her own. Someone more important to her than Draig.

26

LIKE OLD TIMES

"You used to love coming here."

Merlin, resembling an absent-minded professor, long beard, wispy hair sprouting in all directions, circular glasses making his eyes look like those of an owl, wore his usual corduroy pants, button down, cardigan sweater, and blazer with patches on the elbows. Different colored patches of course.

"It was the only place I could go to gain a little perspective." Draig didn't pull his gaze from the view atop the Empire State Building's observation deck. Central Park to the north. The Hudson River to the west, the East River on the other side. The Upper Bay, Governor's Island, and the Statue of Liberty to the south.

"Probably easier for you to do in the mountains when you were staying with your mother. A little less pressure on you when you were with Tiamat."

"A different kind of pressure," Draig replied, turning toward his friend and mentor. He offered Merlin a warm smile. The Sorcerer was like a father to him, even more so than Arthur. Merlin had taken responsibility for his care and his education until he had begun training to become a Knight of the Round. As a result, out of all the Teg other than Gaheris, Merlin knew him better than anyone else.

"I can only imagine."

Draig nodded, not wanting to take that road. Needing to take one that didn't involve memories that would only slow him down. "So when did you put all this together?" His warm smile shifted when he asked the question, revealing the cunning for which his mother was known.

Although he knew that it was of little use, Merlin's first instinct was to dissemble. "What do you mean?"

"You put all this into motion, Merlin. Well before Melissa appeared in Kraken Cove."

"That's quite an accusation." Merlin offered Draig a lift of his eyebrows and no more than that, not bothering to deny the charge.

"It's not an accusation. It's the truth."

Merlin pursed his lips, a smile forming. He had never been able to get much past Draig, and he would have been disappointed if he had. "Ever since you disappeared, yes."

Draig nodded. He hadn't decided yet if he was angry or disappointed, because Merlin only put a scheme like this one into motion if he believed that there was good cause to do so. "Why couldn't you just leave me alone?"

"I did," he shrugged, "for a time."

"Not long enough."

"Don't be a grouch, Draig," Merlin said with a soft laugh. "Your father is grouch enough for all of us."

"Why?" Draig had a good idea about how all the pieces of this new puzzle fit together, though not all. And he was getting tired of feeling as if he was always one step behind.

"We need you, Draig."

"Who needs me?"

"The Teg."

Draig found that hard to believe and with good reason. "Most of the Teg want me dead, Merlin. I was my father's enforcer. I killed for him. Often when I shouldn't have."

"That is neither here nor there, Draig."

"Of course it is," Draig challenged. "The Teg don't forget, nor should they."

"The past isn't relevant to what we face in the future," Merlin said in a quiet but insistent tone. "You out of all of us should understand that."

Draig wanted to dispute Merlin's claim, the words on the tip of his tongue. But he didn't. He couldn't. Because Merlin was right. He had seen it all in the Circle atop the Druid's Peak.

"Just because they don't know it doesn't mean they don't need you, Draig." Merlin reached out, patting him on the shoulder in commiseration.

Draig sighed. He felt like he was getting into another circular conversation with Merlin just as had been the case when he was younger. The Sorcerer preferred the Socratic method of teaching, wanting Draig to ask questions to obtain the knowledge he required.

Draig didn't mind asking questions, but he could ask better questions if Merlin provided him with better information. When time was short, he found the entire process incredibly frustrating. "Don't make me ask, Merlin."

"You know it just as well as I do. There needs to be a balance again between Arthur and Morgase."

"And you think I'm that balance?"

"I know that you're that balance."

"That's why *The Book of Whispers* was so important," Draig said, the last few pieces of the puzzle moving into position for him.

Merlin nodded. "That artifact gives you a power that they cannot exercise. That they can't compete against. It requires them to look at the world in a different way and make different decisions as a result. Decisions that they wouldn't make otherwise."

"Why do you think I won't use that power to remove both of them?" Draig's tone was challenging, as if he was actually considering that option. "Why shouldn't I just take the throne for myself?"

"Perhaps you should," Merlin mused in a very quiet tone, his expression just as mysterious as always.

"You feeling alright, Merlin?" Draig hadn't been serious, but he was certain that Merlin was.

"You made a deal with the Daemon King. In fact, he's an ally now."

Draig shrugged. "I guess you could say that."

"Doing that removed one major threat against the Teg. A threat that has existed for a thousand years. Longer than that, actually, releasing some of the pressure that had been building up."

"I didn't make the deal for that reason. The Daemon King earned that gift. I did it because it was the right thing to do."

"Just like you did the right thing when you didn't destroy him, instead confining him to the winery, because you knew that he is the only one who can control the Daemons of his realm. That if you eliminated him as your father demanded, his Daemons would run amok and create even more problems than they would have with the Daemon King still in power."

Draig shrugged again, not liking where the conversation was going. "That thought had crossed my mind."

Draig studied Merlin with a shrewd gaze. Seeing the truth in the back of his friend's eyes.

Merlin was pushing him down this road because he had identified the threat long before anyone else did. Draig knew as well that Arthur couldn't handle the threat on his own and Morgase wouldn't care about it until she displaced her brother and by then it would be too late.

"You never had the patience for a long conversation, so let me tell it to you straight. You know the risk that Morgase and Mordred present. You neutralized them when you rescued Melissa. You showed them what you can do if they demand it of you. You did the same to your father in the Dragon Vault and to Morgase again so that she wouldn't doubt your commitment."

"What are you saying, Merlin?"

"You're doing the job your father used to do. The job he should be doing now." Merlin gave him a pointed look. "Maybe it's time for a change at the top."

27

A NEW DIRECTION

Draig stood on the rocky beach just below the Raptor Bay Lighthouse, pondering what Merlin had told him. The lure his friend and mentor had set for him.

It was a complication that he didn't want to deal with. Not now with everything else that was pressing down upon him.

But just because he didn't want to deal with it didn't mean that he could escape the responsibility of doing so.

Besides, there was no point in hesitating or hedging. He already had decided.

He was just reluctant to go home, knowing what he was going to find there.

"I'm assuming you wanted to talk."

He focused his comment on the water ten yards off the shore, the waves barely more than a ripple. The cove calmer than it had been in quite a long time.

He didn't have long to wait.

Just a few seconds later, Jinx walked out of the surf, her green eyes glowing in the darkness, green hair every so often reflecting the flash of the moonlight.

"Come here often, sailor?"

"Does that actually work for you?" Draig frowned.

"It worked on Seamus."

Draig smiled. "Anything would work on Seamus."

"True," Jinx admitted. She stopped when she was a few feet from the sand, unwilling to leave the comfort of the water swirling gently around her feet.

"You're here for a reason."

"One of the reasons I mentioned earlier, Dragon. I want the Witch."

Draig nodded, his reddish-orange eyes flashing brightly in the gloom, burning with a greater intensity, letting Jinx know that he was ready for anything she might want to throw at him. "You can't have her. I thought that I had been clear about that."

"You're just wasting your time and effort. You can't protect her from me and my Vipers."

"I believe that I can," he replied with an almost unnerving calm that sounded more threat than statement.

"My father always gets what he wants in the end. There's really no point in getting in his way. He will simply roll over you as if you were never there."

"Thank you for the warning, but your father has never gone up against me before."

Jinx snorted out a laugh at that. "You really believe that you can stand against him? One of the most powerful of the Ancients?"

Draig shrugged. "There's only one way to find out."

Jinx studied Draig for a time. He was a dilemma to her, because she was certain that how she normally approached obstacles in her path wouldn't work with him, and that conclusion irritated her. "I could kill you now."

Draig smiled, hearing the lack of conviction in her voice. "You could try."

Butch, Cassidy, and Sundance appeared then, stepping out of the darkness and forming a semicircle around Draig. They didn't growl. They didn't make a move. They simply stood there, having eyes only for Jinx and clearly unimpressed by what they saw.

She took a moment to study the trio. They appeared to be nothing more than small dogs, however she knew that they were much more than that.

She sensed the power of each one. A power that she had no desire to engage without her Vipers at her back.

"You'll allow these three monsters to fight your battles for you?"

Draig didn't fall for the bait. "I don't allow them to do anything. They do what they want, and they've always wanted a taste of Hydra."

Jinx's frown quickly became a scowl. "You insult me, Dragon. You will pay for that."

"You make a lot of promises, Jinx. Do you ever keep them?"

Draig believed that his last comment would do it. That he would goad Jinx into a combat.

He was more than ready for it, and not just because Butch, Cassidy, and Sundance guarded his back. He welcomed the opportunity. Having to contain himself in the Dragon Vault had chafed. He wouldn't have to do that now. He could call upon the energy surging through him and make a point that Jinx's father couldn't misinterpret.

That hope driving him, his walking stick shifted to its original form. Excalibur appeared in his hands.

It was that revelation more than anything else that made Jinx hesitate.

She rarely took on a fight that she wasn't certain that she could win. Examining the Dragon now, seeing not only what he revealed but also what he didn't, sensing the hidden power that he could call upon, she realized that taking up his challenge would be a very bad idea.

"You have made a costly mistake, Dragon. Have no doubt that when we meet again, you will regret it."

Draig didn't bother to reply, allowing Jinx to slide back into the surf and disappear beneath the waves.

"Keep an eye out while I make dinner," Draig said. "I'll let you know when it's ready."

Butch, Cassidy, and Sundance nodded as one then began their patrol along the shore. Jinx, her Vipers, or any other creature seeking to pay him a visit that evening didn't stand a chance of getting by his friends.

Heading up the trail to the lighthouse's back door, he saw that the lights were on inside. He knew, however, that Melissa wasn't there the instant he walked in.

Draig couldn't say that he was surprised by that finding. He just wished that he had been wrong, although he knew that he wouldn't be. Because he had pegged Melissa from the start. Thus his hesitation to seek more from her than just information.

He walked up to his shield, running his hand over the three red Welsh dragons. He didn't need to open the safe.

He knew the truth.

What he had put there was gone.

Melissa had taken it.

She had proven his suspicions correct.

Melissa was working for Arthur and Morgase. He had known that from the beginning.

And now, with her gone and with what she had stolen, he knew that she was also working for a third party that she had not revealed but Jinx had the second she appeared in Kraken Cove with her Vipers.

A disappointing discovery. But a useful one. Just as Jinx appearing in front of him a few minutes before offered additional confirmation and insight.

Melissa's third party, Jinx's father, was impatient to make his move.

Draig had given Melissa a chance to prove herself. And she had. Just not in the way he wanted her to.

"Come here often, sailor?"

Draig smiled, the sarcasm in the strong, husky voice heavy to the point of dripping.

He turned. Riga sat on the couch behind him, a glass of wine in her hand.

"You're looking out for me?" he asked.

"More than you might expect."

"Why?"

"Because we share something that is more important than the both of us, and I still feel something for you that I've never felt for anyone else. I know you feel the same as well."

"That's the only reason you're here?" Draig asked, giving Riga a questioning expression.

"That and because I've been tracking your exploits during the last few days. I thought you might want to talk."

Draig smiled again, then sat down next to her, accepting the glass of wine she offered him. He then told her all that had happened since they had last spoken.

Riga didn't ask any questions. She listened. And thought. Searching for any gaps in his reasoning, she failed to identify them.

"You know what it means?" Draig asked, having just explained what he had learned while in the Circle.

Riga nodded sadly. "I know it just as you do."

"There's no point in fighting it?" There was a touch of hope in his voice.

"There isn't," Riga replied. "Hope has no place in our world. You know that better than most. You can't avoid it no matter how much you want to. And as you like to say ..."

"Forward. Always forward."

"Exactly."

"I need to kill a god," Draig mused, shaking his head from side to side, trying to fathom the challenge that he never believed he would need to face. A challenge he wasn't sure that he could overcome.

How did you kill a god?

Gods were gods in part because they couldn't be killed.

"Yes, before the god kills you," Riga confirmed.

Draig's expression hardened at that, his eyes blazing.

Riga was correct.

It was time for the Dragon to return to the world.

For those who dared to get in his way, beware.

~

THE END
Keep reading for the first chapter of Book 4.

BONUS MATERIAL

If you really enjoyed this story, I need you to do me a HUGE favor – please follow me on Amazon and BookBub. And if you have a few minutes, consider writing a review.

Keep reading for the first chapter from *The Dragon Returns,* Book 4 in my series. Order Book 4 from my author website PeterWachtBooks.com. Also available on Amazon.

AN URBAN FANTASY FICTION SERIES
THE DRAGON RETURNS
THE FALLEN KNIGHT SERIES BOOK 4
PETER WACHT

The Dragon Returns
By Peter Wacht

Book 4 of The Fallen Knight Series

This book is a work of fiction. Names, characters, places, and incidents are the product of the author's imagination or are used fictitiously. Any resemblance to actual events, locales, or persons, living or dead, is coincidental.

Cover design by Ebooklaunch.com

Published in the United States by Kestrel Media Group LLC.

ISBN: 978-1-950236-70-1

eBook ISBN: 978-1-950236-69-5

Library of Congress Control Number: 2025909377

✻ Created with Vellum

1. THE WRONG CATCH

"Do you think we'll have any luck today?"

Seamus stood on the helm of the *Kraken*, rough hands sure on the wheel of the charter craft. "She's close. I can feel her in my bones."

Draig chuckled. His friend's comment made him think of the scene from *Jaws* when Roy Scheider first went out with Robert Shaw to look for the shark terrorizing Amity Island. "How can you be so certain?"

"I know her."

"We're going to need to talk about your choices for female companionship," Draig murmured with a hint of faint disapproval. "The daughter of Typhon? Really? Out of all the women …"

"The heart wants what the heart wants." Seamus gave Draig a knowing look. "Be careful, now. We could have the same conversation about you and your choices, my friend."

By the gleam in Seamus' eye, clearly he was quite pleased with himself for turning the focus of the conversation onto Draig so quickly.

"Fair enough." Draig sighed as he scanned the surface of

the Atlantic Ocean. They were several miles from the coast and a league or so from Kraken Cove. "If you can feel her in your bones, do you know where she is specifically? It's a big ocean."

Seamus shook his head. "No, it's not like sonar. Besides, being atop the water rather than below makes finding her a bit more difficult." He gave Draig a wily grin. "Have no fear, though. Once I go below, Jinx won't be able to resist me."

Draig nodded, giving his friend a lift of his eyebrows and holding back the host of less-than-helpful comments and questions that popped into his mind. "Quite confident, aren't you?"

Seamus nodded with an expression that bordered on fratboy arrogance. "Once a woman gets a taste of the Kraken, they only want more."

Draig had no response to that. At least not a useful one. And he didn't want to encourage his friend. Still, he felt like he should say something. "You do realize that you can't make a comment like that in mixed company, right?"

Seamus nodded quickly, some of the air leaving his sail. "Of course. That's why I save them for you. I'm well aware of what Peggy Rose or Cerridwen would do if I said something like that in front of them."

"I'm glad you still have a little common sense." Nevertheless, Draig was finding it exceedingly difficult getting past Seamus' romantic taste. "But Jinx? Seriously?"

"Would you just let it go?" Seamus grumbled. He shrugged. "I was going through a bad patch. She was as well. It made sense at the time. Looking back, I realize that I may have been thinking with the wrong head."

"Thanks for sharing," Draig replied with a distinct lack of enthusiasm, "although you shared a bit too much."

"It's your own fault. You should have stopped while you could."

"You got me there," Draig admitted, accepting a small portion of the blame.

Seamus perked up then, eyes narrowing. He started to study the waves, spinning slowly though always keeping one hand on the wheel. Draig followed where his friend was looking, not seeing anything other than three- and four-foot swells.

"What's the matter?"

Seamus pursed his lips, although it was hard to see because of his thick beard, the long and scraggly whiskers covering most of his mouth. "Doesn't feel right."

"What doesn't feel right?"

"The ocean."

Draig nodded as he searched around them, not seeing anything that gave him any cause for concern. Still, he trusted in Seamus' senses. Instincts as well. When they were on the water at least. "Could you be more specific?"

"I was kind of hoping that a great white would be our biggest concern."

"How so?"

"We're not alone."

Draig closed his eyes and pinched the bridge of his nose between his thumb and his forefinger, needing to take a breath so that he didn't lose his temper. Whether intentional or not, Seamus had a way not only of drawing matters out longer than was required, but also adding some unwanted drama, and Draig only had so much patience.

"Again, specifics?"

"I can sense Jinx getting closer, just not exactly where she is." Seamus frowned, brow coming together. "If I'm right, I think she brought one of her pets with her."

"Wonderful," Draig muttered. "Any idea which one it might be?"

Seamus shook his head. "There's only one way to find out, although I think what we discover will likely be a lot larger than a great white."

"No idea what to look for?"

"None whatsoever," Seamus confirmed. "She's using the Grym to mask herself and whatever she has with her."

"Yet you're sure that Jinx is close?"

"More than sure."

"How can you tell?" Draig challenged.

"My balls are itching." Seamus offered his statement with complete seriousness, not a hint of a smile cracking his chapped lips.

"I'm sorry I asked."

"You'll be even more sorry if this fog gets worse."

The wispy grey that had dogged them not long after Seamus motored his cabin cruiser out of the Kraken Cove marina was getting thicker by the minute. "Jinx's doing?"

"She doesn't have the power required," Seamus replied. "Probably Neptune."

"Why Neptune?" Draig didn't understand why the God of the Sea would have any interest in why they were on the water now.

"I was playing cards with him the other week."

Draig nodded knowingly, beginning to understand. "You lost your temper."

Seamus shrugged. "It was justified," he offered in his defense. "He was being a pain in the ass, and he kept accusing me of cheating."

"Were you?"

"Of course not," Seamus replied, perhaps a bit too hastily. "Maybe being a jackass, but that doesn't matter now. What matters is that he promised to leave me fogbound if I didn't leave him be."

"You were on him for his name again, weren't you?" Draig couldn't stop himself from smiling. There were certain things in the world that bothered Seamus that he just couldn't seem to let go. No matter how trivial.

"How could I not be?" Seamus growled, unable to contain

his irritation. "He kept talking about himself in the third person. And if that wasn't aggravating enough, he kept switching between his names. Poseidon this and Neptune that. Then Neptune this and Poseidon that. He was driving me crazy."

"I can understand why that was the case," Draig responded in a tone that a therapist might use with a neurotic patient with the goal of not riling up his friend any more than he already was.

"Damn right you can." Seamus smacked one large palm on the wheel to emphasize his agreement. "If you speak about yourself in the third person, then you're a jackass. Plain and simple. Even worse, pick a name and stick with it for feck's sake! Who needs two names anyway?"

"A good point," Draig replied just as calmly as before. He decided not to explain why the God of the Sea had distinct Roman and Greek names. They didn't have the time and he didn't have the desire to dive down that rabbit hole.

"I knew you'd agree." Taking a breath to calm himself, Seamus slowed the throttle.

"Have we found our Moby Dick?"

Seamus nodded. "There's only one way to be sure. You want to take the wheel?"

Seamus stepped out of the way so that Draig could take charge of the helm. Draig kept the engine at a soft purr, then set the *Kraken* on a course to complete a slow circle. He hated the idea of being dead in the water with what might be beneath them.

Seamus nodded in approval. Then he looked over the side. Nothing but a murky grey. That didn't bother him in the least, however.

Once he was beneath the waves, he would be home. He would see and hear everything around him as if it were clear as day.

"Too bad we don't have a camera crew around for this," Seamus grumbled.

"You think that would help to boost the business this summer?"

"Without a doubt."

To ensure that Seamus made good money with his sight-seeing charters during the warmer months, he liked to create some free press by teasing a scientific expedition whenever they were working on the east coast between Boston and Nova Scotia. He gave them just a glimpse, and a poor one at that, but still enough to make them think they had seen something in the water that shouldn't have been there.

The Loch Ness monster of the East Coast as Seamus liked to promote his escapades. A few articles later in the press and he had a steady flow of customers until well after Labor Day.

"You know, I think I might have a Polaroid camera down in the cabin. Maybe you could ..." Seamus made the motion of snapping some photos.

"The daughter of Typhon is in the water below us with one of her pets and you want me to take your photo?"

Seamus didn't reply right away, Draig's expression hinting that he was questioning his judgment. "Not a good idea?"

Draig didn't bother to reply, shaking his head instead.

"Not a good idea," Seamus confirmed with a nod. Without another word, he dove over the side, barely making a splash when he slipped into the water.

Draig kept the *Kraken* moving in a slow circle once his friend disappeared. Waiting. Watching.

There was nothing but rolling waves for as far as he could see. And he was finding it harder to see. The fog was coming in faster than before, making visibility even poorer as the billowing grey covered the ocean like a pale and silent shroud.

Draig knew that Seamus could handle himself. He was more comfortable below the water than above it.

Nevertheless, that didn't prevent him from worrying for his friend.

Draig reached for the Grym, extending his senses below the surface of the briny ocean.

Where had Seamus gone?

He realized his mistake in an instant.

His search was too broad. Instead of looking in every direction, he needed to focus on one.

He needed to go deeper.

Nothing a quarter mile below.

Nor at half a mile.

A mile?

No. Still nothing.

He extended his senses even farther into the deep.

Finally, he located his friend.

Draig turned the cruiser to the northeast.

He had gone no more than a few hundred yards when he saw the first signs of Seamus making for the surface. The waves in this part of the ocean weren't obeying the currents. They were listening to what was going on in the water below.

Then the rolling waves stopped moving entirely, the strange stillness that resulted seeming unnatural to Draig. That same placid pool dropped several feet in just a breath, as if that particular section of the ocean was being pulled down into a drain. To confirm Draig's speculation, the ocean began to swirl in a clockwise direction, churning in its very center in a way that more resembled the beginnings of a boil.

That boil became even more violent just seconds later. The water seethed, transforming into a frothy white.

With good cause.

Just a heartbeat later, the Kraken in one of his many forms erupted from the sea.

While searching for Jinx and her pet, Seamus had chosen to retain a version of his human shape as he had done when he dueled Morgase on Long Island, although he had grown in size. So much so that if the George Washington Bridge towered above him, he was in danger of hitting his head.

His lower half, a massive tail that resembled that of a shark, pushed most of his colossal mass out of the water. Spiky red shells like those on a lobster protected his chest, shoulders, arms, and legs, serving as a flexible armor that was stronger than titanium.

His face hadn't changed. He appeared to be the same craggy old man as he always did. The one change was his hair. The rat's nest replaced by a thick green seaweed.

Draig had to give his friend credit. Seamus had found what they were looking for.

Jinx's pet.

The gargantuan sea serpent, its body thicker than the hull of a submarine, was wrapped around him.

Although Seamus had located the creature, he wasn't having the success that he wanted against the monstrous animal.

In large part because he couldn't bring to bear the harpoon made from the bone of a sperm whale that he grasped in his hand.

The serpent's coils flexed and moved with a deadly menace, not only keeping the harpoon against his side, but also tightening around the Kraken, seeking to steal his breath with every constriction.

And it was working.

Slowly.

Insidiously.

Despite fighting hard to free himself, Seamus' face slowly shifted from a bright red to a pale white. The blue that would reveal his inability to breathe couldn't be more than just a few seconds away.

Yet that wasn't the only threat Seamus faced nor the most immediate.

Even as each breath became more and more difficult for him to take, the Kraken couldn't extricate himself from the sea snake's grip with his other hand. That meaty paw, thankfully well away from his body, gripped the serpent's head, Seamus using every ounce of strength that remained to him to prevent the animal's fangs from plunging into his neck.

Draig increased the throttle. He needed to get closer before Seamus lost his battle. And Draig could tell that his friend was losing the battle. Seamus' weakening free hand was losing its grip on the serpent's nostrils.

Of course the rocking and rolling waves didn't help him. Draig couldn't make much headway through the chop. In fact, just staying on the helm of the cabin cruiser was a huge challenge, the boat dropping precipitously into a deep trough before Draig guided the bow atop the crest of the next wave, a never-ending cycle.

Seamus' face beginning to turn the shade of blue that he feared, Draig realized that he couldn't wait no matter how unlikely he was to hit what he aimed for while motoring through a pot of churning and swirling water.

Keeping one hand on the wheel, worried that if he wasn't careful an errant wave would capsize the *Kraken*, Draig called on the Grym and shot a bolt of the Power of the Ancients through the worsening fog.

Dropping into a trough, he smiled when he came back up over the crest of the next wave. He had missed, though not by much.

The white-hot energy sliced across the sea snake's jaw, taking with it a furrow of scales and leaving scorched flesh in its wake. Draig had missed one of its platter-sized eyes by only a few feet.

Not a direct hit though enough to force the snake's head back and give Seamus a momentary reprieve.

Still, Draig feared that his effort might not have been enough. The serpent was still coiled around Seamus, its muscular body crushing the life from his friend. Worse, the snake's fangs were snapping back toward him with an even greater vigor.

About to slide off a thirty-foot crest, Draig realized that he needed to take a less precise approach before he fell into the trough below him.

Using the Grym once again, a shield of gleaming energy formed right in front of Seamus' face.

And just in time.

Unable to stop, the serpent's fang-filled maw already darting forward, with a nasty crunch that Draig heard even with the hundreds of thousands of gallons of water surging around him, one of the snake's fangs snapped off.

When Draig emerged from the trough just a moment later, he watched with a great deal of satisfaction as the serpent pulled back with an angry hiss.

It was just a temporary victory.

Seamus' difficult circumstances had not improved by much. The serpent was preparing to strike again. Clearly uncon-cerned if another barrier blocked its efforts. Instead intent on its prey, Seamus weakening faster now as he gasped for air.

Draig was about to form another shield and fix it in place. He changed his strategy on the fly when he realized that he had hit a fairly stable patch of water, which really wasn't saying much. Ten-foot waves rather than twenty or thirty, though he did appreciate the boiling ocean now was no more than a simmer.

How long it lasted didn't matter to him.

All he needed was a second.

And he made the most of it.

Without the rocking and rolling, Draig's aim was right on target.

A spear of energy sparked from his free hand and sizzled through the thickening fog. The power sliced across the snake's body, ripping away a large swathe of scales and burning into the flesh beneath.

Then again. And again. And one more after that.

Draig didn't stop until the rough water returned.

Even as the *Kraken* pitched wildly to the side, Draig smiled while turning the wheel to keep the cruiser above the surface rather than giving in to the tremendous power of the ocean and capsizing.

Finally, he enjoyed some success that would aid his friend as well.

Unable to bear the pain of the many wounds torturing its long body, the sea serpent unwrapped itself from the Kraken.

The last spear that Draig threw streaked through the fog, this one aimed for a spot right between the serpent's eyes. It proved to be a harmless throw, the snake sliding beneath the surface before the lance struck.

With the snake ducking away, Draig almost hit his friend. The bolt of energy would have sliced across his ribs if Seamus hadn't stood straight abruptly. Bent at the waist once more, Seamus sucked in as much air as he could into his starved lungs.

"Watch it," Seamus' growled. His deep voice rumbled across the choppy surface, and he gave Draig a look that suggested his last attack didn't need to be so close.

Draig held back his sharp reply, not wanting to antagonize his friend while he recovered. Although he did need to make the point, at least to himself, that hitting his target while captaining a cabin cruiser in rough water that was only getting rougher while a heavy fog drifted in and two leviathans battled atop the surface was far from an easy task.

He shifted his focus back to the sea serpent. It had disappeared, probably licking its wounds. But Draig suspected the animal was not yet done with them.

Reaching for the Grym, Draig extended his senses beneath the surface once again. He didn't have far to look.

The sea serpent was circling Seamus just below the waves and only a few hundred yards away. Using his tail to keep himself in place while he searched for any sign of his adversary, Seamus was turned in the wrong direction.

"Seamus! At your back!"

The Kraken spun just in time at Draig's warning.

The sea serpent burst out of the ocean only a hundred yards away, its long mass of coils propelling the animal swiftly across the surface.

Seamus had less than a heartbeat to react. Heeding his instinct, he threw the harpoon, hoping for a fatal blow. Or at least a wounding blow. At the moment he wasn't all that particular.

Unfortunately, it wasn't to be.

It was a good throw though not good enough. The serpent glided to the side right before the harpoon struck between its eyes, the sharp bone ripping off a few of the snake's scales along its thick hide but doing no real damage.

After that, Seamus had no chance to think about maintaining the all-too-brief momentum he had earned. He could focus only on defending himself as the snake lunged, fangs aimed right at his face.

The Kraken got his hands up just in time, catching the snake by the head. One hand on its upper jaw, the other on the lower, Seamus was able to keep the animal's fangs away from him.

Although not without a great deal of effort.

The sea serpent hissed with anger as the beast bunched the

muscles in its neck, engaging in a battle of strength with Seamus.

But that wasn't the worst of it.

The serpent's long body was curling around Seamus again, seeking to take hold and place him in the same lethal position he had been in just a moment before. And with both his hands occupied, and knowing what would happen if he released the snake's head, Seamus was in no position to prevent it.

Seamus needed to focus not only on maintaining his hold on the snake's head, but also on keeping himself above the water. With the animal's body coiling around him, the weight of the creature was forcing him beneath the waves.

Draig refused to allow that to occur, knowing what would happen if the serpent once again wrapped its heavy coils around Seamus then took him below.

One hand on the wheel as he struggled to control the cruiser in the rough waves churned up by the battle taking place in front of him, Draig blasted a stream of magic from his hand.

Rather than trying to strike the straining animal, Draig guided the energy around the serpent's neck, tying the glowing line into a lasso that he fitted just below the head.

That task done, Draig closed his fist, the lasso tightening instantly into a noose that bit into the serpent's neck.

The effect on the animal was immediate, a bloody and charred line appearing where the Grym burned into its flesh.

The serpent reared back, forgetting about Seamus. Seeking only to break free from the painful and potentially lethal snare.

However, Seamus didn't forget about the snake. No longer worried about the beast's fangs, he gripped the snake around the neck with both his monstrous hands right below where the sizzling lasso burned through scale and meat almost to the vertebrae beneath.

All thought of trying to kill the Kraken fled from the snake's mind. All the animal cared about was survival. And the only way to do that was to dive back into the deep. To escape from what had become a losing combat.

But that was no more than a hope, and it faded swiftly.

Seamus' face a bright red to match his armor, muscles flexing, he squeezed with all the strength that his current form granted him, wanting the snake to feel what he felt before Draig got in the way.

The serpent thrashed wildly, desperate to get away, unable to snap at the Kraken, eyes bulging as the awful pressure increased.

Finally having gained the upper hand, Seamus fought with a lethal efficiency.

The serpent's thrashing became less wild and then ended after no more than a few additional twitches, its forked tongue flicking a few more times before lying still outside its mouth, the creature's throat crushed.

Yet even though the combat was over, Seamus wasn't done. He felt the need to make a point. To himself and to his real antagonist.

He didn't release his hold around the snake's thick neck until he crushed the flesh and then the bone with such terrible intensity that the animal's monstrous head dropped into the ocean and slowly sank beneath the surface. Staring for a moment with a great deal of contempt at the serpent's body, Seamus flung it away from him toward the east.

Seamus didn't bother to watch the splash. Instead, covered in blood and guts, he turned with a grim expression to face the woman who had almost caused his death.

Yet when Jinx rose up out of the ocean just a moment later, sitting comfortably on a watery throne, she had eyes only for Draig and demonstrated not an ounce of interest in her former lover.

That earned an angry growl from Seamus. He made no

move toward her, however. He knew that if he did so, she would likely disappear.

And Draig needed to have this conversation with her. That's why they had taken the *Kraken* out into the Atlantic in the first place.

Jinx appeared to be not the least bit surprised by what happened to her pet, even offering Seamus a nod of respect and a few silent claps before fixing her gaze back on Draig, who brought the *Kraken* to an idle just a dozen yards away from her in what had become a shockingly placid ocean.

"I told you that we'd meet again."

"And here we are," Draig replied. "It's been what ... a day? You couldn't wait longer than that?"

Jinx didn't bother to reply, instead studying Draig. He really was quite impressive, frightening as well, even more so than the Kraken who towered over him, Seamus having glided over to hover behind his friend and offer her an angry glower.

Perhaps it was because of the scale, Jinx mused to herself. Seamus was truly terrifying when he went all Kraken on her. Exhilarating as well.

Although not to the level of when she confronted Axel Draig.

Seamus' power was obvious. Draig's less so, though even more potent. Even more frightening when she considered that he was hiding so much from her.

But that wasn't unexpected after what her father had said about him.

The Dragon.

The King Teg's most famous and most accomplished assassin.

A Teg who many believed could not be killed.

Until he was.

And now a Teg risen from the dead.

The Kraken was impressive. She wouldn't deny that. But he had never died and come back to life.

"You've mistaken my intentions, Dragon. I come here as one seeking an ally. Not to fight, which you would know if your waterlogged friend at your back hadn't antagonized my serpent. I'm only a threat if you don't see the logic in my offer."

"Really," Draig said, clearly not convinced. "I find that hard to believe. You'll have to explain. Because from what I can tell, I'm just a piece to be used. Once you're done with me, you'll sweep me from the game board just as your father usually does."

"What do you know of my father?" She was curious. Her father had been away for quite some time, more myth than reality to many of the Teg.

"More than enough to know what usually happens to those working with him. Concrete boots would be a blessing compared to some of what your father has done to eliminate his enemies ... and many of his so-called and very temporary allies."

"There's no need to be so melodramatic," Jinx challenged, although she sounded more amused than anything else. And she made no effort to correct Draig's characterization of her father.

"You've got the right of it, Draig," Seamus rumbled, staring daggers at Jinx. "That's what he does best."

"I don't need help explaining what I want from an overgrown mix of man and fish. Keep quiet, Seamus, so that the adults can talk."

Seamus growled again, this time more in warning. He hadn't enjoyed his combat with the sea serpent. Although the thought of wrapping his hands around Jinx's throat certainly appealed to him.

Nevertheless, he kept his place, understanding that surrendering to the desire to attack the woman who insulted him and sat so smugly on her throne crafted of seawater would do neither him nor Draig any good. Better to allow this scene to play out and to be ready for any other pets Jinx may have called from the briny deep.

"As you might have guessed, my father and I seek your assistance."

"To do what?"

Jinx chuckled softly, as if his question didn't deserve a reply. "You know what, Dragon. It's the same thing that you desire."

"Right now all I desire are a hot coffee and a freshly baked cinnamon roll."

Jinx stared at Draig even harder, her green eyes burning brightly. Then she nodded. "Yes, I was told that you often got this way. Not just challenging, but also rebellious, as revealed by your attempts at humor."

"I wasn't joking," Draig replied. "I really would like a hot coffee and a freshly baked cinnamon roll."

"Do not test me, Dragon. You won't like me if you do."

"I don't like you now, Jinx. That's not going to change."

Rather than allowing Draig to continue to provoke her, Jinx stayed quiet. Calming herself. Refusing to permit her building aggravation to become anything more than that. She was there for a reason, and she would do what was required of her no matter how hard the Dragon made it.

"Enough with your poor attempt at humor, Dragon. As I said, my father and I know what you desire ... beyond whatever you hunger for in this moment."

"You're going to have to be more specific." Draig knew what she wanted. But he didn't feel the need to make it easy for her. Rather, he wanted to press her, his making the conversation more difficult for her revealing a few breaks in Jinx's composure that he hoped to use against her when the time was right.

"Removing your father from the throne, of course, and you taking his place."

Draig nodded as if he was actually giving serious consideration to the proposal. "I may not like my father, but that doesn't mean I want to take his place."

Jinx laughed. "Of course you do, Dragon. How could you not?"

"I am not like your father. I do not seek to dominate all those around me."

"You know nothing of my father," Jinx countered. "You believe what your father told you about him? What you learned when you trained to become a Knight of the Round? Perhaps what Merlin shared?"

She shook her head, scoffing at the notion that anything close to the truth could emerge from those sources. "My father seeks order above all else. Order. Not control. Because with order you can govern. You do not have to rule, a lesson your father has forgotten or never learned. You can give those you are responsible for what they need to not only survive, but thrive."

"You sound like a candidate for office, Jinx. And not the good kind. The kind that hides their true intentions in a rhetoric that leads only to a terrible end for those foolish enough to believe it and those too afraid to take it seriously."

Jinx ignored Draig's argument, believing that she had identified what she was looking for. "I can see it in your eyes, Dragon. You seek to rule the Teg. You seek to give them the opportunities they deserve. The opportunities that your father is keeping from them."

"I seek to help the Teg," he countered. "No more than that."

"And what better way to help the Teg, Dragon, than to rule the Teg." Jinx leaned forward on her throne, placing her elbows on her knees, hands clasped in front of her. "A fair point, don't you think? You know what your father is doing now. That's why you left him. You know that he is no longer the king he was when he assumed the Teg throne. If you remove your father, think of all the good that you can accomplish."

"Tempting, but ..."

"You are thinking too much, Dragon. It is an easy decision to make. You got in trouble with your father because you chose to help the Teg against his wishes, and you continue to do that now." Jinx's smile broadened, becoming almost predatory. "My father will help you. He will help you take the throne, and he will help you help the Teg."

"He will, will he? No strings attached?"

"The throne of the Teg is there if you want it, Dragon. My father will help you. I promise you that. And that is all he wants to do." Jinx almost pushed herself out of her throne, believing that the moment of truth had come, her excitement at turning the Dragon to her cause almost palpable. "My father seeks from you only one small gift in return. That's all."

Draig nodded, already knowing what Jinx was going to demand and why. "You want the Witch."

"A small price to pay for the throne of the Teg, wouldn't you say? For the opportunity to do what your father should be doing himself?"

"One Teg for all the Teg," Draig intoned.

"Exactly," Jinx confirmed with a smile. "Give me the Witch. She has not met the terms of her contract with my father. She has not delivered to him what she promised, and she must pay for that failure." She gave him a shrug of her shoulders and a lift of her eyebrows. "Not a bad trade at all, wouldn't you say?"

Draig didn't reply right away. He had to give Jinx credit. He had believed after his first encounter with her on the town green in Kraken Cove that she was no more than a blunt instrument. But clearly she was quite clever, although a bit misguided as well and much too sure of herself if she believed that she could turn him so easily.

"I'm sorry, but that doesn't really appeal to me."

Jinx laughed, a throaty sound. "Really, Dragon, you feel the need to play hard to get? I can guarantee that this is the best deal that I'll place before you. The only one, in fact, that does not end in utter despair for you."

"The threat wrapped in the velvet glove," Draig murmured. He had assumed that she was going to start with this rather than offering the sweets first. "And if I don't agree to your deal?"

"Then my father will give me permission to destroy Kraken Cove and kill every Teg you care about."

"An impressive threat." Draig's voice hardened, his reddish-orange eyes bursting into flames. "I don't respond well to threats, Jinx. If you had done more research before coming here, you would know that."

"It's not a threat, Dragon. It's a promise. My father and I have no need of threats."

"Tempting as your offer sounds, Jinx, we've been through all this. My position has not changed. I'm not interested in taking the Teg throne. I'm not interested in working with your father. And I won't give you the Witch."

Jinx leaned back into her watery throne, her expression souring. She had been so close, she believed, until the Dragon inexplicably got cold feet. Perhaps he wasn't really as formidable as her father made him out to be. "I will not ask again, Dragon, and my father will not make this offer again. Decide now. We are either allies or enemies. Choose wisely."

"I much prefer being your enemy, Jinx," Draig replied in a voice colder than ice, not even needing to think about it. "I won't work with you or him. And you can't have her." He saw little need to inform Jinx that Melissa had left Kraken Cove and that he didn't know where she was. He did, however, want to make sure that she understood the consequences of what she was contemplating. "And just to be clear, if you come at the Teg living in Kraken Cove, you will regret your decision. You've already been spanked once. It would be embarrassing if I and my friends spanked you again."

"Is that a threat?" Jinx hissed, hating how Draig talked down to her. A daughter of Typhon! A daughter of an Ancient! Such insolence!

"No, I don't make threats, Jinx. That's a promise."

Jinx stared daggers at Draig, her anger becoming more obvious with every breath she took.

Draig used her few seconds of stewing to appreciate the value of this encounter. When Melissa had entered his life, bringing her chaos with her and upsetting the balance of events in Kraken Cove, he had little understanding of all that was going on behind the scenes. He had viewed her as the protagonist, not realizing until just recently that she was really the catalyst for what was biting at the edge of the Teg world.

Three of the most powerful Teg had been vying for *The Book of Whispers*. All trying to keep that a secret. All intent on using the power contained within the ancient artifact on one, the other, or both.

Two of the three were no longer players in the game.

They knew it. Draig had explained it to them in a way that they couldn't help but understand.

Although that didn't mean they still couldn't cause prob-lems for him. A fact that he needed to address before he took on the third player.

Because he couldn't have those two free to stab him in the back while he assumed the task he had seen for himself while in the Druid's Circle.

Neither of the fates that awaited him appealed. Yet he wouldn't run from them. He couldn't. Not with so much at stake.

He would seek the fate that ensured the survival and the freedom of the Teg, even though that would require more from him than he really wanted to give. He really didn't have a choice. Because that was the only fate that he was willing to accept.

Before he did, however, he would do all that he could to ensure that he removed the third player from the board before he died again. This time for good.

Draig couldn't escape what he had seen atop the Druid's Peak. He had known that from the start. And he wouldn't try. Even so, he wanted to give himself the best possible chance of succeeding before he met his end.

"I expected more from you, Dragon. From what I heard of you, you were harder than this when you slaved away at your father's side. You did not allow your emotions to guide you. Only cold reason." She bit out her next few words slowly, seeking a reaction that she could use. "With this decision you appear weak to me, Dragon. Vulnerable. Ripe for the picking."

Draig gave her no more than a nod. "Feel free to have a go at me, Jinx. Then when I see your father, and I promise you I will see your father before he sees me, I can tell him how you completely and utterly failed at the assignment he gave you."

"You are a sentimental fool, Dragon." Jinx spat out the words, never having been so insulted. "We are done here. I will wipe your beloved Kraken Cove from the face of the earth. I will take the Witch. Have no doubt of that. And when I stand above you with the blade that kills you, you will think back to this very moment and realize that all could have been much different if not for your obstinacy and stupidity."

Before she uttered the last of her threats, Jinx already was disappearing back into the ocean, her throne sliding below the surface with her on it.

"You want me to go after her?"

Draig didn't reply right away, staring at the waves, going through in his mind once again the conversation he just had with Typhon's daughter. "No, I think we got what we needed. Thank you for your help. Great job."

Seamus stood at the helm once more, having shifted back into his human form, soaked to the bone and not caring a whit. He nodded sheepishly, uncomfortable with gratitude or praise, even from a friend. "You think she'll do what she said?"

Draig stared at the ocean where Jinx sank beneath the waves for just a moment longer before replying to his friend with a shake of his head. "No, she doesn't want to look the fool again. Even with her Vipers, she knows she doesn't have the strength to do what she wants. She's more concerned about embarrassing herself than with doing the work to earn a hard victory."

"My thought as well," Seamus said. He and Draig had wanted to tease a reaction out of Jinx. They just hadn't expected to get one such as this. "You know what this means, right?"

Draig nodded. When he turned toward his friend, his expression was grimmer than the grey of the sea right before a storm. "Typhon is almost ready to step out from the shadows."

"The last time that happened the world burned. In fact, it was almost destroyed."

"Then I'll need to do what I can to prevent that from happening."

"And just how are you going to do that?"

"Kill a god," he replied in a voice that suggested doing so would be no more than him taking out the garbage.

"You can do that?"

"There's only one way to find out."

WHAT TO READ NEXT

THE FALLEN KNIGHT SERIES

The Death of the Dragon (short story)*

The Dragon Awakens

Duel With a Dragon

Beware the Dragon

The Dragon Returns

THE REALMS OF THE TALENT AND THE CURSE

LEGEND OF THE DRAGON LORD

A Painful Truth (short story)*

Stealing the Light

Sacrificing the Queen

Roar of the Broken Bear (Forthcoming 2025)

Rise of the Dragon Lord (Forthcoming 2026)

THE TALES OF CALEDONIA

(Complete 7-Book Series)

Blood on the White Sand (short story)*

The Diamond Thief (short story)*

The Protector

The Protector's Quest

The Protector's Vengeance

The Protector's Sacrifice

The Protector's Reckoning

The Protector's Resolve

The Protector's Victory

THE TALES OF THE TERRITORIES

*Stalking the Blood Ruby (short story)**

*A Fate Worse Than Death (short story)**

Death on the Burnt Ocean

Monsters in the Mist

The Dance of the Daggers

Bloody Hunt for Freedom

A Spark of Rebellion

Shadows Made Real

Shadow's Reach

Storm in the Darkness

THE SYLVAN CHRONICLES

(Complete 9-Book Series)

The Legend of the Kestrel

The Call of the Sylvana

The Raptor of the Highlands

The Makings of a Warrior

The Lord of the Highlands

The Lost Kestrel Found

The Claiming of the Highlands

The Fight Against the Dark

The Defender of the Light

THE RISE OF THE SYLVAN WARRIORS

*Through the Knife's Edge (short story)**

JOIN PETER'S NEWSLETTER

This eBook is a prelude to the events in my epic fantasy series *The Tales of Culedonia* and is free to readers who receive my newsletter.

Join Peter's newsletter and get your FREE short story.
PeterWachtBooks.com

www.ingramcontent.com/pod-product-compliance
Lightning Source LLC
Chambersburg PA
CBHW070239200726
48293CB00005B/1689